"This is not the first time you've yawned in my presence," Ave said, tongue in cheek.

"This is not the first time you find me so tired I don't know if I'm coming or going," Ernie responded.

"Ah! Then you should listen to me, my love. I know *exactly* where you're going, or, as the case is now, coming." Ernie blinked and raised questioning eyes to meet his twinkling gaze. "You, my dear, are coming straight into my arms."

"No." She pushed against his hands which held her lightly. "You mustn't kiss me. You must *not.* I cannot fight you because you are too strong. I can only plead with you not to do something which I fear I cannot resist—especially when I am completely exhausted as I am now."

For a long moment he considered her words. "But, for my own sake, kissing you now is what I *should* do."

"No." She shook her head, again pushing against him. "You do not understand!"

"I think perhaps it is you who do not understand," he said and lowered his lips toward hers. "You have not yet understood how much I love and need you . . ."

This time his kiss was a soft exploration which didn't produce knots. Not knots: merely loops of ribbon and bows and a gentle warmth which insidiously seduced her tired senses. Ernie leaned against him, melting into his embrace, almost— but not quite—wanting to feel again those wonderful knots of sensation his first kiss induced . . .

ZEBRA'S REGENCY ROMANCES
DAZZLE AND DELIGHT

A BEGUILING INTRIGUE (4441, $3.99)
by Olivia Sumner

Pretty as a picture Justine Riggs cared nothing for propriety. She dressed as a boy, sat on her horse like a jockey, and pondered the stars like a scientist. But when she tried to best the handsome Quenton Fletcher, Marquess of Devon, by proving that she was the better equestrian, he would try to prove Justine's antics were pure folly. The game he had in mind was seduction—never imagining that he might lose his heart in the process!

AN INCONVENIENT ENGAGEMENT (4442, $3.99)
by Joy Reed

Rebecca Wentworth was furious when she saw her betrothed waltzing with another. So she decides to make him jealous by flirting with the handsomest man at the ball, John Collinwood, Earl of Stanford. The "wicked" nobleman knew exactly what the enticing miss was up to—and he was only too happy to play along. But as Rebecca gazed into his magnificent eyes, her errant fiancé was soon utterly forgotten!

SCANDAL'S LADY (4472, $3.99)
by Mary Kingsley

Cassandra was shocked to learn that the new Earl of Lynton was her childhood friend, Nicholas St. John. After years at sea and mixed feelings Nicholas had come home to take the family title. And although Cassandra knew her place as a governess, she could not help the thrill that went through her each time he was near. Nicholas was pleased to find that his old friend Cassandra was his new next door neighbor, but after being near her, he wondered if mere friendship would be enough . . .

HIS LORDSHIP'S REWARD (4473, $3.99)
by Carola Dunn

As the daughter of a seasoned soldier, Fanny Ingram was accustomed to the vagaries of military life and cared not a whit about matters of rank and social standing. So she certainly never foresaw her *tendre* for handsome Viscount Roworth of Kent with whom she was forced to share lodgings, while he carried out his clandestine activities on behalf of the British Army. And though good sense told Roworth to keep his distance, he couldn't stop from taking Fanny in his arms for a kiss that made all hearts equal!

A Christmas Treasure

Jeanne Savery

ZEBRA BOOKS
KENSINGTON PUBLISHING CORP.

ZEBRA BOOKS are published by

Kensington Publishing Corp.
850 Third Avenue
New York, NY 10022

First Printing: November, 1994

Printed in the United States of America

Prologue

Mr. Matthewson's wispy hair fluttered in the slightest of breezes. Breezes were forbidden entrance to his walled garden with its annual sequence of rioting blooms and sun-filled warmth, but here, if he were not mistaken, was a definite draft. The interruption to a peaceful hour in the rose-scented November sun deepened his perennial mild glower into a full fledged frown. That grew to what could only be called a ferocious scowl when he looked around and observed that the gate stood open and that his still-unwed, younger daughter stood there looking in.

"Well?" he asked testily in his whispery voice. He yanked his blanket up over his thin chest. "Well?" he repeated. "Will you wait 'til I take a chill from this abominable gale or will you shut that blasted gate?" Again he plucked at the woolen blanket, pulling at it until it hid his nose.

Ernestine entered, closed the tight high gate and firmly latched it. She strolled toward her sire, snipping off dead-heads in the border as she came. From her pocket peeked a letter or, more accurately, just the corner of a letter.

"Well?" This time the word was spoken in an entirely different tone. "Well?" Mr. Matthewson avidly eyed that bit of white paper. "What does she say this time? When does she arrive?" His long thin fingers scrabbled at his blanket. "What port will she come in at? Hmm? Hmm?"

Ernie shook her head, her eyes scanning the table beside her father. Where, she wondered, has he gotten that new medicine bottle and what, she wondered, worried, is in it?

"Norry isn't coming," she said when her father again insisted on the news. "She says the report read missing, presumed dead, and that Jon isn't."

"Isn't what? Isn't missing?" Mr. Matthewson's claw-like fingers dug into his daughter's wrist, his voice querulous. "What does she mean he isn't missing?"

"Of course Jonathan is missing," said Ernie with what patience she could muster. "Norry doesn't deny that. How can she when no one has seen him for . . . how long now? It's November so he's been missing for more than three months, has he not? No, it is simply that she once again writes that he isn't dead and that she will, without question, wait in Portugal with the army for his return as he'd expect her to do."

"Oh my poor daughter. My poor dear child." Mr. Matthewson's words were rather garbled since he'd ducked his head into his hands and spoke through them plus the added muffling of the blanket bundled around his scraggy neck. Fortunately Ernie had heard the phrase and variations on it too often since word had come her brother-in-law was missing and easily guessed his meaning.

"What can I do for my poor dear child?" he asked rhetorically.

"Norry was very much in love with Jonathan, Papa," soothed his younger daughter. "Young as I was when they married, even I knew *that*. If she cannot yet accept that he is dead, well . . ."

"No, no, you refuse to understand," interrupted Mr. Matthewson. In his agitation he dropped the blanket and stared up at her. "It is something far worse than paltry feelings of grief. Don't you see, Ernestine? Her poor weak mind has been turned by her torment. It's the only possible explanation for her refusal to accept that he is dead."

"Paltry! Her grief . . . her *mind* . . . ?" Ernie's eyes opened wide and she stared at her father. "Have you lost *yours?*" she asked, bluntly.

"Don't be impertinent, Ernestine," said her father.

The reprimand had lost any force it might once have had, repeated as it was on those far too frequent occasions when he was the recipient of his younger daughter's blunt tactlessness.

"If," he added, "her mind is not lost in grief, then why will she not admit her Jonathan dead and come home? Answer me that, if you please." He glared at Ernie from under bushy brows.

"Or if I dare?" she muttered. Ernie drew in a quick breath before adding, "Papa, I can only tell you what she says—which is that she'd *know* if he were dead. She admits he was wounded in the battle, but says he has healed. He has, she adds, been angry that he can't come to her now he's regained his health. She insists he is not dead."

Mr. Matthewson's red-rimmed eyes looked a little wild. "But this is nonsense! These are the words of a bedlamite!"

He plucked distractedly at the blanket. His eyes wandered, jerkily, from one part of the garden to another. Finally his gaze settled on his younger daughter and his eyes narrowed, his thin bloodless lips thinning still more.

"You," he said.

Ernie's brows arched. "Me, Papa?"

"You. You will go to Portugal and you will bring your poor maddened sister home where we may quietly and lovingly care for her—so that no one," he added in a pious tone, "need ever know her mind was destroyed by grief. No one, I say, must ever hear her speak such nonsense. No one must discover to what straits she has sunk!"

"I think it is you who is mad, Papa. There is nothing in Norry's letter to make you go to the length of locking her up in the tower room above the entrance hall—which is what you would suggest, would you not? It is not so wonderful, after all, that she should dream of Jon, should feel him close, should not wish to give up that dream," said Ernestine as pacifically as she could, given her temper was on the rise.

"You are a fool, Ernestine. I tell you our beloved Lenore has been driven out of her wits by grief. Time may cure her, of course," he said, again adopting the pious tone which Ernie found so irritating. "One may *hope* that comes to pass, although I'll not put my faith in miracles—well look at *me*," he finished, faintly belligerent, although his daughter had made no comment. "No miracle has relieved me of *my* misery and I won't place hope in one for poor Lenore. If only I were well and could go to my beloved daughter's side. . . ." A tear made a wiggly track down the invalid's cheek. He straightened, smoothed his blanket and, catching Ernestine's eye again, said, "You will go in my place. *You* will bring home your poor benighted sister."

"My *what?*"

Mr. Matthewson ignored her half-shocked, half-laughing interjection and continued with his plans. "That Browley boy will escort you when he returns to his regiment. What luck that he's home on leave. When does he go?"

"Bertie?" Ernie's mind had drifted: Go to Portugal? See the things about which Norry wrote? The sere hills and sharp valleys? The olive groves and reddish orange of cork trees which had been harvested? The vineyards and village women dressed in black? The incredible blue skies and . . . "What did you say, Papa?"

"When-does-Browley-return-to-that-excuse-for-a-regiment?"

"Papa!" scolded Ernie, "The 95th Rifles are an outstanding regiment."

"Bah. The boy should be in the cavalry. That's the only real army."

Ernie debated arguing, but resisted the need to defend her old friend's choice of a line regiment. Instead she answered her father's question. "He goes next week. His transport leaves from Southampton Waters on Friday, November twentieth."

"Then you'd best get busy, had you not? I haven't forgotten," jeered her father, "just how long it takes a woman to pack for a journey."

"Papa, you really expect me to go all the way to Portugal with no better escort than Bertie?" Mischievously, Ernie adopted a wide-eyed look. "Papa. What of my reputation?"

"To the devil with your reputation! It is your sister's reputation about which we must worry, do you hear?" Having raised his voice to something close to a normal pitch—almost a shout for Mr. Matthewson—he lay back panting. When he'd caught his breath he added, "You'll go, missy, and you'll return with your sister. Have you understood me?"

Portugal. The army at winter rest.

And at play. Bertie told of wild rides over rough country coursing hare and amateur theatricals—which Ernie adored—and of races and dances. It all sounded delightful, despite the odd quarters about which he'd jested and the difficulties one had at times getting proper food!

Hmm. Food. Should she pack along a good ham of their own curing and several slabs of bacon, perhaps? Christmas was coming . . . maybe she could take the ingredients for a proper Christmas pudding? What else might be of use . . . ? She'd ask Bertie.

"Where are you going?" called her father, breathily, as she wandered off still planning, thinking of possibilities and necessities and even of what might simply be enjoyed by her sister as something from home, enjoyed by someone who had not returned to England since her marriage five years previously. "Ernestine! Answer me."

Ernie turned to face him, but continued, backward, down the path. "Where? Why to Portugal, Papa," she said, her eyes gleaming. "Just as you've directed me to do."

Ernie gifted the invalid with one of her most beatific smiles.

One

In a daze of exhaustion Miss Ernestine Matthewson followed her childhood friend, Lieutenant Herbert Browley, between the close-set buildings of still another Portuguese village. Only by keeping her eyes glued to the back of his green uniform jacket could she force herself to remain upright in the saddle. She'd never been so tired. As their way wended along a narrow crooked street, she wondered if they'd ever arrive at her sister's or if they were forever fated to cross this incredibly rough land with its high, steep-sided hills and narrow valleys.

The lane opened into a roughly squared off area, a well centered in the middle which was surrounded by several of the black garbed Portuguese women she'd once longed to see. Beside a war-ruined church, was a slightly larger house than those among which the way had wandered. This was one of the ones boasting stairs leading to a narrow balcony. The upper walls were partially smoothed and white-washed above a rough-walled lower story. It looked to have at least three separate rooms, perhaps four, above the storage space below.

Bertie stopped and Ernie's roan gelding halted as well although it had received no particular command from its rider. The lieutenant dismounted and tied his horse beside a black gelding which whickered a soft welcome. "Well," he said. "This is it."

Ernie felt immediate relief at reaching the end of three exceedingly long days of difficult riding which had begun and ended in the dark. She relaxed. It was an error. Every aching muscle let her know how abused it had been. Her legs and thighs, her back, her shoulders and arms, all protested the ill-usage they'd received. Worst of all, she felt a prickling under the skin of her face. For a time, she actually feared she might do the unthinkable and faint, and so clutched the front of her saddle, just in case . . .

She'd just decided she would not when the door to the cottage opened and a tall man boasting the insignia of a colonel stepped out and came, immediately, down the steep steps. His hair was a thickly waving gray, but the color, usually indicative of age, was contradicted by healthy tanned skin and a vibrancy which made itself felt even when he stood quietly in repose and looked up at her.

It's a mystery, decided Ernie, how he seems both young and old at the same time. A mystery she'd contemplate at some future date. At the moment she was much too preoccupied with the more immediate problem of how she was to remove herself from her saddle without disgracing herself. At just this particular moment in time she couldn't waste the necessary energy to care who he was or how a gray-beard such as his hair proclaimed him to be could step toward her in such a singularly powerful manner—even if it was with the faintest hint of a limp.

Ernie wasn't required to wonder, again, how she'd dismount. Strong, brown, long-fingered hands reached for her waist, lifted her down. She looked up into the mature face of a very hand-some man—or, at least, he'd have been handsome if he'd not been scowling in that exceedingly nasty way.

Don't be angry with me, she thought, and wondered why it was so important that he not be.

"Lieutenant," said the stranger in a war-roughened voice which sent new ripples up Ernie's spine, "this woman is near to dropping with fatigue. Explain, if you can, why you've al-

lowed a greenhorn to ride all the way from Lisbon—as I assume
you must have done?"

Ernie, hearing a reprimand to her oldest friend, forgot the
strange yearning the tall stranger set off in her middle regions.
A surge of new energy flowed into and through her legs. She
straightened, forced herself away from the colonel's support.

"You stop right there," she said, her forefinger poking his
chest. "Bertie didn't *allow* me to do anything. He told me how
it would be. I'm not stupid. I knew what I faced before I decided
to come on horseback. But the choice was absurd." Ernie's
scowl deepened as the officer's expression lightened, his gray
eyes taking on a most disturbing twinkle. Ignoring that, she
added, "If you have any sense at all, you'll agree it is far better
to be a trifle weary now than to be jounced and jolted in slow
moving wagons which will take forever to arrive. So!" she finished, "It is not Bertie's fault I have ridden so far *and don't you
say it is!*"

"Termagant," whispered the colonel, smothering a grin. He
turned to a red-faced, obviously embarrassed Bertie and said:
"Browley, introduce us."

Bertie snapped to attention. "Ernie, may I present Colonel
Lord Sommerton. Colonel, this is Norry's sister, Miss Ernestine
Matthewson, come to Portugal to take—" He happened to look
at Ernie who shook her head at him and changed what he'd
been about to say "—to *visit* her."

"I see," said the older officer. Somehow, without moving a
muscle, he seemed to withdraw.

Ernie wondered what it was he thought he saw, wondered
why she felt hurt at the distance he'd somehow put between
them . . . but not for long. She lost the impetus anger had given
and was again feeling multitudinous aches and pains. She simply hadn't the energy to ask what it was he saw.

"I'll see Miss Matthewson in, Lieutenant. You run along and
report for duty."

Ernie looked from the colonel to her old friend. A faint sense of panic engulfed her. "Bertie, will you desert me now?"

Bertie's expression was one of profound shock. "You would have me disobey a direct order from a senior officer?" he hissed.

Ernie, equally shocked by what she'd inadvertently done, shook her head. "I'm sorry, Bertie. I won't do it again."

"See that you don't." Bertie reached for her horse's reins before mounting up again.

"Those are new remounts for your string, Lieutenant?" Sommerton, distracted by the unknown horseflesh, looked them over. "Hmm. Excellent form. Very good blood lines."

Bertie glowed at the compliment. "Yes sir. Brought three over with me. The third comes up with my batman and the baggage."

The colonel nodded. "Excellent. Now off with you, Browley . . ."

Bertie saluted, waved to Ernie, and trotted away around a corner.

"Shall we go in, Miss Matthewson?" Colonel Sommerton presented his arm. When she didn't put out her hand, he bowed, deeply, a lurking gleam in his eyes sending unexpected shivers up Ernie's spine once again. "Mrs. Lockwood is at home," he intoned. "If you'll step this way?"

His aping the manner of a well-trained butler was the last straw. The dratted man was clearly mocking her! Ignoring the pain in her thighs by will power alone Ernie swept past him and climbed the short flight of stone steps. At the top she faced the door . . . and then was uncertain if it were proper to just open it and go in. She hesitated. But why should she not? It was her sister's home—even if they hadn't seen each other for nearly five years.

A sudden thought occurred to her: Oh dear. Would Norry even recognize her?

When Norry married her Jon and disappeared into the war

torn Peninsula Ernie had been sixteen and still a hoyden, her hair falling down on those rare occasions she attempted to put it up and her skirts more than likely trailing behind with the hems coming out.

Now she glanced up—way up—at the man standing at her side. She noted that trifling gleam of humor was still evident as he awaited her decision. Her own eyes flashed, had she known, with growing temper. How *dare* he laugh at her! He was a perfect stranger to her, someone who couldn't possibly know how much she feared this meeting with her sister, feared what she might find. Turning up her pert little nose Ernie reached for the door. It opened even as her fingertips touched the latch.

"Is something the matter, Ave? I thought I heard voices . . . Ernie?" Huge brown eyes widened in a thin face. "Ernie!"

Lenore Lockwood opened her arms and Ernie slipped into them, laying her head on her taller sister's shoulder.

"Oh, Ernie," said Norry softly, one long fingered hand laid against the braid coiled at the back of her sister's head, the other holding her gently.

Ernie pulled away and put her hands on Norry's arms. She studied her sister. "Norry . . ." she began, then stopped.

She didn't know what to say to this stranger. This gaunt woman was her lovely sister? Norry's cheekbones seemed to very nearly cut through her skin and her chin—that very determined chin! From where had it appeared? In Ernie's memory, Norry's face was so very nicely rounded, her cheeks smoothly plump . . .

"Norry, you've lost weight," was all Ernie could find to say.

Norry smiled. "Yes. One does in this climate. Especially in the summer, of course. But, my dear, you'll be chilled and tired. Colonel? Will you come in and explain where you found my Ernie?"

"She arrived just as I was leaving. Under young Browley's

aegis, I believe." Again that fleeting scowl which disappeared so quickly one wondered if one had actually seen it. "I hope you think that all right?" One dark brow arched a trifle.

"Bertie escorted her?" asked Norry absently. "Oh well, then. They've known each other forever, of course."

"Forever," repeated Sommerton, a piercing glance boring into Ernie. "Hmm. Yes. Forever."

Again he appeared to have some notion in mind, but Ernie was far too tired to delve into what it might be, even though she felt that chill of disapproval and dismissal and again felt it important to her that he not react that way.

"I won't come in now," the officer decided, speaking briskly. "Not when you must have a very great deal to say to each other." He continued more gently, "I'll drop by tomorrow, Norry, to see how you go on." One last look at Ernestine and he returned to ground level where, leading his gelding, he strode away around the side of the building, his limp very slightly more in evidence than when he'd moved to lift Ernie from her saddle.

Norry pulled Ernie into the house, straight into a dim front room. She shut the door against the evening chill and rising mist and turned, studying Ernie. "You're exhausted," she said accusingly.

"It was a harder ride than I expected—although, I assure you, Bertie warned me," said Ernie, an apology in her tone. "Don't scold, Norry. Your colonel already did that."

Your colonel, repeated Ernie inside her head. She cast a speculative look at Norry who wasn't quite so ugly as she'd first thought, just . . . different. Could there be something between her sister and that very attractive officer? Could that be the reason Norry refused to come home? Ernie pushed away some ridiculous feeling which couldn't possibly be jealousy. After all, for Norry to have fallen in love with Colonel Sommerton would be an *acceptable* reason for her refusal to return home . . . when compared to their father's wild surmises, at least!

But, continued Ernie's wandering mind, if it *were* so, then why did Norry insist, as she had, repeatedly, that Jon still lived and would return to her? Ernie sighed deeply, pushing aside that problem. It was too difficult to be logical just now when bone-deep aches had her wishing for a hot bath and a soft bed and either or both on the instant.

"How stupid of me to keep you standing, Ernie, but I cannot get over that you are actually *here*. Why?"

Ernie grimaced. "To take you home, of course, where, according to our esteemed father, you may be properly cared for. He thinks you've lost your mind."

She stared at Norry from under brows which didn't quite bristle as her father's did, but had definitely been inherited from that side of the family.

"Have you?" she asked.

Smiling, Norry shook her head. "You don't change do you, Ernie? Just as blunt as a butter knife. Have I lost my mind, indeed!"

"I've never thought it particularly helpful to dance around a subject . . . but you do not answer!"

Norry almost chuckled. "I am not mad," she said and screwed up her face, made claws of her fingers and growled. "I am perfectly sane—as you see." She smiled. "There. I have said it. Are you satisfied, love?"

Ernie eyed her. "I don't know. It's been so long, since Jon . . ." She bit her lip. "Norry, don't you see that it would be a miracle if he were to return now?"

Norry smiled a secret little smile. "A Christmas miracle," she agreed, soothingly.

"A Christmas miracle definitely would be needed!" Ernie sighed, her exhaustion again forcing her to avoid an argument at just that particular moment. "Norry, under these ridiculous conditions in which you appear to live, is it possible for one to have a bath? It *wasn't* on the voyage, you see—possible—to bathe, I mean—and then . . ." Ernie's voice was a trifle plaintive when she added, "Norry, between feeling as if I'd never before in the whole of my life known what it was to be clean, and aching deep into my very bones, something I'll admit only to *you,* I'd dearly love a hot bath!"

"You don't want much, do you? I think it can be arranged, however—despite our primitive ways!" A faint grimace fleetingly crossed Norry's face. "Ridiculous conditions indeed! Ernie, dear, will you never learn tact?"

Norry disappeared through a door into the back of the cottage as Ernie absently admitted, "Probably not." Ernie looked around. The bleak room occupied the whole of the front of the house. It was low ceilinged, the open beams black with smoke from the fire in a corner grate which looked as if it had been added as an afterthought. The walls were roughly plastered, the sharp, oddly shaped, edges of the stone of which they were constructed obvious through it. The windows, two, were tiny and one, broken, had been fixed by the simple means of covering the opening with a piece of oiled paper. The room would be dim even in daylight!

Locally-made wooden furniture, what there was of it, looked as ancient as the mountains through which they'd ridden for three unending days. But oft-washed curtains hung to either side of the tiny windows, faded cushions padded one chair, and small, worn carpets were strewn across the floor, adding a pitiful touch of hominess.

Ernie felt a sense of shock. Was this how Norry usually lived? she wondered. Their father must never know! First, he'd die of mortification that his daughter's home was in a worse state than that of his meanest tenant. Then, he'd die all over again of apoplexy that she hadn't asked for his help to make a proper home here in Portugal. He'd not understand that it was not possible to live as if one were in England when one followed the army as Norry did. Or, if he did manage to comprehend *that* much, he'd insist she should *not* have done so, but that, if she would not live in England as any proper English gentlewoman *should* do, then she might have lived in Lisbon, her husband joining her on those occasions when he had no duty!

"The bath will take a little effort to arrange," said Norry, returning to the front room, "but we'll soon get organized. You must understand that we've not got all the conveniences of home," she added, apologetically.

Her sister's sudden reappearance startled Ernie from her preoccupations. "I can see *that*," responded Ernie, hands on hips. "I suppose all the water must be carried from the well and you haven't a bath?" Her eyes widened. "Oh dear. *Do* you have a bath?"

"One exists. It belongs to a newly arrived lieutenant. Would you believe he brought fourteen trunks? I'm not certain how he thinks he'll take it all along when the spring offensive begins. However that may be, while we're here for the winter, we feel lucky to have it and take turns with it but, unfortunately, today isn't mine. Albert Bacon, Jon's batman, will track it down. Water's no problem at this time of year. Maria will soon have enough heating to make you a proper bath."

"No problem?" asked Ernie, wary.

"It is winter and the rainy season, so there is plenty of water to waste on something so unnecessary as a bath." Norry's eyes twinkled. "Since that is so, just this once we'll indulge you . . ." She gave Ernie another hug. "My dear, I don't know how it has come about, but I'm glad you've come."

Ernie grimaced. "I'm glad too—despite my aches."

Norry smiled broadly, very nearly in the old way. "Those are temporary, as you very well know! Tomorrow or the next day and you'll feel your usual self. Now. You sit and I'll get you something to eat. My guess is that the men returning from Lisbon were unwilling to stop even for a moment. You didn't halt for so much as a luncheon, did you?"

"Bertie was very careful of my comfort," said Ernie, evading the exact question. "Supper was always excellent—"

She recalled her shock that first evening that she was expected to roll up in blankets near the fire along with the other two women traveling with the group of officers and men returning from the coast, but Bertie had explained that the small inns or the houses they might enter were almost always infested with fleas and it was better, in decent weather, to sleep out.

"—and we had a sort of picnic about midday each day . . ." she added, coming out of her brief reverie.

That they'd had it, slabs of a strong cheese between two slices of coarse bread, while riding along what Ernie was certain must be a slightly improved goat trail she *didn't* say, but then there had been the oranges to finish with and those—she brightened at the memory—had been truly excellent! The most succulent she'd ever tasted.

"Bertie picked oranges right off a tree as we left Lisbon, great golden globes on branches hanging over a garden wall and weighed down with the fruit. I couldn't believe it. He picked more whenever he saw a tree."

Ernie's evasions didn't fool her sister for a moment. Five years with the army had given Norry ample experience from which to make a judgment. "If you only had picnics, I know you need a cup of tea and whatever can be found in a hurry. You sit." Norry disappeared again.

Ernie was afraid to sit. If she were to relax back into a chair she might never get up again. But perhaps the narrow bench near the smoky fire? Ah, but the armed chair, the one with soft looking cushions, was so much more appealing . . .

Ernie approached the chair and eyed it warily, as if it might bite. She sighed. Would it be such a terrible disaster if she couldn't get up again? If no other method occurred to her she could, perhaps, *roll* out and *crawl* to bed . . . which thought raised still another question: *was* there a bed?

Where *would* she sleep? On the floor? Oh dear, she really hadn't planned this visit at all well, but then it hadn't occurred to her to question the details of Norry's life. Bertie, thought Ernie rather crossly, should have explained! Really. It was very thoughtless of him . . .

But the question remained: To sit? Or not? Did she dare?

The cushion beckoned. Ernie sat . . . and instantly fell into a doze. She awoke some time later to new aches, including a crick in her neck. She moved her head in circles to loosen tight muscles and yawned a huge gaping yawn that had her jaw cracking.

"You're awake."

Ernie moved too quickly and moaned softly. "Oh, dear, Norry, why didn't you poke me? How long have I slept?"

"Long enough that we've heated the bath water, but this pot of tea has cooled," she said, touching the pot sitting on the bench, "Unless you've become overly modest in my absence, I'll bring you a hot cup and whatever Maria finds to go with it once you're in the tub. Come along now, love. Let's see if we can make you feel a bit more human and less like something the cat's been teasing."

Ernie chuckled, the laugh followed by a moan. "Oh, I've not felt this bad since the time I fell off the stable roof when Bertie and I pretended we were climbing in the Cuillins on the Isle of Skye!"

"I remember that. You were two foolish children, were you not? But if that's all the worse it is, you'll do."

"All the worse!"

As they spoke Ernie managed to lever herself to a standing position. She followed Norry through a different door from the one Norry had used earlier and found herself in her sister's tiny bedroom. A gently steaming bath stood there and Ernie moaned again, but softly, and with anticipated relief.

"Norry," she said, "how uncaring of you to suggest I'm feeling nothing out of the way—why, I'm so sore I think I must be black and blue in places a lady doesn't admit to owning!" She began unbuttoning buttons before Norry had shut the door.

Norry hugged her sister again before deftly helping her from her habit and Ernie was soon settled into the healing warmth of the hot water. "It is going to be so good having you here, Ernie. I wonder why it never occurred to me to invite you to visit us. Really, it was quite thoughtless of me. I should have done so long ago."

Norry left her, but returned in a few minutes with a tray on which sat cups and saucers and a teapot. A plate held the promised meal which Ernie eyed suspiciously as, despite the temperature, she drank her first cupful of tea with no thought to lady-like sips. She held the cup out for more. The second she was willing to treat with proper respect. And finally, she was ready to try one of the nibbles fixed in Portuguese style. She found it surprisingly good and ate up the rest—along with the bread and honey—with regret there was no more. Riding had been hunger-making as well as ache-making.

"Tell me all about home, Ernie," suggested Norry, once she'd assured herself her sister was beginning to feel more the thing. Norry leaned back against the head of her bed, her pillow pushed behind her, her ankles primly crossed.

"I've spoken of home in letters. Nothing is different except that Father insists you come back—but that's not news either. You know already his thoughts on that subject." Ernie grimaced and Norry raised eyes toward Heaven. "Instead," said Ernie, "you tell me . . . oh, tell me all about that odd man who was when I arrived."

mean Sommerton? What was so odd about *him?*"

hat hair. It says he's well up in years, but when he

looked at me—no! When the dratted man *laughed* at me with that terrible gleam in his eyes, he looked about the same age as Bertie."

"As old as Bertie indeed—who must be all of twenty-three now, since you are twenty-one! Sommerton is barely into his thirties, Ernie. But now that you mention it, I too once wondered about the gray and was impertinent enough to ask! It's a family thing. The men always turn gray at an early age, their hair becoming white long before most men's do."

"How strange." Ernie moved her hands back and forth in the water, watching the small ripples. "I've never heard of such a thing."

"He told me that when he was a child he believed it a family curse, but he was convinced otherwise eventually."

"Did Bertie call him Colonel *Lord* Sommerton?"

"His father's an earl." Norry grimaced. "From what I've been told, *not* a man one would choose to know. Jon described him as a dissolute gambler and recklessly extravagant."

"I met men like that in London," said Ernie. "The worst one I saw easily made me believe the rumors he was once a member of the Hellfire club, although one would have thought him too young for it. That was in our grandfather's time rather than our father's, was it not?" Ernie shuddered. "In any case, he was . . . almost evil. You could sense it."

"The earl isn't quite that bad, but Jon hates Ave's father for what he's done to Ave. Ave won't speak of his inheritance, but Jon says he feels it deeply that, very likely, all will be lost by his father's gambling. That's why Ave went into the army in the first place and *not* because he was army-mad the way Bertie is. It was that he needed a means of supporting himself and also, according to Jon, that there was nothing he could do to save his people—I mean his father's people—from their suffering. Nor could he bear to watch his lordship destroying them as the man went along the road to destroying himself."

"How do you know all this?"

Norry smiled a trifle sadly. "He's Jon's oldest friend which is why he's been looking out for me in Jon's absence."

"Absence." Ernie caught and held her sister's gaze, her own steady. *"Absence?"*

Norry frowned. "Now don't start that, Ernie. Jon is *not* dead. He'll be returning soon now. Oh, in a week or three. Surely before Christmas. Or Christmas Day? I'm very certain of it."

"But how can you? Norry, he's been missing for going on four months. Surely you'd have had word from him if he still lived."

"My dear, don't you understand? I *have* heard."

Relief flooded Ernie.

"In a sort of funny way, I suppose," continued Norry, thoughtfully. "But I know what he's *feeling.*"

The relief faded and Ernie stared at her sister's dreamy features.

"Mostly Jon's angry. Sometimes he seems rather proud of something." Norry looked up and met her sister's eyes. "Ernie, love, Jonathan is well and very much alive, I assure you." Norry grinned a conspiratorial grin. "Then, too, I occasionally dream about him. I can't tell for certain if what I dream is true or not—although I am, of course, very certain of the emotions, his feelings . . ."

She frowned slightly. "Sometimes I wish I were *not* so closely tied to him. You see, not long ago he was beaten—rather badly—and I too felt his pain. But he's recovering now so you mustn't worry . . ."

As her sister continued, her frown fading, Ernie's horror grew. "He'd tried to come to me, I think," she said softly. "I saw him in my dream sneaking out of a cave not too terribly far from here. Perhaps as much as thirty miles? In my dream he carefully stepped over the legs of a sleeping man, a guard, I suppose. He walked away, climbed down a cliff, found a way across a roaring stream—and then he faced a row of wild looking men. Bandits, perhaps, although I'm not certain. Guerrillas maybe? He lost his temper then and didn't give in to them, which he ought to have done because then he'd not have been hurt so badly."

Ernie's distress continued to grow. Dreams? Emotions? Pain? Could their father be right for once? *Had* Norry lost her reason rather than admit to her grief? This was terrible. What did one do with someone in this condition? Surely it was no solution to just tell a madwoman she was mad and that she was to stop, at once, being that way, because if it were that easy then curing madness would be a simple thing indeed. Perhaps it would be best if she pretended she understood?

"You must understand," said Norry, the word echoing the thought in Ernie's head, "that they beat him because he wouldn't give in when they caught him. It wasn't too badly—almost playfully in a way—although he was sore for a day or two." Norry sighed, then smiled, then frowned again. "That happened—or something of the sort, if the dreams are not true visions—a few nights ago. It seems they will not let him go until they're ready, although, as I said, that will be soon now. I *know* and I wish I had some way of telling Jonathan to be patient, that he'll be allowed to leave any day now."

The frown left Norry's brow and her smile appeared once again. "However the details may be, Ernie, Jon has not taken a fatal wound. *You'll* understand how that can be as no one else might do, although I'm not positive about the visions. There was no mention of visions in Great-great-grandmother's diary so I can't be certain. . . ."

After another moment's frowning thought Norry's vision cleared and she looked at Ernie. "I wouldn't dare tell this to anyone else, of course, but you'll know how it is. I actually think I could very nearly guide you to where that cave lies. I could, if I were half the artist you are, draw a portrait of the madman who took Jon prisoner, assuming, of course, that I've dreamed truly. Jonathan's captivity hasn't been all bad either. I've felt Jon's pride in those men he's training that other man to lead properly. At least"—She frowned again—"I *think* that's what he's been doing."

Ernie hid her dismay behind a very real curiosity about Norry's so-called visions. She couldn't help but be appalled, of course. These were the words of someone far gone in madness, someone for whom the real world had receded dangerously. *And what was that about their ancestress and some diary?* But, when it occurred to her to wonder how those who knew Norry had not recognized her condition, Ernie put that question from her mind. Or perhaps . . . she looked up and met Norry's eyes.

"Norry, am I to understand that you've not told anyone at all what you've just told me? About that bandit camp, I mean, and Jon being prisoner and all that?"

"Lud, no. They'd think me as mad as Father thinks me to be! I've only told you because you have studied our history and will understand." Norry said the last as she checked the teapot and discovered they'd finished it.

What history? Ernie quickly hid her confusion. She'd never been interested in the family history in the way Norry was, and had avoided, as much as she could, her governess's insistence she read records kept in the records room. Turning over in her mind what she *had* read, nothing occurred to Ernie which explained such exceedingly odd behavior in her sister. For a moment she wished she knew to whom the diary belonged, but the question slipped away in a huge yawn.

"Do you want more tea, Ernie? No? Well, I'll just go help Marie with our dinner. I'll add this last can of hot water and you sit and soak for as long as you like. I've laid a warm robe on the bed for you and some of my clean linen. Your baggage can't possibly be here for several days yet, so you'll have to

make do with what I have—which won't be up to the quality
to which you are accustomed, poor dear!"

With another quick smile Norry left Ernie to her own devices
and Ernie wished she hadn't. She'd almost begun to think Norry
as sane as anyone—until she'd started spouting nonsense. No
sane person could possibly dream up such a strange tale and
actually think it true!

Even Ernie knew that if Jon had been captured by bandits a
demand for ransom would have come long ago—immediately
after the battle, in fact. So how could Norry actually think that
Jon, badly wounded, had been found by guerrillas who had first
healed him and then kept him prisoner for some purpose of
their own which made no sense at all?

It must be a trick played on Norry by her grieving mind. A
ploy so she need not admit Jon was dead. And that meant—
Ernie sighed deeply at her conclusion—that, for once in a way,
her father was right in his pessimism. Norry must be taken back
to England, must be cared for by her family, cosseted and loved
and petted and amused, until her mind healed and she was able
to accept the harsh truth that Jon would not return.

But such treatment would not include being locked away in
the tower room over the entrance hall! Not if Ernie had anything
to say to the contrary! A ridiculous notion, anyway. Norry
wasn't *that* mad. She couldn't be. If she were someone here
would have noticed!

So, she thought, what did one do? Ernie lifted her hand, and
watched the water drip from the ends of her fingers, the drips
making circles in the still water of her bath. Should one confront
Norry and explain kindly that she had no choice, that they must
pack immediately and go at once? For a long moment Ernie, always
in favor of the blunt approach, thought that would be best.

Then she thought again. Wouldn't it be better to wait, to get to
know her sister again, to win Norry's trust—and then perhaps . . .
what? Well, perhaps one might pretend a letter had arrived from

home saying their father's health was worse due to his worry? Saying that he wanted them to come to him? At once?

Or perhaps, thought Ernie a trifle cynically, simply wait for a *real* letter to come saying very much that very thing? Mr. Matthewson was nothing if not self-deluding and, while he sneered at Ernie for being unwed, for remaining at home where she watched his diet and his household and, for that matter, the daily details of his estate, he would soon find he could not do without her and would, if necessary, *invent* reasons why she must come home.

Norry, too, of course. *Especially* Norry, who was always his favorite—and especially so once married and no longer around to rouse his irritation!

Yes, Mr. Matthewson would write just the sort of letter required. So, one *would* come, one which she could allow Norry to read. Ernie decided that would be best: She'd wait.

A vision of a tall, powerful, prematurely gray-haired man slipped into Ernie's mind. She banished it immediately. The colonel had nothing whatsoever to do with her decision to stay in Portugal for several weeks.

Nothing.

She convinced herself.

Almost.

Two

Bertie arrived in mid-morning the next day, leading the gelding Ernie had ridden from the coast. He was surprised when he found Norry and Ernie still in dishabille. "But of course you must ride today," he exploded after the women suggested Ernie wait a day or two. "How else can you untwist tied up muscles and rid yourself of the stiffness?"

"Bertie, I swore I'd not admit to a soul how I felt, but I will if you'll only go away. I ache more—and in more places—than ever before in my life." Ernie shook her head. "I don't think I could sit in a saddle if my life depended on it."

"Don't be a fool, Ern, old girl. You know very well the only cure is to ride out the kinks."

Ernie remembered something. "I can't. Norry's Maria brushed out my habit and found spots which needed sponging. It can't possibly be dry, so I can't possibly wear it." She crossed her arms, silently daring him to find a solution to that problem. To her dismay, he did.

"You can borrow Norry's habit. Norry? May she not?"

"She may if she wishes, but if she doesn't want to go I don't think you should bully her into doing so."

"Norry, *you* know the cure is to ride at once!" exclaimed Bertie and went on, accusingly, *"You* always do whenever the Regiment's had a rough trek."

"Of course I do," said Norry in a pacifying tone, "but I must be hardened for my life with the army. Ernie has no such need.

It's perfectly all right for her to rest until she feels more the thing."

"Nonsense." Bertie glowered, crossing his arms to match Ernie's. "She doesn't want to sit about for days moaning and groaning when a little effort could see her right again."

"I don't?" muttered Ernie. Then she looked toward her sister. "Is it true, Norry, that you'd go?"

"Oh yes. But, as I said, there's no need for you to do so."

"If it's the thing to do, I'll do it." Ernie's chin firmed and tilted in a way both Bertie and Norry knew well. The chin lowered. "That is, I will if you'll loan me the habit."

"It's a Spanish design, Ernie," warned her sister.

"What's the difference between a regular and a Spanish habit?"

Norry hesitated and glanced at Bertie who grinned. "You'll find out," he said. "I'll wait while you get ready."

Ernie discovered the difference when she went to pull the skirt over her head. When it didn't go she took it off and looked at it more closely. The skirt was divided into legs, the fullness of the skirt hiding the split. Her eyes gleamed. "Norry! Does this mean you ride astride after all those years you scolded me for doing so? I don't believe it!"

Something over half an hour later Ernie gingerly sat astride Norry's gentle mare. Bertie had decided it might be better, assuming Ernie hurt half so badly as she insisted, if she rode an animal not chosen for its willingness to take any jump its rider put it to. He'd asked Jon's batman's permission to use Norry's mount, Senorita, an animal chosen for staying-power and sure-footedness rather than bloodlines and fancy looks.

The two old friends walked their horses through the village and out into a rolling, plateau, criss-crossed by stone walls and dotted with huge, rounded, cottage sized, boulders. The remains of the morning mistiness softened the view and gave it a romantic look.

" 'Ware rabbit holes, Ernie," said Bertie. "This is rough ground and you won't want to break 'Rita's leg. How are you doing?"

She grimaced. "Wishing I'd never been born, but I don't suppose it'll last."

"It won't," he agreed, callously. "Come along now. I know a high spot from which we may get a view of today's hunt."

"I didn't know there were foxes in Portugal."

"They exist. Wellesley—or, I should say, the Marquess of Wellington—goes out for them. We less notable types believe a good hare can give one a surprisingly long run—and, an even better reason for hunting them, they go well in the pot which a fox does not! Come along, girl. See that low ridge sticking up through the scrub? I'll race you to the highest point. See? There—toward the end."

He took off and, for a moment, Ernie struggled to contain 'Rita to a more decorous pace. She might have agreed that hair of the dog, as the saying went, would cure what ailed her, but that didn't mean she wanted to swallow the whole animal! Perhaps later, when her muscles loosened up and once she'd become reaccustomed to riding astride—something she hadn't done since Bertie purchased his commission and left to join his regiment . . .

Ernie grinned, reminiscing. She and Bertie, when they were mere children, had always ridden astride, but then, when she was about twelve, someone, Bertie's mother, she'd always thought, informed Mr. Matthewson that it was a disgrace, such a big girl riding wild like any boy. Ernie was forced into a much detested habit and, as a result, into a sidesaddle, which was worse. She'd hated and avoided both whenever she could, though she'd become accustomed, eventually, and, once Bertie left for the army, she'd put away her trousers for the last time.

Ernie neared her old comrade. She took a better grip on her reins and straightened her back and then, ashamed, glanced cautiously to see if Bertie had noticed how she'd slumped there for a minute. Her gaze was caught and held by the worried brown eyes of her oldest and dearest friend.

"Is it so very bad? Should we go back?" Bertie eased his horse nearer. "I *did* tell—"

"Don't you dare say it, Bertie!" she interrupted with a hint of the old gleam in her eye.

He laughed. "If I can rouse your temper that easily I don't suppose you'll fall on your nose and embarrass me, but I never thought I'd see the day when you'd back off from a challenge, Ernie Matthewson! That wasn't much of a race, after all." He studied her, the worried look returning. "You *won't* fall off, will you?"

She glared. "If I do, just ignore me. Perhaps no one will notice."

Bertie snorted on a bitten-back chuckle and, eyes narrowed against the glare of a haze-weakened winter sun, looked out over the sere countryside. "Chin up, Ernie. You'll do. You always do. I was proud of you, by the way. I'd say you did damn near as well as—oops, pardon—*very nearly* as well as Norry could do on such a long ride. But I did warn you . . ."

"Oh, no, Bertie! *Don't say it!* We swore an oath when I was ten that we'd *never ever* say 'I told you so.' " She glowered. "Don't you remember?"

"So we did. All right, I won't remind you I said you should come with the wagons," he teased, his eyes asparkle with laughter. "I won't say, again, that the way is rougher than anything you've ever seen—living soft, as you've done in England. I won't remind you that you were warned we Army men stop for nothing and that you'd . . ." He ducked, grinning as Ernie swung her riding crop at him.

"Bertie, can we be serious for a moment?" she asked, when he'd resettled his shako. And then she stared out over the boulder strewn country, wondering how to begin. "Bertie . . . you've never said how you think Norry's doing—not that I blame you, since I didn't ask, but, she's so *thin.* I've never seen her so gaunt and . . . sort of stringy. Do you think she's sick?"

"Sick? Norry? Norry's never sick." he said and asked, curious, "Is that why you demanded I escort you to join your sister, that you thought she might be ill?"

"Not ill. Exactly." Ernie bit her lip, debating. Then, drawing in a deep breath, she said, "Bertie, Father insisted I wasn't to reveal his suspicions to anyone, but I'm so worried—especially after a talk she and I had last night . . . But Father . . ." Her voice trailed off, uncertainty as to what to say making her unusually inarticulate.

"Your *father's* suspicions?" repeated Bertie, scorn dripping. "I don't doubt for a moment the old crock has bats in his belfry as usual, so what are these suspicions that you take them seriously even for a minute? And don't say I've insulted your father because we've both said far worse in the past!" When Ernie didn't respond immediately, he turned. "Ernie? What's he suggested to upset you so?"

Ernie drew in a deep breath. "He's afraid that Jon's death has turned Norry's mind, that she's become mad."

"Norry?" Bertie's outrage was directed *her* way at that. "Are we speaking of your sister?"

Ernie, biting her lip, nodded.

"Surely *you* don't think such a thing?" Bertie asked.

"N-o-o-o." She stared, unseeingly, between Senorita's ears. "Not really"—She turned and looked at her old friend, her forehead screwed into a painful frown—"but why, then, does she refuse to admit he's dead?"

He shrugged. "I assume because she believes he isn't."

"But, Bertie, it's more than four months!"

"So?"

Ernie gnashed her teeth at his willful lack of understanding.

When he still said nothing, she demanded, "So how often does a man simply go missing for anything like that long?"

Bertie's face lit in a quick grin. "There have been some who have disappeared pretty much forever . . . not that Jonathan would do a thing like *that.*"

Curious, Ernie forgot Norry long enough to ask, "What do you mean?"

"I refer to men who run scared and desert, of course. Jon wouldn't."

"No he wouldn't desert." Again Ernie felt that knot of pain in her forehead. "So where, my friend, is he if he is not dead?"

"A French captive?"

"A prisoner of war?" Ernie fell silent. "Oh dear. I'd not thought of that. You think that might be it?"

"No."

Ernie beat her fist against her thigh. "Why do you mention possibilities and then say they can't be? Don't you *know* how worried I am about Norry?"

"No one needs to worry about Norry," said Bertie stubbornly.

"But she insists in the face of no evidence at all—no real evidence—that he's alive and well. She admits he was wounded in July at the battle of Salamanca, but says he's well now and merely angry he can't get home to her. Bertie, she says she *knows* all this but how can she?"

Bertie blinked, ignoring her question. "He's angry?"

Throwing aside caution, Ernie repeated, "Yes. She insists she knows he was badly wounded, but that he's recovered and that now he's angry. She also says he'll be home by Christmas."

"But . . ."

"Now do you see why Father insisted I come? Not that *he* knows this!"

"Nonsense. I still say," repeated Bertie loyally, "that Norry is as sane as you or I."

Instantly more childhood memories surfaced and Ernie

grinned, ducked a quick look his way, and met his grinning response.

"All right," he admitted with a rueful look. "I suppose that *isn't* a good comparison." Again their eyes met and he winked at her, laughter in his voice as he said, "It was fun, back when we were young, wasn't it, Ernie?"

"Back when we were called"—her voice took on a trace of the Kentish countryside—"that pair of bedlamites!" They chuckled. "Remember," she continued, "how Farmer Goodfellow predicted we'd, neither of us, see our sixteenth birthday?" Ernie smiled, reminiscently. "Yes, we had fun. Bertie, did I ever tell you that, once, when he was angry with me, Father swore Mother must have given him horns—that no off-spring of *his* would behave in such an outrageous and mannerless fashion?" Ernie chuckled. "What he *meant*," she said, "was that just watching us wore him out and he couldn't believe any Matthewson could *wish* to tear around as we did"—a lesser version of her former frown appeared—"He'd be shocked if he could see Norry now, so thin, yet whipcord strong. Nanny will say she's old leather and Father won't like that either." She added with no more than an understandable amount of bitterness, "The child of his heart was his softly rounded, lady-like and gentle little Lenore with her peaches and cream complexion and beautifully groomed hair and stylish clothes—and she isn't like that anymore, is she?"

Bertie ignored the bit about Nanny, going back to Mr. Matthewson's accusations. "He had no business saying such things to you even if he was angry—that bit about your mother, I mean. You don't tell a girl . . . such things!" Ernie laughed and Bertie's face flushed. "Well, you *don't*. It isn't done." When she just shook her head, he asked, curiously, "Ernie, has he always been so ill?"

"Father? I guess so. I can't remember when he wasn't surrounded by shawls against the tiniest draft, and his precious bottles of medicine." She sighed and didn't know if it was thinking of her father or if it was this ancient looking land in which her sister now lived, but suddenly she felt very alone and . . . sad?

On their way through the Portuguese countryside they'd passed through villages which had, at first, intrigued Ernie: the women dressed in black from head to toe, just as described, the small houses built largely of rough unshaped rock, small and, from what she could tell from the outside, dark and drear. In what sort of house, she had wondered, would she find her sister? Was there a bigger, better town on ahead? Somewhere with larger homes, decent houses—and water piped into the kitchen? Ernie bit her lip. She'd discovered the answer to that.

It wasn't so bad as some, of course, but Norry had little room for guests. Ernie's bedroom wouldn't make a decent linen closet in England and her bed was a camp cot she suspected belonged to Jon's batman. What he'd sleep on now she hadn't a notion, but she couldn't bring herself to ask, either, since she had no desire to sleep on the floor and that might very well be her alternative!

"Bertie," she asked, "has Norry always lived in such rough places? I mean since her marriage? Or is it only that Jon isn't here and she was given the left-over-bit?"

Bertie turned an outraged expression her way. "What can you mean left-over-bit? Colonel Sommerton saw that she's very well settled, I'll have you know. Once I saw her set up house-keeping in a shed with only part of a roof."

"Bertie!"

"At that she was far better off than *I* was," he said defensively. "Most of us didn't have even *part* of a roof!"

"But how can she live like that?"

"Ernie, she's following the drum. No one promised her feath-erbeds and a dozen servants!"

"She has servants, thank Heaven, although it seems to me she does an awful lot herself."

"She has Jon's batman who does the heavy work and the fetching and carrying." A flush colored Bertie's cheekbones and he looked at Ernie and then, quickly, away. "And, of course, she has Maria who is a great help."

"Bertie, just who is Maria? She can't truly be a servant, can she? She seems better educated than one would expect, more . . . refined?"

"She's a Spanish girl Norry rescued—maybe only fifteen or sixteen, then—from one of our less well liked officers who thought to have himself a little sport. Maria won't talk much about her family. She says she's orphaned and it makes her sad to speak of the past." The spots of red deepened on Bertie's cheeks. "I've tried to get her talking, you see, and once she let slip a bit about a much disliked uncle and some other bits and pieces. She's devoted to Norry, however, and that's good."

"But to live the way she does! There's so much I didn't know," wailed Ernie. "So much of which I'd no idea."

"How could you know?"

She rounded on him. "Why did you never tell me?"

Bertie faced her, frowning. "And why should I? You were never going to live this way. Why would you *want* to know the hard facts? Besides, one doesn't distress one's women-folk without need," he finished rather portentously.

"Am I such a fragile thing I cannot be told a hard truth?"

"It wouldn't be right," he insisted. When she glared he added, "Well? Would you not have worried more about Norry if you'd known?"

Ernie's frown deepened. "Of course I would. Any decent person would worry about someone suffering this sort of deprivation."

"Suffering? Norry? I don't think you should suggest that to Norry. She's been very happy living here with Jon."

"But how *can* she?"

"How could she not? She had Jon."

The simplicity of that reply silenced Ernie for a full half a minute. She drew in a deep breath. "She isn't with Jon now."

"No. Not at the moment."

"Don't tell me *you* believe Jon's alive?"

He stared thoughtfully out across the weather-rounded, lichen-mottled, rocks tumbled over the rolling plain. Finally he turned toward her, a stubborn look in his eye. "Well, I won't then." When she didn't seem to understand, he added, "Tell you, I mean."

"But you *do?*" Ernie's eyes widened painfully. They narrowed as she noted how his jaw firmed. "Bertie, how can you?"

He shrugged. "It's very hard to think him dead when Norry's so very certain he's alive. You'll see what I mean soon enough," he added when she would have argued. "And there go the hounds! Look." He pointed, his other hand hard on his reins, pulling in his mount who was as eager as he to join them.

Ernie looked, but her mind was on their conversation. Was everyone here in Portugal mad? she wondered. How could Bertie believe Jon still lived? It was four months with no word from him. *More* than four months!

A horse and rider broke from the melee of straining horses streaming after a motley pack of hounds. Horse and rider curved toward where Bertie was having great difficulty restraining his mount from taking off after the barking and yipping pack which led the hunt.

"Well met," called Colonel Sommerton. "I suppose Norry urged you to ride this morning—very best thing you could do, of course. I wondered where you'd gotten to, Lieutenant, since I couldn't believe you'd voluntarily stay away from a good day's hunting!"

"It wasn't Norry who urged me to ride. Bertie came by and insisted we go out. You are missing the run, Colonel," Ernie finished with a certain coolness.

Sommerton ignored Ernie's hint he should go away. "Browley, it looks as if that gelding of yours hasn't been out while you were in England. Perhaps you should exercise him."

"Join the hunt . . ." Bertie's eyes glowed. The glow faded. "Oh, but I can't. Ernie . . ." Bertie turned to look at her and she could see how much he longed to be off. His mouth firmed.

"No, I'll stay with Ern," he said, proving how much he'd matured in his years with the army.

"I can find my own way back, Bertie." Actually, Ernie wasn't certain she could do any such thing. When they'd left the village she'd been too preoccupied with her aches and pains to do more than follow where Bertie led. "You go on."

"Yes, do go on," the colonel agreed. "I'll see Miss Matthewson home."

"Oh no," said Ernie, with heartfelt earnestness. She put her chin in the air and turned her head slightly. "I couldn't possibly put you to the bother . . ."

He cut her off. "I'll have to return anyway. I'm afraid Caliph took a slight strain at that last jump—he was just the least bit off when he landed, you see. Caliph is my best hunter and I don't want to chance worsening his leg."

There was nothing more Ernie could say, so she nodded and Bertie relaxed his grip on his reins. She watched as his gelding, freed at last from restraint, took off. She turned and said sweetly, "You really should learn to take a hint, Colonel."

"Hints," he said, his eyes smiling, "are much too subtle for an old campaigner like me. What if you *don't* hint?"

"You mean, what if I say right out you aren't wanted? That I find your presence an intrusion?" She gave him a speculative look and added even more bluntly, "That I want to know what's between you and my sister?" His smile faded, the frown she'd seen the day before appearing. "And," finished Ernie, ignoring that sign of imminent danger—and her fast beating heart as well, "that I want to know what you were doing, visiting her, with no chaperon in sight!"

"I thought you a minx. I was wrong. You're merely a thoughtless and irritating brat, Miss Matthewson."

Her cheeks burned, but she ignored the heat in them. "Fiddle." She tossed her head. "You're attempting to shift the subject to *my* faults—which are at least based in my love for my sister and that is *more* evidence of your perfidy, is it not?"

"Perfidy, is it! You little she-devil, I'll have you know my actions are also based in a sort of love—that of friendship. I first met Jon Lockwood when neither of us could walk without help. We were friends for very nearly as long as we are old! Don't you *dare* accuse me of misbehavior with Jon's wife, you . . . you . . . !"

"I believe you've not yet called me a *shrew,*" suggested Ernie with less heat than formerly. Somewhat relieved and partially chastened, she looked at him sideways from the corner of her eyes.

Relaxing, the colonel choked back a laugh. "Perhaps I was right to begin with." She looked her question and he continued. "Minx I thought and minx I think again!"

They eyed each other, taking in details their preceding meeting had been too brief to reveal. Aware, now, of his age, Ernie wondered that she'd ever thought him old. The gray hair didn't detract at all from his handsome face or rangy form—or from the tightly contained energy that seemed to light the very air around him.

For his part, Sommerton saw a small woman with brown hair and huge brown eyes set in a face which would never launch ships as Helen of Troy's was purported to have done. But it was a comfortable face, one a man could live with, he thought, and she had a form which pleased without flaunting its femininity. All in all she made a picture with nothing in particular to recommend it even as there was nothing about which one would complain either.

On the other hand he'd watched as she'd greeted her sister and, then, her whole being had seemed to glow with her smile, making her into an entirely different person, so vivid, so very much alive . . .

Ave wondered what it would take to make her smile at him

that way . . . "Perhaps," he asked softly, "we might begin again?"

Ernie hesitated, unsettled by the feelings coursing through her at his mere presence. "Perhaps we could." This man was her sister's friend. She couldn't very well snub him—which was really very good, because she didn't *want* to snub him! "I was very tired when I arrived yesterday," she said by way of apology.

Tipping his head, he made his own offer of atonement. "Perhaps I overreacted to seeing you so wan and weary."

"Sir, I find that a particularly ungallant statement," she responded, pretending to pout.

He grinned. "You'll get no gallantries from me, Miss Matthewson. Only the blunt truth from a blunt old soldier. Today, much to my surprise, I find you've already recovered from what must have been the worst ordeal of your life—and very good to look at."

Ernie blushed. She glanced at him and then, quickly, away. How could he just say she'd get only the truth and then hear him say such an odd thing as that? And now what? He seemed to be waiting for something . . . but what?

Ernie sighed softly. If he were looking for a flirtation he'd not find it with her. One of the reasons she'd given up on London after only two Seasons was that she could never learn to flirt properly. It was a necessary talent. It was required for the games that fascinated the young people who were engaged in the far more important game of finding a mate. Whether against the background of a ball, a soiree, a morning call or riding in the park, it was necessary that one flirt. Discreetly, of course. At Almacks, the theater, the opera, or visiting Vauxhall Gardens— or merely shopping on Bond Street—*wherever* one was, one needed to flirt. Decorously, of course.

But all that London nonsense seemed far away and unimportant when one had arrived to visit an army engaged in the life and death struggle to win Spain back from Napoleon. . . .

Sommerton, watching her, hid a smile. A minx, surely, but a rather shy and self-conscious minx, he decided. And what else besides? Would she have even half of Norry's courage? Her sister's intelligence and loyalty? That thought brought him up short. What did it matter if she did? Sommerton decided that perhaps he should back off a bit and think about what he was doing!

"You've seen a little of Portugal now, Miss Matthewson. What do you think of it?" he asked politely.

"Lisbon, what I saw, appeared to be an interesting city," she responded, equally polite. "I'll frankly admit I was rather appalled by the poverty and dirt as one moved through the countryside." Ernie had been trying to make up her mind about the colonel and now decided to trust him . . . and to the devil with conventional manners. "Sir, I think I should tell you that when I suggested you might have an interest in my sister, I rather hoped you did."

Ernie stared straight between Senorita's ears and didn't notice Sommerton's quick shocked look. He opened his mouth to tell her exactly what he thought of that notion, but she went on before he could.

"You see, sir, such an interest between you would nicely explain why she refuses to return to England." Now she did look at him. "I think I should explain that I've come here at my father's behest. He wishes me to convince Norry to return to England, but I find she isn't the least willing to go. I thought that if there was a new interest—you, for instance—it would explain . . ." Her voice trailed off and she gave him another look, this one questioning.

Sommerton shook his head. Now that he understood her odd wish, there was the warmth of approval in the gaze directed her way. "I'm sorry to disappoint you, but my interest in Norry is nothing more, or for that matter, nothing *less,* than friendship." Sommerton sobered. "Mr. Matthewson has the right of it in one respect, I fear. She *should* go home. I've not tried to persuade her for the simple reason I thought it a waste of breath, but perhaps the two of us, together"—He frowned, then nodded as if he'd reached a decision—"I'll do what I can to help you, Miss Matthewson, but I frankly admit I don't think we'll succeed."

"You don't think she'll go?"

His firm nod, his rather grim features indicated that was exactly what he thought.

Appalled, Ernie, said, "But she can't stay here forever, surely."

Again he agreed.

Horror grew. "What will she do, then?"

Sommerton stared out to where a distant yapping revealed the location of the hunt. It appeared for a long moment as if he'd forgotten he'd been asked a question, but finally he turned to her. "I have had the thought that, if the time comes when she *must* admit Jon will not return, that *when* that happens, there would then be no question of her staying. I'd decided that, if necessary, I'd ask for personal leave and escort her back to England myself. Assuming, I must add," he finished on a dry note, "that she still lives so that one might escort her anywhere."

Ernie blanched. For the second time in two days she felt odd prickles under her skin. Moments later she felt herself lifted from her saddle, felt strong arms around her, a hand pressing her head into a wonderfully solid shoulder. After a moment she struggled weakly and Sommerton loosened his hold. Assured she'd not fall, Ernie stepped away from him, turned her back.

In a strangled voice, she said, "You cannot possibly mean what I thought, for an instant, you were suggesting . . ."

"But I did." Audibly he sighed. "Miss Matthewson, I should not have spoken so without preparing you, but I'd forgotten you've no idea of how incredibly, unbelievably, close she and Jon are . . . *were,* I mean." He paused, searching for a way to put words to inexpressible thoughts, to explain his fears for Lenore's life. "Perhaps," he said, at last, "she wrote you about the battle where Jon received his second wound, the one that almost killed him?"

"Yes. They went to Lisbon, I believe. His recovery took some time, did it not?"

"Given how calmly you say that, I'd guess you haven't the whole story. You see, in that engagement, his *plight* rather than his *wound* would have killed him—except Norry forced Jon's batman to follow her right out into the middle of the battle which continued to rage around them. They found Jon trapped half under his fallen horse and bleeding from a shoulder wound. Between them they stopped the bleeding and removed him from the field. She did that with artillery shells bursting hot around her—and later, when I asked if she hadn't been frightened she looked at me as if it were I who was insane. You see, she had no recollection of anything except Jon's condition and his need of her."

Ernie thought about that, proud of her sister. Then a further thought slithered in under the emotion. She turned questioning, wary, eyes toward Sommerton. "But . . . how did she know where to find him?"

"An excellent question. I've asked that one myself. But, more, Miss Matthewson, how, before she went looking, did she *already know his need?"*

They stared at each other. Ernie frowned, shook her head, attempted to sort through her thoughts. "Surely . . ."

"Yes?" he asked when she didn't go on.

"But . . ."

His smile had a wry quirk to it. "I know. Or actually, I *don't* know. Nor does anyone else, except that those two seem to love each other to the point they are more then a couple—they are somehow united beyond that. So, now, perhaps, you'll understand why I haven't tried to convince Norry she should return to England—not so long as she insists Jon is well and will return to her."

"It's been over four months. Surely he isn't still alive," said Ernie, repeating the phrases as if to convince herself. She looked up to find Sommerton sadly nodding his agreement. Frowning, she added, "You *will* help me?"

"I'll do what I can. Just remember that I don't predict success," he said in the blunt manner she rather liked—since she was blunt to a fault herself.

"I won't blame you if we fail," she said. "And I'll thank you in advance, Colonel Sommerton, for any aid you may give me." She held out her hand which he grasped, holding it carefully in his own callused palm, his ungloved fingers warm around hers.

"So formal." He grinned, a quickly fading smile which momentarily altered his face into an exceedingly attractive visage. His other hand came up to enclose hers as well. "Since we've made a pact of such importance, do you suppose we might assume we've become friends and, as friends do, use each other's names?" When she didn't respond he added softly, "I'm Ave."

After a moment, during which she found she could not retrieve her hand, she said, "And I am Ernestine."

"Not Ernie?"

Ernie heard what she considered a rather spurious wistfulness in that question. "I think not," she said, her voice as dry as the surrounding countryside.

"Ah well," he said, his voice taking on a lilt she didn't recognize. "A man can only try, can he not?"

She quickly bit back a smile.

Sommerton was almost satisfied with his morning's work and was ready to give Miss Matthewson room to accept what had occurred between them before he pushed further. He blinked at the thought. Pushed further? What did that mean? Setting aside the personal question, he helped her mount and asked, "Shall we ride on a bit and see what sport the hunt has had?"

Silently Ernie tested her muscles, found that, as predicted, she felt considerably better than when she'd gotten, stiff and sore, from her bed that morning. And perhaps she should do something, anything, to stop the disturbing direction the conversation had taken. "That sounds agreeable."

She didn't await his lead, but set off toward the distant yipping and yapping which indicated hounds well set on a hare's trail. She heard, behind her, soft swearing and wondered at it—until it occurred to her that the colonel might be the sort who objected to a woman taking the lead. If that were so, he'd just have to put up with it because Ernie wasn't about to pander to any man's pride! Not even this one who had such an odd effect on her.

Ernie tossed her head, refusing to let her unsettled feelings interfere with enjoying the run—although, now she felt better, she did wish she had one of Bertie's spare mounts under her. Norry's Senorita was willing, but she simply didn't have the speed Ernie preferred and, never having ridden the mare before, she didn't dare put the poor creature at some quite reasonable jumps because she hadn't a notion if 'Rita could take them. As much as she loved a good hard run, she wasn't about to thoughtlessly harm her sister's mare just to get one.

At which point she recalled that the colonel—Ave, that was—had said his mount had strained something. She pulled 'Rita up.

"What is it?" he asked, reining in as well.

"You said your horse was hurt."

Two spots of red appeared across his cheekbones. "I lied."

"Why?"

"I could think of no other means of getting rid of Browley." He held her gaze with no wavering of his own. "I might, I suppose, have *ordered* him to go on about his business."

Ernie was about to ask for an explanation when it occurred to her the answer might possibly be a trifle embarrassing—however flattering. Instead she turned away and again set her mount to a goodly pace.

They caught up with the others, where she found—much to her disgust and entirely thanks to 'Rita—she was forced to trail the end of the pack, uncomfortable and becoming filthy in the midst of clods of damp orange soil kicked up along with the occasional stone.

That settled it! The next time she came out, she'd have one of Bertie's good English bred mounts beneath her and *then* she'd show this colonel a thing or two. Ernie realized her impulsive thoughts had led her right back to thinking of Ave Sommerton in that odd and unacceptable way.

She changed the last one. She'd show them *all* a thing or two!

Three

The hunt over for that day, Colonel Sommerton and Bertie rode on either side of Ernie back toward Norry's little house. Bertie had two hares tied to his saddle, a gift for Norry. As the three entered the square Sommerton noticed a rider crossing the open area and turning the curve toward the upper town. He frowned. "Browley, was that Lieutenant Torville?"

"Graham? I didn't notice. What would he be doing here? His regiment's billet is beyond anywhere, is it not?"

"I don't quite follow your geography," said Sommerton somewhat acidly, "but if you mean it's a twenty mile ride here and back, then yes, he's beyond anywhere." A crease of worry marred his forehead.

Speaking not quite idly, Bertie asked, "Wonder what he wanted here."

The men spoke over Ernie's head. Tired of being ignored, she suggested, "Very likely he came to discover if Jon has returned." She looked from one to the other. Bertie didn't look any too happy, thought Ernie. "What would be so surprising about that?"

"Surprising? Mostly," said Bertie, "that he and Jon don't get along. Not since Graham got a little above himself dipping once or twice or even thrice too often into the punch bowl last Christmas and, as a result, was more than a little too particular in his attentions to Norry. No, I don't think—after what happened between them—that Graham came by because of concern for Jon's whereabouts. On the other hand, he might . . ." Bertie's frown deepened, his gaze turning to meet Sommerton's. "Colonel?"

"I too wonder if that's it." Ave hesitated. "I don't see any solution but to ask Norry if he's making a nuisance of himself. I don't like to do it, but I don't know what else we can do."

By this time they'd arrived at the cottage and dismounted. Bertie, who hadn't the least notion there was any contest between them, was easily outmaneuvered by Sommerton and it was the colonel who lifted Ernie down. He caught her gaze and, by mere force of personality, held it. She blushed. He smiled and his hands tightened momentarily at her waist, but the frown returned as he turned toward the stairs up to the door.

Bertie tied their mounts and gathered up the hares. Holding them by the thong around their legs, he, too, faced the door which just then opened. Norry stood there, obviously pleased to see them. She invited the men in, easily overcoming their objections that they were in all their dirt and had no business stepping into her clean parlor in their condition, the result of a morning's hard riding.

"Maria laid out one of my dresses for you, Ernie," she said to her sister. "She'll help you change and by the time you've done so, I'll have our lunch finished. Ah, Bertie, are those hares for me? Good. You bring them into the kitchen and Albert Bacon will see they are cleaned and hung. Ave, you sit by the fire and enjoy a moment's peace and quiet, something all too rare in your life, I think—especially with all the hullabaloo since the retreat from Burgos!"

Norry, satisfied she'd organized everyone, was moving toward the kitchen when Bertie, rushing his fences, asked, "Norry, Graham Torville hasn't been making an ass of himself, has he?"

Norry paused, her head half-turning toward Sommerton and then, quickly, away. "Torville . . . ?" she asked evasively, a clenched fist nearly hidden in her skirts.

"We saw him ride away. Is he making a nuisance of himself?" asked Bertie.

Norry stared at the door through which she obviously wished to go. "I don't think . . ." she said, then hesitated, her voice trailing off.

"What Bertie is asking, in his inimitably awkward way," said Sommerton, his eyes narrowed, "is whether Lieutenant Torville has decided to take advantage of your being alone here in order to attempt your seduction?" His blunt question fell harshly into the silence.

Norry blushed a hot red. She whirled and stared at the colonel, her look reproachful. "Ave, how dare you think such a thing of me? Surely you don't believe I'd ever . . ."

Sommerton's stern visage almost frightened Ernie who had no reason to fear him. She'd known he must have great authority to have reached his present rank so young, but this display of it surprised her.

"You know perfectly well," he said to her sister, "that I've no fear you'll succumb to Graham's crude blandishments—but that doesn't change the question." He held her gaze. "Does he come to try his luck?"

Norry's eyes widened painfully. "Would I not have told you if it were so?"

Sommerton stared at her, that aura of authority still hovering around him. "You know, Norry, once I'd have thought so, but now"—his gaze grew speculative—"why, I wonder, would you not?"

With difficulty, Norry regained her poise. Her voice was again firm when she responded. "Since I know of no reason, there must be none. Come Bertie . . ."

She moved quickly and almost shut the door in the lieutenant's face, thereby revealing to those who knew her that she was still experiencing an otherwise well-hidden but unexplained agitation.

Sommerton made a mental note to speak to Ernie about this new problem. Now the situation had been brought to his attention, it surprised him it hadn't occurred to him before. Torville wasn't the only self-proclaimed rake bored by winter inactivity and Norry was, he realized, surprised he'd never noticed, an amazingly attractive woman.

Very slightly too thin, her beautiful bones were covered by clear skin that glowed from a touch of golden sun as well as the natural color of good health . . . but it wasn't entirely her looks. Like her sister Ernestine, the liveliness which characterized Norry's behavior—especially when Jon was around—gave animation to her features and drew men's eyes. The colonel sighed. Looking after Norry was becoming not only a full time job but one beset with patches of exceedingly prickly briars!

So. It was a lucky day, was it not, when Miss Matthewson decided to visit? Ernestine's presence would take some of the pressure off him. But, no matter what, Norry must be made to go home before the spring offensive began. Once the army was on the move his responsibilities would become so heavy he'd not have time to keep a watchful eye on his old friend's wife.

Widow!

Half a moment's confusion settled on Sommerton's mind. Why did he persist in calling her wife when it was obvious to the meanest intelligence that Jon must be dead? As Ernestine had said only an hour or so earlier. Only Norry categorically refused to admit it.

At that thought Ave grinned, the grin quickly fading—because it wasn't true. Somehow, Norry had half-convinced more than a few of Jon's friends as well. Look at his own thoughts: wife, indeed! And yet . . . there was that intangible bond between her and Jon which linked them beyond any reasonable man's understanding. Could Jon be alive? But four months . . . ?

No. Jon *must* be dead. If his friend were alive he'd have returned and one would just have to do his best to help young

Ernie—Ernestine, that was—convince Norry it was past time she returned to England.

That settled, Ave made himself comfortable and stared into the fire. His thoughts turned to Ernie and he smiled again, a softer, much more intimate smile. She'd ridden like the very devil today—even on good old safe-and-steady 'Rita. He contemplated what she'd do with a better mount. More than once his heart had been in his mouth when Ernie pulled some unexpected maneuver on Norry's poor 'Rita, orders which had startled that loyal but placid plodder very much indeed. And if Ernie could pull the very best from 'Rita the way she'd done, then what would she do with a decent . . .

But *no*. He *didn't* wish to see her take her fences flying! Even the low rock fences abounding in this region! He truly didn't think he could survive the strain of worrying about when she'd take a tumble and break her neck!

Ah, another part of his mind insisted: what a soldier's wife she'd make! Everything pointed to that. Everything she did— especially riding like she'd been born to it; everything she said—outrageously outspoken as she was. So the next question for which he needed an answer was did he *want* a wife?

Ave sat up, his spine rigid and his eyes wide, staring at nothing. It had never before occurred to him to ask himself that question. Now it startled him exceedingly when the immediate mental response was a mind-boggling *yes*.

"Yes?" he muttered aloud, blinking. "I said *yes?*" he asked himself. Slowly he settled back into the chair.

When had he begun to think of taking a bride? When Jon married Norry and he'd observed their happiness? Or later, when he discovered just how agreeable it was for Jon to have a woman to whom he could say things, reveal worries and fears, notions one couldn't discuss with one's fellow officers—even one's friends? Or perhaps it was that time Jon almost died and Norry saved him . . . perhaps it was then?

No, decided Ave, it was none of those particular times, but a growing thing which had blossomed fully nearly the instant the right woman appeared before him. Ernie . . .

He smiled again, softly, warmly. The whole notion was so simple, so exactly right. So what now? That was simple, as well, was it not? Now he'd take leave and help Ernie get Norry home—and while in England he'd marry his Ernie and bring her back to the Peninsula in time for the spring offensive. Simple indeed.

So. That was settled. . . .

But while Ave decided their future to *his* satisfaction, *Ernie* was equally preoccupied with deciding her own quite different destiny. While riding at his side across some of the roughest hunting country she'd ever seen, she'd come to the conclusion Ave Sommerton was exceedingly dangerous to her well being.

He made her laugh. That was bad enough, but there was that smile of his which started in his eyes and, even before it was fully formed, sent shivers up her back. That battle-roughened voice could do the same thing and when he touched her—she shook her head, earning herself a mild reprimand from Maria who was doing up her hair.

After promising to keep still for the nonce, Ernie sank back into her reverie and continued analyzing what was happening to her. Something was. Something she'd never experienced before, surely. Something new and decidedly frightening.

She was very much afraid it was something really terrible, something unthinkable—like falling in love with the man.

Because it wouldn't do.

Wouldn't do? The thought brought her up short, straightening her spine and earning her another soft complaint from Maria.

Why would it not do? Even six weeks—six *days*—ago there'd have been nothing she'd have liked better, than to fall in love with a man like Sommerton and have him love her in return.

He was an officer in a very good regiment, no matter what her father would say in that scornful way about the Rifles and that the only real army was the cavalry! Ave was, obviously, an excellent officer or he'd not yet have been promoted to colonel. It was obvious he represented all that was best about the army for which Ernie had a passion—thanks to army-mad Bertie's early and careful attention to her education in such things!

But, it truly wouldn't do.

Even though she felt pride in the man and his achievements, a pride she couldn't justify since she'd only just met him, she mustn't allow her emotions free rein. The fact she'd felt instantly attracted to him, at both physical and emotional levels which had never before been touched, should have been wonderful . . . but where, now, could she find the courage to marry an officer—as Norry had? And then, very likely, lose him—as Norry had?

So, it wouldn't do.

She *didn't* have that kind of courage. Far better that she smother such feelings immediately and allow them no room in her heart, because, when she returned to England, the stronger they'd become the longer they'd fester and the more miserable they'd make her. . . .

Because it simply wasn't in the cards. Nothing would convince her to put herself in the hellish position her sister was in. She would *not* allow her emotions to play out the hand just dealt her when only misery could, at the far end, be the result.

Never.

Never would she chance her lot as poor Norry had. Norry, who was so grievously wounded she wouldn't even admit to grief, wouldn't admit there was a *need* for grief, had perhaps lost her sanity rather than admit it. . . .

Such a relationship was impossible. A military man shouldn't be so selfish as to expect it of a woman. In fact, decided Ernie a trifle peevishly, he shouldn't be *allowed* to marry and put the woman who loved him through the hell of losing him.

So, whatever the temptation, it was decided: Ernestine Matthewson would not, under any circumstances, fall in love with and wed an Army man.

And that was that.

So why did she feel so miserable?

In the kitchen Bertie counted plates onto a tray on which he'd already placed silver. "I didn't mean to anger you, Norry," he said. "Please don't go all stiff and stern and quiet."

Norry turned from where she warmed the teapot. "If I seem angry, it's because I am. What business is it of yours, Herbert Browley, if an old friend comes to call?"

"I don't object to *friends* calling," he responded with alacrity. "It's Torville I object to and so," he added with a frown, "would you if you knew him half so well as I do."

"Fold the napkins, Bertie, and leave Torville to me. I promise you he'll not manage to seduce me."

His ears reddened at her blunt words, but he persisted. "It would be so simple for me to tell him to stay away from you."

"He'd listen?" asked Norry in an overly polite tone.

"Of course he would," blustered Bertie.

"And if he did not?"

"I'd . . . call him out."

"Hmhum." Norry's foot began a slow tapping on the tiled floor. "And how do you think I'd feel about that?"

Bertie stared at her. "Colonel Sommerton, then."

"Colonel Sommerton then . . . what?"

"Let *him* give Torville the word if you think he'd not listen to me."

"I don't believe I'd enjoy learning that Ave had met Torville at dawn some bright morning, either."

"It wouldn't come to that."

"What makes you think it would not?" This time Norry

turned and stared at Bertie, a harsh, almost painfully hopeful, look in her eyes. "Tell me why it wouldn't!"

"Why," said a bewildered Bertie, "because Ave is Torville's superior officer, of course."

"Ah." Norry's shoulders drooped. "But this is not a military matter."

"So?" Bertie looked blank for a moment and then understood. "Oh." He looked up from the napkin he carefully creased. "You mean Sommerton wouldn't rely on his rank to convince Torville."

"Why, Bertie," said Norry, sarcasm dripping, "I do believe you must have learned a bit of logic while away at Eton."

"I don't think I've ever heard you use that tone before." His forehead ruffled with worry lines. "Norry, is it because Jon has been gone so long?"

She sighed, laying down the knife she'd picked up to slice the bread. "Perhaps. In part. It's all so difficult when only I *know* he's not dead." She lifted her hands in hopelessness. "I don't believe I convinced even Ernie and *she* should understand."

"We all want him to be alive, Norry. It is just very difficult to understand how it can be, given how long it's been. No one thinks he'd desert, so it can't be that. And he's been on none of the prisoner of war lists, so he can't be with the French. What else is there? That he's still unconscious, perhaps, and has been cared for in some hovel somewhere by kind-hearted peasants? I'll tell you frankly I can't believe that explanation for the simple reason that I went out hunting for him. I was into every house, hut, barn and lean-to for miles around Salamanca."

Norry flashed him her brilliant smile. "Oh Bertie, I didn't know. How kind of you . . ."

"Well, it isn't something I'd advertise, is it?" said a flustered Bertie. "I wouldn't have told you now except that I don't see how else to convince you he must be dead—you see?" he asked accusingly, interrupting himself at the blossoming of her blazing smile. "I *couldn't* convince you, could I? Norry, if he is no-where, then where is he?"

"In a guerrilla camp in the mountains not so veerrry far from here." She smiled again at his blank look of incomprehension. "Don't worry about him, Bertie. He's fine and will be home in the not too distant future. At the very latest, he'll come for Christmas."

Bertie blinked. Then he pulled a stool closer and sat on it with something of a thump. "A guerrilla camp?"

She smiled a lesser but still sweet smile and nodded.

"In the mountains?"

"Never mind, Bertie," she soothed. "He'll tell us the whole tale when he comes home. Perhaps it would be better if you were to forget I've said anything at all."

"But a *guerrilla* camp?"

She sighed. "Now you want to know why they haven't asked ransom. I don't know, do I? Perhaps they still will. But I think it more likely Jon will simply walk in the door one day and surprise us all." Very gently she put her hand on her stomach and smiled. Then, remembering no one was to know about the baby—if she could possibly continue to conceal it—until Jon could be told, she picked up the knife and sliced the loaf. "Ber-tie, I really don't wish to speak of this again. I'm aware that almost everyone I know thinks me mad as a hatter and knowing that is bad enough without *talking* about it."

"All right. But I still think you should tell Sommerton to tell Torville—"

"Bertie!" Norry turned, waving the bread knife in his direc-tion. "That is *enough!*"

"Oh all right," he said, pouting. "But I wish you'd remember I'm all grown up now and stop treating me like you did when Ernie and I were mere children."

"Maybe when the two of you cease to act—"

"Norry!" he exclaimed in exactly the same tone in which she'd uttered his name a few seconds earlier.

She smiled secretly and, bending over the cutting board, refrained from the mild scold she'd begun.

The simple meal of cold meat, fruit and bread, was soon over and the men, reluctantly, made their farewells. Sommerton, especially, wished to remain, wished to get to know Ernie—Ernestine—at a deeper level than had, so far, been possible. A few more hours in her company . . . but duty called and his free morning was finished. He had to report in for a session in which he must coordinate his current needs with the commissary which never seemed to have quite enough of anything. Sommerton was determined his men would not suffer if he could possibly help it, and, if he didn't leave, he'd be late.

"Coming Browley?" he asked.

The two men mounted up and tipped their hats to the two women. They'd no more than started off, though, when Sommerton, an idea bursting, pulled up. He swore softly but without heat, and said, "You go on, Lieutenant. There's a notion which I must mention to Miss Matthewson."

Bertie too was going to be late, in his case for a duty watch so, with no more than a curious look, he nodded and cantered on.

"What is it, Colonel?" asked Ernie when he'd returned to stare up at her where she and Norry stood on the small balcony, shawls pulled tightly around their shoulders. She stared back, curious, about the officer sitting in his saddle immediately below her.

He decided he hadn't time to explain. "I didn't think to tell you earlier about a small problem we must solve and I've not time to explain now, so I'll send Holles around and he'll do it later this afternoon."

"Who? What?" She stared, uncomprehending.

"A young, hmm, friend of mine. Lieutenant Derek Holles.

He'll stop by when he gets off duty. About tea time, I'd guess. Now I really must go!" Sommerton was off, not looking back to see how the young woman would take what was truly high-handed behavior on his part. He smiled, suspecting he knew very well what her reaction would be!

Ernie stared after him before turning to her sister. "Norry, did that make any sense?"

Norry smiled. "I very much fear that it did."

"So?"

"I'll let Derek explain."

A teasing smile hovered around Norry's lips. When Ernie pouted, the smile came very near to turning into a laugh—but didn't. Quite.

Ernie realized Norry hadn't laughed once since she'd arrived. That was strange since Norry had always, in the past, laughed easily. Just, decided Ernie bitterly, another indication that Norry had changed all out of recognition and she wondered whether to put it down to Jon's absence or, generally, to her sister's life in the Peninsula!

Ernie spent much of the rest of the afternoon alternating between teasing her sister to explain who Derek Holles was and what problem the colonel could possibly expect her to help with and, alternately, quizzing her sister about Colonel Sommerton with whom she was *not* falling in love.

She carefully reminded herself of that fact. Often.

Whenever she remembered to do so, that is.

Norry wouldn't be tricked or cajoled into explaining Holles's visit, but she didn't mind discussing Ave. Surprised as she was by the notion, she suspected Ave Sommerton was more than a little interested in Ernie and had no objection whatsoever to helping his suit along if that were the way of it.

"Ave and Jon practically grew up together. His mother and Jon's were close. When Ave's died, Jon's took Ave under her wing. You see, the estates march along one border, so Ave could ride over almost before he could walk—and did. It is a very special relationship between the men. I admit I was jealous when we first met, but soon got over that foolishness."

"When did you meet Ave?"

"At the very last minute, actually. Very likely you don't recall, but Ave was at our wedding, Jon's and mine. He got leave for it and arrived just in time to stand up with Jon."

"Why don't I remember?"

"I suspect you were bemused by your first grown-up gown and too busy flirting with all those young officers who came to see their major wed."

"I didn't flirt."

"Didn't you? Perhaps I was so very happy it seemed everyone else was happy, too."

"I *was* happy. I just didn't flirt." Ernie giggled. "Bertie would have had my head for washing had I done something so foolishly feminine. My wearing a grown-up gown for the first time didn't change me in *his* eyes! Besides," she added a trifle defiantly, "I didn't know how. To flirt, I mean. It's something I've never learned."

"You don't *learn* to flirt, Ernie," said Norry, giving her sister a curious look. "It is just something you *do.*"

"*I* don't. That's one reason I refused to return to London for a third season. I found such games exceedingly uncomfortable and couldn't join into them. People thought me a slowtop and our poor bewildered aunt couldn't hide her misery that *her* niece didn't take."

"So you stayed home to care for Father." A speculative look sobered Norry's expression. "I always rather thought," she said, "that you were waiting for Bertie to reach an age when he'd wish to wed."

"Bertie?" Ernie stared. "Norry, it would be like marrying one's brother." A thought crossed her mind and she giggled. "Actually, *worse* than that. One might as well marry one's *tutor.*"

Norry bit back a grin. "Would that be worse than one's brother, Ern?"

"*I* think so." Ernie adopted a stern look. "Would *you* want to spend the whole of your life with someone constantly trying to *teach* you things? Be reasonable, Norry."

Norry's grin escaped. "I'll admit I didn't think of it in quite that way. Come talk to me while I make scones. If Holles is here for tea I need something substantial to feed him."

Ernie followed her into the kitchen and wrinkled her nose when she was set to stoning raisins for the scones. "The men do seem to come right at meal times, do they not? There was Bertie this morning who ate half our breakfast and Ave and Bertie for lunch. Now Holles . . . ?"

"Of course they come. Not just *here,* of course, but to any house which has a woman in it. Lady Colonel Barton complains she can't keep her larder stocked, that officers are constantly eating her out of house and home, but I tell her it is her own fault. She and Colonel Lord Barton have a *chef.* Once the army leaves winter cantonments she—and the chef—will return to Lisbon where the Bartons have a house, but during the winter they live in a rather fancy residence, a hunting lodge, on the edge of a nearby forest. They keep open house. Then, another instance," Norry continued, "is Lieutenant-colonel Anderson. His wife hasn't much money for food since he is one of the hunting-mad officers and spends every penny he can on his dogs and horses, but he's generally lucky in his hunting so there is almost always an extra hare or two or three for the pot or he'll have shot fowl or she'll contrive something from next to nothing. They freely share what they have."

"Do *you* have money for food?"

"I'm all right. One quickly learns to plan ahead since the men receive their pay so erratically." Norry grinned in much the old way. "Why? Did you fear I might starve you?"

"Well, I didn't know, did I? I hope you'll not be insulted, but when the wagons come, there'll be some extras. I brought a ham and some bacon slabs and"—She looked at her sister, her head tilted to one side—"Norry, I brought the ingredients so we could make a Christmas pudding. Was that all right?"

"Christmas . . ."

Norry's eyes clouded in a dreamy way and Ernie knew her sister was again thinking of Jon. She took a deep breath, put on as innocent a look as could be contrived, and said, "I didn't know how long it would take us to pack you up and organize shipping everything home and besides, it occurred to me that I'd never again have the chance to see Portugal and I rather hoped to stay awhile. So I thought that if we were still here at Christmas we could have your friends in for a farewell meal before we go." Ernie spoke firmly as if it were a settled thing and only when she finished did she dare a quick look at her sister. She straightened, stared. "Why are you grinning like that?"

"That was very well done, Ernie," said Norry in a congratulatory tone. "How long did it take you to think up that little speech?"

Ernie remembered just how many versions and revisions she'd made before chancing it and blushed.

Norry continued, "Jon and I always have had friends in for Christmas dinner . . . but I'd thought perhaps I'd not do it this year."

"I think you should," said Ernie quickly, hoping Norry would ignore the fact she'd not answered the question concerning her expostulatory style.

Norry hesitated. She opened her mouth, shut it, began again. "I can't quite think it proper," she said.

"Why not? Because you are in mour—"

"Don't. It isn't true. You mustn't say that, Ernie," scolded Norry. "You shouldn't even think it."

Ernie took a deep breath and decided she'd better not push

any more than she had. "Then why isn't it proper to hold a Christmas dinner?"

"Because I might not have a host, silly."

"I don't think you should let *that* stop you. Particularly if it is something you always do. We could save the ham since I don't suppose it is possible to find a Christmas goose here, and we could make the pudding easily enough—so why not? Norry, it sounds like fun."

In fact it did sound like fun and Ernie grew more excited as several new ideas competed for attention in her head. "Can one find proper greens for decorations," she queried, "or is that too much to ask of Portugal? And a yule log. We couldn't have a very large one in that pokey little fireplace, but Bertie could find us something which would fit your grate—could he not? And what about wassailers? Do they come around? Or should we organize some this year? There must be many men with good voices among the troops, don't you think? And if we do do that, should we not get in the necessary for a good big bowl of punch? For the wassailers, I mean?"

"Ernie, Ernie, you go much too fast. I haven't yet said we'll have the dinner party."

"Well?"

Norry's jaw clenched and again she stared at nothing at all. "Well . . . I'll think about it . . . and we *can* find the goose, Ernie. Have you not noticed how they are herded much like a flock of sheep is at home?"

"I've seen goat herds, but not geese. That must be a sight!"

Ernie wondered if anything could be added which might help Norry's mental healing. She decided not to try. One could only go so far so fast and, although she hated to think of her poor sister's state of mind, it couldn't be changed just by wishing.

She cast about for another topic, could think of none, and remembered the expected guest. "We'd better get back to these scones, had we not?" She returned to stoning raisins—not her favorite kitchen chore, but one she was at least competent to do!

Later that afternoon when the tall, rather good-looking, red headed officer had earnestly explained his mission, he finished, "So you see why the colonel volunteered your services. You understand that we really need you," he finished earnestly.

Ernie exploded, "Colonel Sommerton did *what?*"

Innocently, Holles faced her ire, placing his head in imminent danger of a good washing. "But I explained that, did I not? He volunteered you to replace Miss Covington who returned very suddenly to England. She won't be able to take the lead after all. We've only a couple of weeks now, you see. My friend Bertie told us you've done a good bit of acting in amateur performances and might even have taken this part before"—Holles looked at Ernie questioningly but got no response—"he wasn't certain about that, but he also said you were quick to learn your lines and were very good at acting them and that you'd enjoy it and . . . what is it?" he asked, becoming aware, at last, that Ernie was watching him with something less than enthusiasm. "Don't you *want* to take a part?"

Ernie glared. "Just like that? Bertie *told* you I've played in amateur productions and Sommerton *decided* I could do so again? Without *asking* me? Just *assuming!*" Ernie gritted her teeth.

"Did he put your nose out of joint?" asked Holles with uncommon rashness based in an unawareness of the danger in which he stood.

"Did he . . ."

Ernie quite literally growled. She hefted her tea cup, weighing it in her palm, eyeing it, and then the young officer thoughtfully.

Norry deftly removed the cup from her sister's hands. "Ern, love," she said quickly. "*Think.* You *do* enjoy play-acting. You've written me about the parts you've taken from time to time at the house parties you've attended. In fact, you've gone on and on about how much you've enjoyed them. So why are you losing your temper?"

"A couple of weeks? Just *two* weeks?" Ernie asked, ignoring her sister's interference—and also the fact they'd often put on plays with even less time for practice during parties where doing the play became part of the entertainment. "Colonel Sommerton expects me to just walk in and in two weeks play a major role in your play?" Again she growled.

Realizing the odd sound had come from the young woman seated across the table from him, Derek blinked. "But the colonel assured me you'd be happy to help . . ."

"You can go tell Colonel Lord Sommerton—"

"No, Ernie," said her sister with sudden firmness—this time removing a scone dripping with honey from Ernie's fingers. "You stop for just one moment and *think* instead of losing your temper as you're about to do. Besides, it is not Lieutenant Holles with whom you are angry and, on top of that, I thought you outgrew such tantrums long ago!"

Ernie scowled and folded her hands carefully. She pressed her lips tightly together and stared at her fingers. Then, once she'd achieved control, she said, "All right." After another moment she asked lightly, "What's the play?"

Derek, with a thankful look in Norry's direction, dropped a half-eaten scone on his plate and began an enthusiastic description of how, with Colonel Sommerton's help, they'd cut Shakespeare's *A Midsummer's Night's Dream* to manageable size. "You'd play the part of Titania," he finished, giving her a hopeful look.

Ernie nodded. Once.

Holles sighed at this lack of enthusiasm but plodded on, his enthusiasm lagging—but not for long. "There is a sort of barnlike building in the upper town which makes an excellent theater—or will when we finish building the stage and benches. Actually, that's about done. We decided to use screens instead of a curtain. They don't hide quite all the stage, but the idea is there and the scene changes go better when the audience isn't staring at the men doing them. You know how that goes . . . or perhaps you don't?"

Ernie had relaxed somewhat during his enthusiastic discussion of the playhouse and the problems associated with it. "Screens sound like a good notion since it must be impossible to manufacture curtains here where you've no supplies."

A mischievous look made the young man's deep blue eyes sparkle. "Well, actually, we tried that once before"—he grinned—"but the men from whom we stole the blankets complained so we had to give them back."

"So I think they *might.*" Ernie broke into laughter and even Norry went so far as to grin. Ernie sighed. "I suppose I did over-react, but Sommerton really should not have told you I'd do it before he asked me. For all he knew, Norry and I might, like Miss Covington, be on our way back to England long before you actually put on the play for an audience and that would never do, would it?"

"Back to England?" Holles's pleasant features fell into desperate lines. "Surely not? Not right away, anyway. You just got here, Miss Matthewson. I'm certain you don't wish to turn around and go right back. Besides," he wheedled, "at this time of year the Bay of Biscay makes one miserable. Having suffered it once, you can't possibly wish to do so again so soon."

"But I didn't suffer," said Ernie.

"You didn't?" For a moment the young officer looked nonplused. "I did," he finally admitted, "and it wasn't even a particularly stormy crossing, or so they told me. I don't think I believe them, but . . . but that's not relevant," he finished in a rush. "You've just arrived, Miss Matthewson. There is so much to see and do. Besides, it would be unfair of you to desert us immediately now you've come to us like this right out of the blue, so to speak?"

"Like a balloonist landing in someone's five-acre field?"

The lieutenant's fine skin flushed. "No, of course not. I only meant . . ."

"You only meant you are desperate for someone to take the part and you fear I might escape you. All right. Against my better judgment, I'll do it. Did you bring a copy of the play so that I might begin learning my lines? I only hope I can do so in the short time available!"

"Then you haven't done this one?"

"Not Titania. I'll do my best, Lieutenant, but Bertie exaggerated if he said I'd done a great deal of amateur theater."

"Oh, none of us are exactly *experts,* you know. We've none of us had any *training.* You'll do just fine. I'm sure." He handed over the folded and creased pages on which her lines were written. "Besides, I'll be happy to help you," he said earnestly. "In any free time I have, I mean."

He smiled beatifically—a smile spoiled only by the speculative look in his eye. But then he went back to his scone, nodding when Norry offered to refill his cup with tea. He ate three more scones as well and Ernie decided she must have misinterpreted the look which had given her pause.

Eventually Derek looked over the table, discovered there was no more to eat and, telling Ernie he'd come by and escort her to the theater for their first practice right after tomorrow's luncheon. ". . . or, no," he said, recalling that another social engagement would likely interfere. "That won't do will it? You'll be off to the races tomorrow, so practice will be scheduled late in the afternoon." He bowed to Norry and left.

"Looks as if you'll have a full schedule, sister-mine. Hunting with Bertie or Ave most mornings, although not tomorrow when you'll attend the races and that followed by play-acting all afternoon." Norry adopted a thoughtful look. "Now what should we plan for your evenings? Other than the occasional ball to which we'll be invited now and again? We wouldn't want you to chance a moment's boredom, now, would we?" teased Norry.

"Bah. I'm never bored." Ernie frowned. "What races?"

"I can't recall which regiment is organizing them this time. We'll go with Ave, of course. Or perhaps Bertie will escort us, if going with Ave doesn't appeal to you . . ."

"Bertie will do just fine. We needn't bother the colonel who must have far more important things on his mind than *us*," said Ernie with a toss of her head.

Ernie gathered the dirty dishes together with far more clatter than one might have expected. She wished to drown out any laughter she might hear from her older sister whom she'd actually forgotten could be such a terrible tease!

Four

The next morning Ernie woke early. Very early. At first she tried to go back to sleep but, when that didn't work, she wondered whether she might be able to start the kitchen fire and boil herself water for tea. Some years ago when she'd tried to start a fire she'd not been successful. This time, assuming she managed it, perhaps she'd make her sister a morning tray as Norry had done for her the day before.

It was, thought Ernie, rather depressing to discover that Norry, whom one had always thought the perfect lady, was more competent at everyday things than one was oneself. Possibly such discoveries were what happened when one prided oneself on one's efficiency and one's ability to get things done! One could, decided Ernie, learn humility while visiting one's sister . . . and just perhaps one would learn how to perk up a banked fire!

It was with a feeling of adventure that Ernie, her robe tightly belted around her, crept silently across the dark living room to the kitchen door, but when she arrived near it she stopped dead. Someone was already up and busy despite the fact the sun had yet to do more than color the tiled rooftops to the east.

Ernie listened. A soft murmur of voices rose and fell but the words were indistinguishable . . . until, sharply: "But no. It will not do. Truly it will not do. You must *not* suggest such a thing, Señor Lieutenant Browley."

Why did Maria sound both worried and irritated? And how

could she be speaking to Bertie? What was Bertie doing in Norry's kitchen at this hour of the day? With Maria. Suddenly suspicious, Ernie's eyes widened. Just *what* was her old friend up to?

But, dare she interrupt a private conversation—which, quite obviously, this was? Ernie stood in indecision, unable to make up her mind to return to her bed, but reluctant to open the door and discover what was happening on the other side. The voices had returned to the soft murmur that she'd first heard, which was no help when making a reasoned decision.

Ernie sighed. She wouldn't return to the arms of Morpheus if she were to return to her bed. It was silly just to stand in the dark damp morning chill and shiver. So why didn't she knock and open the door? For that matter, why did she not simply open the door?

She did. And blinked in the sudden light. "Bertie?"

He turned, quickly, on the stool on which he was sitting, almost falling off. "Ernie. Oh . . . well, I've come to see if you are still angry with me as Holles told me you were," he said with a quick glance toward Maria. "I've been waiting for you to get up, don't you know?"

She looked from her old friend to Maria who had turned her back to feed twigs to the small fire burning under the kettle balanced on a blackened tripod. She looked back to Bertie, studying him curiously. Bertie never lied to her, so why was he telling a half-truth now?

"That's what you've done, have you?" she asked.

"I'm on duty all day," he explained, speaking too fast. "Which is a bore, of course, but I've just got back from leave and there's no one who owes me a favor, so I can't trade. Actually, it's worse than a bore. *You'll* be off to enjoy the races, of course."

"Races?" Again Ernie looked at Maria's back which seemed

to her prejudiced mind to reveal guilt of no mean order. "Bertie . . ."

He shook his head and used the hand signal from their childhood to indicate silence. She blinked, looked from him to Maria. What was going on?

"The races will be fun," Bertie said in a firm voice, continuing more mildly. "Will that tea be ready soon, Maria?"

"Not long."

"Bring it into the sitting room, will you, please?"

"*Si*."

Bertie rose to his feet and took Ernie's elbow, leading her into the other room. "Don't embarrass the poor girl," he hissed once the door was shut. "Do you think she approves of my arriving here so early? If you think that you've bats in your belfry. She *doesn't*."

"Then why did you?"

Ernie thought it a perfectly reasonable question but Bertie didn't immediately respond. Although dawn had developed from the palest pink to giving the sky a pale wash of blue color, it was still too dark in Norry's small sitting room to be certain if Bertie blushed. Nevertheless Ernie was nearly certain he had.

She peered at him. His skin certainly seemed darker than the mere absence of light could justify. Besides, there was that hesitation in confiding in her which was so unusual between them. They needed light so she stuck a taper into banked ashes, lit it and a sudden thought struck her. "You aren't," she asked, her voice sharp, at the sudden thought, "harassing the poor girl? Are you?"

"Me?" The whites of his eyes showed. "Heavens no! Why would I do such a thing? I *like* Maria."

But Ernie had seen that wide-eyed look of innocence before and, although she thought his last sentence a true one, she was quite certain the rest was not. "You're up to something."

"The only thing I'm up to is a good breakfast. Very likely

it'll be the last decent meal I'll see today. You can't blame me for coming by, can you?" he cajoled.

Ernie knew this maneuver too. No matter how she tried to get him to talk about what *she* wished to discuss he'd change the subject.

The kitchen door opened and Maria entered with a tray—which Bertie immediately took from her. "That's too heavy for you," he scolded softly. "Now be a good girl and fix us omelets and toast, will you? Please?"

Maria pouted slightly but she went off to do his bidding.

"Now," he said, setting the tray on the table and deftly putting around cups and saucers and silver as if he'd had much practice at the chore. He folded napkins as quickly and neatly as any butler ever had and set the teapot, sugar and milk near one place. Ernie thought his mother would be much amazed if she could see him! "There," he said. "Will you do the honors, Ernie?"

She eyed him. "Will you tell me what you and Maria were speaking about?" she said, speaking in the same tone and cadence as he'd done.

"No."

His terse response was also out of character. "Why not?" she asked, now more curious than she *had* been which was already quite a lot.

"It's none of your business, that's why, and you'll get no more from me than that." He scowled. "Now pour, will you?"

"You wondered if I were still angry with you for volunteering me for the play," she said, lifting the pot and carefully pouring the first cup. "Well I'm not."

Bertie appeared relieved, but the relief faded when he noted his old cohort was scowling. He cast her a worried look as she handed him his heavily milked tea.

"I'm no longer angry about that, Bertie, but angry all over

again because of whatever you are doing to tease poor Maria so."

He sighed. "Drop it, Ernie. I won't have you bothering the child. Do you hear me? You aren't to question her."

"You sound more and more guilty, Bertie." He glared. She glared right back. "Guilty of *something.*"

After a moment, Bertie held up a hand, his little and ring fingers twisted together as they'd done when children. "I swear on our old oath that I'm not guilty of harassing her." He looked a trifle conscious and modified that. "Or, at least, that I have no ill intentions toward the child—and she knows it."

His words and action recalled one of their oldest pacts. Swearing on the blood of their first ponies had been the most serious oath they could make. "I wonder who is the child, she or you," said Ernie, unable to help a smile forming.

"It is true that she is very young," he said indulgently, ignoring that Ernie had included himself in her comment. "Watch over her, Ernie, will you? I worry about her when I cannot be near."

"Why?"

This time when Bertie's ears turned that interesting red Ernie knew it was embarrassment. "It's not my secret, Ernie." A rueful grin crossed his features. "Actually *I* don't know as much as I'd like to know. She says she must not burden me. *Me.*" He sighed. "In any case, *don't ask.* Do you hear me, Ern, old girl? Don't pry. It upsets her."

The door to the kitchen again swung open and again Maria entered with a tray, which, once again, Bertie took from her. He seated her at one of the places at table and served her himself and then, piling his own plate, wolfed down more bread and egg than Ernie thought reasonable.

"At the rate you men eat," she said, after eating her own share—which consisted of a small portion of the omelet and two slices of toast, "I think I'll hide the bacon when it comes or poor Norry will get none at all. Maria, when my baggage arrives, will you be sure she gets a nice portion each day until it is gone? I can't help worrying—she's so *thin*."

"*Si.*"

It was the first word the girl had spoken since sitting down, but Ernie had watched her and noticed how easily she handled the table setting and that she swept her napkin into her lap with one accustomed movement. Obviously, Maria had eaten, often, at a properly set table. So why was she reduced to servitude? Ernie wondered. No matter that Norry made the work easy for the girl, expecting no more of Maria than she was willing to do herself, it must still be considered service . . .

"Look, I've got to run," Bertie said, interrupting her thoughts, "but I want you to lay a bet for me on See No Evil." He handed Ernie a thin purse. "Will you do that?"

"See No Evil," repeated Ernie obediently. Then her voice sharpened. "Bertie, I know next to nothing of racing and even less about making a bet."

"Don't worry. The colonel will see to your education. Did I say that Sommerton will be here about nine? Be ready," he ordered as he rose and strode toward the door.

"*Herbert Milford Browley,* don't you dare go off after that bit of information!"

"Got to." He stuck his head back inside. "I'll be late. You can't want that, can you?"

"*Bertie!*"

But he was gone, the door shut behind him with a snap.

Norry, rubbing the sleep from her eyes, came to see what the uproar was all about. She looked at the table, from Maria who stared at her plate, to Ernie, who looked as if thunder had gotten into her scowl. "Did I miss something?" she asked, her hand absently rubbing her tummy and her face looking a trifle sickish.

"That Bertie! If it isn't one thing then it is something just as bad. He'll not stop ordering me about and he knows how I dislike it. Do you know anything more than you've said about this race meeting scheduled for today?"

"What?" Norry accepted a slice of dry toast from Maria with an absentminded smile. "The meeting? I seem to recall telling you the Connaught Rangers are sponsoring a point to point. They're excellent at organization and it should be a good meet." She came to the table and sat at the one clean place setting. "That reminds me, however. Sommerton will very likely be here early to escort us."

"So he will," said Ernie with false joviality. "Bertie was kind enough to *order* me to be ready."

"Ernie, I'd think you'd have gotten used to it by now. Bertie has always *ordered you to* . . . whatever it might be at the time."

Ernie's scowl didn't lighten. She added a pout to the expression. "That doesn't make it right."

Norry smiled. "Perhaps not, but do you really think you've any hope of changing him?" She paused half an instant and added, "Especially when he's been an officer for several years and is still more used to giving orders than when you were children?"

"I won't have it!"

"What will you do about it?"

"Perhaps I won't go." Ernie crossed her arms, the scowl in place.

"Childish. Really childish," said Norry, carefully keeping her smile from breaking through. "You'll cut off your own nose to spite your face, will you not?"

"As Nanny would say?" Ernie uncrossed her arms and reached for the teapot. She filled her sister's cup, Maria's and then half-filled her own. The last drops dripped and she set down the pot—which Maria immediately picked up. The girl picked up her own cup and saucer as well and headed for the kitchen, but then, her hands full, couldn't open the door. Ernie went to help her and received a shy smile in thanks.

"I found Bertie already in the kitchen when I got up," said Ernie as she returned to the table and seated herself. "He and Maria were arguing."

"Bertie has tried very hard to befriend Maria," said Norry. "Maria is no longer afraid of him as she seems to be of most any strange man—with reason, of course, after her experience— but she still will not trust him with her history. Or if she has," said Norry, modifying her statement, "she's sworn him to secrecy. Are you talking about Bertie because you do not wish to talk about Ave?"

"I do not like being told to do this and do that and I seem to do nothing *but* what I'm told. Is it the military mind, Norry, that they must always be giving orders?"

"Perhaps. I think you'll enjoy the race," coaxed Norry. "The Rangers do tend to do such things especially well."

"I'll have to go whether I wish it or no," grumbled Ernie. "Bertie left money and told me which horse to lay it on. Norry," she added plaintively, "do *you* know how to place a bet?"

Her sister shook her head. "No. I fear my education is sadly lacking. Ave will know."

"Does Ave know everything?"

"Everything of importance to this way of life, you mean? Then, yes, I'd say he does."

"It isn't fair."

"What isn't?"

"For several years I've run my own life and Father's and the house and, for the most part, the estate, and doing it all quite handily. Why must I be treated like a child in the nursery *now?*"

"Perhaps because you've not yet proven you're out of it?"

Ernie thought for a moment. "You mean here in this place and time."

"Yes. Things are different here. Very different."

Grudgingly, Ernie said, "I suppose that *might* be it. I still don't think it's fair."

Her sister gave her a half-shocked half-mocking look. "Who ever suggested to you that life would be fair?"

"I don't ask it of *life,*" Ernie retorted. "I ask it of Bertie and any other man who thinks I know less than nothing about caring for myself." She stalked off to her little room to dress, regretting that the Spanish habit she'd ordered only yesterday from Lisbon could not possibly have arrived. Having again ridden astride and rediscovered how much safer she felt, she didn't wish to go back to riding side-saddle. But Norry had said she would go to the races, so her sister's Spanish habit would not be available for borrowing.

It was such a bore, this having to conform to silly rules. Perhaps she might borrow a pair of trousers and be comfortable? But, no. Bertie, who might, with coaxing, organize such a thing for her, was on duty and unavailable. However detestable the notion, it would have to be a side-saddle.

Sommerton arrived soon after the women were ready. "Have you broader brimmed hats?" he asked. "Unlike most mornings when we wallow in a mist if not dense fog, it's going to be a bright day and we wouldn't wish to expose that lovely skin to too much sun—even at this time of year when the Portuguese sun is far less vicious than it is in the summer."

Once proper hats were found, they left, ambling, at Norry's request, along the trails at an easy pace. They'd still arrive in plenty of time although it would not be a long day because Ernie must return in time for her first rehearsal. Derek had stopped in to say he'd come by for her about three.

"I'm sorry to spoil your day for you," she said to the others.

"It may be bad for Ave, I suppose, but I don't believe I'd want to stay for all of it, Ernie," said her sister, thinking of the child she carried. "I'll be quite happy to return soon after we've eaten the Rangers' luncheon. I wonder what they'll serve this year. Ave, remember the time they had those oddly seasoned Spanish meat things? I can't recall what they called them."

"I'm remembering last year's *frijitos.* I hope they have those again."

"I thought those a trifle spicy for my taste, too—although I've come to like most Spanish and Portuguese food—especially Maria's way with the panella. I don't know how she does it, but when she prepares even the toughest fowl in that funny clay pan with its clay cover which she nestles in the edges of the fire, it always comes out tasting like a young bird."

Ave nodded. "If the Rangers have *frijitos,* I'll have them cut you something from nearer the bone which will not have sat in the marinade for long—although it will, of course, be rarer meat. You'll have to choose which you prefer, Norry: over-spiced, or under-done!"

Ernie chuckled and Norry smiled as they reached the top of a long hill where he pulled up, suggesting the women stop as well.

"There!" he said, his arm sweeping from one end of the valley to the other, "You can view the line of the race from here. Do you see, Ernestine, how they've managed to include nearly every type of barrier one would wish?"

Ernie followed his pointing finger and saw men on horseback going slowly along what must be the steeplechase over which they'd soon be racing. It looked like fun and she found herself bitterly jealous of those who would be riding it.

"What's the matter, Ernestine?" asked Sommerton.

"I wish I could join them," she admitted.

Norry, overhearing, broke in. "You wouldn't!"

"Why shouldn't I?" asked Ernie, her eyes sparkling at the thought of the exciting ride it would be.

"It is no more proper here than at home," scolded her sister.

"I've raced at home." Ernie noted a shocked look cross Sommerton's face and grinned to herself. For some reason she enjoyed shocking him.

"What you mean," scolded Norry, "is that you and Bertie have indulged in racing each other. That is not the same as joining in an organized race over a set course. As you know. You are bamming me just to see me worry!"

"Is that true?" asked Sommerton quietly.

"That my racing has been with Bertie or that I wish to worry my sister? Certainly not the latter!" she added quickly.

"I didn't think for a moment you would wish to upset your sister. It's the racing I worry about. Racing is dangerous. I don't think Bertie should have allowed you—"

"Allowed me . . . Bertie allow me . . . !" Ernie gritted her teeth. For an instant she was ready to take off and ride the route spread out below her in the valley into which they were making their way simply because the effort involved might cool her easily roused temper.

Ave noted the stubborn set of her chin. "If I've said the wrong thing, I'm sorry. But if you didn't know the danger, should it not have been made clear? Like a child in the nursery fascinated by fire, one must be taught . . ."

"Grrrr."

A sharp glitter of anger that flared in her eyes startled Ave anew. For a moment he was silent. "Do you find it annoying that someone is concerned about you?" he asked.

"I've been riding for years." Her voice was low, vehement. "I do not cram my horses. Nor do I put them at jumps which are too much for them. I am not foolish."

"I know you can ride," he said with surprising cajolery. "I watched you with the hunt yesterday, remember?"

"Was that just yesterday?" The sudden thought slid in over her anger, the surprise drowning the strong emotion. "It feels like *weeks* ago."

"Do you, too, feel that way . . . ?" he asked softly.

Norry, watching the two, knew Ave well enough to know he hid relief that the argument seemed ended. Since Ave was not one to back down from a fight, she wondered at that.

". . . that we've known each other forever?" he finished.

Ernie threw him a startled look, felt her cheeks heating. She didn't respond, maneuvering her gelding closer to Norry's 'Rita.

When they reached the valley floor Ave joined them on the wider track and gestured toward a hillside where spectators had assembled. The men were in many different uniforms, the strong red and green hues of their tunics lightened here and there by a woman's finery in plaids and pastels. It was a cheerful scene and one had to remind oneself that this sort of occasion was merely a break from the serious business of war—a war which, under the incredible blue of the winter sky and a surprisingly warm sun, seemed far away and nothing more than a bad dream.

The Rangers were everywhere. What appeared chaos at a casual glance soon sorted itself into a well organized sort of chaos in which all ran smoothly. Threading a way through the press of spectators and organizers, answering greetings and, occasionally, introducing Ernie to a particular friend, Sommerton eventually found Lady Colonel Barton, a woman Norry liked very well.

Once he'd settled the women with her ladyship's party he took the horses over the back of the hill to a picket line where he could strip their tack and water them. Sommerton soon returned and, before Ernie quite knew he was there, settled himself very near to her. Somehow, without ever saying a word, he made it clear to the young officers already surrounding her, that he would put up with only so much where she was concerned. Ernie, still irritable from their earlier exchange of fire, suddenly discovered she knew how to flirt after all.

Flirt she did—with everyone but Ave Sommerton. The colonel eyed her for a long moment and then grinned, knowing full well she was fighting a rear-guard action which would not succeed. Ernestine Matthewson might not have accepted the fact, and perhaps it was unreasonable to wish she had, but she was his. Eventually he'd make that clear to her, but for the present it wouldn't hurt to allow her room.

It occurred to him that those were, to Ernie, fighting words: the notion that he *owned* her, that he had a right to *allow* her anything at all! Still grinning, he quietly took himself off to where a group of friends stood. Although reluctant to lose sight of her, he kept his back to Ernie. He entered into the joking and betting going on amongst those around him with all the verve he'd have shown at any other race meeting—perhaps even a bit more.

Ernie, seeing Ave well occupied elsewhere, immediately confused her would-be suitors by quite suddenly, and with no explanation whatsoever, refusing to respond to any of their sallies.

She decided she'd been right all along: flirting was not for her.

$\mathcal{F}ive$

Shortly before the first race Ernie recalled she was to place a bet for Bertie. She turned to Norry to ask her what she should do but Norry was deeply involved in a conversation which, shamelessly eavesdropping, Ernie discovered concerned the annual midnight Christmas service. There was no end, it seemed to the details which must be settled, the most important of which appeared to be the choice of location. The difficulty was to make it convenient to all, an impossibility, Ernie would have thought, rather than a difficulty, given the army was spread out along a hundred miles of hillsides, each regiment centered in one or another village.

She turned back to look speculatively at the young men who still surrounded her—although somewhat sullenly at this point, having lost her attention. It would not do for them to stray too far from the newest female to visit the army, she guessed, cynically. Who knew when, was their obvious thought, they might have another opportunity to meet her?

Ernie was unaware of the renewed interest she roused by that casual glance during which she tried to remember an officer's name and found she'd not caught a single introduction. *So how did she ask one of them to escort her to Sommerton's side so she could ask* him *about placing Bertie's bet?* Before she could become too irritated by her problem, Sommerton himself approached and deftly removed her from her circle of admirers.

"Such a crowd as you've drawn to yourself, Miss Mat-thewson. One feels lost among so many."

"Don't tease," she said, waving away his comment. "I need help with something of importance. You see," she said, looking up resolutely, determined she not allow her confused emotions for this man to interfere with her need of his advice, "I very nearly forgot that Bertie asked me to place a bet for him and I don't know how."

"Hmm. A difficulty indeed." His eyes caressed her intense features. "On which horse did he say to lay his blunt?"

"Blunt?" For half a second Ernie looked confused. "Oh. His money, you mean. Some absurd name, I thought." For reasons she didn't wish to understand, she pretended she had to search her memory. "Gossip No More? No, it wasn't that. Tell Me No Lies . . . ? *See No Evil*. That's it. Where do men find the names they give their mounts?"

"I think we must have run out of simple ones long ago, do not you? It becomes more and more difficult to think up some-thing new." Ave's fingers grasped his lower lip and tugged slightly. "Ernestine, I'm not sure I should allow you to place that bet—and don't fall into a distempered freak that I use the word allow! In this particular case it is apt! Browley was gone for weeks and, obviously, he hasn't yet caught up with the tit-tle-tattle. The difficulty we have, you and I, is that See No Evil is running in a private match against a new arrival and the odds are all on his rival's winning." He eyed her, his brows arched queryingly.

Ernie's, on the other hand, snapped together at the bridge of her nose. "But if I *don't* do as he said and See No Evil wins Bertie will blame me." She looked at him from the corner of her eyes and, a trifle saucily, added, "I don't dare *allow* you to place the bet on another animal." Dropping the teasing note, her irritation returned and she added, "On the other hand, if the rival wins and you do convince me to change the bet, then *you'll* get all the credit. Why are men so illogical?"

Sommerton smothered a chuckle. When he could speak without laughing, he suggested, "Should I cover Bertie by splitting his bet between the two?"

"No matter what I do, it will have exactly the same result." She moped her brow and muttered, "It's a question of damned if you do and damned if you don't!" A conscious look crossed Ernie's face and she glanced up at Sommerton from under her lashes. Had he heard? Would he be disgusted by her use of a word which should not have passed her lips?

"What would you suggest, Miss Matthewson?" asked Ave, one brow higher than the other, but otherwise ignoring her use of bad language.

She handed over the little purse she'd earlier tucked into her reticule. "We'll split it—assuming that means what I think it means."

"I'm sure you've an exact notion. But there is still a decision to be made. *How* should it be split?"

Ernie tipped her head, pursing her lips thoughtfully. "Just how likely is the new horse to win?" she asked, her brow deeply crinkled in thought.

Ave found the expression particularly endearing, to say nothing of tantalizing. He very much wished he could reach out, rub away those worry lines, touch those lovely lips, lift her chin slightly, lower his head and . . .

And was forced to clear his throat before responding. "That's rather difficult to guess," he said after a pause he hoped had not been too long. "I can only tell you that the odds have shifted completely to the newcomer." He watched as she contemplated that information. Just what would her next question be, he wondered.

"How often has the new horse raced here?"

"Not at all. He's judged entirely by his record in England—which is excellent. So far, his owner has kept him under wraps."

"Under wraps?" Her look sharpened. "Just how long has the poor creature been here?" She lifted her handkerchief to pat her upper lip where a dewing of moisture had appeared.

Curious as to what was on the young lady's mind, Sommerton answered slowly. "Not quite a week . . ."

Again Ernie's lips pursed into the contours of thoughtfulness. She obviously hadn't a notion that Ave found the expression a difficult one to resist. She'd have been quite shocked to discover just how easily the expression roused in him a desire to kiss her. After a long moment's cogitation, she smoothed her expression and said, "I've changed my mind. Do as Bertie said and put it all on See No Evil."

"Why?" asked Ave, almost as curious as to her logic as to just how her lips would taste.

"It is my belief the new animal has not had time to become acclimatized. I think he'll find today's hotter sun and the higher temperature which we are experiencing as enervating as I am. It is my contention that his energy will flag before the course is half over." In actual fact, she'd found it necessary to unbutton the top two buttons of her high necked habit as the morning progressed. She hoped the bow of her broad brimmed bonnet hid that fact from casual observers!

"Hmm." Ave's brows rose, his surprise at her exceedingly rational notion obvious. "An interesting point. Perhaps I'll put a little blunt on See No Evil myself."

Her initial desire to start an argument about his expectations of female intelligence which had been raised upon seeing how his brows expressed his thoughts, was just as quickly lost at hearing his suggestion. Ernie looked alarmed. "You would do that on my assessment of the situation?"

"Should I not?"

"But what if he loses?"

"Have you no faith in your logic?"

"Of course I have," she huffed. "But . . ."

Ave chuckled. "Fear not. I'll not blame you."

Moodily, she responded, "Oh yes you will. Even if you say you won't. Men are so unfair to us ladies, I think."

Suppressing a chuckle Ernie would not have appreciated, Ave assured her that he was not so prejudiced. "You appear to have had the wrong sort of men around you, that you judge us so unfairly! Believe me, Ernestine, it is my decision and mine alone to agree with your excellent logic. You've not twisted my arm, nor held a gun to my head, have you? Then it will be entirely my fault if the logic is false. But I do not foresee that to be the case." He offered his arm and gestured to where bets were still being laid.

"We'll see. Or, if See No Evil loses," she amended. *"Then* we'll see."

She hesitated, wondering if she'd imagined the odd sensation she'd felt earlier when she'd touched him, then lay her hand on his offered arm. She sighed softly. It had not been her imagination. She did have the odd sensation she was somehow connected to him, that they were one individual, that an energy flowed back and forth between them . . . and, most surprising, she felt all that through no better contact than her gloved hand on his coat-covered arm.

What would she feel if her hand were bare and his arm . . . but no. That would not do. Such thoughts were unacceptable. No well brought up young lady would think such things!

Still thinking them, however, she allowed Ave to lead her to where bets were being placed as time for the first race approached. Bertie's bet was entered and another for Ave. Several young men who looked to Ave for a lead made new bets as well. Ernie began to feel quite alarmed, forgetting the odd sensations Ave roused in her even when he wasn't trying.

"Will you lay out any of your own blunt, Miss Matthewson?" he asked politely.

She bit her lip. *Wouldn't it be cowardly to shake her head no as she wished to do? But wouldn't it be totally unladylike for her to place a bet?* In a quandary, she stared at Ave. "Is it proper?" she whispered.

"Not for you to do it yourself, but for me to do it for you? That is acceptable."

"Then please do. Not too much," she added when he turned back to where bets were still being laid at a furious rate.

"I'll put two Spanish dollars on See No Evil for you," he said, and proceeded to do so.

The first two races were wild melees from Ernie's point of view. Too many men tried to push their mounts into too small an area so as to be as close as possible to the starting pole. She feared for the horses more than she did for the riders, believing the men should have known better and deserved whatever they got. But that did not stop her from gasping just as loudly as any other woman when a horse did, some moments later, go down. Soon, though, man and horse were off again and, wonder of wonders, came in third. Ernie thought it ridiculous the officer riding should actually be rewarded for treating his horse so badly.

See No Evil's race was just before luncheon was served. Delicious odors rose from the pits where two young bullocks, culled from a herd raised for the Portuguese bull fight, broiled. The tempting smells very nearly made Ernie forget she'd an interest in the race about to begin, but an overheard comment to the effect that See No Evil finally had a rival worthy of his prowess brought her to her senses.

The new animal was surely a strong and well formed beast, she thought. Ernie feared she'd erred in not following Ave's first recommendation to put Bertie's money on him. The animal caracoled, obviously just for the joy of living, and she grew certain she'd made a mistake.

"I don't think I want to watch," she told her sister.

"But I thought this was the race . . ."

"It is, but look at that creature. He'll win by a mile and I'll be in disgrace for days."

"Do you think so?" smiled Norry.

"Think so? I know so." Ernie sighed dramatically. *"Both* Bertie and Sommerton will blame me and neither will forbear to tell me so."

"Bertie maybe . . ."

Ernie gave her sister a sharp look. "Why not the colonel?"

"He takes responsibility for his decisions. He's well known for it," said Norry promptly.

Ernie tipped her head. "He said something of that sort but I didn't believe him."

"You'll see—or maybe you won't!" Norry pointed to where the current race was nearly half over. See No Evil had taken the lead. "In fact, I doubt very much that on this particular occasion you need worry about a thing!" she finished, grinning.

Ernie, who had had her back to the course, spun around. "Oh!"

"Just oh?" asked the dusty voice she was beginning to know so well. "Perhaps you'll wish I'd laid a larger bet for you?" Ave teased.

"No. Oh no. I'm just pleased . . ." she gasped. "Oh dear!"

"No, no. Only a slip. He's all right, but it is true that a race isn't over until it's over! You see? He's coming along just fine. He only lost a few feet by that stumble. See? He's catching up again. Now if that next jump . . ." A roar went up when the new horse refused the jump. "Chin up, Miss Matthewson, we'll do it yet."

Around them male voices were raised, some encouraging See No Evil, as others encouraged his rival, who, when brought around, took the jump in stride. The excitement grew until Ernie wished she dared scream out her own words inspiring greater effort. The animals made the turn and worked over several low jumps in a row where tiny fields were arranged one after another.

The rider of the new animal began then to use his crop—too viciously, thought Ernie, and, revenge in mind, wished the beaten horse would unseat his rider! However that might be, and even to the most optimistic eye, the favorite *was* flagging.

Those who had bets on him were falling silent, many turning away, unwilling to watch the horse's sure defeat. One voice, however, could be heard swearing roundly. The swearer ignored those who attempted to shush him on the grounds that ladies were present and he must not say such things. Ernie glanced around but couldn't tell from where the curses arose.

"Your education is being seen to in ways you never expected, is it not?" asked Ave, his voice a combination of amusement and chagrin.

"If you refer to that gentleman's meager expressions of irritation, so far I've not learned a thing," she said, acid etching her voice. "We've a head-groom at home who has a far wider ranging vocabulary. Perhaps, when Norry and I have returned home, I should send him out to give lessons. Just think of the variations he could supply so that such tirades would not become repetitious and boring to those of us who are forced to listen."

Ernie had meant her biting words for Ave's ears alone. She'd not realized her court of young officers still hovered nearby. When she heard chuckles and the men repeating her words to those who'd not heard, she felt her face flush and her eyes lifted to see just what she'd expected: Ave's eyes danced with unsuppressed humor. Colonel Lord Sommerton was laughing at her. Again!

Well, she thought, vaguely dispirited, at least he isn't disapproving or disappointed. Then it occurred to her that it would be far better if he were. It also occurred to her that Ave Sommerton was courting her in his rather odd fashion. And, she reminded herself, it would not do . . .

See No Evil did not lose, of course. Ernie and Ave collected their winnings with a smug feeling which they could not hide. Thinking about it later, Ernie was rather surprised to remember that Ave had actually attributed their astute betting to her—not that he explained her thinking. He whispered, as they walked away, that the notion gave him an edge he didn't wish to lose when placing future bets.

Their chuckles at this secret conversation further exasperated some of the losers—not excluding Lieutenant Graham Torville, who made no secret of the fact he'd expected to cover previous losses by a sure bet on the new entrant. His tirade carried clearly after them. Obviously he was the man others had tried to shush.

For reasons Ernie could not discover—no matter how hard she searched her mind—he blamed Ave and her, just the sort of male illogic of which she had complained earlier.

An excellent lunch was served, the meat more to Norry's taste this year, and then the colonel brought their horses around. Other women were also ready to leave so their little group was much enlarged over the early morning ride.

"You look glowing," said Norry, observing her sister's happy expression.

"Glowing? What a strange expression."

"Not at all," said Ave. "I've noticed it before. You both do it."

"We do?" asked Norry as Ernie asked, "Do what?"

"It comes from inside somehow," he said. "When you are happy or excited or—I don't know. You glow. Don't they, Lady Barton?"

Appealed to, that lady had to have the conversation repeated and then she nodded. "Yes. I don't yet know Miss Matthewson well, of course"—she smiled at Ernie—"but you, Colonel Sommerton, are not the first to note how our Lenore's expression can actually light up a room, making all who observe it happier and more contented. It is a very special gift, I think, and one I envy."

Both Matthewson girls blushed furiously and Ave chuckled. "I don't believe that that new color is the glow to which Lady Barton and I refer," he teased.

Ernie, still more embarrassed, lay her crop lightly across her roan's flank. Bertie's gelding responded, happy for the run. Ave, laughing, followed after and they were soon well ahead of the others. Gradually he caught up to her and set his mount to pacing hers. Finally, she looked at him, grinning, her temper settled by the wildly exhilarating ride.

"What a soldier's wife you'll make!" shouted Ave.

Ernie's grin faded instantly. Equally quickly she pulled up. Ave took a moment to realize he'd gone on without her. He turned, trotting back to her, facing her, his thigh mere inches from her own. Ernie, wishing he were not so near, scowled.

"What is it?" he asked, his own frown in place. "Why did you stop?"

"Don't ever suggest such a thing again."

"Suggest what?" Ave, forgetting his impulsive comment, was truly bewildered.

"That I'd make a good wife for a soldier."

"But you would," he said, recovering quickly.

"My competency one way or the other is irrelevant. What's important is that I'd never be so foolish."

He frowned in earnest now. "Foolish?"

"To deliberately put myself in the position in which Norry finds herself? To experience the sort of pain that little Mrs. White, whom I met today, is suffering? To consciously decide to place myself into a situation where such pain and horror and desperation are exceedingly likely to result? Foolish beyond permission!" Ernie drew in a deep breath forcing the next words from her reluctant mouth. "I'll never *ever* marry a soldier, Colonel Lord Sommerton. And don't you forget it."

For a long silent moment they stared at each other. Her eyes trumpeted defiance; his demanded she not be so foolish. Ernie, unable to stare Ave down, turned to see how far behind the others were and noted that it would be some while before they caught up. Ernie had no desire to remain alone in Ave's company now she'd told him how she felt. She feared he might attempt to dissuade her from her vow and, given the unruly state her emotions were in, she doubted she could keep from reacting in an unacceptable fashion.

She turned her mare away from the colonel and trotted back to ease into place beside her sister—and stayed there for the rest of the ride, despite the fact Norry insisted on keeping Senorita to an exceedingly boring pace.

Once the others had gone on and they were home alone, Ernie recalled Lieutenant Torville's illogic and, in an attempt to avoid the questions she could see in Norry's eyes concerning herself and Ave, complained that she didn't understand such men.

"How can they," she asked, "twist the facts to suit themselves as Lieutenant Torville did today?"

"Do not attempt to understand that particular man, Ernie," said Norry. She went on with a great deal of bitterness. "Graham Torville is incapable of doing anything which makes sense."

"You do not like him?"

"He is not a gentleman in the true sense of the word and will go to exceedingly devious lengths to achieve his ends."

Norry's tone roused Ernie's suspicions. So, she decided, Sommerton and Bertie must have been correct in their suspicions about Torville. "What devious lengths has the monster tried so that he might achieve his goal with *you?*" asked Ernie, astutely.

"Nothing particularly interesting. At least not yet." Norry bit her lip. "Ernie, I'll admit I'm glad you've come to visit at just this particular time. Torville has made something of a nuisance of himself for a couple of weeks now. I simply don't understand the man—but one thing is obvious: he is incapable of hearing anything but what he wishes to hear!"

"I see."

"Do you?" Norry eyed her younger sister. "Perhaps you do." After a moment of looking at her twisting fingers, she glanced up. "Ernie, I insist that you not tell Ave or Bertie that his persistent attentions upset me."

"It would seem to me they are exactly the ones who should be told, so why not?" asked Ernie, although she was thinking she wouldn't have to tell them: They were already aware that something was going on.

"Because I'll not be the cause of one or the other meeting Torville on the field of honor. Not that it *is,*" added Norry tartly. "It's more a field of hurt pride and stupid acts of revenge. Or, at least, that's the way it seems to me."

"You fear a duel?"

"Have I not said so? In any case, I've had it out with Bertie and I don't think Ave will make such a spectacle of himself, so forget I've said anything at all, if you'd be so kind. Please don't worry, Ernie. Jon will be home soon and Graham will hedge off quickly enough when my husband is returned. He only comes around because he thinks any woman who has been married cannot help but miss"—she glanced at her unwed sister and blushed—"well, never mind *that.*"

"Miss the marriage bed." At her sister's shocked look, Ernie grinned and, when Norry appeared to find that nearly as shocking, she explained. "Obviously you didn't get to know our aunt very well. She doesn't think young women should remain ignorant of the act of love between male and female. She claims ignorance only leads to exactly what lack of knowledge is suppose to prevent for the simple reason the young lady doesn't know what's happening until too late!" Ernie waved away her aunt's unusual philosophy, returning to their discussion of Torville. "While your new admirer continues to make problems, we'll just have to see that you are never alone when he visits. Cannot Maria sit with you when he comes and I'm not near?"

"She does, but then I find it necessary to send her to the kitchen for tea or more bread and butter or whatever and Graham is very quick to take advantage of her absence. You don't know how often I've tried to convince him I'm not interested, but he'll not believe me. You wished to know how he could blame Ave or yourself for his losses today. In my case, I wish to know how he can continue to believe I'll become his mistress when I've told him no and no again. His way of thinking must be very strange indeed, don't you agree?"

"Very strange." A knock sounded. "I suppose that is Lieutenant Holles." Ernie's concern for her sister led her to ask, "Will you be all right now, or should you perhaps come with me to the rehearsal? We could always say I need a chaperon!"

"I've been perfectly all right without you for months, Ernie. I'm quite certain I'll be fine for the week or two remaining until Jon is back." She opened the door. "Ah. Lieutenant. Ernie is just ready to go. You'll escort her home again when you've finished, will you not?"

"I will unless practice runs on until I'm to go on duty, in which case, Colonel Lord Sommerton has offered himself in that capacity. He directs the play, you know."

"He does?" asked Ernie, her head coming up with a snap.

"Now, Ernie!" said her sister, a warning note in her tone, and laying her hand on the younger girl's arm.

Ernie looked at Norry, noted an exceedingly wary expression

and, her temper cooling as quickly as it had become hot, she chuckled. "Well," she said, "someone should have told me."

Then she recalled their confrontation on the road home from the races. Could she, she wondered, face him so soon after her blunt words? And if she did not? It seemed she had no choice—and, reluctantly, she admitted she was glad.

Ernie's heart beat faster and she knew it had nothing to do with fear of the man's reaction to her implicit rejection, but everything to do with seeing him so unexpectedly soon. Would she never learn sense, she wondered? And how would he react? Would he be angry? Would he take his irritation out on her? But that was surely nonsense. Colonel Lord Sommerton was a gentleman and surely she was lady enough she could control the ridiculous inclination she felt to step into his embrace and never leave it!

"Come along, Lieutenant Holles," she said. "If Colonel Sommerton is directing, I'm very certain we should not be late!"

Why, wondered Ernie, as she strolled beside the lieutenant, did her interest in doing the part increase with the knowledge that Ave had a hand in things? As if her increased interest were really such a mystery!

But why should she suddenly anticipate the next few hours, why did her heart beat faster and her breathing become irregular when he must now, after her words, hold her in disgust? And what was there about the colonel that had her wishing to see him when he was absent, but shy and unsure—not to say perverse—when he was near? But that was no secret either, was it?

Not that she would allow any man to know he had such an effect on her! That would never do at all. Besides, Bertie would laugh his head off if he ever discovered Ernie felt shy about anything and, she grinned to herself, she couldn't have *that*.

But, she remembered suddenly, whatever it was she felt for the man, *it would not do.* Marriage was not to be thought of—not when the man involved was an officer in the King's Army.

She had reached a decision on that, had she not? She would *not* put herself through the hell her sister must be experiencing. However at peace and contented Norry *appeared* to be, her stubborn insistence Jon was alive could not keep her blind to his death forever. At some point she'd have to admit he was gone, that no miracle would occur, and then she'd fall into that pit of despair awaiting her. The same pit that poor Mrs. White, as white as her name and drawn taut with unhappiness, experienced now . . .

But Norry. Norry's latest piece of idiocy was her comment that her problems with Torville would end soon because Jon would come home in a week or two. Ernie sighed. What did one do with a problem such as this? she asked herself. How did one make another see a truth to which that person dared not admit? If only Ave could help convince Norry she must go home. There must be something they could do . . .

"What did you say?" she asked Holles, when he lightly pinched her arm, drawing her attention back to the present.

"I *thought* you had your head in the clouds," he said a trifle sulkily.

Why, wondered Ernie, did men think one should hang on their each and every word. Especially men one didn't know and didn't particularly wish to know.

"You are quite correct. My thoughts were somewhere else." She glanced sideways and discovered her agreement hadn't appeased him. "I don't suppose you'd care to repeat your remarks, whatever they might be?"

"It was merely that I thought we could get together to practice our lines sometime tomorrow. I have duty later, but early— say ten?"

Oh dear, thought Ernie, remembering past experiences with men who wished to practice, preferably unchaperoned. There'd been one particular man who'd made such a nuisance of himself she'd very nearly left that party and gone home—which memory made her think of Miss Covington who had preceded her in this role. Had Lieutenant Holles made a similar pest of himself? Lud! I've enough problems without an infatuated leading man!

"I suppose we *should* practice," she said, mendaciously, "but I've already promised Bertie I'll ride out with the hunt tomorrow. I'll be long gone by ten. When do you get off duty?"

"Just in time to get to rehearsal. The next day, perhaps?"

Ernie desperately sought another lie and found one, desperation giving her a new capacity for invention. "Norry has asked that I help plan the Christmas Eve service along with her and Lady Colonel Barton," she said, making it up on the instant. "I don't think it'll be possible for us to have private rehearsals, Lieutenant," she added in as kindly a voice as she dared. Not too kind, as she feared to give him the least sort of encouragement. "I very much fear we must rely on those rehearsals which are scheduled."

"Perhaps if we have difficulties with the roles as the first performance nears . . . ?" he asked, a trifle diffidently, but with a sharp touch of concern in his tone.

"Perhaps," she said, but with no encouragement at all in her voice or expression. Ernie had given up private rehearsals when she'd discovered they were far too often an excuse for attempted dalliance. After that one really irritating experience, she no longer allowed such opportunity to arise—although, perhaps, if Ave, as director, asked for one . . . ?

No. What could she be thinking? She must not encourage Ave to anything more than friendship. Whatever was meant by that gleam she'd noted in his eyes, if it *were* more than laughing at her—as, more often than not, she suspected it was—then it must be stifled! Just as she must avoid any more of his leading comments concerning herself and the army!

She would not allow herself to succumb to his charm, to his appeal to her senses . . .

"Yes? What is it?" she asked impatiently.

"I merely pointed out that we've arrived," said the lieutenant very much on his dignity.

Ernie blushed. "So we have. I apologize that I'm preoccupied, Lieutenant Holles. Something my sister said shortly before you arrived . . . it bothered me a great deal and I cannot seem to think of anything else."

Holles looked alarmed. "You'll have forgotten your lines?"

Ernie chuckled. "I assure you, once I'm on that stage I will think only of the play."

"Oh, well then." He eyed her, unsure. "In that case . . ."

"You take your acting very seriously, do you not, Lieutenant?"

It was his turn to flush rosily. "I sometimes wish I'd not been born the younger son of an earl," he admitted. "I've often thought I'd enjoy the life of a player. The smell of paint! The smokey foot lights! The magic one makes with words and action! Oh, yes, I'll admit it. I love everything to do with the theater."

"I will try not to disappoint you. Shall we go in?"

Holles hesitated. "I rather hoped that we might get to know each other somewhat better than merely as players in the play," he said, rushing his fences.

"I am very sorry, Lieutenant," said Ernie as carefully as though she were speaking to an easily insulted dowager, "but I've vowed to have nothing to do in that way with any man connected to the army. Do not take it personally, sir. It is a matter of principle, you see. I've vowed I'll never wed an army man and, therefore, I don't wish to find myself in a position where I'll be tempted."

"Then you are *not* engaged to Browley?" asked Holles eagerly. "He has denied it, but no one quite believes him." Ernie could not help revealing her surprise at such nonsense and he added, "It is rumored, you see, that you came out with him because you are to be wed soon."

"Where do such rumors arise? Bertie must be mad as a wet flea that such a notion is going around. He and I are far too nearly brother and sister to ever wish a different relationship."

"That's what he says," said Holles, suddenly complacent. "I won't worry about your vow, then. Women get silly notions and men must ignore them. We'll do fine together. You'll see."

Ernie stared at him. Her mouth firmed into a grim line. "Lieutenant Holles, do you wish to lose another female lead for this play?"

Alarm returned to his mobile features. "Good heavens *no.*"

"Then I suggest you do not ignore my 'silly notion.' I assure you, however silly you may think it, I take it very seriously indeed." She turned on her heel and entered the make-shift theater and the first person she saw was Ave. He was sitting straddling a bench, a young man in shirtsleeves facing him. They were rehearsing the fellow's lines.

Sommerton shook his head. "No, no. Try it again and this time try to ask a question rather than just say the words. 'If he come not, then the play is marr'd. It goes not forward, doth it?' There. Like that. Now try it."

Ernie listened to another botched attempt, and, at her side, heard Holles groan. She giggled. Sommerton heard her and looked around. He rose to his feet immediately and came to her. She looked up into his eyes, noted that now familiar gleam—and very nearly turned on her heel to leave. He mustn't! She *wouldn't* allow it! Ave Sommerton must not invent a tendre for her just because he was lonely and she had arrived just when he wished for romantic companionship!

Besides, it was nonsense, this feeling they had been made for each other, that they'd known each other forever and were destined to spend the rest of their lives getting to know each other still better, and besides that, he knew how she felt. She'd told him only that afternoon that . . . She was again horrified by the memory. How could she possibly work with him after her tirade in response to his impulsive suggestion she'd make a good Army wife. Ernie quickly lowered her gaze and refused to look at him even when he reached out and touched her chin. After a moment he moved away.

"Well. Here you both are," said Ave, a slightly overdone jovial note in his tone. "Now we may begin, may we not? Have you had a moment to work on your lines, Miss Matthewson?" She nodded, still not willing to look him in the face. After another moment he added, "We'll begin with the first scene then. I believe you are on stage, Miss Matthewson?"

Holles, his hand possessively on her arm, led her forward and gallantly aided her climb the three rather shaky steps to the newly built stage. The cut version of the play began when Titania enters and calls for a roundel and a fairy song, saying she will rest. Oberon enters soon after.

Holles, as Oberon, moved up behind where Titania sat on a chair which, Ernie was assured, would later become a green-covered hillock. As Oberon, intent on teaching his Titania a lesson, Holles reached around Ernie to squeeze a pretend flower over her eyelids, pressing far too close for Ernie's comfort but perhaps, she thought, he was merely worried about his lines which he muttered just a trifle hesitantly.

> What thou seest when thou dost wake.
> Do it for thy true-love take;
> Love and languish for his sake; . . .
> When thou wak'st, it is thy dear.
> Wake when some vile thing is near.

The play practice continued with the arrival of Bottom and his cohorts. Bottom, also played by Holles, was soon supplied, by Puck, with his ass's head although, at the moment, there was none available so, again, they must pretend.

Practice stumbled along as such practices do until finally

Sommerton called a halt. "We've done enough until we've more props—and until more of you know your lines! Only Miss Matthewson has any excuse for not knowing them and she, one finds, already has hers better than some of you who have had well over a week now to learn them. We must do better. Next practice will be tomorrow at four. Good night."

Ernie was helped off the stage by Holles who had, she thought, taken far too many liberties with her person during practice. It was possible, of course, to construe every individual touch as an accident. Ernie believed otherwise. She excused herself a trifle coldly from Holles, deciding she'd rather take her chances with the colonel's less objectionable pursuit.

She joined Ave who was talking earnestly to a young man who made one note after another, jotting each in tiny print into a small black leather covered book. The officer nodded firmly after each direction, writing furiously, but seemed relieved when Ave said that was all.

"You are dismissed," said Ave, looking at cast and crew. "I've a word or two to say to your sister, Miss Matthewson, so I'll escort you home."

Ernie fumed at his high-handedness, but even with that, she preferred Ave's escort, dangerous as it was to her heart, to Holles's more physical approach to wooing her.

She waited patiently as the others filed out.

Six

Once they were alone, Ave offered his arm—which Ernie took after half a moment's hesitation. He led her from the theater. "Are you enjoying yourself?" he asked.

"I think you've made an excellent job of the cuts," she said, not quite answering his question.

For once Ave didn't notice her evasion. Instead, he jumped into an enthusiastic explanation of just why he'd dropped certain characters and why he'd started his version with the Fairy Queen's entrance. "We cannot go on for too long, you know. We've neither a large enough cast nor a proper stage nor, for that matter, an audience interested in anything more than entertainment of the most casual sort. One must offer only the most humorous parts and what has more humor than Bottom with his ass's head?"

"How many roles does Holles play?"

"Just Oberon and Bottom. He'll do them well, too. I haven't any worries where he and you are concerned, but"—his expression was one of humorous despair—"have you ever seen such a collection of bumbling idiots as the rest of the cast appear to be?"

"It is always that way just at first . . . or even at second or third," said Ernie, unable to resist an encouraging squeeze to his arm, "but somehow things always do come together at the end, do they not?"

"That has been my experience but I always forget. Thank

you for reminding me." Again he looked at her with that satisfied gleam in his eye. "I'll not worry so much," he added before she could comment on his expression.

He wouldn't push her into doing or saying anything which shouldn't be done or said, thought Ernie. He was, she decided, a gentleman. Satisfied with her thoughts, Ernie relaxed. They strolled on toward the square and Norry's house in a surprisingly comfortable silence.

When they'd gone around a curve and were well out of sight of Lieutenant Holles and the others, Ernie couldn't resist asking, "Do you really have something to say to Norry?"

Ave immediately frowned and slowed his pace. He tucked his free hand behind his back, his fist clenched. "Yes. I do. I was warned of something while at the races today that has me rather worried."

"Can you tell me?"

"I'd rather discuss it only once."

Ernie bit her lip. "Does what you heard have to do with Graham Torville and my sister?"

Sommerton halted, reached for Ernie's other arm and turned her toward him. "How did you guess?"

"I could think of nothing else which would disturb you so deeply as your frown indicates. Besides, something . . . oh, I too heard something"—she hedged, knowing Norry would be angry if she told Sommerton that she'd had it from Norry herself—"which bothered me."

"Tell me."

She shrugged. "I don't suppose it is so very unusual, really. Only that Torville isn't likely to be dissuaded in his pursuit of Norry by means one would apply to any normal gentleman!"

Sommerton snorted on something which might have been a laugh. "How true. Ernestine, it isn't proper to discuss this with you, but I think you must be warned if you are to help protect her. The bastard has laid at least one bet he'll have seduced your sister and made her his mistress before Christmas," Ave explained, led by his concern into greater bluntness than he would normally use before an unmarried woman.

"I'd wondered if something of the sort were at stake. A man doesn't usually persist in such untoward behavior in the face of persistent rejection unless pushed to do so."

Sommerton blinked at Ernie's easy acceptance of a situation which should have her swooning in horror, but it was only one more indication, if he needed any, that she'd make a splendid wife for a man such as himself, whatever she thought of the notion! Now, however, was not the time to push his suit. "Norry has said something to you."

Ernie wondered if she'd ever learn how to equivocate and evade. She was simply incapable, it seemed, of avoiding an admission of the truth in answer to a direct question. "Yes," she said, sighing. "She'll be angry you've discovered as much as you have. She seems to think she must protect *you* from what Torville has in mind."

Ave stopped dead and, when Ernie walked on, pulled her back. "Protect *me?* Did I hear that correctly?"

"Oh yes." Ernie glanced at him, noted the frown and wished she'd somehow managed to keep her mouth shut. Airily, she added, "From engaging in a duel, you see. Please don't let her guess I've told you."

Sommerton understood Ernie's dilemma. "I needn't reveal that I've had some of my information from you, my dear," he said, his tone filled with understanding.

Ernie sighed at his use of the endearment, but otherwise ignored it. Instead of beginning an argument of that point, she admitted, "I'll very likely tell her myself. That's what she fears most, you know, that you or perhaps Bertie will become involved to the point of a duel. She doesn't want that—in fact she'll do practically anything to avoid it."

"I can't answer for young Browley, of course," said Ave

soothingly, "but I'm not so foolish. Dueling is an out-dated and illegal means of settling an argument."

"When you discuss your latest news with Norry, you might bring that up if you can find a way to introduce the point. It might reassure her a trifle."

"A duel is definitely out of the question—although given this situation I can finally understand why men are occasionally driven to give a challenge! It is never a true solution, however. No. I'll have to come up with some other method of controlling Torville and protecting your sister . . ." The colonel started walking again.

Ernie, pacing along at his side, glanced up at his frowning face. "Norry insists that now I've come he'll have far less opportunity to play his tricks, but I don't agree. Not if I continue going out with the hunt and taking part in such long play rehearsals and going to races and everything else that goes on around here. Ave," she said, a sudden revelation striking her, "it is as bad as the Season in London! Just like it, in fact. One hasn't a moment to oneself in which one may stop and think!"

He chuckled at her wry tone. "Do you *wish* time to think? Are you so unlike most women that you don't enjoy a constant round of distraction and entertainment, shopping and gossiping and . . . and I've no notion what else?" He placed a hand over hers where it lay on his arm.

Ignoring the warmth and comfort of that hand, Ernie slowed her pace, pulling Ave's long steps down to a more reasonable rate. "You know, I don't think I do. And, yes, I do want a minute now and again to think. I wonder if that is the true reason why I refused to go up to London for a third season and my excuses to my aunt only that: excuses." Ernie pondered the thought, but still heard Ave's quiet reply.

"Someday you'll have to tell me what excuses you made, but here we are, almost to your sister's. And wouldn't you know it!" he said, instantly alert, "Your sister appears to have company!"

"Torville is here?"

"Yes. I recognize that mare. Come along now. Don't dawdle."

Since Ernie had already picked up her pace she made a face at him, but, since his increased speed was just that much more than her own and he was a half pace ahead of her, he didn't see it. She jerked on his arm as they started up the steps to the door, however, and swung him around to face her. She put a finger to her lips.

"You'll come in for coffee, Colonel?" she said a trifle loudly.

"I'll be pleased to do so," said Sommerton, going along with Ernie's pretense.

The door opened and, although it wasn't terribly obvious, Ernie read relief in the look Norry sent her way. "Yes, Ave. Do come in and see who is visiting. I've been telling him it is too long a ride to come here so often, but he seems to think the twenty or so miles round trip a mere nothing."

"Torville." Ave took the seat next to the younger man when Norry and Ernie seated themselves across the table. "You must be a real glutton for punishment. Don't you fear you'll fall asleep while on duty tomorrow?"

Torville laughed harshly. "Nonsense. I don't know how many times I've gone on duty with no sleep at all," he bragged.

Ave turned a cold look his way. "Then I'd dislike being one of the men depending on you. No man is at his best when he lacks sleep."

Torville scowled. "Doesn't affect *me,* I tell you. I can go days with only snatched bits of sleep. Besides, there isn't an enemy within several days march, so why worry?"

"Army discipline is not something one puts on merely when it is needed, Lieutenant. It is part of the way of life."

The argument, with Torville making himself look worse and worse, if he'd only known, continued until the coffee arrived. Maria carried it in, the cups and saucers, and a plate of sliced cake on a tray. Sommerton rose to take it from her and place it on the table. He drew up a fifth chair and seated Maria.

The girl didn't say anything although she gave the colonel a sharp look after a quick glance at her mistress. Maria, decided Ernie, was an exceedingly intelligent young woman. She'd guessed she was to be more a friend than a servant in Torville's eyes so that she could be more effective as a chaperon for Norry. That she really *was* as much friend as servant was irrelevant, of course!

Once the late supper was ended Torville made his excuses and rose to leave. He asked Norry to walk him out to his horse. She went, as a good hostess should do, but Ernie tagged along as well, and he lost the opportunity to try for a kiss—or whatever he'd had in mind. Ernie didn't like the expression which he gave her as he mounted. Dark with irritation, it boded no good.

"He's getting impatient, Norry," she said, watching the man ride away.

"Yes." Norry sighed. "I fear he is."

Ernie put a hand on her sister's arm. "Come back in now or you'll catch a chill. I hate like anything to worry you more than you already are, but you'd better hear what Ave has to say."

Maria was clearing away the dishes when the sisters returned. "Leave that for now," said Ave. "I've something to say and I think you'd better hear it, too, Maria. Mrs. Lockwood will have special need of your close attentions, I fear."

He soon laid out his news about Torville's bet which made Norry flush an ugly bright red. "How dare he!" she said.

"He's no gentleman, Norry. You told me that yourself," said Ernie, soothingly.

"Yes, but I assumed he kept the forms of gentlemanly behavior among his own kind." There was a bewildered look in Norry's eyes when she raised them to look around the table. "How can a true gentleman have anything to do with him?"

"True gentlemen do not," said Ave, his tone dry. "Unfortunately there are too many unlicked cubs and would-be gentlemen who are less discriminating. Torville finds his friends among that sort. If I were his commanding officer, I might order him to remain in camp or something equally inhibiting. Unfortunately, the man who is Torville's superior is not an officer who interferes in his men's private affairs—even something so dishonorable as this."

"Something must be done to protect my sister," said Ernie glaring around the table.

"Yes. I agree." Ave spoke in soothing tones. "Something must be done."

"Well?" challenged Ernie. No one spoke. She sighed. It seemed to her she was doing a lot of sighing recently. When no one offered an idea she suggested, "The first thing is that I'll no longer ride with the hunt. That is several more hours a day when I may be at Norry's side. Now that we know how serious it is, someone *must* be near at all times. At least I assume that as long as she is not alone, he cannot hurt her?" She looked toward Ave for an answer. Before he could respond, her sister did.

"You must not give up something you enjoy so much," said Norry softly. "I'll not have it."

"I don't think your ceasing to ride will help all that much," Ave agreed. "It is the wrong time of day for such a night creature as Torville, so you needn't give up your pleasure. And," he chuckled, "you needn't insist your pleasure is unimportant when compared to your sister's need because we know it is. The thing is, I've finally thought up a solution. I'll have a little talk with his commanding officer and discover just when Torville is on duty and when not. Then, once we know when he's free to appear, we can arrange among Norry's friends to make calls or they can invite her over for an evening. If you were to simply dog your sister's steps, Ernie, it might have the effect of making our sly friend more determined than ever—and therefore, more dangerous. He might decide that mere seduction was not the only route to his goal." He looked from one sister to the other. Solemnly, he added, "He might conclude more extreme measures were necessary."

"On the theory that once I've been *forced* I'd have no reason to forbid him my bed and he'd have achieved his goal of making me his mistress?" Where Norry's anger had merely made her flush before, it now left her white. "The man is despicable."

"Is there a worse word than despicable?" asked Ernie softly but with a viciousness which startled those who heard her.

"I didn't wish to actually *say* what you've just expressed so clearly, Norry," said Sommerton after a moment in which, open-mouthed, he stared at Ernie. "I nevertheless believe your conclusion a distinct possibility. You must not find yourself alone with him, but to avoid setting his mind toward such extremes, we'll have to be more subtle than Ernestine suggested she be."

"In that case, someone needs to inform Bertie he's taking me out on the hunt tomorrow," said Ernie.

"Bertie will not be available tomorrow."

Wide-eyed, Ernie insisted. "But he must be. I've told Lieutenant Holles that Bertie will escort me to the hunt."

"You'll now discover a problem with lying to someone in the military, Ernestine," teased Sommerton, a laugh in his voice. "Your fib to young Holles will be discovered, I fear, as soon as he discovers Browley stands duty tomorrow morning—which he is scheduled to do."

It was Ernie's turn to flush, but her blush added becoming color to her complexion. "It's what I get for relying on old habits," she admitted ruefully. "Bertie and I have always gotten each other out of scrapes and I simply used him as I'd have done long ago when we were children."

"If you'll not object to my escort," suggested the colonel politely, "I'll be more than happy to take you out. Your words to Holles need not be entirely a lie."

"I'd enjoy that," said Ernie just as politely, but wishing she could fall through the floor.

"If Holles becomes a nuisance, do not fail to tell me," ordered Sommerton. "Does it seem to anyone else that the women in this house are prone to drawing the wrong sort of attention?" he asked rhetorically.

Ave didn't notice Maria flush and duck her head, but Ernie wondered at it.

"In any case," he continued, "I'll have a chat with Holles which will settle him down. I hope! It's a bad habit with him that he invariably develops a passion for his leading lady. If he were not such an excellent actor, I'd cast someone else for the lead, but he is the best amateur I've seen and really very good."

"The best *I've* played against. If he behaves, I'll enjoy the part of Titania." Ernie smothered a yawn, noticed her sister was also trying very hard not to yawn. "Oh dear. It has been a long day and tomorrow will begin excessively early if I'm to go out with the hunt. I hate to make a show of poor hospitality, Colonel, but I would, at this particular moment, enjoy your absence far more than your presence!" She made nothing more than a half-hearted pretense at hiding a second and more gaping yawn.

Sommerton laughed, chucked her lightly under her chin as he might a child and asked that Maria see him out. Norry and Ernie, curious, awaited the maid's return.

"What did he say to you?" asked Norry.

"No more than what we had decided already." The maid returned to the table and stacked the small plates. "It is only that I am not to leave you alone." She shrugged.

Ernie yawned again. "Good. I don't know how it is, Norry, but I truly am exceedingly sleepy."

"Only a long ride this morning to the races, an exciting time watching Bertie's horse come in, all the strain of rehearsal this evening—however much you enjoy acting, do not attempt to tell me it is not a strain—and add to that a rather emotion-laden discussion of my problems . . . no, I haven't a notion why you might be ready for your bed."

Ernie chuckled, but sobered when a thought crossed her mind. "Oh, Norry," she said, turning away from the tiny room which was hers, "You'll be happy to know that Sommerton does not believe in dueling. He thinks it an out-dated and foolish way of settling problems."

"And just how did you discover that interesting bit of information?" Norry crossed her arms and tapped her foot.

"Don't be angry. Ave said he wanted to escort me home because he'd overheard that conversation about Torville while at the races and he wished to warn you about the man's motive. His attitude toward dueling came out when we were discussing it. That's all."

"You have that wide-eyed not-so-innocent look you always wore as a little girl when you were lying through your teeth, but never mind." Norry's posture relaxed and she smiled. "However you learned it, it is a relief to know that Ave, at least, will not be getting up before dawn and meeting our fine villain at twenty paces. Oh, go to bed, Ernie, and stop feeling so guilty. I'm not angry with you although I've a notion I ought to be!"

Ave Sommerton was met by his batman who held out a letter to him. "Came from London by special messenger not an hour ago," said Riley.

"Did you see to the man?" asked Ave, staring at the thick cream-colored paper.

"Yes, sir. He's all taken care of right and tidy." Riley unobtrusively helped Ave out of his tight coat and, when the colonel seated himself, pulled off his boots, his hands covered with soft white cotton gloves. A man's boots, after all, were to be treated with the utmost respect and care.

"That'll be all," said Ave. "I'll get myself to bed."

Ave's eyes trailed toward the missive he'd laid on his traveling desk. Not his father's seal so not from him. What could it be?

"Riley," he called to his retreating batman. The man turned. "The messenger, was he a military man?"

"No sir. More likely a clerk, I thought. At least," grinned Riley, "he's a scrawny creature, not in uniform, and an unhappy little man who jumps at a shadow and cringes at any unexpected noise. Likely thinks there's a Frenchie hiding behind every bush, poor bastard!" Riley chuckled but then sobered. "Almost came a'hunting of you, sir, a private messenger coming that way— thought it might be important."

"Very likely it is, but you'd probably not have found me so that's all right." Sommerton nodded. "That's all, then. Thank you."

A clerk, Sommerton thought. Was the message from his father's solicitor then? Sommerton's lips compressed. Had his father finally done it? Had he—not unexpectedly—landed himself in a sponging house, held in one of London's many jails for non-payment of bills? Ave felt a distinct disinclination to discover the worst. In fact—he allowed himself to admit it—a cowardliness he never felt when in battle and under fire chilled his blood.

But he was *not* a coward and avoiding the letter would not change the facts concerning whatever the Earl Mowtrey had gotten up to. Still reluctant, however, Ave reached for it, slit the seal and unfolded the thick missive.

Ten minutes later the heir to the profligate and normally destitute Earl Mowtrey lay back on his hard cot and stared at the ceiling of the room he had managed to arrange for his own use for the winter. He fingered the heavy paper, rubbing the tips of his fingers up and down the stiff edge finding it impossible to believe the news revealed there. For a moment he didn't dare believe it. It was too opportune, too unbelievably timely—in fact, far too good to be true. In one way, at least. Besides, Ave didn't trust the fates to be busy in his behalf. Not to this extent.

On the other hand, it was also impossible to believe that anyone might have organized such a cruel jape in order to make a May-game of him. *Why would anyone have done so, anyway?* He'd told no one of his determination to marry Ernie. Nor was it common knowledge that Miss Ernestine Matthewson was equally determined she'd not wed a professional officer dependent on his pay. Not that she'd mentioned wealth or comfort or any of those things which *should* be in a woman's mind when she thought of marriage. No, she'd spoken only of the emotional hell that anticipated widowhood would bring her!

Little idiot, he thought cheerfully. Who had promised her she'd ever be a widow anyway? He certainly had no notion of dying to oblige such maudlin and muddled thinking!

Pushing that thought from his mind, he spread the pages flat against his bent knees. Once again Ave read the incredible words. "So sorry, your lordship, to be required to inform you of the late earl's, your father's, demise."

Ave wished he could feel differently toward his father, feel some proper grief, or, at the least, a sense of loss. But his father had never encouraged such feelings as would lead to grief. He had, actually, done all in his power, by his behavior and his lack of care, to be undeserving of them. Ave sighed and looked down again to the lamp-lit page.

The letter went on to describe—although not in so many words—how, blind drunk, his father had walked into the path of an on-coming gig which as ill-luck would have it was harnessed to a half-trained colt which, startled, had, not unexpectedly, reared. The colt's descending hooves had been the instrument of the late earl's death. The last paragraph was full of flowery verbiage which, when one managed to work through it, meant no more than that the writer hoped to continue in his position as the new earl's solicitor.

And well he might. Over the years the poor frustrated man had done his best for the estate in the face of an employer who had been doing *his* best to ruin it! So. Fine. The man might as well be retained.

Ave set that aside and returned to an earlier section, hoping to determine if there was anything a solicitor might do at this point in time? By his first quick reading, it appeared there might be. If he hadn't misread the thing, the *utterly* unbelievable information was that the late earl had died a wealthy man! It seemed that during recent weeks he'd had an incredible run of luck at tables and turf.

The solicitor was not yet certain of the total, but would soon have full information as to the exact amount of the late earl's winnings, which findings he would forward to the new Earl Mowtrey. It was thought already, however, said the letter in carefully convoluted and wishy-washy language, that it was possible that maybe, just perhaps, there would be enough from the deceased earl's winnings, even after all current debts were paid, to make a very large dent in the mortgages. It was not completely impossible that they might be paid off entirely. Although, if doing that were the new earl's decision, the solicitor feared it likely there would then be anything left with which to put the ruined Mowtrey estates in order.

There was more, written in the ridiculous language which solicitors find impossible to avoid, all of it suggesting and then recanting, making allusions to possibilities and then warning of the dangers . . .

What it boiled down to, decided Ave, was the never-expected possibility that he might actually be able to go home . . . more, that there might be a home to go home to! A vision of the old place deteriorating in a hundred different ways, as it was the last time he'd seen it, filled Ave's mind. A mix of emotions followed: sadness it should be so; love for his home; a barely allowed hope that he *could* save it after all, and then, to top off his confusion, a vision of Ernie standing in the curving drive, staring up at the long Palladian frontage and shaking her head at all the work which needed doing. . . .

Ernie would not marry a soldier; would she marry an impoverished earl? Sommerton gritted his teeth. He didn't want to think she might marry a peer when she would not wed the man he was now. He was a soldier, a career officer, dammit, whose future was bound to be unknown however careful he'd be of his skin. Even though he loved her he could not promise that a serving officer's life might not, at some point, be lost. Again the gritted teeth. Blast it, he would *not* go to her hat in hand and beg her to marry a poverty-stricken peer instead. She *would* agree to marry the soldier or . . .

Or what? Ave stared again at the cracked ceiling. Could he give her up if she stayed firm to her principles? On the other hand, did he want a woman who could be easily swerved from what she considered a firm belief?

Ave grimaced. Ernie's belief was based on the wrong end of the stick, dammit. Ernie was forgetting that if they did *not* marry, then they'd have nothing at all! Surely that should mean something, the time they *could* have together. . . .

And he wanted that time with her. Badly. He threw an arm over his eyes and groaned softly, because now the growing physical and emotional desire for her was muddied by another need. *Now* he needed her in a new and more complicated way as well— and perhaps, or so some might say, an insulting way? Because now he needed her mind and experience as well as her presence in his life! From things Norry had let slip over the years or had read in snips and bits from Ernie's letters, Ernie knew far more than he did about estate management! How demeaning that was, but how very true. He would *need* that expertise.

But how would she react to that selfish need? *Would* a woman find it insulting that he didn't want her merely because he found her desirable? He discovered he didn't know the answer to that one. Maybe, he thought, most women would be insulted, but his Ernie was a different sort altogether and he hadn't a notion how she'd react.

However that might be, he did not wish her to agree to marry him already aware he'd give into her desire that he leave the army. Very possibly he was merely being foolishly stubborn, but he wished her to want to marry the man he was and not the man he might have to become.

Was that so very selfish? He sighed. Likely it was, but however ridiculous, it was the way he felt: Miss Ernestine Matthewson had better say yes to Colonel Lord Sommerton and not to the Earl Mowtrey—or else. And there would be no *or else.* He *wouldn't* lose her—she *would* say yes.

Satisfaction filled him at that, but it rapidly faded, because once she'd said yes, he had another problem on his hands. By every honorable consideration, it would be immediately obligatory to free her from her commitment to him. He would have to explain that his father was dead and that she'd actually agreed to become a poverty-stricken countess rather than a poverty-stricken officer's wife! Ave grinned wryly. He knew his Ernie well enough to know she'd be furious! So, with Ernie in a temper, he'd have to chance his luck all over again. It didn't sound promising. . . .

Ave found emotional release in a long sigh. The fact he must give her a chance to say no to that alternate life in England which would be as hard as life here in the Peninsula—at least until they'd put the estate in order—was frightening. Because what Ernestine must be made to understand was that, even if he left the army, as he was gradually accepting he must, given the chance of saving the estates he'd long believed lost to him, even then he would be the man he was now and it was to that man Ernie must agree to be wed!

Satisfied with his muddled reasoning, Ave finished undressing, readied himself for bed and blew out the lantern. Too few hours remained between now and the morning when he would again meet his love. He'd sleep and then think about it all all over again. Then, too, he'd think about the letter he must write the solicitors who were now his. . . .

The new Earl Mowtrey closed his eyes and images of his old home, returned to its former grandeur, filled his mind. Somewhere in the background, the scene was alive with childish voices. His children's voices. His and Ernie's. Ave smiled as he drifted off to sleep.

The next morning after lighting the stub of the candle in her candlestick, Ernie got into her sister's habit which Maria had brushed and laid out for her. Dressed, Ernie strolled through the dim sitting room. Only a faint gray light, seen through the mist outside the windows, indicated dawn was at hand. Once again she paused when she heard voices in the kitchen accompanied, this time, by the unmistakable odor of frying bacon. English bacon, which must have arrived with the wagons, which meant her trunks had arrived!

"Bertie," she said accusingly as she unhesitatingly opened the door, "it is too bad of you, coming here and eating up all the food I brought from England for Norry's enjoyment!"

Startled, Bertie jumped away from Maria. The girl looked over her shoulder and Ernie caught a glimpse of a tear-stained face before it was averted and Maria crouched over the skillet poised on a tall trivet over the fire. The wonderful smell from the cooking bacon made Ernie's mouth water, but that didn't stop her from glaring at her old friend.

"Just what do you think you're doing here, anyway?" she asked.

"It isn't what you think," he said, a worried glance toward Maria and a second, defiant one, cast toward Ernie accompanying his words.

"Since I've known you forever," said Ernie pacifically, "I'll take your word for that. So," she added when neither spoke, "if not the obvious between a man and lovely young woman, just what *is* going on?" Bertie opened his mouth. "And do not try to tell me it is nothing!"

"You must not pry, Ernie," he scolded. "It is *not* your business."

"I think it is very much my business when I find that someone, whom I like as much as I like Maria, is crying. And do not deny it," she added when Bertie shook his head. "I saw her tears." Ernie moved a step or two toward the Spanish girl. "Maria . . ."

"It is nothing." The girl spoke softly but insistently. "I am quite fine. It was only a moment's weakness, truly."

Silently, Ernie made a vow to get to know Maria better. Something was very much *not* fine and certainly not a *nothing*. But what it could possibly be she couldn't think. Maria seemed content working for Norry, if not ecstatically and outrageously happy. She appeared to like and admire Norry and she never gave the impression she resented anything she was asked to do. In fact, it seemed to Ernie that Maria tended to do far *more* than asked. So what could it be?

"Ernie?" asked Bertie, a warning in his tone.

"If you are certain nothing is wrong . . ." said Ernie, postponing, for the moment, any attempt to draw the girl out.

"Nothing," insisted Maria.

At the same moment Bertie firmly insisted, "There is nothing wrong about which you can do a thing," which roused Ernie's curiosity to a still higher pitch.

She gave him a straight look and was satisfied when a red tinge colored his cheekbones. "Very well then." Silence followed her words. Finally she asked, "Bertie, *are* you here for breakfast? Again?"

" 'Fraid so. I'll not eat much bacon," he offered, looking a trifle rueful at the knowledge his thoughtless anticipation of the treat might have deprived Norry. "Also, I'm here to tell you that when Holles accused you of lying when you told him I was taking you hunting today, that I assured him I had offered, forgetting I was standing duty. Told him I arranged for the colonel to ride with you. Was that all right? After all, since you lied, I supposed you did not want him coming around . . . ?"

Ernie, forgetting her worry about Maria in her disgust at Holles, responded, "In half a moment Holles has convinced himself he has conceived a passion for me. Bertie, why do men do it? It has happened too often to be an accident. We are only playing parts in a play when suddenly my opposite thinks the play-acting is for real and pursues me amorously." She grimaced. "If it were not so irritating, it would be exceedingly humorous, would it not?"

Bertie tipped his head, eying her. "Can you not believe they might actually have fallen in love with you?"

"With *me?*" She laughed so freely it brought Norry into the kitchen, pulling her robe tightly around her and blinking in the sudden light. "Bertie," Ernie added, with a spurious frown and chiding tone, "the army has not been good for you. You have developed rocks where your brain should be." When he looked as if he didn't understand she added, "You know very well that men do not fall in love with me."

Remembering the silly incident which had, however irrational, convinced Ernie of that fact, Bertie opened his mouth to argue. Norry's hand on his arm stopped him. She shook her head at him and responded in his place. "You obviously believe that, my dear sister, but someday you'll discover it's not true." It was her turn to tip her head questioningly. "I wonder where you got such an odd notion."

Bertie exchanged a look with Ernie. Again he faced a woman shaking her head at him. He grimaced. "Maria, is that food about done? It's no fun when everyone demands that I not say what I think . . ." The Spanish girl didn't respond and he turned toward her. "Maria?"

She, too, solemnly shook her head, revealing she'd been more observant than one might have guessed from her seeming concentration on the bacon. Bertie groaned and rolled his eyes in disgust.

Ernie chuckled drawing their attention. "Maria, you mustn't tease our poor Bertie so. Have I not just said his brain has turned to rocks?" She pretended compassion. "One must be kind to him and pat him on the head and tell him he is a good boy and encourage him to do his very best . . . no matter how bad that may be!"

"You watch out, Ernestine Sara Matthewson!" said a half angry, half laughing Bertie, "I'll find a way of getting even for that."

"Will you Bertie?" For a moment she pretended concern. The look faded. "But no. You've become such a perfect block, I needn't concern myself, need I? Here Maria, let me dish that up while you set the table." She knelt next to the fire, removing the platter and fork from the girl's hands. "Good heavens, you've cooked enough for the whole army, have you not?"

As Ernie finished loading her tray a knock sounded at the front door. She carried the food in from the kitchen just as Norry asked Colonel Sommerton to come in. "Ah," said Ernie, nodding portentously. *"Now* I see why so much food! It *is* for the army!"

Blinking, Sommerton came on in. "Have I missed something?" he asked.

"Nothing worth repeating," Ernie insisted. "If you still plan on taking me to the hunt you need not, you know. Bertie will be free one of these mornings and when he is he'll escort me."

"I go in any case," said Sommerton a trifle off-handedly, still a trifle bemused. "I see no reason why you should *not* go."

Ernie glanced sharply his way, a knife-edge of hurt sliding between her ribs. She looked down at the tray she still held and turned to put it on the table. There was no reason on earth that she should feel the slightest hurt. There *wasn't*.

"And," added Sommerton as she turned away, "I would very much like escorting you"—

Her spirits rose . . .

—"since Bertie may not."

. . . and took another swift dip at his last words. "I think, after all, that I must stay with Norry. We must not forget her danger."

"Oh no you don't!" said the older sister as she entered the room with a plate, this one loaded with freshly toasted bread. "You won't make *me* your excuse, Ernestine Sara Matthewson!"

It was the second time that morning she'd been addressed by her full name, something which happened only when she'd somehow offended or was being reprimanded. She sighed. "Very well," she agreed, her voice prim and her gladness well hidden that she was forced to give in and go. "Colonel Sommerton, I would be pleased to accept your very kind invitation—such as it was."

He chuckled. "Someday you'll cut yourself with that sharp tongue."

"I've been warned of that problem." Ernie shrugged. "So far I've not wounded *myself.*"

"Have you not?"

There was a gentle questioning look in eyes which were far too kind and saw too deeply for Ernie's peace of mind. Remembering the various men she'd driven away by speaking too freely, she shook her head and turned to Maria. "You will be in the market today, will you not?" Maria nodded but looked a trifle wary. "Will you see if by any chance my new riding habit has been delivered at that place we'd call a receiving office in England? I don't know what you call it here."

No one enlightened her. Maria merely nodded once again and

exchanged a glance with Bertie who was finishing his second cup of tea. He stood, picked up a last piece of toast, and made his excuses. For some reason Maria followed him out. She came back in almost immediately and resumed her place at the table.

"Did Bertie forget something, Maria?" asked Ernie, her curiosity burning still hotter at this further evidence of something between the two. What *was* going on there, she wondered.

Maria stared into her teacup. "I merely ascertained that he would, as he'd promised, meet me in the market to carry a rather heavy item home," said the Spanish girl softly.

"Doesn't Major Lockwood's batman do that? I thought it part of his duties, to help with your heavy work," said Ernie. And how could Bertie go to market if he could not go to the hunt? she wondered. Mystery on top of mystery! "Well? Does not Mr. Bacon do the heavy work?"

Norry answered Ernie's question. "I've sent Albert off to take messages for me to women in several units around and about. The Christmas Eve Service committee, you know." Norry also looked as if she were curious about Maria's unexpectedly close relationship with Bertie. "I doubt if Albert will be back until evening—although he may plan to stop here around noon for a rest and refreshment before going in the other direction," she added.

"The lieutenant is very kind," said Maria softly, her eyes on her plate, "to offer to help me in just this little way." Her fork made patterns in the remains of her eggs.

"Just so long as that is *all* he offers," said Ernie under her breath. She heard a soft chuckle and looked up, finding Sommerton's amusement-filled gaze on her. She blushed as she realized her comment, totally unacceptable in its insinuations that Bertie might offer Maria a slip on the shoulder—as the saying was—had been overheard. She stared at him. Defiantly.

"If you've finished mangling that toast," he said, ignoring

her discomfort, "perhaps you'll find your hat and crop and we may be off."

Ernie stood up immediately. "Certainly. We wouldn't wish to keep the hunt waiting."

"Do you think they would?" Sommerton asked, almost as if talking to himself. He also answered himself. "Very unlikely."

"All the more reason to hurry," suggested Norry, grinning at the neat way Ave had turned the tables on her sister.

Later that morning milling riders, the heavy ground mist swirling around their horses' legs, waited, impatiently, as the hounds were set to casting for a new scent. A very young man— Ernie doubted very much that he found it necessary to shave above once a week—approached the colonel and drew him off for what appeared a very solemn discussion. A second man, who had been introduced to her as Brigade-major Osgood, forced his restless animal nearer to her equally restless roan.

"Watch it there," said Ernie sharply when his bay reached out to nip her mount. She backed a few steps away but the young officer again moved nearer—this time more carefully controlling his horse.

"I've hoped for an opportunity to speak to you," he said softly, his large, long lashed eyes staring deeply into hers.

Ernie blinked. "And is this your chance?"

He chuckled and Ernie liked him a little better. "I sincerely hope so. It appears that young Hazelwaite has drawn off your guard dog quite thoroughly and that allows me a moment of which I'll take advantage . . . if you allow?" His very expressive eyes hinted that he'd like to take more than merely verbal advantage.

Ernie noticed that whatever his words and expression promised, he occasionally cocked a wary eye toward the men's conversation. *Was Sommerton such a bear? Or was it assumed by his men that she was the colonel's property?*

Ernie frowned. If that were the case, it was a totally unacceptable situation. She belonged to no man! Certainly not an officer. And most certainly not to Sommerton, no matter how foolishly her mind and body felt drawn to him. Ernie drew in a deep breath and turned back to Osgood. "Hazelwaite's the young officer speaking to him? I don't believe I've heard the name."

"He's just out from England and convinced he sees a Frenchie lurking under every bush. Besides this very natural nervousness felt by all new arrivals, I fear some of the wags have filled his innocent ears with tales. Now he is emptying his budget into the colonel's."

Ernie sent a compassionate glance toward the boy. "Sommerton should be warned the lad's been teased, should he not?"

"Colonel Lord Sommerton is an old hand, Miss Matthewson. He is well aware of the problem, which is on-going, and he'll handle Hazelwaite with his usual tact. Luckily for me that may take some time—time which I can spend with *you*." He beamed at her, those eyes again expressing things he'd not dare put into words. "Do tell me, Miss Matthewson, have you heard that the Light Division plans a ball?"

"A ball?" Ernie blinked. "Bertie told me there are balls, but now I've arrived here and see how it is, I wonder . . . is it *possible* to give a ball under conditions such as exist in these camps?"

"Not just possible, but often done. I would very much like the privilege of escorting you—and your lovely sister, of course." Osgood caught her gaze and again stared deeply, suggestively, into her eyes.

He'd have been insulted if she told him, as she wished to do, that she found it humorous rather than intriguing! But the fact Osgood remembered the need for a chaperon was much in his favor—despite his insistence on flirting with her in such an imbecilic fashion. Then it occurred to Ernie that if she did not say yes she would undoubtedly end up going with her sister and Colonel Sommerton. Even Osgood's idiotic batting of eye-lashes was better than that.

It was ridiculous, but she very much feared, from Osgood's hints, that she was already, even in the few days since her arrival, marked as Ave's. It would not do. Not only must the regiment not perceive that it was so, Colonel Sommerton must not be allowed to think such a thing.

The first excited yip of hounds broke into her thoughts. She looked up from her hands to find Osgood watching her, his expression shadowed by those jealousy-inducing lashes. "I would be pleased to accept your escort," she said and added as a broad grin crossed his even features, "but with the caveat that my sister must also approve." Her gaze was firm and straight and totally unflirtatious.

He nodded, still grinning. "That will do. I'm certain Mrs. Major Lockwood will agree. I'll stop by this evening if I may? To discover her decision?" he added when she seemed about to question that.

Satisfied, Ernie nodded her agreement and noted that young Hazelwaite, red around the ears, was trotting off toward the encampment. She felt sorry for the lad, but had no time to think about his situation as Sommerton returned to her side. There was something about Sommerton's manner which bothered her although she could not quite put her finger on it . . .

"Osgood," he said crisply, merely nodding by way of greeting.

"Colonel," said the Brigade-major just as curtly. He doffed his hat to Ernie and, with another grin, turned his restless mount toward where the hounds had just rousted out another hare.

Sommerton reached for Ernie's reins when she would have followed. "What did that young fool want?"

"Is it any of your business?" she asked.

"Yes." When Ernie pursed her lips and narrowed her eyes, he added, "If for no other reason than that I'm your protector at this moment and I don't wish to see you hassled in any way by men who see all too few young ladies. Osgood has rather a reputation for flirtation." He eyed her when she didn't respond. "I warn you, he'll have no serious intentions."

"That's a good thing, is it not?" she asked softly.

"Is it?"

"Yes. For I'll have no serious intentions toward him, either. You do not seem to have understood, Colonel, that I'm not looking for a husband. Particularly, as I said yesterday, not a soldier-husband. Not that I blame you for thinking it," she said with false sweetness. "I've been informed that the young ladies sent out to visit female relatives traveling with the army generally *are* looking for one. Please remember that I came because of my sister's situation *and for that reason only!*"

With her crop Ernie lightly tapped his fingers which still held her reins. For a moment he didn't remove his hold. Their eyes met and a silent battle ensued. Then, shrugging, Ave allowed her her freedom.

Ernie immediately set her gelding into a canter at an angle which would bring her up the quickest to the streaming race of horses. The colonel's gray matched her roan stride for stride. The horses took each jump eagerly and soon set her irritation to naught as pure enjoyment of the physical demands of the rough ride took over and exhilaration filled her.

She found herself grinning at Ave who grinned back just as broadly, obviously understanding and sharing her delight in the hard riding. Catching herself, she turned back to watch for hazards, again telling herself the man was a worse hazard to her state of mind, than any physical hazard she'd met while out with the hunt!

Seven

The morning's hunt continued with no further irritations, the hounds rousing four more hares and catching three. Sommerton managed to collect one for Maria's magic earthenware panella in which she would stew the animal to a delightfully tender point of perfection along with vegetables and various spices. Made hungry by the long ride, Ernie's mouth watered at the mere thought of one of the Spanish girl's interesting concoctions!

A little later, standing in the kitchen, having finished a bowl of thick soup, she bit into a slab of cheese between two slices of freshly baked bread and studied her lines for the play. She was repeating a particularly difficult line when Norry returned from her latest meeting with Lady Colonel Barton. Ernie glanced up from the hand-written script. "You look tired, Norry," she said, worry putting a crease between her eyes.

"I am. I'll rest this afternoon while you are at your play practice. Ah, Maria, is that for me? Thank you." Norry dropped onto the bench near the fire and lifted the first spoonful of soup from a bowl to her mouth. She savored it, her head back and her eyes closed. "Hmm, that is good. I don't know why doing so little or sometimes nothing at all seems to tire me. It is quite ridiculous."

Maria gave her a quick disbelieving look and Norry blushed. Ernie looked from one to the other but, at Norry's shaking her head at Maria decided she'd not probe. At least not at the moment. But here was another mystery to add to the one about Maria!

"I met someone new today," she offered as a red herring.

"Did you like him?" asked Norry.

"I thought him pleasant enough. However, Sommerton warned me he is nothing but a flirt." Ernie grinned. "Poor Ave couldn't know that that actually *added* to my positive feelings for the young man. He's offered to escort us to a ball."

"Ave has? And whose ball?"

"Not Ave and it is the Light Division's."

"Ah," said Norry, comprehension dawning, "their annual Christmas ball, no doubt. I wonder where it will be held this year? Did you say *who* offered to take us?"

"A Brigade-major Osgood." Ernie watched for Norry's response and wasn't surprised when her sister smiled. "I told him I'd like to accept his offer, but must ask your opinion first."

"Well done. Needless to say I agree with Ave that Osgood is a charming rogue; but if you wish us to go with him, then we shall." For a moment she thoughtfully studied her sister's unrevealing features. "Just out of curiosity, what did Ave have to say to all this?"

Ernie turned to hide anything which *might* be revealed by her expression. "He hasn't said a word because he doesn't know," she admitted.

Norry's brows arched. "I wonder how Osgood managed to get you away from Ave long enough to work up to asking you!"

"He didn't have to manage anything at all. A *very* young man—in fact I wonder that he isn't still at Eton!—cornered Sommerton and bent his ear quite badly. Stories about the French with which the wags had filled the poor boy's head, I think. It didn't take Osgood long to take advantage," said Ernie. "A very fast worker, the brigade-major."

"In more ways than one," said Norry dryly, but added, "He's an honorable young man, I think. Not like our Terrible Torville who truly takes advantage. Osgood, I believe, will take no for an answer, but I warn you, Ernie, if his reputation has been honestly earned, he *will* attempt your seduction."

"Men are the very devil, are they not?" asked Ernie. She was surprised to hear an almost silent but quite vehement agreement from Maria. She turned a frown toward the girl. Had Bertie, after all, been up to some nonsense which upset the girl?

Ernie decided it could not be that. Bertie had denied it, and Bertie didn't lie to her. So just which man had upset the Spanish girl so badly? Ernie made a mental note that she really must find time to befriend Maria and discover her secret . . . and still more time in which she might probe her sister's!

She looked at Lenore who leaned against the wall, eyes closed, hand resting on her waist, her expression dreamy and a silly smile hovering around her mouth. Ernie blinked. She looked at Lenore's middle. Was she breeding? Was that why so little expended effort made her tired? Dared she ask . . . ?

Well, not just now. She hadn't time for something so wonderful as news of a baby! Her rude lunch finished, Ernie licked the last crumbs from her fingers and hurried off to her room where Maria had just set a can of hot water. Ernie stripped out of her sister's habit. Turning to lay it on the bed, she found her own new riding outfit laid there.

Almost, she was tempted to try it on, but the realization she didn't have time held her back. Either Holles or Ave would arrive shortly to escort her through the winding lanes of the village to the theater. Biting her lip in frustration, she reached for a walking dress in a good weight wool instead. Designed high to the neck and with long tight sleeves, she thought it about as off-putting as any dress in her wardrobe.

Ernie wasn't aware that what Holles would see, to say nothing of Ave and every other man with eyes in his head, would be shoulders hugged closely by finely woven dark blue material, young breasts neatly encased by it and her naturally fluid movements setting the skirts to a graceful sway. And if she *had* been aware, there was little she could have done about it. The dress truly was the most off-putting dress in her wardrobe!

Practice went along as it had the day before with Holles using any excuse the play offered to touch Ernie.

"No, no," shouted Colonel Sommerton, finally, his exasperation clear. "You must not hover so close to Titania. Give the poor queen enough so room she may breathe!"

"But I am supposed to be in love with her."

"Languish at her feet or worship from afar!" Sommerton shook his head in disgust. "That's enough for today. Everyone dismissed except for Miss Matthewson and Lieutenant Holles. Miss Matthewson, will you work on the lines for the last act for tomorrow's practice?" Ernie nodded. "And you, Lieutenant, your interpretation of Bottom's love is far too amorous, too lustful. You must remember that this is idealized love, courtly love . . ." Sommerton's brow' rose. "How is this? You look as if you have never heard the term. Surely that cannot be . . ."

Holles's whole demeanor expressed confusion. "But I haven't," he said a trifle diffidently.

Summerton huffed. "Well. That explains a great deal, I suppose. Now listen to me. The object of your love—Titania—is so far above you, so perfect, so . . . so . . ."

"Unattainable?" suggested Ernie softly.

"Unattainable," repeated Sommerton nodding, "that you know your love can never be returned. Therefore you worship the ground she walks upon. You sigh and make up poetry in her honor. You may go so far as to secretly touch her skirts—but you do *not* try to grab her or some portion of her at every opportunity!"

"Portions of her?" whispered Ernie, choking back a giggle.

"Leave her hands alone," ordered Ave, ignoring her. "Don't

put your arm around her shoulder. Do not under any circumstances try to kiss her."

"It was only her cheek," grumbled the lieutenant.

"Nevertheless it is out of character."

"Besides," said Ernie, "it will look exceedingly silly when you are wearing your ass's head!"

Sommerton, quickly suppressing the grin that that comment roused, held the lieutenant's gaze until the younger man's eyes fled. "You will *not* use this play as an excuse to embarrass Miss Matthewson," the colonel said in a softly dangerous voice. Unspoken but known between the two men were the words: *as you did Miss Covington who has since left us.*

Holles blushed. "Yes sir. I understand, sir." He sent a hopeless, mournful, look toward Ernie who had wandered away, belatedly realizing it was not proper in her to listen to Sommerton lecture the younger man. He sighed. "But, I . . . she . . . oh, to the devil with it." He scowled and exited quickly before he could say something he shouldn't.

"Weren't you a little rough on him?" asked Ernie when he'd gone.

"Not at all. If anything I was far too easy."

"I do know how to handle him, you know. It is not necessary for you to interfere."

"Is it not?"

"I'll take care of Lieutenant Holles when the time comes." Ernie met Ave's eyes and held his gaze. "Believe me. I know exactly how to teach him a lesson he'll not forget."

"Then why not do it?

"But, did I not say?" She deliberately widened her eyes, giving herself a falsely innocent look. "The time must be exactly right."

Ave lifted her chin and stared at her. "All right. I'll believe you. Besides," he added, a grin appearing, "I don't think you'll have so much of a problem as you have had."

"You don't?" Her expression, now, was one of spurious tolerance. "Ah well, how comforting to believe what you wish to believe." Ave questioned her with a look of his own. "*I,* on the other hand, think you'll only have driven him to be more subtle in his harassment."

Ave studied her, his head tipped slightly to one side. "You find it harassment?"

"Oh yes. You realize it is not the first time this sort of thing has happened, do you not? I'm quite experienced with leading men who suffer from unrequited love. Or what they call love," she said on a bitter note. "I find it quite as irritating now as when it's happened in the past."

"Not embarrassing? Not frightening? Not at all gratifying?"

"Why should it be any of those things? In the first place, it is Holles who is making the perfect ass of himself, is it not? Perhaps *he* should be embarrassed. As to frightening—why, you, the cast and the stage helpers are all around us. How could he possibly do anything that the thought of it should make me fearful?" She tipped her head. "Gratifying? Perhaps"—Ave stiffened—"assuming I took more pleasure in the game of flirtation. But I have never liked that particular game, so, no, I cannot say that his all too obvious interest is the least gratifying."

Her final comment had Ave relaxing. The mocking words which had set off his fears that perhaps she was more attracted to the actor than he'd thought couldn't have been explained away more thoroughly. "Miss Matthewson, you are the most sensible and logical woman I've ever known."

Ernie grimaced, a mere instant's expression, but Sommerton noticed.

"I have *not* insulted you," he said, "but given you the sincerest compliments I've ever given any woman. A man like me appreciates those qualities, Ernestine."

She didn't respond.

Suggestively, he added, "What would a soldier do with a

wife who was forever falling into megrims or was so wooly-minded as to never know how to handle a difficult situation? No," he continued, allowing a degree of portentousness to enter his voice, "logic and good sense are far more important to someone like myself then those characteristics our class usually consider proper accomplishments in a young woman. Oh, and one other," he added. "A sense of humor so that one finds it possible to laugh at the problems life tosses one—which in the army are many and varied."

His last words brought a sudden gleam of sympathy to her eyes which washed away the anger aroused by the not-too-subtle hints Ave was tossing her way concerning marriage.

"Was a sense of humor the solution when the men marched for three days without food because the commissary went off on its own and was nowhere near?" she asked. Ernie referred to a recent disaster when the army pulled back from Burgos after failing to take the citadel there.

Having to withdraw from that siege, Ernie had learned, was only the first irritation. Retreating without supplies in very bad weather with the French on their heels had been barely tolerated as part of war. But, when the Marquess of Wellington finally found his lost troops and immediately lost his temper, the resulting intemperate memorandum to his officers had sent most everyone else's tempers soaring as well. Low morale had dropped to, and stayed at, rock bottom until shortly before Ernie arrived when things had rather settled back into regular form.

Now Ave grimaced wryly and rolled his eyes. "Don't, for the good Lord's sake, mention the retreat from Burgos! We're trying very hard to forget it. Thank goodness Norry was coming from Madrid with the baggage. She didn't suffer as did one wife, brave little lady that she is! You'll meet Mrs. Brigade-major Smith at the ball her husband's division is hosting. Since you and Norry will want to wear your best gowns we must arrange for you to guest with someone." He paused momentarily. "The

Smith's household would be excellent—if they've found quarters worthy of the name." He grinned. "Knowing Harry, I've no doubt they have! He married a young Spaniard straight from the convent and everyone predicted disaster to his career, but little Juana Smith is the best of soldiers." He chuckled. "Just ask any of Harry's men!

"It sounds as if you admire her very much," said Ernie, something between curiosity and hurt filling her. Her conflicting emotions made her forget Sommerton had just made a rather back-handed invitation to take her and her sister to the ball.

"I do. However, I would not wish to be married to her. She's a fire brand with a temper like you've never seen—but courage and stamina and a great number of excellent qualities. Harry Smith is a lucky man in a lot of ways, but I'd not be in his shoes for anything! Nor could I treat Mrs. Smith as he does. The fact it seems to work, that he expects her to handle all that is thrown at her, does all asked of her, is irrelevant. I would wish to protect my wife from such horrors and very likely worry myself to death if she were to stay with the unit as Mrs. Smith does." Ave shook his head. "No, I could not like to have such a one as that for wife . . . but, of course"—his grin was quick and his brows arched—"I *do* admire her."

"What *would* you require in a wife?" asked Ernie, curious.

"Someone like you."

Ernie's gaze was caught by his and for a long moment she couldn't look away. Finally she managed it, darting quick glances everywhere but at Ave. How could she have allowed that to happen? How could she have given him such an opening? "We must go," she said, looking around and realizing they were alone.

"That is all you have to say?" asked Ave, noting her discomfort and wondering at it. Had he rushed his fences? Again? But her question had seemed to suggest . . . had appeared to be an invitation . . . and he had thought that perhaps she'd already come around to changing her mind about the military . . .

"I hope you find the woman for whom you look. Someday," said Ernie stiltedly and stalked toward the door. "Are you coming?"

He sighed. Softly. Obviously she had *not* . . .

They walked out into the street and discovered Holles and Torville in earnest discussion. Torville, noting their arrival on the scene, said a few more words before he mounted the horse he held by the reins. He nodded at Holles and glared at Ernie and Ave.

"I hope you are not becoming involved with that set of men," said Ave to Holles.

"What? Oh no. Graham is no friend of mine"—he glanced at Ernie, curiously—"not that he can't make good sense once in awhile . . ."

"Had that man been visiting my sister again?" demanded Ernie, her sternness startling Holles.

"He said he tried, but Major Lockwood's batman opened the door to his knock and reported that Mrs. Lockwood was sleeping and could not be disturbed. He had to come away, of course, although he says he doesn't believe it to be true."

Ernie grinned. "Good for Albert! Best of all," she added, "it may very well have been true. She's been doing too much—or worrying too much"—Ernie thought again of her suspicion Norry might be pregnant—"or something," she finished awkwardly. "I really must discover a way to convince her to go home . . ."

"You are leaving?" asked Holles abruptly.

"We must in the not too distant future." She glanced up. "Oh, dear, is it raining again?" Ernie stuck a hand from between the edges of her cloak and held it up to the increasing drizzle.

"We'd better hurry or you'll be soaked," agreed Sommerton. "Good day Holles and, although I fear I speak only to hear my own voice, I suggest you keep away from Torville. He's not an example I'd like to see my officers use as a model—far too ramshackle by half, I assure you, and with less sense of duty and discipline than any other officer I've ever known. *Not* the sort of officer I admire!"

Holles looked thoughtful but then, after a glance at Ernie, a mulish look replaced the gentler expression.

As they walked away Ernie, reminded by seeing the man, asked if Ave had discovered Torville's duty schedule.

"Yes, but it will do us little good, I fear. His commander says Torville will exchange duty with another at the drop of a hat, so one never knows where he is or exactly what he's doing."

"Which does not sound to me the sort of man on whom one could rely in a battle."

"Oh," said Sommerton, giving his hand a deprecatory wave, "I've heard no complaints of him in battle. He isn't a go-on if that's what you're suggesting."

"I certainly wasn't suggesting any such thing!" She paused a moment. "I couldn't. Just what *is* a go-on?"

Sommerton grinned. "The men, discussing officers, will tell you that a go-on is quite different from a come-on. A come-on—"

"Never mind," said Ernie, shuddering. "I do not wish to hear of the different methods of leading a charge into battle. I hate to think of men going into battle. It is such a waste. So many lost or wounded, so much heartache . . ."

"War is not pretty, but there are times when it is necessary. Or perhaps," he said politely, "you are one of those Whiggish types who believe we should allow Napoleon to rule the world as he wishes to do? That we should give up our sovereign rights and freedoms to his over-weaning ambition without a struggle?"

Ernie grinned. "I don't think the Whigs put it quite that way!" She was silent for a few steps. "But you are correct. One cannot allow a madman to do as he pleases and no more can one allow a tyrant to reign—no matter what good he may do in between periods of his own particular form of lunacy. You will, I think," she asked, brows arched queryingly, "admit that Napoleon *has* done good for France when not obsessed with conquering more territory?" She drew in a deep breath, not waiting for his answer, and let it out. Staring straight ahead she added, quickly, "The difference, I think, is that it takes only a few men to subdue a madman and so very many where a tyrant is involved. I cannot like war and what it does to the man or to the soldier's dear ones."

Sommerton gave her a quick look at that last comment but Ernie continued before he could say anything.

"At home," she said, sadly, "there is a man with no leg. He was a seaman and lost it at Trafalgar. His father is a very good farmer and comfortably well off. He can care for his son, but what of those soldiers who are wounded and can no longer fight, but, sent home, have no one to care for them? Aye, I saw beggars in terrible condition, obviously ex-soldiers, at Southampton where Bertie and I took ship." She turned on him. "How can our government allow the men, who fought to keep us free, suffer as they do when they return home?"

Sommerton grimaced. It was a subject which worried him and he forgot her comment about a soldier's loved-ones. "I too have seen such men when on leave in London. I agree that it isn't fair. But, Ernestine, the government is deeply in debt simply pushing forward the war. Supporting our wounded would raise that debt so fast and so far . . ." He sighed and shook his head. "No, I see no immediate solution, my dear."

She debated objecting to the endearment but, as usual, decided it was, perhaps, better ignored. "Nor do I," she said. "But having seen the misery, I've concluded I'll never be able to accept the constant sight of it, the constant reminder before a battle that, for far too many, tomorrow will not come . . ."

Sommerton eyed her bent head. Ernestine, he was certain,

liked him very well; it was sad such thinking kept him at arm's length—although he could see her point since she'd not been raised to accept the bad as well as the good of war. In fact, it occurred to him, very likely she'd no notion of the good, the incredible camaraderie, the feats of heroism . . . He must think about that. But when he was near his Ernie he couldn't think, so . . . Later, he decided.

"Here we are, Ernestine. Since Norry's napping I'll not come in. Try to put such serious thoughts as we've been having from your mind and enjoy your dinner. Later, get a good night's sleep and I'll see you tomorrow some time . . ." He snapped his fingers, a frown crossing his brow. "Oh, no, I will *not,*" he said. "Blast! I forgot there is a meeting at headquarters for which I must leave early and from which I'll not get home until late. Ah well." He flicked her under her chin. "I'll see you the next day. Take good care of our Norry," he ordered and stalked away into the drizzle which, suddenly, turned into a downpour.

Ernie did not stay to see him go. She dashed up to the little balcony and opened the door, rushing under cover before she too would be soaked to the skin! Then, alone in the front room, she stood stock still, wondering why the knowledge she'd not see the man for a full day should have such a shocking effect on her. Why did she feel suddenly as if she were very young, very small, very unsure and . . . very unhappy?

Ernie compressed her lips. *It would not do.* She would *not* miss the man. She would not yearn for his voice, for his presence . . . That decided, why did she continue to feel so miserable?

She was not in love with him. *Not.* Then why . . . ?

Because it wasn't true, that's why. She did love him.

Eight

Norry, yawning and stretching, came from her room. Her arms dropped and her mouth closed when she found Ernie in the middle of the floor. That in itself would not have startled Norry, but Ernie was simply standing there, staring at nothing. "What is the matter?" she asked.

"The matter?" Ernie turned to look at her sister. "Should anything be the matter?" Her gaze sharpened. "You have a problem, Norry?"

"Not me. I want to know what is wrong with *you*."

"Me?" Ernie shook away her shock. Despite all her resolutions she'd done the unthinkable and fallen in love with an officer and now she hadn't a notion what to do about it. "Not a thing in the world," she lied, and, for once, did not give herself away. She forced herself to study Norry's face. "What is far more important is that *you* look more the thing."

"I feel better." A sudden flashing smile lit her face. "Oh, Ernie, I'm certain my dreams of Jon are true dreams. I've felt his contentment flowing around me for a day or two and this afternoon I've had another dream and he appeared happy—almost at peace. I'm certain that monster of a guerrilla has finally told him when he may come home!"

Ernie's hope that her sister's improved looks was based in something of another sort, namely that a pregnancy was progressing normally, was shattered. Once again Norry was talking like a madwoman.

"Oh?" she asked cautiously. "Do you wish to tell me about it?" That rather fey look she'd seen before returned to Norry's face and Ernie sighed, softly, silently, and settled down to listen to what she didn't wish to hear.

"Jon sat in the sun outside a cave. He carved at a piece of wood. I couldn't see what exactly it is and perhaps," she said, her head to one side, "that is just as well. I had an impression it was a Christmas gift for me and I would not wish to spoil his surprise. Every so often he'd look up and grin, almost as if he were looking right at me . . . you know?" Norry looked at Ernie and lost her dreamy look. "You don't believe me, do you?" She shook her head and waved an admonishing finger. "You'll see. All you doubters will see. Jon *will* come home. And soon now.

"Shall we," she went on when Ernie opened her mouth to argue, "see what Maria is fixing for supper? There will be a rabbit stew. I can smell that and doesn't it smell good? I must learn to fix that dish myself. Jon is particularly fond of it the way Maria does it and we won't always have her to work for us I'm sure."

Shaking her head at the abrupt change of subject, Ernie followed Norry into the kitchen which was replete with pleasant smells and greater warmth—a very welcome warmth since the day had gone so very damp and chill. She suggested, "Maybe we should eat here."

Ernie took another look around the pleasant room. A rough set of shelves held Norry's few dishes and other tableware which she'd purchased from the sutlers in Freinada—a market to be avoided if at all possible since such were always more expensive than elsewhere. The shelves held the pots and also the panellas Maria had acquired for her cooking and baking. Strings of onions, garlic and dried peppers hung from the rafters. Baskets of fruit and nuts stood on the broad window ledge. There was another shelf with the large tin of precious coffee beans which

Ernie had brought with her, the contents carefully hoarded. Another tin sat beside it full of fragrant tea—at twenty-two shillings the pound—and still another held chocolate. The white-washed walls were clean-looking and the room was far more light than the living room.

Norry looked around, too. "I wonder why I never thought of that. Oh, not when there is company, of course. One cannot ask one's friends into one's *kitchen*." She paused, smiled. "Well, maybe some friends?"

Ernie nodded. "Bertie, for instance. He spent enough time in our kitchen at home in England, so why not this one?"

"He did have a penchant for Molly's gingerbread, did he not?" Norry's dreamy look returned. "Remember how she would let us help? I learned a lot from Molly—thank heavens. Things far more useful to my present way of life than the globes Miss Winston made us learn or her insistence on proper posture!"

"Gingerbread! Oh dear, that makes me think! Norry, we've not yet made the Christmas pudding."

Norry nodded. "I've discussed the problem of boiling it up with Lady Colonel Barton's chef. He says he will do it for us in his pudding basin, which is adequately sized. Colonel Lord Barton and Lady Barton have been invited by the local hildalgo to dinner along with Lord Wellington and some other of the top command—Ave, perhaps—and we'll do it that day."

"Colonel Sommerton? Is he that important? That he's invited to dine with such exulted company?" After she'd asked the question, Ernie wished she'd not. Surely Norry would wonder . . .

"He has been, but I don't know for certain if he will be this time, of course." Norry got that teasing look. "If you're that interested, you'll have to ask him." Before Ernie could think up an unrevealing response, her sister went on. "But however that may be, we will mix the pudding and take it to the Bartons' chef while he has nothing else to worry about."

"We must warn your friends, Norry, so that as many as possible can give the pudding a stir."

"Hmm. And I must ask Ave to find me a decent bottle of brandy. That was one ingredient you forgot to bring with you, Ernie, my love!"

"When Father discovered what I wanted to do, he'd not allow it. He said he'd only a very few bottles of good brandy left and he wasn't about to spoil any of it by allowing it to travel when we would very likely be home for Christmas in any case."

"I do wish he'd get the notion out of his head that I'm returning home," said Norry a trifle crossly. "Jon will be back by Christmas."

"And if the miracle does not occur and he is not?" she asked quietly.

"Then he will be home by the new year," was the instant calm response. "Maria," Norry asked and turned to the Spanish girl, "what is there that I may do?"

The conversation was over. Norry would not discuss the possibility—the *surety*—she was wrong.

Ernie moved to the window to stare out at the crowded, helter-skelter of cottage roofs, the houses facing every which way. What was she to do about Norry? What *could* she do? Maria hummed one of the popular songs of that winter and Ernie began to sing. She broke off abruptly when she recalled the ball and that young Osgood would be coming by that evening. "Norry, is it proper to serve something when someone such as Brigade-major Osgood drops by in the evening?"

"I'd forgotten he was coming."

"I will fix *formas com laranja*," offered Maria.

"Those fancy waffles are too hard to do since they must be eaten immediately." Norry frowned. "How about *queijadas da Sintra?* I haven't made those little cheese tarts for a long time and now that I've thought of them I find they really appeal to me."

"Have we time?" asked Ernie.

"Oh yes. Evening visitors arrive late since most have adopted Portuguese hours and dine late—although no where nearly so late as the Madrilene's did. Madrid became something of a penance for me," said Norry solemnly, her eyes twinkling. "I never could get used to dining at very nearly the hour when I was thinking of going to my bed! But as it is, certainly we'll have time. Do we have everything we need for those tarts, Maria?"

The Spanish girl frowned. "I think we have no more of that soft cheese."

Norry frowned as well. "But I have my mouth all set for *queijadas!* What shall we do?"

Out of character, Norry looked a trifle pettish, but that was excusable due to the pregnancy Ernie was more and more certain existed.

"Maria," coaxed Norry, "is it too late to buy more?"

Ernie noted how Maria's body twisted ever so slightly in rejection of the notion. It occurred to her the girl did not wish to go and, since Maria never seemed to object in any way to anything asked of her, she wondered at it. "Can one no longer buy something of that sort today? I would be happy to go if only I knew where and what I was to ask for . . ."

Maria squared her shoulders with a determined look. "I know where to get what is needed. I will only get my shawl and I will go."

"I'll go with you," said Ernie, suddenly wondering if Maria was afraid.

"Yes, I would like that," said Maria softly, her overly stiff shoulders relaxing. "Señor Bacon was home for awhile before he went off again to deliver the rest of the messages. He dealt with Lieutenant Torville when the man insisted he see Norry, but Señor Bacon, he has gone again and I do not like to go alone. I admit it," she said, looking straight at Ernie, daring her to scold.

Once again Ernie realized Maria was an exceedingly obser-

vant young woman. She had seen and interpreted Ernie's expression at the moment when Ernie saw and interpreted *hers!*
"I, too, had better find something to wear. I had not thought Portugal would be so cold."

"We are in the mountains," said Norry absently. "I didn't know you didn't like going to market," she added to Maria.

"It is nothing." Maria shuddered and, clearly, it *was* something. "Just that I do not like strangers." She cast a glance toward Norry. "Not since . . ." She trailed off but Ernie thought the look she'd sent Norry's way was speculative, changing to relief when Norry nodded and held out her hand in a kindly way.

"Maria, you must not fear all men. That officer who attacked you was drunk. He was sorry afterward. I didn't let him approach you, but I did tell you he came around." Norry grinned. "Even if he did it partly to get back in Jon's good graces, he *did* apologize. One must remember that."

"I know I must not fear *all* men," said Maria, her tone a bit grim and her eyes flashing.

She left then to find her shawl and the sisters looked at each other. "Now why," asked Ernie, "do I get the feeling it truly *isn't* all men she fears? Some particular man, though, whom she has reason to fear . . . ?"

"I don't know if anyone has told you, but I found her in a distressing situation—luckily I was in time. I cannot think who might have approached her since then, although she is a pretty little thing, is she not? I suppose someone may be harassing her when she is out and about." Norry's head rose sharply. "Not Bertie, surely . . ."

"Bertie assures me it is no such thing." Ernie thought for a moment. "It's a mystery, Norry."

"Oh, I'm sure a very common one," said Norry, lightly. "Here's Maria, all ready and you are not. Off you go, Ern, girl."

Ernie started toward her room and then paused. "Norry, I didn't think. Will you be all right?"

"It is very simple, is it not?" She grinned. "I will simply not answer the door!"

That solution relieved Ernie's mind of one worry and she left quite happily, following Maria through the twists and turns of the village lanes. Eventually they turned off the main way into a narrow passage between two houses which tilted above them in such a way they hid the sky. The passage opened into a slightly wider lane leading almost immediately out among stone walled fields. Maria stepped carefully around and over evidence of the presence of farm animals. A little farther and she crossed the lane to climb the stairs to a closed door. Ernie could hear the low contented sounds made by comfortably housed animals coming from the lower rooms.

Maria knocked. A weathered, dark clad matron opened the door. She looked from one to the other and folded her arms. She and Maria then had an involved conversation during which Maria wheedled and the woman shook her head. Then the conversational style changed. Maria offered some comment which included Norry's name. The woman hesitated, answered more politely. Finally the matron sighed, turned on her heel and returned with the soft cheese.

Maria took it, volubly thanking the woman and, after carefully placing the bowl in her basket, equally carefully counted small coins into the waiting hand. The door closed with a snap.

"I didn't think you'd manage to convince her," said Ernie, showing her amazement Maria had done so.

Maria smiled. "I, too, wondered. Senorha tends to be quite rigid about when she will sell her wares—but she has the best cheese for miles, so I told her my mistress was with child and had one of those cravings a woman gets at such a time."

"Is she?"

"Is she what?" asked Maria, evasively, as she turned and lifted her shawl to put it around her head. Suddenly she turned back, pulling the shawl far forward so that it fell over her forehead, her skin paling to a dirty white. "We must go."

Ernie forgot her probing question, as she realized just how frightened Maria suddenly was. Maria's fear pushed it from her mind. "Who was it, Maria?" asked Ernie quietly when they'd escaped down the narrow passage and were walking quickly away down the village's most major street.

"Who was what?" asked the girl evasively.

"Back there. You saw someone and you are frightened."

"You speak nonsense," Maria insisted.

"No I don't. Someone is looking for you, are they not?" Maria shook her head. "Someone you fear," persisted Ernie.

Maria stopped. She studied Ernie's face for a long moment. "I will tell you because you are Lieutenant Browley's friend, but I cannot allow you to become involved. You must promise, because I see that you are the sort who will try to do something. It is too dangerous. You must not try to help me." She looked sternly at Ernie who looked just as sternly right back. "You will promise?"

"Maria, you are in need of help. I do not see how I can promise, but, even so, you've gone too far not to tell me the truth."

Maria pursed her lips. "I will tell the lieutenant. He will make you see reason and you will do nothing to put yourself into danger." That settled to the Spanish girl's satisfaction, she walked on, speaking as she went.

"I will tell you my story," she said. "You have guessed it. There is a man whom I fear very much. He is my uncle, my guardian. I have monies, you see, which he will control until I marry a man with his approval or until I am twenty-five and far too old to marry anyone. My uncle would have me marry a friend of his, an old man with oily hair and a tummy like so"— Maria made a descriptive movement with her free hand— "which I could bring myself to agree to if he were a good man, but he is not. He is like my uncle, hard and cruel and never kind or generous—not even to his daughter by a former marriage."

Maria shrugged. "I told my uncle I would not marry the man. My uncle said I would live on bread and water and be kept in a small room at the top of the house until I agreed."

Maria tossed her head. "I thought not. Instead I pretended to fear that so much that I would agree and then I ran away"— she tossed her head again, but, immediately, her bravado faded—"and I ran right into an army on the move. Your sister saved me from horror. She is wonderful, your sister. I would give my life for her," finished Maria dramatically.

"Well, I hope it never comes to *that*." Ernie stalked up into the rough square before her sister's home, skirting the well and thinking of all Maria had revealed. "Then it was your uncle you saw in the market?"

"Not my uncle. My uncle is far too proud and—what is it Lieutenant Browley has said?—too high in the instep? *Mio tio* would not stoop to search himself. It was but one of his men I saw." She sighed. "I keep hoping they will stop searching for me. Unfortunately, one man saw me a few weeks ago when the army first arrived here and I was stupid enough to think myself safe. I was careless to forget my danger. Even so I managed to make the man believe I was going to another village, to another unit, and for some time they have searched elsewhere. Now they are back. Some day they will see me again. They will capture me and take me to my uncle and I do not believe I could bear it." She shuddered.

Ernie thought of the ins and outs of the story, then asked, "What has Bertie to do with all this?"

"The lieutenant has been unbelievably kind. He is quite wonderful, is he not?" asked Maria wistfully.

"Have you fallen in love with him?" asked Ernie—and then mentally kicked herself for her blunt and tactless tongue.

Fortunately the question did not appear to upset Maria. "It

is the dearest wish of my heart that I might wed with him," she said, obviously speaking from great emotion. A sadness entered her voice as she added, "But, of course, it must not be."

"Why not?"

"It would never do"—Maria cast a sideways look at Ernie—"would it?" she asked hesitantly.

"I don't think I understand. Why would it not?"

But they had arrived at Norry's house and, at Maria's urging, the conversation was allowed to lapse until they were again alone. Ernie made a mental note to tell Norry that Maria must not do the shopping from now on, but that Albert must take a list and do the best he could.

Unfortunately, thanks to the contretemps into which they walked, the thought slipped her mind. In the center of the living room Lieutenant Torville held a white faced, struggling Norry and was attempting to kiss her. Ernie took one look and, flinging caution to the winds, walked up and poked him in the back just above his belt.

Startled, Torville released Norry and turned, already swinging his fist. He could not stop the movement and Ernie, not expecting it, didn't move quickly enough. The fist connected with the side of her head and Ernie fell. For a moment she was stunned, but she came to hear her gentle sister, while kneeling at her side, ranting at the rake.

". . . You brute! You monster! Leave this house at once! Don't you ever come here again!"

Aghast at what he'd done, Torville stuttered, "But I did not mean to hit her. I'd never ever . . ."

"You never *mean* anything, do you?" interrupted Norry, full into the tirade she'd previously felt too ladylike to deliver. "But you never see anyone's point of view but your own; you never believe others might disagree with you; you never allow another his way if it interferes in what *you* want. You are a ridiculous excuse for an officer, the most odiously selfish man I have ever met and no gentleman. I *wish* I knew the language to tell you what I think of you!" Norry paused, adding, her voice dropping to a threatening level. "When *this* story gets around . . ."

Pale under his ruddy tan, Torville interrupted. "You would not tell. Surely you must know that it was an accident!"

"Why should I not tell the tale far and wide? If you had accepted that I did not wish your attentions it would never have happened. Because you would not believe me, it did. *It was not an accident.* Accidents don't happen when they might have been prevented by the situation never arising. Oh, you awful man, *get out of my sight* and stay away from where I ever need look upon your face again!"

Maria stalked to the door and held it open. She too glared at Torville but the man ignored both her expression and the door.

"Your sister," he said quietly. "Will she be all right?"

Ernie decided to add a further dramatic moment. She groaned. Loudly.

"I've no idea," said Norry crushingly. Although she pretended she was still worried, relief filled her. Ernie had opened her eyes for an instant, and winked. "Another thing. You needn't try that door ever again. I will, from now on, have it barred. You see, it didn't occur to me someone might be so brutish as to simply open the door and walk in."

She glared at Torville who, seeing his bet lost, a bet he could not afford to lose, lost his head in yet another way. "Damn you, Norry Lockwood," he swore. "You know you are not adverse to my attentions. If you do *not* know it yet, you would soon enough if . . ."

As he spoke Norry, who had knelt beside her sister, rose to her feet and turned to face him. "Are you deaf?" asked Norry. "How, otherwise, can you be so wrong. When Jon returns—"

"Fool!" he roared, the last remnants of emotional control slipping completely from his grasp. "Lockwood is *dead. Dead,* do you hear me?"

"I would think the whole regiment could hear you," Norry answered, her chin rising. "My husband is not dead. You will discover that to your cost if you do not leave me alone."

"Dead," taunted Torville, but, at the look in Norry's eye, he turned on his heel—only to swing back for one surprisingly worried glance at Ernie, who was still sprawled on the floor. Then, his shoulders oddly slumped, he went quietly out the door.

Maria shut it and rushed to Ernie's side, but Ernie was already sitting up. The blow had been pulled just a trifle and she had moved just a fraction, enough so that, although it had knocked her out for a moment, it was not enough for her to forget what had happened. Hopefully, then, she had managed to take advantage of his blunder to help her sister.

"Are you all right?" asked Maria as Norry said, "That man should be taken out and shot."

Ernie put her hand to the side of her head, pressed lightly. "I'll have a headache to end all headaches, I fear, but other than that I think I'm right as a trivet." Ernie touched her temple, winced, touched it again. "Perhaps a rather glorious bruise as well?"

"I fear that may be so," said Maria, leaning closer and gently probing the hair over Ernie's ear.

"Did Torville really just open the door and walk in?" asked Ernie, the headache beginning to manifest itself and her eyes finding even the light allowed in by the small windows too much for comfort. Soon she'd have to go to her bed and rest.

"He did. He walked right in without knocking. He saw you two on your way to buy the cheese and thought I was still sleeping—and, of course, alone. I think he assumed it would be an excellent time to force his attentions on me. He was quite astounded to find the bedroom empty and to come face to face with me when I came from the kitchen to discover who had arrived." Norry sighed. "I fear I may actually have encouraged him—not that I meant to. When I heard the footsteps I thought it was Jon, come sooner than I expect him, so I came out in something of a welcoming rush! It was quite stupid of me. And then, of course, you arrived."

"Not quite soon enough," said Ernie, remembering the scene. Her hand returned to her head. "That settles it. You truly must never be left alone again. That man will obviously stop at nothing to achieve his ends." She pressed both hands to her head, and, leaning over, moaned softly.

"Your head is so very bad?" asked Maria. "I will make you a tisane and perhaps tincture of arnica for the bruise? It will help." She disappeared into the kitchen.

"She is very good at such things," said Norry soothingly. "She had a convent education and the nuns teach many practical things our governesses wouldn't think to teach. Here, Ernie, you come along now and I'll help you into your nightshift and, once you've drunk Maria's concoction, you take a nap. I think you'll find your head is much better when you wake up. Do come, love," finished Norry, an arm around her sister's shoulders to lead her to her room.

"You comfort me when it should be I comforting you," said Ernie ruefully. But the headache she'd predicted had taken full hold. She could barely keep her eyes open to see where she was going.

"I'm fine. When you arrived I was more angry than afraid. I suppose fear would have come, but he'd only just grabbed me. I'm truly all right. I'm just sorry you must suffer because of his nonsense."

"Remember it is not nonsense to him. He has a bet riding on the outcome. A rather large bet, if rumor is correct."

"I haven't forgotten."

Norry refused to discuss it further. By the time she had Ernie ready for her bed, Maria arrived with her tisane. Obediently, her head hurting more than she cared to admit, Ernie drank it, thanked the Spanish girl and, lying down, turned her face to the wall, a cold compress laid across the bruise.

* * *

After a short sleep, however, Ernie felt well enough to get up and dress again. She was sitting in the front room with Norry and Maria when Osgood arrived late that evening, he was all agog with news. "Is it true?" he asked.

"Is what true?" asked Norry, laying aside the shirt she was making for her missing husband.

"It is said that Graham Torville burst into Lieutenant Holles's quarters where a number of men in the play were working together on their lines. He went straight to where Holles keeps his carefully hoarded store of good brandy. *No one* gets into that bottle but Holles. In fact"—Osgood chuckled—"I think Holles believed no one was aware he had it! I heard he was completely out of temper when he saw Torville gulping down great drafts of it and jumped up to take it away from him."

Ernie thought of Torville's chunky shoulders and Holles's slim form. "Did he manage to do so?" she asked politely.

Osgood grinned. "Yes, but only because Torville had had enough, or so it is said! It's also said he managed to drink nearly half the bottle in that brief time, which *should* be enough for any man. Although," he turned and bowed to Ernie, "if he truly did what he said he did, then brandy is too good for the villain and he deserves to be whipped at the very least." Osgood grinned. "Would you believe it? The man himself says so!"

"And so he does deserve," said Norry. "He hit my sister so hard she was unconscious."

"He didn't say that. Only that he hit her and knocked her down. He was, one is told, absolutely horrified that it had happened."

"Did he send you as his messenger to apologize for him?" asked Ernie, curiously.

"Me? I barely know the man except from hearsay. He *is* talked about, you know. And now we've this new story . . ." he looked around. "This is only what I've heard although I've already had the tale from more than one source. Unusual as it seems, it is always the *same* story. Perhaps the truth is so odd no one feels a need to embroider it?"

Ernie and Norry exchanged a glance before urging him to tell them what he'd heard.

"It seems Torville babbled about his father hitting his mother and that he once swore a terrible oath he'd never ever hit a woman. And now he has. From what I've heard, the man has a rather strange sense of honor, at least from the point of view of most men, but he holds firmly by the few principles he has."

"What an oddity he must be," said Norry.

"A very good officer under fire," said Osgood hurriedly. "He just can't seem to deal with normal discipline and routine detail when there is no fighting."

"However that may be, it is my wish he'd never come out to the Peninsula," said Norry. "He had no business hitting Ernie even if she did startle him."

"You mean he didn't even look? He just turned on her, swinging as he came?"

"Yes."

Osgood sighed. "That's the story, but I couldn't bring myself to believe it." His forehead was creased into long horizontal lines. *"Why* would he just start swinging? Especially in a house full of women? What could he have feared that he didn't stop long enough to see who was attempting to get his attention?"

The three women looked at each other. *Was Osgood unaware of Torville's bet that he would seduce Norry?* Since they themselves, as decent women, should be unaware of such things, it was not their place to enlighten him.

"I have no idea why he didn't bother to discover whom he was fighting," said Norry mendaciously, "but I've told him he's no longer welcome in this house. Unfortunately, I suspect he'll not accept that I'm serious. Major, if you happen to see him coming this way and you happen to be free of duty, might we rely upon you to come calling as well?"

"Oh, very well done, Norry," said Ernie. "Major? We dislike it that we've no man on whom we may rely to see we're safe from such as he. You would be doing us a great service if you were to aid us in this way." She didn't quite bat her eyelashes at him, but very nearly—and smiled a sweet conciliatory smile.

"A great service?" Osgood's answering smile had a slight edge to it, his eyes very slightly narrowed, as he looked at Ernie in a way she couldn't quite like, but then the expression vanished and he grinned freely. "The devil! When a woman asks a service of a man, how may he deny her? Of course I will come along to see that you are not troubled." He bowed toward Norry. "I would be delighted to help in any way I may."

"Thank you," said Norry.

Ernie analyzed Osgood's reaction to her request and was no longer sure she should have backed her sister's impulsive suggestion. Surely the man wouldn't use protecting Norry from Torville as an excuse to make his own advances toward herself? Or to blackmail her into agreeing to them? She sighed. Very softly. He couldn't know it, of course, but even if he tried such a silly trick, it would do him no good.

"Would you care for coffee, Major?" asked Norry politely, although the answer was obvious. She went off to the kitchen to bring in the tray prepared earlier by Maria. Included was a plate of the tiny cheese tarts which Norry and Maria had made while Ernie slept.

"These are delicious," said their guest, reaching for another. "Have you"—he turned to Ernie—"told your sister of my invitation?"

"Yes she did," Norry responded for her, "and we'll be happy for your escort, Major. Traditionally, I've always gone with Jon and Colonel Sommerton. I suspect the colonel assumes he'll escort me this year. Since I must stay with Ernie, I hope you'll not object to his presence as well?"

"Colonel Sommerton?" Osgood's mouth tightened for a moment before he gained control. "No, of course not. How could I object to his being your escort," he added, looking straight at Norry.

She smiled an understanding sort of smile and he grinned.

"Well," inserted Ernie, feeling left out of the conversation, "that's settled, then. Colonel Sommerton mentioned that he would try to arrange for Norry and me to stay with Brigade-major Smith and his wife."

"Then I'll try to remember to coordinate our travel with him," said Osgood, obviously wondering if he might manage some arrangement which would *not* include Norry and the colonel. He turned the conversation then to more general topics, occasionally picking up another of the tiny desserts. When the plate was empty he looked startled, glanced at Norry and actually blushed. "I fear I've a terrible sweet tooth. Please forgive me for eating so many of those delicious tarts!"

"We'll forgive you," said Norry kindly, fully aware there was another plate in the kitchen awaiting her own sweet tooth!

"I'd best be going, then. I've duty in the morning. Will you hunt tomorrow?" he asked Ernie. "I will be sorry to miss it, if you do."

"I don't know," said Ernie, startled by the thought. With Ave gone to his meeting, she had no escort. Unless Bertie was free? But he'd said nothing of going out. "Perhaps not." She'd have to wait another day before she could try her new habit. What a shame, she thought.

"Do you know I'm selfishly glad you may not ride? I cannot be there to watch you, you see," he said softly, looking deep into her eyes.

"Lud, Major," laughed Ernie, her blue mood evaporating as her sense of humor was touched. "What nonsense. You cannot be watching me when you must take care your horse doesn't step in a rabbit hole or stumble over a jump!"

"Not true. I manage to watch you often. I've never seen a woman ride so well."

Ernie knew she rode well—but not *that* well. She gave him a skeptical look. "I think I'd best inform you I do not care to have the hatchet thrown my way. Please desist from telling such bouncers."

"Why do you think I lie?" he asked. When she merely gave him a skeptical look, his brows rose. "Are you so different from other women, then, that you dislike compliments?"

"Very different," she said firmly. "Now you'd better go. Good night Major."

Osgood managed to exit gracefully even in the face of Ernie's obvious displeasure, but he was unhappily aware that he'd left behind what he felt was a bad impression. He was about to mount when Lieutenant Torville loomed up out of the dark startling his animal. "Whoa! Who's there—oh." He grimaced. "You."

"You cannot think worse of me than I think of myself," said the rake bitterly, his posture emphasizing his rue. He straightened, stiffened as if expecting a blow. "Please tell me," he said, "that Miss Matthewson is all right."

"She has a rather large and hideous bruise on the side of her face"—Torville groaned—"but, otherwise seems to be well enough and her own cheerful self."

"Thank you." Torville turned away and, mounting the animal he'd left near the well, rode off.

"Did you hear?" asked Osgood, whispering in the direction of the balcony.

"We heard." Norry spoke through the crack, speaking for them both. "I am glad he feels badly. It is not that he should *not,* but that one wondered if he *would."*

"I think he feels very badly indeed," said the officer slowly, obviously surprised.

"Well," sighed Norry, "I doubt not it will do him good, but I also doubt it will change him much. Good night once again, Major."

This time she closed the door.

Nine

When Ernie woke the next morning it was with the unsettling feeling that she'd very much like to turn over and go back to sleep, that the day ahead of her was without interest and would be flat and gray and boring.

This feeling was so unusual she flopped onto her back and stared at the ceiling. It was so very odd of her to wish to dawdle in her bed that she wondered if perhaps Torville had hit her harder than she'd thought. Perhaps this was the way one felt when concussed? Rather as if it would be far too much effort to get up and dress and face the day?

She thought back to when one of her father's tenant's sons had fallen from the hay loft onto his head. The boy had been unconscious for more than a day and then he'd had a funny look about the eyes . . . what was it? Ah. The dark part had been overly large in one eye and he'd complained of seeing two of everything. The doctor had insisted on a darkened room and that the boy stay quiet and, although Ernie thought she might like the darkened room which would match her mood, she'd never been one for staying quiet. Nor were her eyes producing two images of anything at which she looked. Reluctantly, to say nothing of sorrowfully, she admitted it was not concussion inducing this irritating listlessness.

No, not concussion. Ernie sat up and hugged her knees, her nightcap falling down over her face. She blew at it, but the soft cotton material only fluttered a bit. Not concussion, but an extreme case of stupidity. She was feeling pulled about for no better reason than that, today, she'd not see Colonel Lord Avenel Sommerton!

It would not do. She must not allow it. Ernie forced herself up and over to the makeshift washstand where water was to be found. She splashed the sleep from her eyes and, in the process, the chill water roused her a bit from her lethargy. The words emerging, muffled, from her towel would have shocked her sister if Norry had been awake to hear them.

Truly, she told herself, she must not allow herself to suffer unrequited love for a military man. In fact, she added, ruefully, she must not allow herself to feel *requited* love! Something Sommerton had said made her think he too had been stung by Cupid's arrow and *it would not do.*

Determined not to give in to her mood, Ernie put on her brand new habit—although she feared she'd not be riding. She was pleased with the sense of freedom the split skirt and slightly shorter hemline gave her, and looked down to her booted feet. She nodded. Such sensible dress for the rough world in which she found herself!

Ernie picked up her hairbrush and thoughtfully pulled it through her brown hair. The length of her skirts was not important. Her love for Ave was . . . important because it was *wrong.* Feeling love for an officer was stupid. She must push the colonel from her mind and heart as quickly as she could manage and agreeing to have Brigade-major Osgood as escort to the ball was certainly a step in the right direction. Not only would Osgood distract her from her own unruly emotions, but Sommerton could not believe she loved him if she went about with another man.

Ernie brightened. She *could*—in fact *should*—go with the morning's hunt! She merely needed to locate some *other* officer's escort. Safety in numbers, she thought idly . . . but how was one to manage it when it was already within an hour or so of time to go?

Ernie wandered out to the kitchen, wondering if Bertie had, as was his usual practice, arrived to sit in Maria's pocket. Ernie, newly sensitive to tender feelings, had decided Bertie was in love with Maria which was quite the most wonderful thing possible since the Spanish girl had admitted to a tender passion for Bertie. Ernie decided she would have to see what she could do for the two of them.

For once Ernie was the first to arrive. She knelt before the grate her hands on her thighs and wondered how one went about using the banked coals to bring about a new day's fire. Once, long ago, she'd tried to revive the fire in her bedroom when she'd awakened at an unconscionably early hour. She'd simply poured coal from her hod all over what was left from the night before, but all she'd managed was to quickly, if not so neatly— given the dust she raised—put out all sign of any heat at all.

So. Putting several of the little logs stored in the corner directly on top of these coals was not the answer. Something smaller perhaps? Rising to her feet, she wandered around until she found some neat folded brown paper which, she guessed, had been tied around her habit. She tore off a bit and stuffed it at glowing coals she could see through the ashes. An immediate flame very nearly caught her fingertips—but it died down before she could reach for a length of wood.

It wasn't hard to guess that even the whole of the paper, wadded into a pretend log, would not burn long enough to achieve her goal. Ernie bit the end of her finger and scowled at the pile of ash-covered coals. There must be a way. Maria managed it easily enough. There was no reason at all that *she* could not manage it too . . .

So, why could she not think how to go about it? It couldn't be so very difficult, after all. Her first problem was that the logs were too big . . . Ernie looked around and there, near the logs, was a basket with just the sort of bits and pieces of wood and bark she needed. She chose some thin bits. They lit—but she had forgotten to bring bigger bits to add to her first success. More bits, bigger bits, bigger and bigger until she dared add a real log and some smaller branches . . . and then, soon, another. She'd done it!

Quite proud of her achievement, Ernie looked around for the tripod on which Maria set the kettle in which water was boiled for tea. She found it and looked from it to her pleasantly crackling fire. She groaned. Her seeming success was not so great after all. The fire was now too big and there was no way she could fit the tripod over it. So much for making tea.

Silently, Albert Bacon came in from the back carrying a bucket of water. He looked under his shaggy brows from the fire to Ernie and back again. Ernie tried to look helpless and girlish, but doubted it would soften the oddly silent man who had been with Jon for years.

Grunting softly he approached and Ernie moved back. Using tongs she had not noticed, he removed one log, resettled the other, and set the tripod into place. He filled the kettle and put it on the tripod. Then he gave Ernie a look as if to ask, "Can you handle it from here?"

"Thank you, Albert." He didn't respond. She tried again. "I'll be able to make the tea now."

He merely nodded, went back out the door and disappeared. Ernie hadn't the slightest notion where he had gone or why. She set about making tea and, using the long handled fork, a few pieces of toast.

Again the quiet sense of pride in a job well done filled her. Ernie finished setting a tray for Norry just as Maria came into the kitchen. "Albert helped," said Ernie. "I mean, I managed to start a fire, but it was too big and Albert had to fix it for me."

"Have you never made a fire before?"

"I tried once when I was thirteen or fourteen, but merely

PRESENTING AN IRRESISTIBLE OFFERING ON YOUR KIND OF ROMANCE.

Receive 3 Zebra Regency Romance Novels *(An $11.97 value)*
Free

Journey back to the romantic Regent Era with the world's finest romance authors. Zebra Regency Romance novels place you amongst the English *ton* of a distant past with witty dialogue, and stories of courtship so real, you feel that you're living them!

Experience it all through 3 FREE Zebra Regency Romance novels...yours just for the asking. When you join *the only book club dedicated to Regency Romance readers,* additional Regency Romances can be yours to preview FREE each month, with no obligation to buy anything, ever.

Regency Subscribers Get First-Class Savings.

After your initial package of 3 FREE books, you'll begin to receive monthly shipments of new Zebra Regency titles. These all new novels will be delivered direct to your home as soon as they are published...sometimes even before the bookstores get them! Each monthly shipment of 3 books will be yours to examine for 10 days. Then, if you decide to keep the books, you'll pay the preferred subscriber's price of just $3.30 per title. That's $9.90 for all 3 books...a savings of over $2 off the publisher's price! What's more, $9.90 is your <u>total</u> price. (A nominal shipping and handling charge of $1.50 per shipment will be added.)

No Minimum Purchase, and a Generous Return Privilege.

We're so sure that you'll appreciate the money-saving convenience of home delivery that we <u>guarantee</u> your complete satisfaction. You may return any shipment...for any reason...within 10 days and pay nothing that month. And if you want us to stop sending books, just say the word. There is no minimum number of books you must buy.

GET 3 REGENCY ROMANCE NOVELS FREE

An $11.97 value.
FREE!
No obligation to buy anything, ever.

smothered the coals and never tried again. Until now. I feel so foolish and helpless. It is silly I cannot do even the simplest thing."

"You cannot start a fire. I cannot be an English lady." Maria shrugged. "It is all what one is taught, is it not?"

"Why can you not be an English lady?"

"Because I am a Spanish lady," said Maria patiently. "It is quite different."

Ernie thought it through. "Are you saying that because you are Spanish you cannot marry Bertie?"

Maria nodded. "It is true. His family would not wish him to marry a Spaniard. They would be quite shocked and might even tell him he must never come home again." Maria looked exceedingly sad at that thought. "He would not like that I think."

"No, he would not, but I know his family, Maria. I do not think they'd say any such thing."

"Can you promise me that?"

Ernie grimaced. "No. I wish I could. It is true, however that all his family love him. They would want him to be happy."

Maria digested that as she cut slices from a slab of bacon. "Bertie hesitates when I ask if his mother would approve our marrying. He does not know I have seen this. He would have me believe she would love me as her other daughters, but I know he does not truly believe it. I will not marry him only to destroy his happy family. It would not be well done when I love him and only wish the best for him. It is not good to lose the love of one's family. I *know*," she finished, her eyes flashing fiercely.

There was nothing Ernie could respond to that except to ask what had happened to Maria's family. ". . . if it will not pain you too much to tell me?"

"My mother I only remember a little. I was quite young when she died giving birth to a child which did not live long. My father was, I am told, inconsolable. He gave me to the good sisters at the Convent of Our Lady and went off to join the patriots, not caring, my uncle told me once, if he lived or died. I suspect because he did *not* care, he lived to fight for—oh, for many many years."

"Did you live with your uncle, then?"

"Only in the convent until very recently," said Maria. "The nuns were kind in their way. I did not mind. Too much. And when my father was nearby, then he would visit me. And he would write." Maria, looking very sad again, turned back to the bacon.

"When did *he* die? Your father?"

Maria glanced up. "Did I not explain? I am not at all certain he *is* dead. Only Uncle is certain." She gave a wise little nod. "I think because he *wishes* to be certain."

"I don't understand," admitted a confused Ernie.

"You did not hear that a Spanish general attempted a coup late this fall? No? My father was in the general's army—fighting the French, you see. But he did not believe his general would be good for Spain, so he did not support his coup."

"How do you know that?"

"But it is obvious, is it not? It all came out in the trial when the general was caught."

Ernie was silent for a moment, thinking. "Then, did the general have him executed when he would not support him?" Having asked the question, Ernie once again wished she'd think before speaking. Asking anything of the sort was, she thought, unbelievably cruel. She bit her lip, but soon forgot her rudeness in Maria's response.

"That, you see, is unclear. The general would be a fool to have allowed him to live—or so my uncle insists. But the general insisted equally strongly he could bring himself to execute no one. He swears he gave those who wished to leave an opportunity to escape."

Maria wiped a hand over her eyes. "I do not know, you see, if my father lives or not," she went on earnestly. "It is very difficult not to believe my uncle when he is so very certain, but me, I *wish* to believe the general. There is also the problem that I heard nothing from him to tell me that he lived and how, and surely my father would have written."

"If he wrote to the convent, would the nuns have sent the letters to your uncle?"

Maria straightened slowly, staring all the while at Ernie. "You are saying that my uncle would not wish me to know my father lived until he had me safely wed to his friend and they had shared my inheritance—my mother's fortune, you must know? At least that is what I believe they meant to do, you see." Maria looked pensive and stared at nothing at all. "That may very well be a true thing you suggest. I had not thought of that." Maria appeared far more happy than she had at the beginning of their discussion and was humming a bright song while bent over the sizzling bacon when Bertie knocked lightly at the back door before entering.

"You appear to be quite the thing. Ernie, I feared I'd find you laid upon your bed!"

"I'll carry a bruise for several days, I think, but, as you see, I am not badly hurt."

"Torville should be shot," said Bertie sternly.

"Perhaps, but then he'd cease to suffer, would he not? I think I prefer to have him alive so that every time he sees me he'll remember he hit me and once again feel badly. Although I do not quite understand why, he really is upset."

"You would rub his nose in it, would you? You, my girl, are an exceedingly cruel lady!"

"Perhaps," said Ernie, "but, it is more in the way of tit for tat, I think."

"Did that make sense?" asked Bertie, looking from Ernie to Maria and back again.

Ernie chuckled. "It is only that he doesn't feel the slightest guilt for what he wishes to do to Norry, so I want him to suffer doubly for what he did to me!"

"Hmm. Something to that way of thinking, I suppose. I see you're ready for the hunt this morning. I remembered when I got up that I forgot to tell you I was going. Then I remembered Torville's dastardly behavior. I hadn't a notion if you'd feel up to it or not, but I brought along your horse, in case."

"Then *you* are going? Excellent."

Somewhat later, as they rode through the thick early morning mist and out of the village, Ernie wondered if Maria would tell Bertie that Ernie now knew her secrets. Or most of them anyway. Ernie was in a quandary as to whether she should mention it herself. On the one hand, she needed to discuss Maria's fear of her uncle with Bertie. On the other, it would be rude to speak of the pair's matrimonial problems and Maria's qualms concerning his family's reaction to it unless Bertie were to ask her advice . . .

Ernie decided she *could* ask him about the problem of the man in the marketplace. At which thought she recalled that she'd not told Norry that Maria must not go to the marketplace!

"Bertie," she shouted, "we must go back." She pulled up her nervous roan.

"What?" he called, turning in the saddle to look over his shoulder. He too reined in and trotted back to her. "Now no megrims, my girl. Don't you go telling me your head hurts or something of the sort. I haven't been out with the hounds since that time when we first arrived and I don't want to miss a run now just for some silly complaint from you!"

"It isn't me. I just remembered I meant to tell Norry that Maria must not be sent to market. Not ever. Albert must go instead and do what he can for us."

"Maria . . ."

"So, you see, Bertie, we must go back. Maria must not be allowed to put herself in danger."

"Just what do you know of her danger?"

"Only what she told me of her uncle's plans for her and that she has seen his men looking for her. Yesterday when we were out together she saw one and I saw her fear. I made her tell me. But why has she not told us before this?"

A young officer who had previously given Ernie admiring looks, but had never been introduced to her, noticed they were stopped and approached. "Is there a problem? Not due to that madman, Torville, I hope . . . ?"

"Ah." Bertie's scowl lightened. "Good. Ensign Greystone, will you be kind enough to escort Ernie today and see she is returned safely to Mrs. Major Lockwood. I must return to the village immediately. Ernie," he said quickly, "Ensign Greystone. Greystone, Miss Ernestine Matthewson. Have fun, Ernie . . ." he added, already setting his horse back toward the village.

Ernie glared after him. "Well!"

"I'm pleased," said her new acquaintance softly.

Ernie turned back to him. "What a bouncer," she said. "You cannot possibly wish to take on the responsibility of seeing to my safety. Besides, it is totally unnecessary. Shall we go? We'll pretend we are merely new acquaintances and have no more interest in each other than that."

She didn't notice his rueful look at her words and wouldn't have cared if she had. Ernie set her roan to a canter, allowing the gelding to lengthen his stride to a full gallop. Reveling in the speed, Ernie recalled something a hunting acquaintance of her father had once told her. She turned to look at the young man keeping pace with her.

"Do you know," she called out, "why a canter is called a canter rather than a slow gallop?"

"No," he shouted back. "I never thought to wonder."

Conversation was difficult and yet seemed to add to the excitement so Ernie yelled, "The canter used to be the Canterbury-gallop because of the easy pace at which the pilgrims rode to Canterbury, like in Chaucer's tales."

A new look in Greystone's eyes gave her pause until she realized she'd given him the impression she was a blue-stocking. She grinned. It wouldn't hurt to have that word go round. It might make some of the gallants making asses of themselves whenever they were anywhere near her think twice and draw back. Perhaps they'd not make such nuisances of themselves!

But then Greystone eyed her again, dropping back slightly to watch her ride before catching her up again. Any woman who could ride like that couldn't possibly be one of those absurd women who spent all their time pretending to scholarship, he told himself. A faintly confused look passed over his face. Actually, of those he'd met, many of them did seem to know a great deal. He took another look at the rider at his side. Was she truly one of them? But there was that equestrian skill. Could she possibly ride like that and be a scholar as well?

Greystone decided he'd reserve judgment.

Then they caught up with the hunt and there really wasn't time to worry about things like a lady's interest in books and writers like Chaucer who were so famous even Greystone had heard of him . . . although he could not quite place exactly who he was or what he'd written. But under present circumstances it made no difference, did it? The hares were running in long straight runs and the motley group of hounds were in fine voice. And soon the sun broke through the haze and shone brightly for a change, giving one a rest from the frowning clouds which tended to drizzle all over one with no notice at all and on this fine day he was escorting a lovely woman who could ride like the very devil!

No, decided Greystone. It made not one bit of difference if she also had tendencies of a very different sort. She couldn't very well do anything about intellectual pursuits while following the pack!

Ernie enjoyed the outing. She was quiet as they rode back toward the village, a couple of hares over Greystone's saddle for Norry. The exercise had worked off some of the tension and worry she'd been suffering since her realization she'd fallen in love with a man with whom she could not wed—or perhaps one should say *would* not wed.

It was too bad, really. Sommerton was so much the man she had always hoped to meet. A man who could honestly say he preferred a sensible woman to a beautiful one, for instance! The men she'd met in London who were looking for brides would have thought him quite demented if he'd suggested they look for sense rather than sensibility in the women they would wed. And it was that very insistence on sensibility, among other things, which had decided her she would not return for another season under her aunt's kind but misguided chaperonage, was it not?

"Are you very tired, Miss Matthewson?" asked Greystone, a worried tinge to his tone.

"No." She glanced at him. "Not at all. Merely thinking." She said the last with a hint of humor which Sommerton would have caught in a moment. Greystone—as she'd expected—pokered up, immediately assuming she was again admitting to bluestocking tendencies. "Have you never tried it? Thinking, I mean? You really should," she said kindly. "It is amazing what a little thinking can do for one."

"I remember my uncle telling me that one could think too much and to watch that I did not fall into the temptation," said the young man stiffly.

"Hmm. I suppose it is possible. I have heard of lads studying themselves into a brain fever when preparing for university. Such a pity. I suppose it is impossible to tell in advance if a boy has a weak mind which must be coddled and not allowed to function fully?" She suppressed a giggle at Greystone's look of horror. "Surely you were not such a lad?" she asked as innocently as she could manage.

It occurred to her that Sommerton would not be taken in by her teasing for a moment. The young man was clearly a slow top and she really should not bait him. The desire to giggle returned with her next thought. Why, she might push *him* over the edge and into a brain fever!

"Miss Matthewson," he said, clearing his throat and blushing deeply, "it is terribly rude of me to ask, but are you, er, hmm, well, is it possible you are one of those women who are called a blue-stocking?" he finished in a rush.

"I can't remember that anyone ever suggested such a thing to my face," she said, calling on an innocence of demeanor that would have had her sister immediately suspicious. But the implication that someone might have said such a thing behind her back was so clear even Greystone could not avoid making the connection. His horrified expression returned.

"I don't suppose," she added, "that I would mind the appellation. It does indicate I might be more than a pretty face, does it not?"

"But," he blurted, "why would you want to be?"

Ernie could not suppress a laugh at that. "Why indeed. Mr. Greystone, perhaps it is something only a woman is able to understand, but, there is a great secret most men can't seem to be made to comprehend even when it is explained to them."

He looked a question, so, looking one way and then the other, pretending to check they could not be overheard, Ernie lowered her voice. "We women are humans. We are each an individual person and wish to be treated as such. And occasionally we wish that the men who appear to admire us would realize there is something *behind* the pretty face, that we are something more than, the externals—the hair, the shape, the color of one's eyes—which seem to be all that interests most men."

Greystone actually thought about that. "You mean you have

a life and interests beyond catching a husband and having his children?"

"Perhaps that is a trifle crudely phrased," she scolded gently, "but you have hit the nail quite firmly on its head nevertheless."

"I don't suppose I ever thought of it before." He looked at her oddly. "What interests have you?" he asked.

"Any number." Perhaps it was time to stop teasing the boy. "Obviously, I am addicted to riding to hounds—although I must admit I do not care for the mobbing which is occasionally allowed to occur. I understand Wellington's only fox so far this year was mobbed?"

"Yes. But I don't think Lord Wellington cares if he comes anywhere near a fox. It is the strangest thing, but I've heard that he only goes out for the exercise and is quite content with the lack of actual sport which has been his lot this winter."

"I was surprised to hear there were foxes in Portugal."

"Oh yes. And wolves. I wonder if there is anywhere the fox is not."

Wolves? Ernie shuddered slightly and remembered his comment on the fox. "Australia, perhaps?"

"Oh, Australia. And . . . India?" he suggested daringly. Since neither knew for certain in either case, that promising line of conversation was allowed to drop. "Will you be attending the Light Division's ball which is to be held very soon now?" he asked.

"Yes," responded Ernie and then, fearing he'd ask to escort her, she added, "Our plans are pretty much complete, I think."

"Then will you," asked Greystone politely, "save me a country dance?"

"I'll do that."

"And perhaps a waltz?" he asked, a sly look turned her way.

Ernie straightened in her saddle. She had, of course, heard of the German dance which was sweeping the continent. She had heard murmurs of the immorality involved. She wondered if it were true that the man actually embraced the woman during the dance.

"I think not," she said.

"Then I shall be satisfied with a second country dance," he said. "Perhaps the Lancers?" Again he looked at her from under his lashes. The Lancers was an exceedingly exuberant dance which could, if it were not well under control, turn into a romp.

"We'll see," she said repressively, her mouth shutting tight and her lips a firm straight line.

Another line of conversation was closed off. On the other hand it didn't really matter since they'd reached the outskirts of the village and were starting through the winding lane. They would very soon reach Norry's house and that was, thought Ernie, all to the good.

Ernie dismissed her escort at the door much to his distress. He'd heard that Mrs. Major Lockwood had good English bacon and had hoped to sample some. And if not that, then at least a bowl of the justly famous stew which was nearly always available—or so he'd been assured. But, hiding his disappointment as well as he might, he bowed and, taking Ernie's horse's reins, to return it with his own to the grooms who would care for them, he mounted and trotted off.

"Thank goodness," said Ernie when the door was firmly closed behind her, "that that is over. Norry, *does* one waltz here in Portugal?"

"Of course. I'll teach you if you have not yet had an opportunity to learn it. Of all the dances I have ever had opportunity to perform, the waltz—with the proper partner, of course—is by far the most exhilarating. I only dance it with Jon . . ."

A sadness crossed her features and Ernie wondered if, at last, Norry were beginning to accept that her husband was dead.

Norry forced a smile, her gaze returning to meet Ernie's. "There is no reason why you shouldn't enjoy it, however. I'm certain Ave will partner you." She frowned slightly at a further thought and added, "Ernie, I'm not certain you should allow Osgood a waltz. I cannot be certain he'll hold the line . . ."

"I would like to learn it, but I think perhaps I haven't the courage to dance it with any man. Not in public where all would see my blushes—if it is half so immoral as is said—to say nothing of my mistakes!"

"Done properly, it is merely fun. We'll have a lesson with Bertie for your partner just as soon as maybe. But that can't be today. Ernie, I received a note after you left and you've been invited to come with me to Lady Colonel Barton's while we make our final plans for the Christmas Eve service. Will you come?"

"I'd enjoy that," fibbed Ernie, hiding her reservations. Ernie had little liking for the way committees organized things—or didn't organize them! All too often it would be far simpler to do the job herself. Norry assured her, however, that the work was almost finished, so surely there could be little left about which this committee might argue?

"Is there only one such service for the whole of the army?" she asked.

"Heaven's no! Wherever did you get a notion such as that. There are many all through the region in which the army is spending the winter. This one is just for our own regiment."

"I don't remember exactly where I got the idea. Something was said, I think, which I must have misunderstood . . . but it is not important. Where is our midnight service to be held?"

"Just outside the village here, which is central for our men. We went out recently and surveyed an area which seems very nearly a natural amphitheater. A field altar will be set up at the bottom of the rise and the congregation will either stand or sit on the hillside."

"It will be very cold."

"Yes. It is as well you brought that fur lined cloak with you." Was there just a touch of wistfulness in Norry's voice? Suddenly Ernie determined to give her sister her cloak for a Christmas present. Even if they returned to England . . . Ernie blinked and quickly changed that: *when* they returned to England, it would be good for Norry to wear it on board ship. Especially if she was carrying Jon's child. In that case her sister must have all the protection Ernie could give her.

Will there ever be, wondered Ernie wistfully, the thought sneaking into her consciousness without her permission, someone to take care of me?

Ten

Carrying an umbrella against the cold drizzle which had started up again after lunch, Lady Colonel Barton met Norry and Ernie in the enclosed garden before the red tile roofed house. "This weather! I will almost be happy when I must return to the more salubrious climate in Lisbon."

"How can you say that?" inserted the unhappy Mrs. White who had arrived at the same moment. "It will mean that our"—if anything her face became more ashen than ever—*"your* men will have returned to battle!"

A grimace crossed the older woman's face. "My dear, you must know I wasn't *serious."* She came closer to Ernie. "That poor dear. She has no sense of humor whatsoever. So sad . . ."

They entered the foyer. Here, as in Norry's cottage, were white-washed walls and open beams in the ceiling. There the comparison ended. The floor was tiled in two colors, the pattern neat and unobtrusive. Overhead was a wrought iron chandelier with fat white candles, unlit, the watery light streaming in tall uncovered windows beside the door providing sufficient light. More wrought iron formed a banister for the curving staircase which ended at a balcony above where one could see that heavily carved, dark wood doors shut off rooms above and, on either side of the wide entrance hall, more doors, double this time, closed away ground floor rooms.

"Come along," urged their hostess. "We are meeting in the solarium—not that there is any true sun today, but I love the scent from the lemon flowers, so clean and awakening, is it not?"

Lady Colonel Barton herded her guests down a short hallway to an arch which opened into the solarium. Perhaps half a dozen ladies of all ages sat there in a circle, a low brazier in the center giving off heat. Each woman held a tall glass of some light colored drink. Lemonade? guessed Ernie and was partly correct. The drink also contained lime juice and she took a moment to decide she liked the combination of flavors. She sat back, determined to listen with good grace to Lady Colonel Barton's report.

Ernie's detestation of committees was long standing and she had no expectation this one would be better than those at home. She was mistaken. The meeting was far shorter than she'd steeled herself to endure. There was only one argument and that concerned the candles to be lit by the congregation toward the end of the Christmas service.

"You don't think it a trifle popish?" asked the objector.

"I've discussed that very question with Reverend Stark. Whenever I see candle-lit processions in Lisbon I find them quite beautiful and very moving. I feared my suggestion that we, too, use candles upon certain occasions *might* be turning too far from Anglican principles. Reverend Stark reassured me. He reminded me that candles are used in our churches at home and, that at an outdoor service such as we hold here at Christmas, we cannot depend on the cooperation of the wind. Candelabra would be an absurdity. If there are to be candles at this service, then each must light his own. I found his argument quite comforting. It relieved my mind completely of my fears that I have, in my years in Lisbon"—her voice dropped—"turned popish!"

"Oh well, if Reverend Stark approves . . ."

And that ended the one and only argument. There were still a few decisions to make, but here again the women followed Lady Colonel Barton's lead. Perhaps, thought Ernie, much impressed, it is the discipline their husbands must maintain leaking over into their lives?

Everyone appeared pleased the meeting was over and many surreptitious glances were turned toward the arch, which Ernie didn't understand. All became clear when she heard sighs of pleasure as refreshments were pushed in. The Portuguese maid, dressed in a stiffly starched uniform which crackled when she moved, served from a tiered, wheeled cart.

Lady Colonel Barton's chef lived up to his reputation and Ernie found herself agreeing to a third serving from a magnificent creation which involved fruit and a thick creamy sauce layered between several thin rounds of a pale-golden lemon-flavored cake. Embarrassed by her greed, she looked toward Norry—and relaxed. Norry was spooning up a third helping of the créme brûlée. Obviously *she* suffered from no thought of possible accusations of gluttony!

When everyone had eaten their fill—over-eaten, in many cases—the women turned to gossiping. One rather pushy woman, the one who had wondered about the candles, moved to sit by Mrs. White. "My dear, do you think it wise to remain with the regiment as you've done? Can't help but remind you every instant of your Adrian, can it now?"

Tears filled the white faced Mrs. White's eyes. "I've just received a letter from my—my father-in-law who has very kindly invited me to come live with them. In Kincraig. It's on the river Spey near Lock Inch . . . I will go, of course." Her lip trembled. "What else can I do?"

"Have you never met him?" asked another woman kindly. "Your Adrian's father, I mean?"

"No." Mrs. White looked around at kind faces, curious faces, one or two indifferent faces. Almost in a whisper she added, "Adrian didn't get on with him, you see. His father, I mean. His father didn't want him to go into the army so . . . so they argued . . ."

No one had a response to that. One could guess that Mrs. White went in fear of her father-in-law. Such a situation was still another reason, thought Ernie, feeling bitterness for the poor woman's plight, that she herself would never marry an army man. Not even one so wonderful as she believed Ave to be. Not even when she herself would never find herself in a position where she had no home to go to, even if widowed.

"How did you meet your Adrian?" asked Norry, hoping to turn the grieving woman's thoughts to happier times.

The thin white face roused to a bit of animation. "Oh, it was so very wonderful. My mother had taken me to Bath to recuperate from a bad case of measles and dear Adrian was there getting back his strength after a terrible wound. Both of us were so pulled about we didn't feel like joining the riding parties or the dancing parties or what not. We simply enjoyed talking together and playing chess and reading books from the lending libraries . . . and then . . ." again she had that lost bewildered look.

"Then?" prodded Norry.

"Then Mama was run down by a run-away wagon. The driver hadn't properly set the brakes, you see, while he unloaded. The poor horses were simply pushed in front of it down one of those terrible Bath hills. At first we thought she'd recover . . . and then she didn't." For a moment Mrs. White was still, but then a little smile returned to her face. "Adrian said he'd intended to wait until his next promotion and then write and ask me to come out to him, but because Mama died and I would have to live with the most terrible cousins who didn't really want me at all and would have made my life perfectly wretched, he proposed. Which was just the thing to do. Because I had him that much longer, don't you see?" she said, looking around.

Ernie, also looking around, noted several firm nods of understanding. Ernie couldn't see it. The Whites had been foolish beyond permission—Ernie even wondered if Mrs. White hadn't taken unfair advantage of her officer. If she had looked at him very often with that soft bewildered look, he'd very likely had no choice but to marry her or be beaten by his conscience forever and a day!

"Do you need money for your trip back to England?" asked Lady Colonel Barton brusquely.

Mrs. White, mortified, shook her head. "My father-in-law has very kindly sent me what I need." The bewildered helpless look returned. "It isn't that . . ." Again that helpless, begging, look.

Ernie heard a soft sigh from the colonel's lady. "Then, Mrs. White, if not that, just what is it?"

"I don't know what to do. How to go about? Adrian took care of such things. He saw to moving our things and arranging for passage on the ship and post-chaises and I don't know what to do . . ."

"You poor child," said Lady Colonel Barton. "Why have you not asked for aid? As soon as Christmas is over I'll see you right, my dear, but I can't do much before then . . . ah, but where are you living? Right now? Hmmm. I remember." Her ladyship's mouth tightened. *"That* situation won't do."

Lady Colonel Barton looked around the room. For a moment her gaze settled on Norry, then, with the tiniest shake of her head, passed on to another woman whose name Ernie had not caught. "You, Mrs. Major Weston. I believe you have room, do you not? You must take Mrs. White in until after Christmas when we can arrange for her to return to her family."

Although Mrs. Weston faintly grimaced at the notion, she was a kindly woman and it was soon arranged for Mrs. White to move in with the Westons until suitable arrangements could be made.

"Where," asked Ernie when she and Norry were on their way home, "has that pitiful Mrs. White been living?"

"I haven't a notion, really, although I must remember to ask

Bertha—Lady Colonel Barton, that is. But pitiful?" Norry turned a curious look on Ernie. "Do you truly think so?"

"Do not you?"

"No, I do not. She trades on that helpless act. In my opinion she's worked to perfect it and, again in my opinion, she is one who takes any opportunity to get others to do the needful for her."

"You think there's another reason she's not returned, yet, to England? It's been quite some time now since the retreat from Burgos, has it not?"

"She wasn't there. She was in Madrid, enjoying herself no end. You don't think she'd allow her husband to give her permission to follow the army anywhere near a dirty, dangerous siege, do you? Not that he'd know he'd been maneuvered into making such a decision, of course—or not making it, depending on how you look at it?"

"You don't like her."

Norry sighed. "I should not say such things, but it seemed to me she was more a hindrance to her husband's career than a help. She didn't love him, I think. She married him to escape those cousins she mentioned. Now she has no wish to return to England because she fears she will not like her husband's family—or, more accurately, that they will not be appropriately impressed by her helplessness! And there I am, doing it again. I simply cannot abide women who will not accept responsibilities and take charge of their lives, but must depend, always, on someone else to care for them. And, especially, such women should not be allowed to join the army!"

Which, wondered Ernie, leaves us where? Wasn't her sister's belief her husband would return to her no better than Mrs. White's inability to face, alone, the difficulties in her life? Could she make Norry see that? Should she point it out? Ernie sighed. She had no desire, just at this moment, to try. Except for the interlude concerning Mrs. White, it had been a very enjoyable afternoon—far more diverting than she'd expected, given her antipathy to committees. And, given it had been a good day, she wouldn't spoil it with a sisterly argument.

The argument, when it came, was of an entirely different sort and not between the sisters. As they turned the last corner into the open area before Norry's house, Norry pulled up poor placid Senorita so sternly the usually docile mare actually danced a bit.

"You!" she said, glaring at the mounted man waiting near the well where a few dark-clad Portuguese women gossiped.

"I came to see if Miss Matthewson had recovered. And to apologize," said Torville, his back stiff and straight as a poker.

Norry's face was cold and stern. "I told you I never wished to see your face again. You struck my sister! How *could* you?"

"Very easily when she poked me in the back as if with a gun. I didn't think. I merely defended myself . . . as I thought."

"Thought? Didn't think? Not only are you despicable, you are totally illogical. You've seen Ernie will survive. Now leave."

"I would also like to apologize to you for any upset you felt because of my ill-considered action."

Torville's formal speech given, as it was, in bitten-off words made Ernie think apologies came hard to him.

"If I thought you truly repentant I might accept your apology. Since I don't, I won't."

Ernie had never heard her sister so unyielding.

Torville's ears were brilliant red. "I *am* repentant. Long ago I vowed I'd never strike a woman. I cannot forgive myself for breaking that vow."

"Good."

Torville blinked. "Good!" He shook his head as if he hadn't quite believed his ears. "Why do you say that?"

"Because I don't believe there is much which rubs against your conscience and there is a very great deal which *should*— although you would not agree, of course. Therefore, if you suffer because of what you did to my Ernie, then I think it a very good thing indeed."

He gave her a baffled look. "I'd no notion you were so vindictive, Norry."

Norry straightened in her saddle, that cold hard look in her eyes, her features stiff. "I've never given you permission to use my name."

"I must take such permission for granted, since you'll not admit you want me—or, at least, have a need for what I can give you," he said slyly.

Norry growled. "Men! Sometimes I think they should all be drowned at birth—ah, Jon, not *you,* my love," she added, but not so softly Ernie didn't hear her. Deepening her glare for Torville, Norry said, "You are disgusting. Leave us now."

The sound of clattering hooves coming along the stones of the lane had Ernie turning in her saddle. "Bertie!" She grinned a welcome and felt far more relief than she thought sensible. *What, after all, could Torville do to them under conditions such as these?*

"Afternoon, Ern old girl. Norry." He frowned. "You here?" he asked Torville. "Why?"

"Why I'm here is no business of *yours."*

"It's my business if you're upsetting my friends," said Bertie with a dignity which surprised Ernie no end.

"I've no desire to upset any one! I came to see that Miss Matthewson was no longer suffering."

"No more than one would expect," said Ernie. She lifted the hair she'd carefully arranged to hide the bruise.

Torville saw the purple and greenish flesh and his skin took on a greenish tinge of its own. "Mother . . ." he whispered. He wheeled his horse and whipped it up. Within moments he'd raced up the lane and out of sight. Gradually the sound of pounding hooves faded into silence. The silence stretched tautly for a long moment.

"Mother?" asked Ernie. "Is that what he said? Did I hear correctly?"

"I couldn't hear him, but I'd be surprised if that's what he said," said Bertie, dismounting and going to help Norry from Senorita's back. "I've never thought him the sort to *have* a mother."

"I *almost* feel sorry for him," said Norry slowly. "I mean, I do if he meant what I think he meant."

Bertie turned to Ernie when Norry didn't go on. "Does *that* make sense?" he asked.

"Maybe," said Ernie. "At least, it does if she suspects Torville often saw his mother with bruises such as mine."

"That's exactly what I suspect. I detest men who knock women around and if Torville witnessed such behavior while still a child. . . ." Norry shrugged. "Well, you can see, can you not, how it might affect him? It is sad that women have no choice. They are weaker physically and, legally, have no rights. I mean, what could his mother have done? The law is on the side of men such as his father, allowing them to beat their wives as they will."

"It is?" asked Ernie, forgetting she'd been about to say she'd not have put up with such a life.

"I believe," continued Norry, "it is still legal to *sell* one's wife."

"Truly?" Ernie had never thought about such things. Now that she did she couldn't believe her sister. "You're bamming. You must be."

But Norry didn't tease about things of this sort and shook her head.

"But that's awful."

Bertie looked thoughtful. "Maybe that last isn't possible anymore. I mean, it's now illegal to buy or sell slaves and wouldn't selling one's wife fall under the same sort of law?"

"One would think so," agreed Ernie, "but I'll bet half my next year's clothing allowance you'd find any number of men who would say a wife and a slave are two entirely different things."

"Well, of course they are," agreed Bertie. "That isn't what I said."

"It is too what you said," began Ernie, but Norry interrupted.

"Stop arguing like a pair of bewigged barristers and come inside. It is far too chilly to stand around out here." Norry shivered.

"Yes, do come in, Bertie," said Ernie sweetly. "I'd quite forgotten you'd got rocks under your skull these days. I forgive you for being so illogical."

"But I wasn't!" said an exasperated Bertie. "If you'd only shut up and listen . . ."

He and Ernie were off and running and Norry, knowing of old that such arguments could continue, on and off, for days, left them in the sitting room and went on into the kitchen to see if all was well with their supper.

"Maria!"

Norry's voice was loud enough it penetrated Bertie's concentration and, in mid-sentence, he closed his mouth and turned toward the kitchen. Before Ernie could comment, he'd crossed the room and also disappeared. Ernie followed. Albert Bacon, mopping his face as if relieved to have been saved from some horror, stood near the back door. She saw Norry hovering around Bertie who held Maria in his arms, his broad back bent over her, protectively. Maria sobbed harshly and clutched at Bertie's coat, borrowing her face into his chest.

When, after a long moment, no one did anything sensible, Ernie moved on into the room and went to the precious store of coffee beans. She found the mill and the small pot and started coffee—which she'd noticed was Maria's preferred drink. As soon as Ernie had made a well-sugared cup of strong black coffee, she turned to Bertie. "Maria will feel better if she'll drink this. See if you can get her to do so."

A few minutes later Bertie sat on the stool near the table with Maria on his lap. The girl would not let go of him. Carefully he held the coffee so she could drink, urging her to take another sip and another—until the whole cup was finished and, except for the rare hiccough, Maria had calmed herself. But she still wouldn't speak, once again hiding her face in Bertie's shoulder.

"Albert," said Norry, "tell me what has happened to put the child into such a state?"

"Don' know."

It was the first time Ernie had heard the man's voice. She had previously decided he was a mute but now thought a more taciturn creature didn't exist. "Where were you when whatever it was set her off?" she asked. "At least, I assume she wasn't somewhere on her own?"

"Inna market," said Bacon, obviously grudging each syllable.

Ernie glanced toward Maria who, it appeared, was attempting to burrow into Bertie's coat. "She saw someone there? Someone who frightened her this much?"

"Maybe . . ."

"Albert, surely you know if someone menaced her," said Norry.

He shook his head.

"You don't know or no one did?" asked Norry patiently. She'd dealt with the man's dislike of talking before.

"Dunno."

Ernie sighed. Getting information from Albert Bacon was worse than pulling teeth from a hen. "Did Maria leave the market in rather a rush?" she asked.

"Hmm."

"She did?"

He nodded.

"Did she seem frightened?" asked Norry.

He nodded.

"Damn."

"Ernie!"

"Norry, this is no time to worry about my language. Maria," said Ernie, softly, her hand on the girl's head. "You must tell us. Did you see one of those men trying to find you?"

Maria held up three fingers.

"Three of them? Oh dear. And they saw you?"

Maria nodded, rubbing her forehead against Bertie's shoulder. His arms tightened around her. "That settles it," he said. "Maria, my girl, you no longer have a choice. You'll marry me now or else."

Norry straightened. "Bertie—"

Ernie waved her to silence. "I wondered if you felt for her what she admitted to me that she felt for you. How long have you wanted to marry her?" she asked, giving Maria time to think.

"I've known ever since I first saw her. But she's always said it will not do. It'll do now, my girl," he added, putting his hands on Maria's shoulders and pushing her away from him so he could look into her tear-stained face. "No arguments, hear me?"

"I am too frightened to argue, I think," the girl said in a soft but strained voice. "He will come and he will take me away and he will force me to marry that awful old man and I *won't*. I'll kill myself first. I will! I won't marry him. I *won't*. . . ."

Ernie slapped Maria's cheek, a sharp stinging slap. "Enough of that. He can't take you away if you are already married to Bertie. Much as it amazes me, for once my old friend has the right of it and you've no choice now but to marry him. I understand your fears, Maria, but you are wrong. Bertie's mother will not reject you because you are Spanish. She will fear, far more, that she'll offend you in some way, and that you'll turn Bertie from his family because of it."

"Nonsense," growled Bertie. "Why would my Maria do any such thing?"

"Maria fears your family will turn *you* away from your home for marrying her. Hasn't she told you that?"

"Is that what you meant by all that nonsense?" Again he had her by the shoulders and was shaking her gently. "Maria, love, I thought you meant I wasn't good enough for you!"

"Not good enough . . . ! No, no. It is I who . . . but we will argue such things later." Maria turned in his arms to stare at Ernie. "You are very certain my Bertie will not be disinherited?"

"For marrying you? Of course not. Now that I think of it, his mama is much more likely to take you to her bosom in *relief.*" Ernie's eyes twinkled roguishly. "She's always feared he'd end up married to *me,* you see, and that, she considers a disaster beyond anything. She didn't like it at all that I sailed here under his protection and will be pleasantly surprised to find he's married to someone quite different."

Norry smiled and Bertie chuckled.

"So, you see, Maria," said Norry gently teasing, "you'll be doing Bertie a good deed if you agree to marry him. You'll save him from my hoyden of a sister and will be considered, at least by his mother, to be a heroine!"

"But there is his father . . . surely his father . . ."

For an instant Ernie thought her sister would join the laughter which escaped both Bertie and herself, but Norry merely grinned broadly. When she could, Ernie gasped, "You don't understand . . ."

Bertie's initial comment was no more helpful. "My father?" His chuckling overtook him again and he could say no more.

Norry took it on herself to explain. "Maria, in Bertie's family it is his mother who rules such things. Bertie's father runs the estate and does it magnificently well, but his mother has control over the family and all its doings—except for Bertie, of course."

"But why not my Bertie?" One of Maria's small hands still clutched his lapel.

"M'mother knows I'll not be ruled by her. Inherited a bit from my godfather and immediately bought my commission. She'd been trying to make me go into the law ever since she was forced to admit I'd make the worst sort of churchman! But she's known I've wanted nothing but the army since I first learned to play with tin-soldiers and she should have known that's what I'd do—one way or another."

"Who," asked Norry, "taught you to play with tin-soldiers?"

A flush colored Bertie's ears. "M'father. Mother didn't know. She didn't come much into the nurseries, you'll remember. Or maybe you wouldn't. Ernie would."

"But she sounds a monster, this mother," said Maria, sitting up and glaring at no one in particular.

"Ah, then it's your duty, m'love, to save me from her machinations," chuckled Bertie with a wink at Ernie. "I *do* need your protection, m'dear. Who knows what platter-faced chit Mama might try to marry me off to when next I'm home? This last time it was a witless lass from the north. The daughter of an old friend from m'mother's first season whom she'd not seen in years."

"Is that why Lady Lennex-Storn was visiting?" asked Ernie. "Your mother truly thought you might develop an interest in that pasty faced, spineless, and utterly dim-witted chit of a—"

"Ernie!" said Norry just as Bertie, once again chuckling, warned, "Better *not,* m'girl."

Ernie pouted. "Well," she said once she'd managed to control her temper, "she *was,* you know."

"But you must not say so," scolded Bertie. "It isn't nice for well brought up—" he ducked, raising one arm to cover his head. "Maria, protect me! The devil's in her!"

Maria looked from one to the other. "But Bertie, of course the devil is in her." She frowned at her beloved. "It would be in me too if you were to scold me in that silly way."

This time Ernie doubled over with laughter. "Oh dear. Be warned, Bertie! You've just been told you'll wed a termagant!"

"It is no such thing." Maria scowled. "Me, I am not a terma . . . a ter . . . that thing you said!"

"No. Only if the devil gets in you," teased Bertie. He stood and set Maria on her feet, keeping her close to him. "Enough of this nonsense. We've no time for such jesting. Norry, do *you* know how we should go about getting married? I want it proper so there'll be no question her uncle can set it aside," he warned.

"Oh Bertie, I've just thought," interrupted Maria. "He'll not give up my dowry! I cannot marry you without a dowry. It would not be right to come to you only in my shift, as they say."

"Maria, your dowry would be nice, but it is *you* I love and *you* I want. It will make not one iota of difference if he keeps everything—except the shift, of course."

Maria relaxed. "Ah, then if you do not demand my dowry, he'll have no reason to want me back. He'll have what he wants."

"Don't be such a child, Maria," scolded Bertie. "Of course I'll demand it. It is my right."

The Spanish girl seemed to curl into herself. "But Bertie, don't you see? He'll never allow that. He'll insist the marriage is not legal. He'll do anything to see that—"

"Silly chit," said Bertie, touching her cheek gently. "I don't expect to *get* it. It is simply that he must not be allowed to steal your property with no threat of a comeuppance. He must not believe it is securely *his*." Bertie's voice softened still more. "Who knows, Maria, love? Your father might come back from wherever it is he's disappeared and your uncle should not be allowed to forget *that* either. Then if your father does come and *he*, too, disapproves our marriage and will not give us your dowry"—Bertie shrugged—"well, we never expected to have it anyway, did we, sweetheart?"

A silence followed Bertie's little speech. Then Maria spoke. "I am afraid."

"What do you fear?" asked a new voice.

Everyone whirled to find Colonel Lord Sommerton standing in the kitchen doorway. Ernie, a warming gladness filling her at the sight of him, even took a step toward him before she caught herself.

"I *did* knock," he said, looking around apologetically, "but no one heard me, I guess."

"You are very welcome. In fact, you're just the man we need!" said Bertie.

"I thought you were not to be back until late," said Ernie, more breathless than she thought reasonable. But, since she'd not expected to see him at all today, the warmth filling her at his sudden appearance seemed to make it hard to breathe properly which was quite ridiculous. She devoured him with her eyes, absorbing the long lean length of him, the hard muscles, the stern expression . . .

"As Bertie said," inserted Norry, drawing everyone's attention, "you, Ave, are *just* the man we need. How does one go about getting married quickly when one is with the army as we are? I mean, you can't just pick up and go to the consulate in Lisbon where the ambassador could do the trick, can you . . . ?"

"Married?" Ave's brows snapped together and his gaze stabbed into Ernie.

"Not *me*," she said, backing away a step at the fierce look.

The frown disappeared and he returned his gaze to Norry. *"Quickly* married?"

"Bertie and Maria must marry and marry quickly."

This time Colonel Lord Sommerton turned to glare at Bertie. "How *dare* an officer in my unit behave so!"

"How dare . . . ?" Bertie tugged at his collar and looked wildly anywhere but at his threatening superior. Then a bewildered look crossed his face. "How dare I *what?* Marry my Maria? Why should I not?" He looked at the others. "Is he making sense?"

Maria giggled, tugged at his arm until he bent and she could whisper in his ear. "He thinks me with child, Bertie."

Bertie, in turn, glowered. "I'll meet you for that insult! Name your friends!"

Sommerton relaxed. "Don't be more of an ass than you are, Lieutenant, and explain what the devil is going on here?" He looked from one to another and back to Bertie. "*Why* must you marry quickly if not for the usual reason?"

"Because my Maria is in danger."

"Danger? Nonsense."

"It is not nonsense," said Ernie. "She has an evil uncle who would marry her off to an old friend so the two of them can share her dowry. She ran away from that situation and Norry found her and now her uncle's agents have located her. The wedding notion isn't just a response to that, however. Bertie has been trying for weeks to get Maria to agree to a wedding."

"I'll not have the child forced into marrying this young idiot if she doesn't wish it," said Ave.

"Oh, but I wish it very much," said Maria softly. "It is only that I have not thought it proper, but Mrs. Lockwood and Miss Matthewson have said it is all right, so I will do it."

"All right? Nonsense. It offends propriety on all counts, rushing it this way. I see no reason why you cannot wait until your uncle comes and ask his permission so all may be in order."

"Ave," said Norry, "you haven't been listening. Her uncle would *not* agree. He would immediately take her away to marry a man old enough to be her father—"

"My *grandfather.*"

"—who has grown children by another marriage and is fat and balding," added Ernie, "which, Maria once told me, she could agree to if only he were a good man, but he *isn't.* I didn't care to ask her what she meant by *bad* in this particular case . . . ," she began, glancing at Maria.

"He beats his daughter and he starves his peons when they cannot pay their levies and—"

Ave had turned from one to the next as each woman spoke.

"We see what sort he is, Maria. But, Browley, am I to understand you wish to wed Maria merely to save the child from a marriage her uncle approves and she cannot stomach?" His eyelids drooped and his mouth twisted slightly in an ironic way. "I find that too chivalrous for words, Lieutenant!"

"We wish to wed because we are very much in love," said Bertie with a degree of dignity Ernie would have thought him incapable of achieving. He stared, steadily, at his commanding officer.

For a long moment there was silence. Ave's brows arched and he held Bertie's gaze until something seemed to satisfy him and he shrugged, but his mouth was still a tight line.

Finally Norry asked, "Ave? Do you know how one goes about it? What one must do?"

Sommerton drew in a deep breath and let it out through his nose. Again his eyes went from one to the other and on to the next, finally settling on Norry. "You approve this romantic idiocy?" he asked cautiously.

She smiled the old mischievous smile. "I think it wonderfully romantic, Ave, and not idiocy." He grimaced. "I think they are well matched in all ways which count and will get along well together."

"If you are thinking of little Juana Smith . . ."

"I wasn't," admitted Norry, "but isn't that an excellent example that such marriages can work well?"

"*That* one does, but Harry Smith understands the Spanish in a way no one else in the British army seems able to do. Sometimes I think Harry must have *been* Spanish at some time in his wild career—although of course that is impossible! What I *don't* think is that Bertie has a notion of what he's getting into." They all stared blankly and he explained, "He won't know what Maria will expect of him."

"No, no. That is not important," said Maria. "It is far worse that I do not know what is expected of an English lady. I will be a terrible wife to him. Because I am ignorant I will do it all wrong. I fear it!"

"You'll do just fine," soothed Bertie, drawing her back to his side, his protective arm around her waist. "What you don't know you'll ask Norry, won't you? Norry will know."

"At least," said Ave, "Maria knows English. Juana still speaks only Spanish and French which is crazy and so I've told Harry, but he just says there's plenty of time for such nonsense." Again he stared at each of them. "Lieutenant, I can't say I approve because I don't—"

Everyone drew in a deep breath to argue but let it out again when Ave went on.

"—but if all of you are certain this is what you want, then we'd better lay our plans."

So that is what they did. The most important decision was that Maria must not leave the house for any reason until she was safely married to Bertie. They thought it could be arranged in two days at most if they all worked to that end and Ernie noted that, at that, Maria relaxed a trifle more. Even so she was still very tightly drawn and Ernie was certain the poor girl would not feel entirely safe until her uncle had come and been forced to accept she was married to her Bertie and safe from his machinations.

Married. Strange how, whatever way she turned, the subject intruded. How ironic, thought Ernie, when all I want is to forget that marriage to Ave would be the most wonderful thing in the world . . . if only he were not in the military. But he is. And she won't. And that, thought Ernie, is that.

It was important that she remember she was the sensible sort and the sensible thing to do was to forget such a silly notion . . . except, of course, that for once in a way, she couldn't seem to be the least little bit sensible.

Eleven

Once they had discussed their plans from every possible angle, Norry fixed a late supper. Maria's stew was barely enough, but with lots of bread and fresh, uncooked, vegetables fixed with olive oil and vinegar in a way Ernie had never tried, there was enough food that no one actually felt hungry. There were even a few tarts to pass at the end of the meal.

As they sipped their tea, Norry asked, "Did those men try to stop you from returning here, Maria?"

"No. They merely followed us. I think at least one of them is still out there." Maria shuddered.

"Maybe we could do something about that," said Bertie, with a suggestive look toward Ave.

"And maybe it would be better to let them wait in the cold with no suspicion that Maria has friends who will help her," responded Ave, equally suggestively.

Bertie opened his mouth to object but Maria laid her hand on his wrist. "That is a very intelligent thing to do, I think," said Maria. "They will not know we have a plot to save me, but if one of them is hit over the head and disappears, the others will know that someone has done it and if someone has done such a thing to one of them, then the others might become dangerous. They might even try to abduct me." Her hand tightened on Bertie's wrist. She turned a white face his way. "No, no, Bertie. Do not interfere with those terrible men. Please. I fear them. I wish to marry you now. Mrs. Lockwood assures me it is . . . is *comme il faut* to do so. I do not wish to be kidnapped. Bertie?"

"Shush Maria. I won't do anything which might interfere with our wedding, I can assure you of *that*. But *afterward* . . ."

"No, *no*. Not then either. We must await my uncle. We must convince him it is too late and he will go away and then I will be safe."

Bertie scowled. "But I don't like it that you are frightened. Anyone who frightens you should be punished!"

Ernie looked at Ave who looked back and shrugged his shoulders. "The thought is properly lover-like, Browley, but impossible, nevertheless. You listen to that sensible little woman of yours. She's very obviously got better judgment than you have."

"My Bertie has very good judgment," insisted Maria, and hugged Bertie's arm close. "You will not say my Bertie hasn't good judgment!"

Bertie grinned. "Wildcat! He's right and I don't. I will listen to you—unless I'm too angry to listen to anyone which does happen occasionally."

"Whenever you rub him up the wrong way," said Ernie wryly. "Maria, are you sure you wish to marry Bertie? I think it quite possible that Colonel Sommerton could, if you preferred it, arrange a suitable escort for you which would take you safely to Lisbon where you'd be put on a boat for England. Norry and I would provide you with a letter of introduction to Lady Browley who would take you in for Bertie's sake. She's a very kind-hearted lady, really—if we write the letter properly, I mean—and then, when she knows you and grows to love you as she couldn't help but do, then Bertie may get leave and go home and marry you there. Properly." She looked around. "In the village church, I mean."

Maria had begun shaking her head halfway through Ernie's little speech. Bertie began to glower at much the same moment.

They spoke together. "I will not leave my Bertie," said Maria just as Bertie said, "My mother? Kindhearted?"

"She is, Bertie. You know she is. She's just a bit of a tartar about propriety and the conventions."

Maria again lost color. "She will not approve! I *knew* she would not approve. She will want a proper English lady for her son. Oh, Bertie, I must not marry you. I must *not!*" She pushed him away when he would have taken her into his arms. "Oh, what will I do!"

Norry set about soothing Maria who turned to her and put her head on her shoulder. Ernie glowered at Bertie who again wore that what-did-I-do look as he watched Norry talk softly to his love.

Ave touched Ernie on the shoulder and moved her away from the others. "Maria is Roman Catholic, is she not? Will that be a problem?" he asked. "The religious men with the army are all Church of England, unless there are priests for the Irish. I don't know if her uncle *will* accept a Church of England marriage . . ."

Ernie rolled her eyes. "If it isn't one thing it is another. I haven't the least notion. If it will be a problem, I mean. I do know she was raised in a convent . . ." She looked trustingly at Ave who groaned softly.

"Don't look as if you thought I could find a solution to any difficulty. I can't even seem to solve my own problems which are caused by *you*—"

Ave gave Ernie a meaningful look which she avoided, but she had more difficulty ignoring the tingles running up and down her spine at the insinuation she heard in his words. *Could he mean what she thought he meant? But it wouldn't do . . .*

"—so how," he continued, "can I possibly solve theirs?"

. . . *Oh dear.* Ernie pushed this further clue that Ave was falling in love with her from her mind. They had far too many other problems which must be solved. Forcing herself to think of Bertie and Maria reminded her of another wedding. "How did that Harry Smith solve his problem? You did say he married a Spanish lady, did you not?"

"I think they had a drumhead marriage . . . Ernie, tomorrow, perhaps you and I should ride over to where the Twenty-first is bivouacked and find out how they managed it. If what they did seems suitable, then I can arrange another such wedding here and that will be that."

"Until the uncle arrives. Ave . . ."

"One problem at a time. If those men saw Maria today, then they'll have sent off a messenger. Unless the uncle is waiting somewhere nearby for that message—and I think it unlikely—he'll be a week or more getting here. We'll have plenty of time."

For a fleeting moment Ernie suspected something was wrong with that reasoning. Something about the men seeing Maria earlier . . .

"We'll leave about eight, Ernie." Then he hesitated. "It is a rather long ride. . . . Perhaps . . ." He eyed her speculatively and shook his head, obviously about to change his mind.

Instantly up in arms, Ernie forgot her objections to Ave's reasoning. "Don't you dare say it will overtire me. I came up from Lisbon, did I not? I am not the frail sort who cannot stroll around the garden without a man's arm on which to lean!"

Ave's eyes narrowed, humor lines scrunching up the corners. "No, you are not. Thank God."

As with his earlier insinuations, Ernie didn't wish to have that fervent prayer explained. She ignored it as she'd done his other comment. "So," she said, "we leave at eight. You said it was quite far," she added in a completely serious way. "Will we need a trail picnic?"

This time Ave laughed. "You learn quickly, do you not? No. Trail picnics are only for journeys such as you suffered coming up from Lisbon, the day long marches where one may not stop for more than a moment along the way. I'll not ask that of you. Not tomorrow anyway."

She could no longer ignore his hints. "Not ever. Not if you are suggesting . . . suggesting . . ." Oh dear. Now what? She couldn't ignore such very pointed comments, but what could she say when he'd not actually done more than hint?

"Suggesting?" he asked politely, humor evident only in his eyes.

She glared, feeling heat coming up her breasts, up her throat. She *couldn't* ask him outright if he were thinking of their marriage. "Oh never mind." She crossed her arms and looked at where her toe dug into one of Norry's old carpets.

"But I do mind." A spurious solemnity cleared his face of all expression. Unfortunately, his eyes continued to twinkle merrily. "You see, Ernestine," he said with a patently false patience, "a soldier's wife must expect long treks occasionally. When the army is on the move, it does not ask if the women are ready to go or politely wait for them if they are not. So you see, there will be times when—"

"But," she said in an overly sweet tone, *"I* will never be a soldier's wife, so there will never be a time when I need worry about such things, will there?" She felt his fingers touch her hair just where it was pulled up from her neck, just where tiny strands would never stay properly straight and tended to curl back down onto her nape. More heat rose up into her throat but the reason for it had changed. She turned, wary. "I need not concern myself with such problems, need I?" she insisted.

"There is only one error in that argument, Ernie."

"An error? I see none."

"The error, my dear," he said softly, all humor gone, "is that you *will* be a soldier's wife. It would be far too much of a waste if you were *not* and of all things, I detest waste."

"I fail to see what *you* have to do with it." Ernie immediately wished she'd not gone quite so far.

In the mood Ave was in, he'd not let that pass—and he didn't. "I? Ah, Ernestine, my very special Ernestine! You've never shown signs of stupidity, so I must assume you are deliberately and consciously appearing obtuse. Once we get those two idiots wed, then you will marry *me*. Of course."

"There is no of course about it!" A touch of panic oozed through Ernie. She very nearly hissed at him in her intense need to convince him while constrained by the need to keep her voice low so the others would not hear. "I have told you I will never put myself into the position in which Norry finds herself. Or that pitiful Mrs. White. That poor woman is miserable. Why," she asked, "would any presumably sane woman wish to chance such . . . such *horror?* Why, for that matter," she continued, eyes narrowed, "would any *gentleman* presume to ask it of her?"

Ave's brows rose. "You believe a soldier should not take a wife?"

"A soldier should ideally have been born an orphan," said Ernie, turning away to hide sudden bitterness that he couldn't see her point. "It is not merely wives who suffer, but mothers and sisters and—"

"Ernie," he said, using her nickname without permission. He waited half a moment to see if she'd demand he retract, but she didn't. "Ernie, love, you are foolish beyond permission. I've a cousin who is a widow after only six years of marriage and her husband was no nearer to war than one visit, which he made with me, to the Horse Guards. He died of an inflammation of the lungs, Ernie. Death does not hover only over battlefields!"

"But," she responded promptly, "the skull-faced gentleman spends far more time there than at home and you cannot argue *that* point. I'd be foolish to listen to you. Foolish!"

"And Maria? Is she foolish?"

Ernie sighed. "Yes, of course she is. But the alternative for her is worse. I have alternatives."

Norry approached. She looked from one tense face to the other. "What are you two arguing about?"

"Whether Maria is being foolish to marry Bertie," said Ernie promptly, her gaze catching and holding Ave's, daring him to mention that he had as much as proposed and been turned down. "I think she is, but that she's justified because the alternative is worse."

Norry turned to her husband's old friend. "And you, Ave?" she asked, her head to one side.

"Me?" His brows rose. "I merely asked how Ernie felt about it." He turned the subject, telling Norry he'd invited Ernie to ride to visit the Smiths on the morrow. "We'll leave early."

"Ah. I will have Maria fix you a picnic."

"A trail picnic?" asked Ernie sweetly, with a look under her lashes at Ave.

"Heavens no," said her sister, drawing her gaze. "A real picnic, of course."

Ernie subsided, avoiding the twinkle in Ave's eyes which she suspected would be there because he knew she'd been discomforted by Norry's backing his assessment.

"We should be back shortly after three," said Ave. "I'll set play practice for four which should give you time for a rest, Ernie."

"We agreed I am not a frail creature, did we not?" she asked a bit belligerently.

"Yes, but if you don't wish a rest, dear, then understand I'll have work to do before practice and, my love, don't argue the point."

Norry's brows rose at the first endearment and still higher at the second.

"Grrrr," said Ernie, furious with him.

"Yes, love?" he asked, that sham sobriety again in evidence. "You wished to say something?"

Ernie found herself with too many contrary and roiling emotions to find her tongue.

Norry, understanding, grinned. "You, Ave Sommerton, are a tease. Ernie, dear, don't let him get to you that way. He is enjoying himself hugely, I fear."

"Ah. You mean he doesn't mean it when he uses such objectionable terms in reference to me?" Ernie asked, relaxing and finding herself able to respond.

Ave's brows snapped together and the twinkle instantly disappeared from his eyes, but, again, it was Norry who answered. "Ernie, it is not objectionable to be called someone's love. It is merely that, in this case, it is done to rouse your temper."

"Who says so?" asked Ave. He marched Norry away from Ernie's side and, softly, warned her, "Norry, watch your tongue. Don't you *dare* queer my suit."

Norry blinked. "Ave . . . ?"

"Stay out of it?"

"Out of *what?*" Norry looked from Ave to her sister who was, unlikely as it seemed, blushing. Norry didn't bother to keep her voice down. "Ave, are you courting my sister?"

"Would you object if I were?"

"Of course not." Her eyes widened. "Now I think of it, it's perfect!"

"It is no such thing," said Ernie from across the room. "Norry, don't encourage him. I'll not have it!"

"It?" asked Ave, tongue in cheek. He felt drunk on happiness now his intentions were out in the open. "You'd have the rest of me, then, if it weren't for *it?* Ernie, that's ridiculous."

"*That*, Ave, is enough of *that*," scolded Norry, firmly controlling a smile. "You behave yourself."

"I can't. I'm feeling too much like a boy with his first infatuation and very nearly as completely out of control. See you at eight, Ernie, love. Be ready." His brows rose as she looked ready to explode. "Ernie, this is the Army. You'd best get accustomed to taking orders!"

"One more reason why I'll never marry a soldier!"

He chuckled, called Bertie to order, and the two of them took their leave—Ave returning almost immediately. "Norry, there is a man lurking out there. Perhaps I should set a guard on this house. Perhaps one would discourage Torville as well as Maria's ungentle watchers."

"Nothing," said Norry with more bitterness than Ernie had ever heard, "will discourage that . . . that . . ."

"Bastard?" asked Ave. When she didn't respond with more than a tightening of her lips, he added, "Jackanapes, perhaps? Or cully . . . ? You'd prefer ding boy maybe?"

"A what?" interrupted Ernie.

"Ding boy," repeated Ave. "In other words, a bully."

"He's that all right," muttered Norry.

"And what's a cully?" asked Ernie.

"A blockhead," Ave promptly explained.

"That's enough new vocabulary, Ernie," scolded Norry. "Ave had best leave. Ave, I don't think I want a guard here. I can't like the look of it and I truly believe it would do no good."

"We've no notion what Maria's pursuers might do. I can't like it that you are unprotected."

"We have Albert Bacon and I'm capable of using a gun. I'll keep my pistol primed from now on and will have no qualms about using it if it becomes necessary."

"I know you're an excellent shot, but you've never had to shoot at a man . . ." When Norry only shook her head Ave sighed. "All right, Norry. However, as I said, I cannot like it."

He made his adieux all over again and left, taking the reins from Bertie who had mounted. He rose into his saddle and the two men trotted off.

For a moment Ernie could not keep her eyes from following after, her senses filled with the sight of broad shoulders and straight back. But only for a moment. She forced herself to go in and to close the door behind her.

"So," asked Norry, before Ernie could so much as breathe. "Just when did Ave propose?"

"Colonel Sommerton proposed?" asked Maria. "What did he say? How did he do it? How very romantic that he should have fallen in love with you the very instant in which he laid eyes on you—which I am very certain he did do!"

"*I* cannot think it, Maria. That he has fallen in love, that is. What's more, he has not, in truth, proposed. He's merely informed me that I'll marry him. He's *impossible.*"

Norry laughed. "Not at all impossible—merely up to your tricks."

"*I will not marry a soldier,*" said Ernie.

Maria blinked. "But why? If you are in love with him—and you are, of course—what does it matter what he does, who he is?"

Ernie did her best to ignore Maria's calm certainty that she, Ernie, was in love with Ave. When she didn't respond, her sister again stepped in, and, this time, asked Maria a question. "I thought the Spanish were very strict about such things, Maria, as who and what a girl's suitor might be. I would think you'd assume it very important indeed."

"But it is well known that the English are *not* so strict and that parents do not tell their daughters whom they must marry. I would," said Maria, "much prefer that I be English, which"— she brightened—"I *will* be when I marry my Bertie, will I not?" She looked from one to the other and was angry when they laughed. She stamped her foot. "But it is true. I *will* be. Bertie has said so!"

"We don't laugh because you'll be English, but at the thought we may marry where we please! I can just see my father allowing me to wed our head groom, for instance!" said Ernie.

"Or perhaps young farmer Gross?" teased Norry, remembering an incident with the smitten young man that she knew Ernie would much prefer forgotten.

"Or the curate," suggested Ernie, in turn teasing her sister about an old beau. "Or, for that matter," she added, "the new vicar whom our father cannot abide!"

"Or—"

"I do not understand," interrupted Maria.

Ernie, controlling her giggles, turned to the Spanish girl. "It is only that while we may have greater freedom of choice in England when it comes to marriage, it is not true we may marry wherever we have fallen in love. Norry and I were merely thinking of men we would never be allowed to marry no matter how well we loved them."

"Then why does one hear otherwise?"

"I suppose," Norry suggested thoughtfully, "because a Spanish girl is married off much as our grandmothers were. Back then, all marriages were arranged marriages. It was still quite often true in our father's time and one occasionally hears of it even yet—usually for financial reasons, the merging of estates, for instance. The difference is that, now, if a girl is truly against the marriage, often she may prevail in saying no and some other match is arranged for her. It is rarely the case, in our modern times, that a bride meets her husband for the first time at the altar at which they are wed. In fact, I've never heard of such a thing, have you Ernie?"

Ernie shook her head. "Never."

"But that is very often the case in Spain," said Maria. "If I had not met my uncle's friend and if he had not told me, gloating and looking at me in *such* a way, that he and I were to wed, I might have had no opportunity in which to escape." She trembled and looked wildly around the room. "Oh, I wish I had not thought of that. I wish I had not remembered that my uncle might arrive before I can wed my Bertie!"

"Maria, we will not let him take you away," said Norry, going to hold her. "You must trust us."

"But he has the right of it! The law can make it so!"

"Not if your father lives," insisted Norry. "You must believe he lives and that he will come to your rescue."

"Instead of worrying about what has not happened and is not likely to happen, why don't we do something more interesting," said Ernie. The others looked at her expectantly. Ernie grinned. "For instance, we might look at the dresses I brought from England and see if there is one we may alter for Maria's wedding gown."

Maria turned toward Ernie, but not so that she was out of Norry's comforting embrace. "Wedding gown?"

"I will give you a gown for a wedding present," said Ernie. "But we will have to work very hard to have it ready in time for you to wear when you say your vows with Bertie."

"I can do it. I am very good with a needle," said Maria firmly. She drew away from Norry. "But you must pick one which is not a favorite. I would not take from you a favorite gown . . ."

"No, no. You must have any one you wish." When Maria still looked as if she would object, Ernie added, "Maria, I can easily have it replaced when I am home again if your choice is a style or a pattern of which I am particularly fond."

Maria hesitated. "You are very certain?"

"Very."

"Well, then . . ."

"Come and choose it," coaxed Ernie. "Bertie insisted I not pack too much so I haven't a great number, but surely there is something which you have seen and liked?"

Maria, reassured, glowed. She smiled shyly. "I unpacked your things when you arrived and there is one I thought so beautiful . . . oh, if I may truly have which I wish! Come, I will show you."

Not very much later Maria was settled by the kitchen fire

with needle, thread, and the gown. It had been tried on and marked where adjustments must be made, and, as Ernie had thought, it would be something of a job to make it fit the smaller and much slighter Maria. Maria, however, seemed to have no fears she could not manage.

"The nuns, you see, they taught us very well—all those things which one must know to properly run a house."

"But surely a Spanish lady does not do her own cooking or sew her own gowns," said Ernie.

"No, no, of course not, but if one does not know how oneself, then how can one properly oversee those who *do* do the work? And a very good thing I *do* know how. Poor Bertie, if I did *not!*"

"Which reminds me," said Norry. "Before you are wed, I wish to learn how to properly make that rabbit stew you do so well. It is, as you know, a favorite of Jon's and it would not do that *I* not know how to make it once you are gone, would it?"

Jon. Ernie glanced at her sister who had hold of the hem, shortening the skirt of the rosy colored wool walking dress while Maria ripped at the side seams and the gathers under the bust. Once again Norry had mentioned Jon in that complacent way she had of expecting him to walk in at any moment. Was now the time to start that argument which she'd avoided as they rode home from Lady Colonel Barton's?

But no. Maria was chattering away about the herbs and spices she used in the stew and how it really made little difference just what vegetables one put in so long as those ones used were fresh and wholesome. Ernie sighed. Maria had had too many upsets today. It would not be fair to add another to the list just because Norry would not admit to the fact of her husband's death.

"He isn't, you know. He'll be home for Christmas," said Norry softly, and smiled at Ernie's startled expression. "You think I read your mind, Ernie? Not that. I've never been good at that. It is your face which gives you away. In case you did not know it, it is a very expressive face. I can almost always read what you are thinking just by looking at your face. Our great-grandmother may have had the ability to see into another's heart and mind, but I cannot."

"Our great-grandmother?"

"On Mama's side of the family. *You* know."

Norry turned back to the conversation with Maria while Ernie searched her mind concerning their family. Why, she wondered, had she paid so little attention to the family history? But now Norry mentioned it, she remembered nursery tales about witches in the family. There'd been an ancestress who barely escaped burning at the stake and another was believed very good at healing the sick . . . but what did that have to do with Norry's insistence Jon still lived?

Ernie stared at Norry. Could it be true? Could she have some . . . some *connection* to her husband which kept her aware of how he felt, when he was hurt . . . that he lived or died? But no. Such tales were told to entertain children in the nursery. One didn't grow up and still believe them . . .

Ernie's frown deepened as another memory rose to the surface. The story Ave told, the one where Norry had gone to Jon on a battlefield, rescued him, saved him from death. Nonsense. Not that Norry had not found and rescued Jon. That was fact. But that she had somehow known . . . surely nonsense?

And, if it *were* nonsense, as it *must* be, then Norry couldn't know that Jon lived and must be convinced to go home, must be cared for, loved and coddled and helped. Ernie sighed. Why, when it was so awful, must their father finally be right in his assumptions? Norry, poor beloved Norry, was obviously mad. There could be no other explanation . . .

Could there?

* * *

Only after she and Ave arrived at the Smiths did Ernie remember Ave's comment that Mrs. Smith knew no English. Desperately, she dredged up every bit of the French she'd done her best to forget from the day her father dismissed their French-born French teacher for frightening both girls half out of their wits.

Mademoiselle had insisted Napoleon was a warlock who, once he'd conquered the rest of Europe, would waft his army across the channel! The woman had been explaining the whims of conquering soldiers in graphic detail when Mr. Matthewson happened to pass the schoolroom.

It was the only occasion on which Ernie remembered her father moving that fast or speaking that loudly. Mr. Matthewson had instantly dismissed Mademoiselle and some days later Ernie had heard the poor woman was locked away in a Bedlam, her mind completely turned by her fears of French invasion. Looking back, Ernie suspected the only thing which kept Norry and herself from nightmares was the fact Mademoiselle had been speaking exceedingly rapid French and half the words she'd used were unknown to her students.

But all that had been years ago. French. She must remember her French. Ernie turned her head from Ave to Juana and back. She managed to understand just enough to know that Ave explained the situation to the young woman. Woman? She was so young. Nearly a child. Or was she? Ernie blinked, confused. Just what age was Juana Smith!

Juana shook her head. Her words went on and on with Ernie catching only a few—and most of those were names. She looked to Ave.

"She does not know what Harry said or did to arrange their wedding," he translated. "There is one important difference to their case, however. Juana's aunt was with her and gave permission that the wedding go forward."

Ernie sighed. "And we have no convenient relative whom we may consult. Will it, do you think, make a difference?"

"I don't know. Harry should be back soon. Juana has invited us to eat with them. Since we must be on our way, she says we'll eat early so that we'll not be late returning for practice. And here," he added, lifting his head, "is Brigade-major Smith himself. Hello, Harry!" he added as his friend opened the door and, still talking rapidly to someone who remained in the hall, backed into the room.

A self-contained whirlwind seemed to enter. Finally Ernie managed to overcome her initial impression of tightly leashed energy and see the man. He was smaller than she'd expected, given the stories Ave told as they rode the fifteen or so miles to where the Twenty-first was encamped. Somehow, she'd expected a more heroic figure. But, as she took in the sun darkened skin, the fined-down wiry body, the impression grew that Smith would normally be doing at least three things at a time and was merely being polite by setting himself to do nothing but talk to them in that rapid way he had, words spilling out one after the other in a fast flowing stream.

"My Henri!" said Juana entering the room in almost the same sort of rush as her husband had come in from outside.

"Juana!" More tumbling words, this time in Spanish. A giggle from the petite Spanish girl and the faintest of blushes.

Ernie thought Juana told him to behave himself because they had guests and he must not put her to the blush. Perhaps, thought Ernie, my French returns. She chanced a few words. Juana nodded and encouraged her, occasionally offering a word when Ernie could not go on. The two women went out to where Juana was fixing their meal. When they returned somewhat later, each carrying a tray, Ernie looked toward Ave, her eyes asking a question. He nodded, which meant, she hoped, that he'd discovered what they very much needed to know!

Despite Ernie's problems with her French, the meal was ex-

ceedingly enjoyable. She decided she and Norry would be quite
comfortable staying with the Smiths when they returned for the
regiment's ball. Thinking of the ball and Ave's arrangements,
she wondered if he yet knew that Brigade-major Osgood would
be her escort while he came along with Norry. She decided she
hoped he didn't know—not when she had a long ride ahead of
her, alone with him, all the way from this village to their own.

They left soon after eating and were well over half way home
by a different route when, at an easy pace, they started down a
narrowing trail into a steep sided valley. The valley was filled
with scrub trees which Ernie didn't recognize and heavy underbrush where the trees were not. They'd just reached the bottom
when, swearing softly, Ave grabbed Ernie's reins and pulled their
horses up.

For an instant Ernie felt her temper rising that he should do
such a thing. Then she heard what Ave had heard: the snick of
metal against metal, the clink of a rock hitting another . . . and
then a man stepped into the path some twelve feet in front of
them.

"I speak no Spanish," lied Ave, repeating the words in very
bad Spanish indeed.

"Then we will speak French," said the man in educated tones.
"I must meet with your English command," he added in an
authoritative way. "It is imperative that I organize with them
where it will do the most damage when my men harass the
French."

Ernie was amazed when she managed to follow most of that
and actually understood what was going on.

"You are not bandits, then, but guerrillas?" asked Ave.

The tall, distinguished, but badly dressed gentleman chuckled. "I am no bandit, certainly. I cannot speak for all those with
whom I now make my life. On the other hand, I do know there
are none who have any fondness for the French." His eyes nar-

rowed. "But you have not said you will take me to those in authority."

"I think you'd better tell me a bit more, had you not, before I agree to anything so foolish? How am I to know that you are not a French spy?"

Ernie heard a noise to one side and flicked a glance that way. The face which peered at her from between the trees was the ugliest, most fearsome, face she had ever seen. She bit back a scream, but could not suppress a gasp. The face disappeared. Quickly she looked back toward the man who must be the leader of the creatures hidden by the brush.

"It is an insult, what you suggest!" The man slowly relaxed. "But understandable, perhaps, that you think me a spy. We will speak together," decided the man. "You will dismount and walk forward. If you will give me your parole, you may keep your weapon. If not, you must allow yourself to be disarmed before we meet." The man whistled twice and suddenly eight or ten raggedly dressed, but heavily armed men surrounded them. "You are surprised at the discipline shown by that maneuver?" asked the leader, looking pleased. "You will tell those who command you I am not just the ordinary sort of guerrilla, will you not?" He whistled once and the guns were raised, aimed just over Ave and Ernie's heads. "Your parole?" the stranger asked politely.

Ave gave a glance to Ernie, swore again, and nodded. "My parole."

"Then dismount and follow me. My men will see to the horses."

Ave turned to Ernie. "We must do just as he says, love," he said softly. "Do nothing foolish. Please. This trail was a short cut I took so you'd not have quite so long a ride. It is rarely traveled and we cannot expect help. We must hope the man is what he says he is and truly wishes to set up a liaison with our headquarters."

Her nerves as taut as the strung bow one of the men held, Ernie allowed Ave to help her dismount. She wasn't surprised when he slipped her a knife in the process. She managed to hide it in her skirts before turning toward their host—if one could call him such, given the circumstances. She took Ave's arm and attempted to look as calm as he did as they strolled toward the leader.

"So? Now?" asked Ave.

The gentleman bowed to Ernie and gave his name—one of those exceedingly long and complicated Spanish names as she'd heard was often the case. She nodded and looked to Ave. Ave sighed and introduced first Ernie and then himself. "So, Señor," he said to the Spanish grandeé, one of the highest in the Spanish aristocracy, assuming he wasn't lying about his name, "I think we should get on with this meeting for the simple reason that you will not wish to be discovered by English troops. Our rescue will be organized very soon if Miss Matthewson and I do not return as expected."

"I fear we are late already," said Ernie softly in her stumbling French and looking fearfully—she only had to pretend a very little to produce the expression—around the empty clearing. "We stayed longer than we should have done with our friends."

The foreigner grinned, his teeth white in his deeply tanned face. "You have trained your lady well," he told Ave. "I would not have believed if you had made such a claim, but how can a gentleman doubt the word of such a lovely young woman?" Again he bowed.

Ernie blushed, glanced at Ave who adopted a sardonic expression. "But I am not his lady," she said. "I barely know him. I met him less than a week ago."

The Spaniard sobered, his features stern and his chin lifted aristocratically. His eyes were cold when he asked, "And yet you ride with him with no chaperonage? You are then, no lady?"

"She most certainly *is*," said Ave. He scowled at Ernie. "I have proposed marriage and Miss Matthewson's sister, who is married to my closest friend, has approved. As you know, much greater freedom is given English girls than to your Spanish daughters."

A bittersweet expression crossed the man's face, giving him the look of a sad-eyed hound. "Ah. Daughters. Such a problem as *they* can be. My own daughter has disappeared. My brother searches for her, but what will he find, *if* he finds her? How will she have lived, if she survives? How can she ever hold up her head again among those who should be her friends? Ah, my Maria . . ."

"Maria!" repeated a startled Ernie.

The Spaniard suddenly had a pistol in his hand. Around them others appeared from the brush and raised their weapons, aiming directly at the two English. Menace hung in the air, cooling it, chilling . . . the formerly pleasant gentleman seemed to have turned to ice.

Ernie bit her lip, glancing at Ave. "I shouldn't have said that, perhaps?"

"What do you know of a girl named Maria?" demanded the Spaniard.

"We know a Spanish girl who escaped from her uncle who expected her to marry his friend so that the two of them could share her dowry," said Ernie carefully and in English. "Tell him that," she said, looking to Ave to translate. With a sigh, he did so in the stumbling fashion he'd adopted when first speaking to the Spaniard.

"And this Maria, describe her," was the next demand.

Ave did as well as he could, but since he was pretending his French wasn't all that much more fluent than his Spanish he couldn't make his description anything but what could have been any moderately pretty Spanish girl of good breeding.

"Your *enamorada's* friend says she escaped a marriage arranged by her uncle? She did not run away from her convent?"

"She was taken from her convent by her uncle when her father was thought to have been killed by his general for not supporting him in a coup. Tell him that, Ave."

The man's skin, under his tan, took on a grayish look, revealing he'd understood Ernie's English. "Her full name. What is her full name?"

Ave's face wore a startled look. For a moment he searched his memory, shook his head and then translated the question into English. "Do you know Maria's name?"

Ernie's brows drew together and she shook her head. "I haven't a notion, Ave. My sister didn't introduce her as anything other than Maria. Nor has Bertie . . ."

"My brother told me my foolish romantic child ran away from the convent when she heard I was missing, that she had some thought of finding me." A frown creased the Spaniard's high brow. "It is true, however, that the nuns returned my last letter to my daughter, telling me that in future I must write to where her uncle tells me to write, which is not exactly the same as telling me the child has run away, is it?"

"You believe our Maria may be your Maria?"

"I have had to trust my brother who has overseen the family estates while I've been at war. It is a trust which I gave reluctantly because my brother is a greedy man. Yet there were others to see that he did not cheat the estate too badly and he *is* my brother." An elegant shrug indicated one could believe what one would believe, that that was all he would say on the subject. "But," he continued thoughtfully, "those others should also have seen to the protection of my daughter . . ." He frowned. "But, perhaps this all happened while they were moving to their winter homes . . . ?"

The man seemed to be thinking out loud more than explaining to Ave what he believed. Ave translated softly for Ernie as the Spaniard spoke.

"But if this *is* my daughter . . ."

"*This* Maria was told her father was dead, that her uncle was her guardian and that she must do as he said and since she preferred death to marrying the man chosen for her, she ran away. Tell him that, Ave, please."

For a long moment the Spanish gentleman was silent, thinking. "So your Maria ran away rather than marry her uncle's choice. I wonder," he said, again in that thinking-aloud voice, "just who that choice might have been." He glanced up, around, and said, stiffly, "Assuming, of course, that it is my brother of whom we speak?"

"Again we have no names but . . ." Ernie gave the would-be groom's description as Maria had given it to her. "There is a further problem, perhaps—if this is your daughter. Our Maria has fallen very deeply in love with a British officer of good family. She wishes to wed him. Particularly, she wishes to wed him before her uncle finds her and that must be quickly, because the men the uncle set to find her have. Found her, I mean."

The man looked at his hands, fiddled with the pistol, and put it away. The others in the band relaxed, letting their aim move away from their captives. They faded back into the underbrush and disappeared. "I must see this girl." A haggard look appeared around the man's eyes. "I must know for certain whether it is or is not my daughter."

"And her love for the young officer?" asked Ernie in her bad French, speaking softly and holding the Spaniard's gaze.

A proud arrogant look took possession of the man. He held himself sternly straight. He opened his mouth, obviously to deny that his daughter would ever marry an Englishman—and then Ernie's steady gaze seemed to pierce through to the man's heart. His mouth closed. His stance softened slightly. The arrogant look faded to one of sadness, of resignation.

"He is young," said Ernie, "but he is true and honest and loves our Maria very much."

"And is he wealthy?" asked the Spaniard a trifle sardonically, an ironic expression in his heavy-lidded eyes.

"He is not without income, but he is not wealthy," said Ernie.

"He is, I presume, not heir to his father's estate?"

"He is not the heir."

"Bah," said the grandeé. The father in him, however, sighed. "I will meet this Maria's young man. If she is my daughter, then I will think seriously about their marriage. Times are changing. Things will never be the same ever again. Perhaps it would be best for her to live a new life elsewhere instead of one where the oldsters try to bring back the past and the young fight for a new age. Besides," said the realist, "she's been gone, either from the convent or from her uncle's protection, for so long it would be very nearly impossible to arrange a proper match for her in Spain. It is not possible to have kept secret her disappearance—particularly if my brother and his friend did not wish it kept!" He looked up and met Ave's eyes. "Our discussion concerning my need to arrange liaison with your command will be postponed until we have settled it about this young woman. Ah," he said in an anguished voice, "I must know . . . I *must*. Whatever has happened to her, whatever she has done, she is my daughter and I love her very much."

For a moment silence reigned. Then Ave asked, "We are several miles from the village." He named it. "Will you trust us enough that you will leave your men here?"

For a moment the Spaniard remained perfectly still, his eyes focused on nothing at all. Ernie wondered what went on in his mind, how he reached a decision. When he looked up he had done so, whatever the means. "I will trust you," he said.

Soon the three rode on, this time taking the trail at a faster pace then before. Ernie found, at first, that she was shaking, a tremor of fear passing through her, then fading away, only to be followed by another as she recalled, again, that face peering at her from between the branches. A face, she suddenly recalled, that was not among the half dozen men who surrounded them when they dismounted or again when several stepped into the clearing to train guns on them. It was a face she could not have missed if it had been there.

The band of guerrillas was bigger, must be bigger, than Ave knew. How *much* bigger, only Heaven knew! Ernie told herself she must not forget to tell Ave when they had a moment alone. Not that it mattered, she supposed. If the Spaniard and Ave's superiors came to some arrangement, then surely the size of the band would be revealed so that numbers could be taken into account when plans for its use were made.

Shortly after those thoughts, the three rode up onto the plateau and galloped toward the village. They quickly wended their way through the oddly angled village passages toward Norry's cottage, soon reaching the large open area before it.

A group of men on horseback milled before Norry's house and immediately drew Ernie's attention. "Look," she shouted and whipped up her mount, speeding across the square at a reckless pace.

Swearing roundly, Ave set off after her. The Spaniard, his horse in less excellent condition than the British steeds, followed along as best he could.

Twelve

Ernie had seen that roughly dressed men were attempting to hand a struggling Maria up to a far better dressed man, while others held Norry back. She rode straight into their midst, laying her crop about her in every direction. Maria was released when her captor attempted to protect his head from Ernie's fury. The leader, however, had a cooler head. He raised a wicked looking long barreled pistol and shouted something in Spanish which Ernie couldn't understand. It was easy enough to guess however: the pistol was trained straight at Norry's breast. Defeated, Ernie pulled her mount down, lowering her crop.

"Now," said the Spaniard in heavily accented English, "you, Maria, will come to me or you will watch a bullet destroy that exceedingly ugly gown when the whore's blood is shed."

"No, Tio. No, no."

"Now, Maria. At once . . ." Maria's uncle stopped speaking, swung around in his saddle, swearing, as Ave pulled up, his own gun out and cocked.

"I think you'll have to forego your plans, Señor," said Ave pleasantly. "We have made other arrangements for this afternoon and Maria will be very busy. She cannot go for a ride with you."

A rapid spate of words alerted the milling men and, suddenly, the uncle swooped, picking Maria up and holding her close. "I will kill her if you do not drop that pistol. I will not be interfered with. She is mine to do with as I please . . ."

"I think not," said a new and very cultured voice, speaking coldly in Spanish.

"You." The villain's eyes seemed to pop. "But you are *dead."*

Ernie decided that as soon as possible she *must* set herself to learning Spanish. This not knowing what was going on was not to be borne.

"Papa! Oh, Papa, you are *not* dead. I did not think it. I did not believe Tio when he insisted it was only good sense that you must have been shot by the general."

At least, thought Ernie, that was clear enough. Or at least a very important part of it: the Spaniard they'd met along the trail was indeed Maria's father! So now what? Again Ernie wished she knew Spanish and again watched one speaker and then another, and was exceedingly frustrated to learn little from what was said.

What their new acquaintance was saying was: Those of us who would not follow our general into a coup were given one brief opportunity to disappear. I have never been completely certain whether it was an accident or no." The Spanish grandeé rode closer. "You will, gently, place my beloved daughter on the ground. Then you and your men will leave. I care not where you go, but it must not be to any property to which I lay claim."

His brother sputtered.

"You have betrayed your trust, Carlos. Do you truly expect forgiveness for what you would do?"

"She is a woman. She is nothing. Why should she not marry where it will do the most good? It is the way of the world," blustered the uncle.

"Put her down."

Reluctantly, the uncle did so, letting Maria slide down until her feet touched the ground—but his pistol was still aimed at her head and she obviously didn't dare to move.

The younger man, the uncle, Ernie decided, had something of the look of the grandeé—but more in the way an echo has to the real voice, or a shadow to that which casts it. It must always have grated on the younger man that his brother was taller, more handsome, and with more natural authority and true pride—to say nothing of the inheritance and all that must have meant to a second son of such jealous temperament!

"She is a woman," said the older Spaniard, "but she is also my daughter. She's my responsibility and I'll make any decisions for her future."

A wild ugly laugh broke from the uncle. "Future? But for my friend who is still willing to take her in spite of her undoubtedly impure state, who would have her?"

"I would," spoke a new actor on the scene and Bertie rode out from between two rough rock-walled houses. Maria, forgetting the gun pointed at her head, ran to his side and he lifted her up before him. "You will apologize, at once, for your insult to my fiancée!"

Ernie didn't know what Bertie was saying, exactly, but it was her impression her old friend had, on the instant, matured a dozen more years or so. She wished she dared dismount and go to Norry who seemed to understand what was going on and might translate—but she didn't dare. Any sudden movement might explode the obviously unsettled and ugly situation.

"Apologize? To a whore?"

Bertie rode forward. His crop rose, fell. A slash of red creased the uncle's face. The pistol was raised. A shot fired . . . but it was the Spaniard who screamed, clutching a bleeding hand, not Bertie or Maria.

Ernie turned to where Ave calmly put his pistol into its saddle holster and drew a second from the other. He held it steady on the villain. Bertie, who had thought himself a dead man, slowly untwisted from where he had turned Maria so that his back protected the young woman. He straightened, white of face, but stern of feature.

"All right, Browley?"

"Thanks to you, Colonel."

"Hmm. Set Maria down so that the three women may go into the cottage while we decide what should be done with these men. Señor, your brother is indeed a greedy man. He is also a stupid man. No one of any intelligence would insult another man's daughter to his face in such an idiotic way. I dislike suggesting this when he is your brother, but I do not feel you can trust him to see for himself where his best interests lie . . ."

"I fear you are correct," agreed Maria's father staring sadly at the younger Spanish aristocrat.

The younger wore a hunted look, but had enough pride he didn't whine about his wound, which he had wrapped in a handkerchief.

Ernie, at a nod from Ave, who only looked an order her way, dismounted and went to Maria whom she led up the stairs to the door. Norry quietly opened it, and the three, Norry, Ernie, and Maria, went inside. Once inside Ernie demanded instant translation of what had passed outside, but Norry said that she would have to wait. Instead of recounting the tale Ernie wanted, Norry headed for the kitchen and Maria, suddenly remembering that poor Albert Bacon had tried to protect her, gave a small cry of horror and followed after.

Ernie, after a look to see that Albert had recovered consciousness although obviously not to the point he could do much more than moan, left the others to care for him and returned to watch out one of the small windows. The men had been herded into a small group. They stood passively, awaiting their fate. The uncle waved his unhurt arm, obviously arguing. Maria's father only shook his head, his expression closed and cold. Ernie wished she knew what had been proposed and why the uncle disliked the notion.

She gnashed her teeth. It was stupid to be left out of things this way. Hadn't she, Ernie thought, by recognizing what was happening and by quick action prevented Maria's abduction?

Wasn't it due to her and her alone the men had been prevented from carrying out their foul deed? So why should she be banished to this ignominious position of spying on them!

Her shoulders slumped. Even if outside she'd not understand a word. She didn't know Spanish. Her French was abominable. She'd always been far more interested in horses and the proper management of the stables than in her studies and now she was paying the price for that . . . not that she would have been taught Spanish, in any case. Italian, perhaps . . .

The door opened and Ave strode in. "Are you all right, my dear?" he asked.

"Other than dying of curiosity, you mean?" said Ernie in a biting tone.

He chuckled. "All is well in hand. We must take the scoundrels to our military prison for now. Once we have them under lock and key we'll return and tell all. Do you think Norry can provide a meal for three hungry men?" he asked, teasing.

"I haven't a notion what she can or cannot provide." She waved the point away. "What you are telling me, in fact, is that you'll tell me nothing!"

"Not now. Later, once we've seen to the care and feeding of the villains!" His grin faded as he took another step and reached for her. He pulled her close pushing her head into his tunic. "Damn you, Ernestine Matthewson don't you ever frighten me like that ever again." He pushed her away and shook her gently before pulling her close again and crushing her mouth under his in a brief hard kiss. "Don't you *dare* do anything, ever, to frighten me like that."

Ernie, fighting feelings such as she'd never experienced which had been roused by that brief kiss, glowered at him. "Do you still wonder why I believe a military man should not wed? *Now* do you see just how their wives feel every time there is a battle?"

For half a moment Ave stilled to complete immobility. Then

he seemed to recall something and grinned a cocky grin. "We'll discuss *that* at some future time, too. For now, we'll return soon, my dear. Don't," he added, just before he shut the door behind him, "forget we'll want a good supper waiting."

Maria returned to the front room. "I heard Colonel Sommerton's voice, did I not?" She looked around the room, rushed to the door and opened it. "Where have they gone? Where is my father?" She swung around. "Why is he not here?"

"They are taking your uncle and his men to be locked up until a decision can be made as to their disposition. Then they, including your father, will be back. Ave has ordered that we have a meal prepared for them. A substantial meal."

Maria tipped her head and stared in wonderment at Ernie's angry face. Deciding she'd never understand her new friend, she shrugged. "But of course they will want a meal. They will be hungry, will they not?" One more curious look and she turned away, returning to the kitchen where she immediately began rattling her pots and pans.

Ernie, laughing at herself for over-reacting to what she now believed had been Ave's teasing, followed after, but stopped half way to the door, sobering as she remembered that kiss and the way it had instantly scrambled her insides into knots—hot knots that melted in hot searing waves and were instantly retied, only to dissolve again in the heat which followed. *Was this why women became subservient to men? Because the creatures could induce those fiery, wanting feelings and a woman hadn't the strength of will to fight them?*

Ernie turned away from the kitchen and walked as a sleepwalker walks to her room. She lay down, throwing her arm over her eyes. Faint but clear, she relived those moments when the heat of Ave's mouth had coursed in and through her. A moment's panic reached in to twist her innards into entirely different sorts of knots. Ernie sat up and hugged her knees.

The solution was obvious, of course. She must never again

find herself in Ave's embrace! If he never again kissed her she'd never again feel that melting, the weakening, a sense that she must have more . . . more. . . . So she must not allow it to happen. And she wouldn't.

Such a simple solution, really.

So why, then, was she experiencing this equally ridiculous feeling of regret?

Ten minutes later, after washing her face and hands, Ernie was setting the table when a knock sounded on the door. For a moment she hesitated, remembering that ugly face peering from the brush, remembering the men milling around Norry's door . . .

"Who is it?" she called.

"Lieutenant Holles. I've come to see if Miss Matthewson is ill . . . Is that Miss Matthewson?"

Ernie opened the door, faintly embarrassed. "In all the excitement, I fear we forgot practice, did we not?"

"I think you must have done," said Holles, frowning, his features stiff with outrage. When he continued, it was clear to Ernie he was on his high horse. "I, personally, don't see how anyone could forget something so important, but I suppose, in other minds, there might be some acceptable excuse . . . ?"

"After being temporarily captured by Spanish guerrillas and later occupied with interfering in an abduction, I haven't a notion why we managed to forget something so crucial, so utterly important, as play practice," responded Ernie, bitingly.

"Guerrillas? A kidnapping?" He eyed her suspiciously. "You jest, of course."

Ernie wished she were not quite so ladylike and that she could kick him in the shin. "I jest not."

"But there are no guerrillas within many miles of here and surely they haven't taken to kidnapping English women."

"You speak with a great deal of scorn, Lieutenant Holles, as if you thought I'd made it all up." Ernie glared. "I do not make up tales for children. You, however, are enough to make one think it might be just the thing, you with your childish involvement with the theater. Perhaps," she added when he'd have spoken, "I should add that there was an evil uncle and a lost father and a brave lover involved."

Relaxing, he chuckled. "You have such a delightful sense of humor!" When she didn't laugh he gave her a wary, questioning look. "Surely you are jesting?"

The door opened and three men strolled in. Ernie turned to them, passing quickly over Bertie's glowing face and Ave's questioning look to the Spaniard's obvious agitation. "Your daughter is through that door, Señor," said Ernie in her bad French. She added a gentle warning. "She awaits your return both very anxious to see you and exceedingly fearful of your decision for her future."

"She will be anxious for no longer than it takes to explain," said the Spaniard. He disappeared into the kitchen and Norry, after a moment came out, leaving the father and daughter together.

"Maria's *father?*" asked Holles, scratching his head.

"Did you," asked Ernie, turning to Ave, "get those villains under lock and key? Is Maria truly safe from her evil uncle's machinations?"

"Evil uncle!" Holles grew very red in the face.

"He'll never bother her again. Several officers have leave to spend time in Lisbon, going along while Wellington is there for the ceremony where he'll be made Duque da Victoria. They'll be detailed to put the Spaniard and his men on board one of the ships in a convoy which leaves for Brazil soon. Letters will go both to the British consulate there and to the Portuguese court-in-exile. Our villain will find a cold welcome, but he'll not be allowed to leave, either. Maria need never again fear she'll be kidnapped."

"Kidnapped." This time Holles sounded resigned. "I suppose," he added, "that the villains were guerrillas?"

"Heavens no," said Ernie, all wide-eyed innocence. "Whatever gave you that idea?"

Holles looked befuddled. "But you said . . ."

The Spaniard and Maria returned from the kitchen in time to hear the last exchange. "I," he said in stilted English, "am the guerrilla."

Holles spun around to face the tall man, distinguished looking even in his badly damaged and dirty clothing.

"I told you a few minor things happened to put play practice out of our minds," said Ernie softly.

Ave heard her and slapped his forehead. "Practice! We were to get back in time for practice. Hell and damnation—excuse me, Norry, but it is enough to make any man swear. We've so little time . . ."

"I put the others through their scenes and we worked on their lines," said a subdued Holles diffidently. "I didn't think you'd want to waste the time, wherever you happened to be," he added bitterly, still certain in his own mind that the practice was far more important than an obviously over-dramatized story of guerrillas and attempted kidnappings.

Norry bit her lip. She and Maria had had great difficulty putting together enough food for three extra. She truly didn't have enough to invite Lieutenant Holles to dine as well. She looked toward Ave, toward the table and on to Holles.

Ave nodded understanding. "Well, Holles, I'd say you did well under difficult conditions. We'll practice tomorrow and, hopefully nothing else will come up so that I miss it again! Tonight, however, we've family problems which must be sorted out and I must ask you to remove yourself from Mrs. Lock-

wood's home—if it were otherwise, of course, you'd be welcome
to stay, but as it is, I fear you're not."

Holles sent a startled look around the room, settled on Bertie
who might possibly be able to enlighten him, and said as casually as he could, "Well, Browley, in that case, should we be on
our way?"

Bertie looked at his fingernails. "Sorry, old man. I appear
to be part of the family problem. See you tomorrow when we
establish the pickets?"

Defeated, Holles bowed to Norry, moved gracefully to grasp
Ernie's hand which he raised to kiss. She jerked it away before
he could do so and he eyed her with a sorrowful, I-forgive-you,
look that angered her the more. A faint scowl creased Holles's
brow when he turned to bow to Maria who immediately sidled
a step nearer her father . . . and then, totally routed he departed,
retaining what dignity he could manage.

"I am glad *he's* gone," Maria said naively. "We've barely
enough to feed the rest of us and I very much feared we'd find
it necessary to ask the lieutenant to join us and then we would
have all gone hungry." She frowned fiercely. "It was very bad
of him to arrive just at this very moment, I think."

"Quite unthinking of him," agreed Ernie solemnly.

Ave's eyes twinkled and he added, "I'll really have to speak
to the cub about his atrocious manners, will I not?"

"He is very young," said the Spaniard, not quite certain
whether his new acquaintances were serious.

Norry took in a great breath and let it out. "I believe our
best course is to serve the meal now before anyone else comes
to the door—someone a trifle harder to be rid of! Wellington
himself perhaps?" she queried after a moment's thought and
most everyone laughed. Again the poor Spaniard couldn't be
certain of the jest.

The meal passed with little conversation, as everyone stilled
appetites roused by danger and successfully overcoming it. Af-

ter dinner Norry brought in more of their precious coffee and everyone settled around the small fireplace. Ernie remembered her desire for a small yule log, but put the thought from her. Now was no time to worry about Christmas even though it was fast approaching.

A silence filled the room. Finally Maria, who had seated herself on the floor near her father's legs, looked up. "Papa?"

"Hmm. My dear, I only wish that you would agree to a longer engagement. You have known this young man for only a very brief time."

"We wish to wed, Papa. We wish it very much."

"I want to have her where I can care for her," inserted Bertie, his fond gaze resting on Maria's features.

"War is uncertain and you a soldier . . ." said the father.

"Which, Papa, is why we must marry *now*. We cannot know what the future brings to us. We would have the *now* for our own."

"The impetuosity of youth," said the Spaniard softly in his native tongue.

Norry softly translated when Ernie looked at her questioningly.

"The sad, unthinking impetuosity of youth." The Spaniard slapped his hands down on the arms of his chair. "And who is to say they are wrong? I had so little time with my own dear wife . . ." He trailed off and memories made shadows in his eyes.

"Papa?" asked Maria. Her hands moved to cover one of his and his turned to clasp hers in return.

"Ah," he said, smiling sadly, "all that is gone now. And, as my wise little daughter has said, who is to know what the future brings. Perhaps, if we survive, we will go into a future so different we'll none of us understand it, or have a place in it." His head snapped up and he looked at Bertie. "Which is another way of saying that I haven't a notion whether Maria's property, that which I've set aside for her dowry, will ever come to her. I can have brought to her her mother's jewels which she is also to have upon her marriage. That I can easily do. There are several valuable pieces which, if sold, and the money invested, should bring you in a reasonable income. I do not know . . ." He shook his head. "No, one cannot know whether Maria will ever have the income from her estates in Spain as she should be able to expect because, even if they survive this war, they will be in such condition money will need to be put *into* them . . . no, I do not know . . ."

Bertie diffidently explained his financial situation which was better than Ernie had known. "I will set up as generous a widow's portion as I can—just in case something happens to me. I would want to know that Maria was financially secure," he said with dignity. "And I will not put conditions on it. It will be hers. I would wish her to remarry if I were to die young and a suitable portion will always help any new marriage which she might wish to enter."

"Bertie . . . no!" Scrambling along on her knees, Maria leaned against Bertie's knees. "How can you even think such things!"

"But you have already said that one cannot know the future, my love. If I were to die, I would *want* you to find love again. Do you think me so selfish that I'd wish you to grieve forever?" He touched her hair gently. "Maria, Maria, have we talked so often and about so many things and still you do not know me?" He lifted her face until she was, reluctantly, forced to meet his eyes.

Again Ernie had the feeling that the Bertie she had known was gone, was somehow, against all expectation, grown much older and far more mature. Such philosophy was so unlike the Bertie she knew, the childhood playmate, the enthusiastic young officer. Obviously he was not so impervious as she had thought to the dangers of war and no longer reveled in such things as glory and heroics and all they had played at as children. Ernie looked toward Ave, but his sober gaze was on the pair of young lovers.

"Forgive me, Bertie?" asked Maria.

"Of course," he whispered.

Again the Spaniard slapped his hands down on the arms of his chair. "Maria, you will come to order. Such behavior is not suitable for my daughter, as I'm quite certain the good sisters taught you well. You are my daughter and you will behave as such"—he smiled a rather wry smile—"at least you will until this marriage may be arranged between the two of you, which I understand will not take long?"

Wide-eyed and hopeful, Maria looked around. "It is settled then? I may marry my Bertie?"

"It is settled. I believe him a good man and that he will treat you well. I approve your choice, child, but I'm not quite certain I forgive you for having the audacity to make it all on your own. Children can not be trusted in such things. They should leave the choice of mate to older and wiser heads."

"Such as my uncle's?" asked Maria daringly.

The Spaniard threw back his head and laughed. "I see you have already been corrupted into the English miss's pert ways, my child. Well, I forgive you that, too, for you are soon to be English, are you not?"

"Soon. Oh, very soon!"

"I think we may arrange it in a day or two," said Ave. "Harry Smith gave me the details and now that we have you, Señor, for legal permission, then there should be no problem. Have either of you," he added, looking from Bertie to Maria, "a suggestion as to when and where this wedding should be performed?"

"Wherever and whenever my Bertie decides," said Maria promptly.

Bertie grinned. "Now? Here?" He laughed. "I know that's impossible." He was silent for a thoughtful moment. "There is

to be a review of troops day after tomorrow. The Marquess of
Wellington is to honor the regiment with his presence for a time
after he reviews us." Bertie turned to Ave. "Do you think he
would also honor Maria and myself by attending the marriage
service? It will be brief and nothing like the formal service and
decorated church and half-dozen attendants—all those things
you deserve, my love—but I would like it if the commander
could attend . . . ?"

"I'll send him a message to that affect," said Ave. "He has
a romantical side, you know, and I think will enjoy witnessing
your wedding. Señor, will you attend?"

"Would it, perhaps, be a proper occasion to introduce me to
Wellington?" asked the Spaniard. "I cannot, must not, in fact,"
he added apologetically, "forget my duty even with the excitement of seeing my daughter properly married. I think the special
circumstances would make a good opportunity for an introduction . . ."

"I will make mention of that as well, when I write to headquarters." Ave nodded. "And your men?"

"I will return to them now and they will make a camp until
I return. It is easily arranged."

"They will need supplies . . ."

The Spaniard's sardonic expression stopped Ave's offer of
help. "I think you need not worry about supplies."

He spoke in such a dry way that Ernie wondered again what
had been discussed. Norry translated for her and again Ernie
vowed she'd begin studying her languages . . . although why
she should wish to when, very soon, she would take Norry
home to England where they needed nothing but their native
tongue . . . !

Ernie forced herself to listen and do her best to follow a
conversation which took place in three languages and drove her
just a little bit crazy. The intense concentration needed to do so

made her excessively tired—or so she discovered when everyone but Ave had gone. She yawned.

"I do wish I didn't have this effect on you," said Ave softly from far too near.

Ernie looked around and discovered she had been left alone with him. She looked up to meet his eyes, a faintly worried expression in her own. "What effect?" she asked cautiously.

"This is not the first time you've yawned in my presence," he said, tongue in cheek.

"This is not the first time you find me so tired I don't know if I'm coming or going."

"Ah! Then you should listen to me, my love. I know *exactly* where you're going, or, as the case is now, coming." Ernie blinked, raised questioning eyes to meet his twinkling gaze. "You, my dear, are coming straight into my arms."

"No." She pushed against his hands which held her lightly. It did no good, his fingers only tightening slightly.

"No? But you said you didn't know and now I've told you and you do know." As he spoke he drew her closer and her panic grew. "What is it, love? Why do you look so?"

"Let me go."

"Not just yet."

"Ave, you must let me go! Please!"

It was his turn to frown. "Why does this not sound like my Ernie? My Ernie would not beg," he added.

"Ave, please."

He heard panic in her voice. "Ernie, you must tell me what is wrong."

"You mustn't kiss me. You must *not.* I cannot fight you because you are too strong. I can only plead with you not to do something which I fear I cannot resist—especially when I am completely exhausted as I am now."

For a long moment he considered her words. "But, for my own sake, kissing you now is just what I *should* do."

"No." She shook her head, again pushing against him. "You do not understand!"

"I think perhaps it is you who do not understand," he said and lowered his lips toward hers. "You have not yet understood how much I love and need you . . ."

This time his kiss was a soft exploration which didn't produce knots. Not knots: merely loops of ribbon and bows and a gentle warmth which insidiously seduced her tired senses. She leaned against him, melting into his embrace, almost—but not quite—wanting to feel again those wonderful knots of sensation his first kiss induced.

Then, remembering those intriguingly frightening sensations, she pulled back. He looked at her and she looked back. Their gazes locked, each searching for they knew not what. Not knowledge of the other's love. Each was now quite certain they had that. No, this was a search for something different.

Perhaps it was a hunt for Ernie's trust on Ave's part.

Perhaps it was for assurance he'd go no more into danger on Ernie's.

Whatever it was, neither found that for which what they looked. With a sigh Ave loosened his hold; with a matching sigh, Ernie backed away.

"I'm sorry," he said.

"I, too, am sorry. It will not do, Ave," she said sadly.

"Think you not?" he asked.

"I'm a coward. I fear losing you far too much to ever want to wed you in the first place." She eyed the widening grin on the man's face. "Ave, you wouldn't wish to take a coward to wife."

"A coward rode pell-mell right into the middle of a bunch of villains today and hit about her with her crop?" He chuckled softly, his eyes bright with laughter.

She shrugged, waving the humor away impatiently. "I was in no particular danger. I knew you'd be right behind me. Besides, that is not the sort of danger I fear. I know I can be hurt physically. That I might even be killed." She shook her head. "Ave, it is the emotional pain I fear to the point of panic. You must not continue pressing me this way. You *must* not."

"Ah." Again his gaze caught hers and held it. "You would wish on *me* the emotional pain of losing *you*."

Her face crumpled and she turned away, her shoulders slumped and her head bowed. "Unfair," she said.

"Yes. I suppose it was. Men are not expected to have deep emotions or to reveal that they can hurt. Perhaps you did not know, but one reason a man needs a wife is that, to her, he *can* reveal and discuss those weaknesses he won't allow another man to suspect he feels. We all feel them. Despite the barriers convention sets up to prevent us from turning into maudlin heaps of emotion, the emotions are there." He eyed her, but didn't find the weakening he'd hoped to see. "I need you more than I can say. Don't ever believe otherwise, my love," he said softly.

Ernie ignored his covert invitation to discuss his fears, his hopes, his emotions . . . the panic rose higher within her. "I must convince Norry to go home. Soon."

"Norry must go home, yes." The softness in that comment was hardened in his next. "You, my love, are destined to be my wife."

"It is a fate I'll not allow."

"Will you not? We'll see. You mistake your courage, my dear. You have more courage than any other woman I've known. You will find it is true and you will marry me. You'll see."

Ernie drew in a deep ragged breath. "I will not marry a soldier. I will *not*."

For a long moment Ave held her gaze, then looked away. He could settle this so quickly if only he could bring himself to tell her that he as well as Norry must return to England, that she would *not* be marrying a soldier.

A silent if derisive chuckle shook him: when that happened she'd find herself wedding something as bad if not worse, a nearly impoverished peer! His lips compressed. He had this irrational desire to be wed for himself, the man he was . . . and that, simply, was the soldier, the life he'd chosen for himself and not the one thrust on him by his birth.

"What have you planned for tomorrow?" he asked, abruptly changing the subject.

"Tomorrow?" Ernie blinked. "Tomorrow . . ." She forced her mind to consider the coming day. What, she wondered, did they have planned for tomorrow? Ah yes.

Very politely she responded, "We make the Christmas pudding. All our friends must come by to give the pudding a stir and make a wish. Just as is being done in kitchens all over England."

"I'll look forward to it," he said.

For a moment Ernie thought he was being merely polite. Then she saw he truly meant it. For the first time she believed what Norry had said, that the troops tried in every way they could to celebrate Christmas just as they would if they were at home.

He smiled down at her, his eyes promising things she wished she dared allow. "It's been many years since I made a wish on a Christmas pudding, my love. I certainly won't waste this one!"

Ernie closed her eyes against her intuitive understanding of the wish he'd make: she'd not marry a soldier, whatever he wished.

And that was *that*.

Wasn't it?

Thirteen

Ernie looked around the crowded noisy kitchen and, for the first time since she'd arrived in Portugal, Christmas felt real, something to which she could look forward. She wondered how soldiers such as Ave who had not been home for many years managed to retain the abiding love of Christmas, the wonderful closeness of family. How did women who lived abroad—such as those in the heat of India or the wilds of the new world—manage the traditions to which, in England, one never gave a thought . . . unless, for some reason, they were missing, as they had been the first year her mother died.

Since that awful year Ernie had had an extra special feeling for Christmas. It had somehow, by its very disappearance from her life, become far more important to her than it sometimes appeared to be to others. Too many seemed to Ernie to take this very special day for granted.

Ernie leaned against the kitchen wall and folded her arms across her chest. The satisfied feeling inside her grew as she watched still another young officer give the Christmas pudding a stir. He had his eyes closed very tightly, his face screwed up in concentration. No one laughed at him, however. Too many of these boys—she couldn't help but feel they were only boys, although some were her own age or even older! But too many of them were away from home for the first time and were, quite obviously, missing it very much indeed.

Poor lads. Ernie had begun by feeling bewildered when a

small group of near strangers arrived at Norry's door and asked, diffidently, if they might give the pudding a stir. Before those finished and left, another pair had arrived. And then arrivals, both known and unknown, came in a steady stream. Ernie's teeth flashed in a sudden grin: this was, surely, the best stirred pudding in the whole of Christendom!

She looked across the room to where Norry stood in much the same posture as her own. Their eyes met. Norry smiled. That very special closeness which had been theirs in childhood returned to flow back and forth between them, warming her.

Beside Norry stood Bertie, his arm around Maria, holding her close. Maria's father, bemused by this strange English custom, had found a corner for himself. Bemused, yes, yet he obviously approved whatever it was he was thinking. That warmth inside Ernie billowed into a great pillow of softness which she wondered if she could contain or if, perhaps, she'd simply burst all over Norry's clean kitchen—or maybe float away and hover, like an angel, up against the ceiling.

Ernie looked once again toward the door and the billows settled, collapsed. *One* person had not come to make his wish. A wish he said he'd not waste. A wish he'd assured her was important to him.

Where was Colonel Sommerton! Why had he not yet come? They couldn't allow the stirring to go on forever! At some point, the pudding must be poured into the pudding bag which Ernie had packed with the necessary ingredients. It must be carried to Lady Colonel Barton's where the chef had a proper pudding basin in which to boil it. Ernie sighed. Softly. One small problem with using Lady Barton's kitchen was that the lovely smells, another tradition of Christmas, would permeate the Barton house instead of their own . . .

But one was living with an army. One counted the good things and pushed from one's mind the bad. It had, after all, only been a lucky thought that she could bring what was needed which had allowed them to have the pudding at all. She would remember that.

As the time arrived that men now on duty must be relieved, Norry cleared her house of strangers. "Hurry, now," she said to Ernie. "We'll fix this for Albert Bacon to carry to Lady Barton's where the chef has assured me it will be done to perfection. But with it gone, we must stir up something else as quickly as we can."

"Stir up more of this strange thing you call a pudding?" asked Maria, curiously.

"What we stir up won't be a pudding because we've used up some of the special ingredients, but whatever we make, we must hurry and do it quickly. Something, anything . . ."

"But why?" asked the Spanish girl.

"Isn't it obvious?" asked Norry, the old mischievous smile crossing her face. "As soon as those coming off duty wash up and change into their very best uniforms, we'll be inundated by more visitors! This pudding," she said, as she poured it carefully into the bag Ernie held for her, "will be ruined if we do not get it off now. Those who are coming will not know or care for the difference—that what they stir is not this one. They will only care that they have *had* a stir and made their wish. Don't you see?"

Ernie had already understood and asked Maria to measure out more flour and some of their precious butter. "We've spices and raisins," she mused and set Bertie and, much to his surprise, Maria's father to stoning the latter. "Surely we can come up with something which, if not a pudding, will still have the smell of Christmas about it!"

The afternoon proceeded much as the morning had done . . . and still no Colonel Sommerton. It was more than a little disturbing, although Ernie refused to admit that to anyone but herself.

Actually, whenever she remembered she should *not* feel such disturbance, she'd not admit it to *herself* either!

* * *

Colonel Lord Avenel Sommerton—or Colonel Lord Mowtrey, as Wellington persisted in calling him—sat with his commanding officer going over lists and making notes and, figuratively, gnashing his teeth.

The message from headquarters had arrived as Ave shaved. It demanded the instant presence of the colonel, but, regardless, he'd taken time to write a note excusing himself to Norry from his promise to stop by that morning. By then his favorite hack was tacked up and he rode to the village of Freinada where his initial confrontation with Wellington would ever burn in Ave's memory.

"Colonel Lord Mowtrey," had said Wellington, nodding permission for the younger officer to take a seat facing the windows overlooking the long narrow balcony just outside the room.

Ave remembered drawing in a deep breath. "I've not yet announced that, my lord. I've no desire for the news to be spread at this time. There are reasons . . ."

"You do, I presume," interrupted the stern-visaged, newly invested field marshall, "intend to resign your commission and return to England?"

"Yes sir," admitted Ave. "Just not quite yet."

"Hmm. And just when might you have deigned to inform us of your intentions?" asked his cold-eyed commander.

Ave swallowed. He'd not thought that far ahead, his involvement with Ernie the only item of importance in his view. Foolishly, he'd assumed his decision affected no one but himself—and he should have known better! *Did* know better. *Should he explain?* Ave eyed the faintly disapproving face staring at him from across the field desk. Inwardly, he sighed as he decided he must.

"Sir, I am in something of a muddle just at the moment. There is a young woman, you see. I wish to marry her. She . . .

she says she'll not marry a soldier, and yet I believe she loves me. I've this irrational need for her to say yes to *me*. To the soldier, I mean. I do not *feel* like Lord Mowtrey. But worst of all," he added, a wry grin escaping at the thought, "once she's said yes to the soldier, then I must release her from her promise and explain that I will no longer be one—and that the so-called honors I go home to are a run-down and heavily mortgaged estate, a home which has been allowed to deteriorate for far too many years, and nearly no money with which to set things right. I *think* she'll say yes to what will be a difficult life for far too many years . . . You see, I'm determined to bring my estate back to what it was in my grandfather's time. If she is *not* willing to help me . . ." Ave shrugged.

Ave had gone into rather more detail than he'd meant to do as he'd made his confession to Wellington. Now, when he focused on his commanding officer, he found Wellington staring at him with that faintly pop-eyed look he got when he concentrated fully on something. Ave felt a flush rise up from under his tight collar and heat his ears.

"Sorry, sir," he said. "Didn't mean to run on so . . ."

"Chosen a good little woman, have you?" asked Wellington. "Do I know her?"

"She's Lenore Lockwood's sister, sir, come out to take Mrs. Lockwood home. If I were to remain with the army, she would make an outstanding wife for a soldier. She rides like the devil and does not panic under difficult conditions . . ."

He told Wellington of their meeting with the guerrillas, adding that setting up a meeting with the Spaniard was something which must be discussed before their conference was over.

"As you see, she's a wonderful woman and would do very well when we're campaigning." He chuckled. "It is, however, Miss Matthewson's contention that no soldier should have a family at all. She's gone so far as to say they should all be born orphans!"

Wellington nodded, a smile hovering around his mouth. "There is, perhaps, something to what she says. Lockwood, you say . . . ahh." His brows rose queryingly. *"Major* Lockwood?"

"Yes. Missing for months, but no one can convince his wife—widow!—that he's dead. Ernie, Miss Matthewson, that is, finds her sister's refusal to face facts more than a little distressing which does not help my suit. Unfortunately she's also met that impossible Mrs. White who lost her husband in the siege at Burgos." Ave shrugged, loosening tight muscles. "But none of this is anything with which you need concern yourself, sir."

"Except for one thing, Mowtrey," Wellington reminded Ave. His eyes took on that ice-blue look and his voice that cutting tone which could turn a man of long experience into the rawest recruit. "I must think of a replacement for you for when you decide it is time to admit to your new rank, your inheritance, and your imminent departure from our midst."

"Er, yes sir. Sorry sir."

"At least," said his commander with a hint of humor, "you didn't say 'Sorry sir, *I didn't think, sir'* which is an excuse I am exceedingly tired of hearing." Wellington scrabbled around his desk, found a particular piece of paper and scanned it. "What, by the way, does this memo mean? Since you were the deciding officer in this case, perhaps you can explain it."

He handed Ave a tightly written officer-of-the-day report and pointed to the section concerning the transfer of six Spanish non-combatants to Lisbon and their further transfer to one of the ships leaving soon for Brazil.

"A civil matter," said Ave, a muscle jerking in his jaw. "I'm sorry it was brought to your attention."

"We have procedures for dealing with civil disturbances," said Wellington, his eyes again round and protruding.

"Yes sir." Ave's jaw tightened.

"You do not feel you should have gone through proper channels in dealing with these men?"

"No sir."

Wellington stared. "I'll have the whole story, if you please," he said.

Ave wondered what would happen if he were to say he didn't please. Instead, he explained about Norry's original rescue of Maria, Maria's problems with her uncle, and the nearly unbelievable coincidence of meeting Maria's father along with the guerrillas.

"It has been settled for the best, sir. Maria and young Browley will be married tomorrow after you've reviewed troops. Ah! That reminds me. He asked if I would pass on an invitation to you to attend their wedding, sir. He would very much appreciate your presence." Ave drew in a deep breath. "It would also be an opportunity for you to meet our Spanish gentleman. He does not wish to have it gossiped about that he is acting as liaison between our troops and his guerrillas. He'll have to explain to you why he feels such secrecy would be to his advantage. I'll have to admit I didn't understand it myself, but I've never felt my Spanish entirely adequate and he wasn't speaking French when he explained."

Wellington shrugged. "It is, very likely, merely one more instance of the Spanish love of intrigue of which we've seen so much. Even the best of them can seem to do nothing in the straight-forward manner which we blunt English prefer. I'll meet the man, of course. We'll see what we will see. *After* we've witnessed the wedding that is. I do like a wedding now and then. Does for a rise in morale, although I cannot tell you why . . . now, about the distribution of the new tents!"

The discussion turned to details concerning the apportioning of new equipment such as the large tents which were designed to be easily raised and taken down. There were also new kettles to distribute—a vast improvement over the old to which neither man referred: those heavy old kettles, which took forever to heat, had been, by implication, the subject of one clause in a scathing memo from Wellington written after the disastrous retreat from Burgos but before he'd learned of the errant commissariat. The memo had very nearly been the cause of mutiny among his officers and morale had been lowered to what one hoped would be a nadir in the final history of the Peninsular war.

The meeting with Wellington, who was departing within the next few days for the coast, finally ended, leaving Ave with a thick handful of orders which he must now see executed. Exiting the commander's chilly office, he searched for the three staff officers with whom he must now deal. That meeting went on for more hours than he cared to remember but had, finally, resolved all the problems raised by the orders.

As Ave trotted back down the road to where his regiment had its winter quarters the darkness was only partly relieved by a half moon seen now and again through skittering clouds. Ave's disappointment was partially soothed by the thought that Ernie knew where he'd been all day. Thank Heaven I wrote to her that I'd no idea at all when I might return . . . but I do wish I'd had my chance with the pudding, he finished sadly to himself.

Since it was so late, Ave went directly to his own room. He felt one more twinge of regret that he'd not managed to stir Ernie's pudding, but the twinge faded. He was tired from the long day of paperwork, the incredible difficulty they'd faced, working out logistics for re-provisioning the army. Thank Heaven the new officer in charge of the commissariat was competent. With any luck, this next spring's push into Spain would be the final assault against the French and remove them from Spanish soil forever . . .

Ah, thought the drowsy man, but it will not be my problem, pushing the frogs over the Pyrenees . . . strange, he added, just before slipping over into sleep. How very strange. I don't feel the least bit of regret I'll not be here to help. I'll be in England—with Ernie. An amused smiled played around his lips. With Ernie, so . . . Perhaps not so very strange after all . . . ?

* * *

Ernie, who had not received Ave's message, had far more difficulty falling asleep. She could not believe Ave Sommerton had merely forgotten. He wasn't the sort to forget anything. Besides, she was certain he'd looked forward to it . . . so why had he not come to give the pudding a stir? What could possibly have kept him from something so important . . . or was she wrong. Had he forgotten for the simple reason it was unimportant in his scheme of things?

No matter how well she sometimes thought she knew the man, it was true that theirs had not been a long acquaintance. She counted up and was surprised to discover it was no more than weeks! Perhaps, thought Ernie wearily, I am merely making up the person I wish the colonel to be and he is nothing like that at all . . . perhaps he has been flirting with me, teasing me, acting the part of the sort of man he thinks I most admire . . .

Oh dear. What a terrible notion *that* was. But how could one know another's mind and heart? Really *know?* Ernie flopped over on her other side, managing to do so without falling off the narrow cot as she'd done the first time she'd rolled over on it. Very likely, decided Ernie, bitterly, he isn't anything at all like I think he is and not really anything special and perhaps even no one I'd ever wish to know if we were at home where he didn't wear that uniform and he didn't look at one as if . . .

But no, one wasn't to think of Ave's eyes and how they looked at her in that special way he had . . . except that that sort of look was one reason why one had begun to think . . .

But it *wouldn't do.* Whatever it was she'd begun to think, and Ernie didn't wish to examine the rest of that particular thought too closely, it simply wouldn't do. Ave Sommerton was involved in the theater, was director of the play they were putting on all too soon, so very likely he was also an actor. Perhaps that look

she found so enticing, so very heart warming, was merely acting . . . ?

And there she went again. *It wouldn't do.*

Having come to that firm decision—again—Ernie wondered
why it seemed to take forever before her tired body relaxed and
her tired mind drifted away into sleep.

The next morning Maria was in the kitchen washing her hair
and unaware when an altercation outside their door roused
Norry and Ernie from their breakfast. Norry was now wearing
her pistol in a holster slung from her shoulder, across her
breasts, and hanging at her side like a baldric. This time when
she opened the door she had the gun in her hand: never again
was she going to have rough men come uninvited into her home
and very nearly carry off one of her household as had nearly
happened to Maria!

"What," she asked, "is the meaning of this?"

Lieutenant Holles and Brigade-major Osgood fell away from
each other but, although they were no longer very nearly nose
to nose, they still glared, not at all pleased the other was there.

"Well?" asked Norry, holstering her pistol.

Osgood bowed. "I've come to offer my escort to Miss Matthewson and, of course, to yourself, to this morning's Review."

"I," insisted Holles, "have come at Colonel Sommerton's
orders and with his compliments to escort the two of you to the
Review! Surely you must see that this . . . this . . ." Holles,
never at a loss for words, seemed, for once, unable to finish his
sentence—at least, in a manner suitable for feminine ears. He
snapped to attention. "Mrs. Major Lockwood, you must see that
I must be allowed to do my duty as ordered."

Norry's eyes twinkled and opened her mouth to reply. Ernie
feared what she might say.

"It is very kind of both of you," responded Ernie before her

older sister could interfere, "but we've arranged to go with—"
At the last instant she remembered Bertie would be busy and
unavailable—"Lady Colonel Barton and will have no need of
either of you for escort. Thank you just the same." Rudely, she
pulled Norry into the house and shut the door. She leaned back
against it and glared. "Norry, don't you dare suggest they might
both go with us. I don't want either one of them."

"No, I can see that. But Ave will be busy for hours and
unavailable. You've no notion of the complications which can
arise organizing a Review. And we've made no arrangements
of which *I'm* aware to go with Bertha—Lady Barton, I mean."

"Of course we have not, but do you really think it would be
at all comfortable to have those . . . those . . ."

". . . poor bennish clunches?"

Ernie, about to agree, stopped, her mouth open. She closed
it and, after a moment, asked, "What?"

"Poor bennish clunches," repeated her sister agreeably, the
impish smile Ernie loved playing around her lips.

"Is that cant?"

"Of course," she answered and hastened to add, "Of the
milder sort and not at all nasty."

"Well, when we go home, you'd better not let Father hear
you using it—even if it isn't the nasty sort." Before Norry could
object, again, to the notion of leaving Portugal, Ernie went on
to ask, "What does the expression mean?"

"Poor foolish clowns."

"Hmm. Foolish yes. Clowns? Do you think . . . ? Well . . ."
she continued, answering her own partially phrased question,
"Perhaps Holles. If it were on a stage, he'd gladly play the clown
if that were the only role available to him." She tipped her head
thoughtfully. "Come to that, he is Bottom in the play we're supposed to be doing, you know, and there are few parts in Shakespeare more clownish."

Norry peeked through the window. "They are still out there."

"Still prepared to come to blows?"

"I don't think so. Ah . . ."

"What? What's happening?"

"Nothing. Or, nothing important, anyway. Osgood just produced a pair of dice. I don't think they intend to leave, Ernie. Now what?"

"Now what about what?"

"You told them a lie," said Norry patiently. "How are you going to get us out of that?"

"Easy," said Ernie, her fertile mind immediately finding a solution. With a quirk to her mouth, she went to the door. "Gentlemen, I think you must, yourselves, get to wherever the Review is to be held?" They nodded. "You had best be off then. We intend to go much later. Norry finds long days far too tiring, you know. Goodbye." She closed the door and then leaned against it.

"Did you have to add that last?" asked Norry. "I'm *never* tired."

"When," asked Ernie, "will you admit that, at times, now, you do?"

Norry's expression became one of extreme wariness. "Whatever can you possibly mean?"

Ernie sighed. "Am I wrong? Ah well. Never mind then." For an instant she stared at her sister's middle, but then turned back to the table and her now cold breakfast. "Have you noticed that since we ran out of bacon, we no longer seem to have so many visitors arriving in time for breakfast?"

Norry waved that away, thinking. "Ernie," she asked after a moment, "What do you have in mind for us to do if we do *not* accept their escort? I mean how are we to get there?"

Ernie paced from one side of the room to the other, a piece of toast in her hand. She took a bite, chewed, swallowed—and turned as Maria came into the room, her hair wound up in a towel.

"Let me brush that for you," Ernie offered, shoving the last bite into the mouth. She settled Maria on a stool by the corner fireplace and began brushing. Then she paused, the brush hovering over a long tress. "Norry," she said, "it is obvious what we do! Maria, is your father not coming to escort you to your wedding?"

"He comes, yes, but not until after lunch . . ." said Maria, blushing.

"Ah. My sister and me, as official bridesmaid—we must go with you, must we not?"

"I would like that," said Maria, smiling a bit shyly. "I truly wish to marry my Bertie, but now that it is almost time . . ." She looked around at Norry. "Did you, perhaps, feel the butterfly in your tummy and wonder if you did the right thing?" she asked.

"On the morning before I met my Jon at the altar?" asked Norry. "I never doubted but that we were doing the right thing. However I did have flutters and twitches and fears of the unknown which was only sensible, was it not? It is not easy to turn one's life upside down and begin it all over again. Marriage very definitely is a new beginning because one can no longer think only in terms of oneself but must think as two together. It is not at all easy!" Norry took herself to the breakfast table and looked at her cold omelet. She sat and absently took a bite.

"Was it worth it?" asked Ernie softly, referring to Norry's recent widowhood.

"Marriage? To my Jon?" Norry looked at her sister, her surprise evident. "Of course it is worth it."

Is . . . ? Pulling the brush down through Maria's lovely long hair, Ernie found herself still again wishing to avoid a confrontation. But how would she ever convince Norry to go home, if she could not bring herself to mention the subject? Norry *must* be made to face her widowhood!

"Norry . . ."

"If you are thinking, again, that Jon must be dead, I tell you, still again, he is not. He lives and he will come home. Soon."

"If only such a miracle were possible." Ernie brushed and brushed. "Norry, if he does not?" she finally asked.

"I don't understand why you will not believe me," said Norry, almost plaintively. "He is coming home. I *know*."

"How can you know?"

"How can I *not* know?" asked Norry with great simplicity and returned to eating her breakfast.

"Is that supposed to make sense?" asked Ernie as she continued to brush Maria's long dark locks of damp hair.

Norry lifted her head and for a long moment stared at her. "Ernie, can it possibly be that you *don't* know about our ancestress? Either of them?"

"I remember a few tales told in the nursery for the entertainment of children."

Norry shook her head. "Poor Ernie. I wish you too might have the art, but quite obviously you've none at all or you wouldn't argue with me. You too would know—or at least know *how* I know."

Ernie paused in her brushing. Could Norry actually have some witchy power? she wondered. But how could it be? Such things were nonsense, were they not? Tales for children? Of course they were!

Maria reached up and touched Ernie's hand. Ernie glanced down and met her eyes. Maria shook her head. "Do not distress her," she said softly. "She speaks truly."

Ernie went back to brushing. What did Maria mean by that? What could she mean?

Ernie decided she must remember to ask—when Norry wasn't seated a few feet away chewing on cold egg. Ernie repressed a shudder. How could anyone eat it? The remains of her own omelet sat congealing on her plate, swirls of the oil in which it was cooked surrounding it. Then Ernie remembered

Norry's tales of traveling with the army, of days of steady rain when no fires could be built, when even hot water for tea was unavailable! Ernie shook her head. Perhaps, under those conditions, even cold omelet would be desirable!

As the morning progressed, time, which had crawled, began to pass much too quickly. Maria carefully pressed her wedding gown which must somehow be transferred to the parade grounds. Ernie wondered if a tent would be available in which the bride could change. She shrugged. If nothing else, there would be a grove of trees or a clump of bushes—or, if necessary, a circle of women with skirts and hats and parasols!

All too soon Maria's father arrived. Someone had helped him clean his clothes, mending the worst rips and replacing lost buttons with others which nearly matched. His leather was polished to a shine and the three horses brushed to a fare-thee-well, a Spanish pillion saddle found to put on Maria's father's large boned roan so she might ride behind him. Flowers had been tied to the bridles and all looked very festive.

The Spanish gentleman smiled at his daughter. "I feel both happy and unhappy on this auspicious day, my child."

"Unhappy?"

"You go from me to another's care. Because of my duty to Spain, I have, it seems, always left you to another's care and have done so for far too many years. Now, when I foresee my duty ending, foresee the French chased from our land, and a time coming when I might have been able to get to know you again, child . . . ah, it is like everything in life: too late for what should have been."

"When this war is ended, you will visit us."

"When this war is ended, my child, there will be another," he said gently. "Somewhere. There are always wars, it seems."

Maria's eyes widened and her skin paled slightly. "You mean my Bertie will *always* be a soldier . . ."

"Not necessarily," said the Spaniard, seeing how his words

frightened his daughter. "You will inherit broad estates. You already own a goodly estate, for that matter. Once the French are gone, perhaps you and your husband will return to me." He smiled, chucked his daughter under her chin. "I like that notion. Very much."

"Will you discuss it with my Bertie?" she asked shyly.

"Yes. We must have a long talk about your dowry and your inheritance. There has been no time for any detail about such things, but he and I will find time in the next few days before I must return with my new information to my band of guerrillas."

"Do you lead these guerrillas, Papa?"

"No. I call them mine, but I'm no more than a messenger between their leader and the leader of the British forces. I will tell the guerrillas where they may do damage which will help the British. It is what they wish to do." He shrugged.

"Then you will not be fighting?"

Her father hesitated. "Perhaps not."

Maria didn't really notice that he qualified his statement. She'd felt instant relief at the belief her father would no longer be in the midst of battle and turned her thoughts to her wedding. "Had we not better be going?" she asked, looking around nervously.

"Yes. I think we must leave now or we'll have Bertie thinking you've changed your mind," teased Ernie.

Maria paled at the thought. "We must go. At once. I will not have my Bertie worrying about such stupidities and he *would*. *Men*. They never think, do they?"

She looked quite surprised when her father and Ernie, their eyes meeting, laughed at her.

Two hours later Ernie stared across the regimental drum which had become a makeshift altar and straight into Ave's com-

pelling eyes. As the minister read the service she saw the colonel's lips mouthing the responses, felt, as if a warm cloak were
surrounding, warming her, along with the vow he made to her
as Maria and Bertie made theirs.

Deep inside her a conflict waged a war as desperate as any
battle Ave had ever fought. How could she give up this man
who had come to mean so much to her? But how could she do
anything else . . . ? She was the same woman, a *sane* woman,
who had seen and railed about what happened to the women
war hurt, their scars one could not see but felt as if they were
one's own. She was far too sensible to put herself into their
position. Was she not? And yet there was this yearning, this
need, this feeling the two of them were meant to be one . . .

But it could not be.

Ernie forced her attention away from Ave, turned to look at
the young couple standing before the altar, their wedding nearly
over. Bertie, sterner, paler, more determined . . .

Maria, young looking, stars in her eyes and, from somewhere,
a new maturity, new stature, an instant matronliness . . .

Maria's father stood nearby, proud, a little sad, a lot weary
from too many years of war. Bertie's friends, waiting to celebrate this sudden and unexpected wedding, full of anticipation
for the party which had been quickly arranged for that evening.
Wellington, too, standing by, indulgent and patient and very
likely—or so Norry had warned Maria—the first to kiss the
new bride before going off to his duties elsewhere . . .

For a moment Ernie stared in awe at the man who, in, a few
short years, had risen from a second son to a position equal in
rank to that of his brother. Richard, the older, was by birth the
Marquis of Wellesley—Arthur, the younger, had not so very
long ago been created the Marquess of Wellington. This rather
short man, then, with his pale-blue eyes and smiling face, his
loud laugh and pleasant manner, was the great man Bertie ad-
mired so much . . . ?

The great man congratulated Bertie, bussed a blushing Maria on the cheek and, a hand on the Spanish gentleman's arm, walked off with Maria's father as if the whole had been arranged just for that purpose. Twenty minutes later Maria's father was introduced to a middle-aged officer who spoke fluent Spanish and, indeed, had Spanish relatives distantly related to Maria's father.

While that new friendship was quietly arranged, everyone who could manage it wrangled an invitation to Norry's little house where a celebration of the wedding went on far into the night—long after the bride and groom, looking deeply into each other's eyes and completely uninterested in anyone but each other, wandered off to Bertie's quarters.

In the end, the most difficult guest to be rid of was Graham Torville. Finally Ave drew the brooding man away, and, as a result of the necessity to rid them of Torville, left as well.

Ernie watched them go, sobered by a heavy feeling of regret that she and Ave had had no opportunity to talk. The things he'd said with his eyes when their gaze met and mingled at the wedding didn't count. Not when she needed to know and understand why he'd not come to stir the pudding! She no longer believed his absence had to do with regret for his announcement that he was courting her—or that perhaps his not coming had been an unsubtle way of telling her he'd changed his mind.

No. What his eyes had said to her across the altar threw out that notion entirely.

So why had he missed stirring the pudding?

Fourteen

The tempo of life increased over the next days. Ernie still rode in the mornings, when the morning mist hadn't turned itself into outright rain. But then the weather deteriorated and she, along with everyone else, began to worry about the outdoor service at midnight on Christmas Eve. When she wasn't riding, she suffered through long play practices during which she rebuffed Holles's more subtle approaches, made whenever the young man thought Ave not watching him, by stepping on his foot or kicking his shin.

His behavior grew exceedingly irritating, however, since he pretended to believe each such contact was an innocent's untutored encouragement—to be regarded, as he smugly told her, like a village boy's pulling a village girl's hair! Ernie refused to ask Ave to step in. She had her own revenge in mind—assuming she could survive Holles's heavy-handed pursuit until the evening the play would be presented!

At home, she and Norry stirred up fruit cakes which should have been made a month earlier and set to properly aging. They made gingerbread men and decorated them, and other baked goods of various sorts. They planned the Christmas dinner which Norry had finally agreed to give and sent out invitations to particular friends.

And, because Torville was still making a nuisance of himself, Norry spent a great deal of time with her friend Bertha, Lady Colonel Barton, and the other women who were knitting stockings and scarves, Boxing Day gifts to a variety of people who were not family or closely dependent on them, but were important to their lives with the army.

Then Torville was not seen for several days so that Ernie, returning from a late practice, was shocked to discover him sitting in the corner of the kitchen simply staring at Norry. His hang-dog look would have amused Ernie if she hadn't been so worried about her sister. Ave, following Ernie into the warm kitchen, was also put out of countenance.

"Haven't seen you for a while," said Ernie to Norry's bete noire.

"No," said the bemused looking man, lifting a haggard face to stare blankly in Ernie's direction.

"Been busy with your duties, I suppose," she said, not totally able to keep a sneer from her voice.

He didn't seem to notice her tone, his eyes following Norry's graceful movements from table to cupboard to window ledge to table. "No."

"No you've not been busy with duties?" she asked.

He glanced at her, back to Norry. "No duties."

"Then why have we not had the displeasure of your unwanted company?" she asked, exasperated.

Torville finally turned to stare at Ernie, a disquieting emotion in his red-rimmed eyes. "Stayed away," he finally muttered. Again he looked back, staring broodingly, if a trifle blearily, at the object of his desire.

Norry ignored him—or, at least, seemed to do so.

Ave cleared his throat. Torville seemed not to hear. The colonel stepped between Norry and Torville, blocking the younger man's view. "How long have you been here, Graham?"

"Here?" Torville seemed to think about it, then shook his head. "Don't know."

"Are you ill?" asked Ave, his tone sharp and commanding.

It hadn't occurred to Ernie that Torville's odd behavior might indicate an illness. She too stepped closer and put her hand on his flushed forehead. She looked up, startled. "Ave, he's burning up."

"Hmm. Torville, have you had the fever before?"

"Fever?" Torville craned his neck to look behind Ave and catch a glimpse of Norry.

"Damn," said Ave under his breath, gazing at Torville through eyes narrowed by heavy lids.

"What is it, Ave?" asked Norry, the first words she'd allowed between tightly clenched lips.

"Have you any bark you could infuse for him?"

Norry set down her bowl and spoon. "Bark! You think he has *that* sort of fever?"

"I think so. If I'm right, he'll soon be shaking like an aspen and, if it is truly bad, may become unconscious—assuming it *is* what I think it is, of course. I wish I knew if he'd had it before."

"He must have done so if that's what it is. This isn't the time of year one first comes down with it." Ave turned to look at her and Norry explained further. "First-time sufferers always get it in a hot wet summer—usually when working in flooded trenches during a siege. They don't get it in winter. Not for the first time."

"You certain of that, Norry?"

"As certain as I can be." She was headed for the door. She soon returned with the Lockwoods' private stock of medicines. "Ernie, put water on to boil and see if there is any honey or if I used it all yesterday in that batch of snaps."

"The jar is very nearly empty, Norry." Ernie showed it to her sister who was shredding a dry substance Ernie assumed was the bark from which the medicine would be made.

"Fiddle. Well, maybe he's so far gone we can get the stuff down him even if it is bitter as the devil himself. Ave, I won't have him left here," she added quietly when the colonel joined them beside the table. "I won't nurse him."

"No. That wouldn't be at all suitable—especially since so many know he's pursuing you. Unfortunately, under the circumstances, too many would think it a lie that he's sick—or at least pretend to do so."

Angry spots of color appeared on Norry's cheeks. "Exactly. And I won't have it, Ave. There must be no nasty whispers for Jon to hear when he comes home!"

Ave's jaw tightened at mention of Jon, but he only said, "We'll get Torville to other quarters as soon as maybe and"—he brightened—"I've finally thought of a way of ridding us of his presence altogether!"

"Is that water boiling yet?" asked Norry.

Ernie checked, returned to say it was just beginning to get the little bubbles that meant it soon would.

"If this were a winter like some we've had, I could infuse this, and then take it outside and cool it in snow." Norry poured steaming water over the material she'd placed in the bottom of a bowl. "As it is . . . Ave, I don't know how long it will take before it cools enough to become drinkable."

"Make it as strong as you can. I'll get fresh water from the well and we'll dilute it with a little of the cold."

He went out the back door with a bucket and Ernie turned to look at Torville. Suddenly the big bad villain no longer seemed the least bit evil. At this moment, he was very obviously nothing more than a sick man. "What is wrong with him, Norry?"

"It is a fever which, once one has caught it, comes back again and again. That's what we call it. The Fever. With capital letters. Perhaps the doctors have another name for it. He'll likely be delirious and difficult to handle, wanting to get up and go somewhere or do something. In fact, that may be how he got here. If he was left alone, he may have gotten up and just come!" Hands on hips, Norry stared at Torville. "He'll sweat buckets, complaining that he's burning up and moments later shake as if the flesh were to come off his bones, so chilled he'll believe he'll never be warm again. And ache. He'll ache as if all the imps of hell were beating him."

"And that bark you're soaking, that helps? Like willow bark, maybe?"

"It's bark off a tree they found in Brazil. The natives there use it. You can't believe how awful it tastes, though, which is why we need the honey. Bitter! You've never tasted such bitterness."

Ernie touched a finger to the hot liquid and put it to her tongue. She spat, making faces, and poured herself a cup of tea from the long-cooled teapot. She gulped it down, swishing it around in her mouth between swallows.

"He has to drink that?" she asked when she could speak again.

Norry grinned. "Yes. If he weren't so sick I'd say it serves him right for making such a nuisance of himself."

Ave returned, set down the bucket, and turned just in time to catch Torville as he tumbled, almost gracefully, from the stool. "Blast and beda—" His mouth snapped shut cutting off the oath. "Norry, he just passed out."

"Lay him on the floor. He'll not know the difference. You'd better strip off his coat and shirt and start rinsing him down." Norry turned to Ernie. "Off with you. This is no place for an unmarried woman."

"I can help. I've nursed our father often enough."

"It still isn't right. You take yourself into the other room," said Ave. He was already undoing buckles and buttons and hooks. "Norry, hold him while I get this tunic off."

The two working over the sick man ignored her and, reluctantly, Ernie removed herself from the kitchen. But once in the living room, she was restless. Twice she opened the kitchen door and peered in. The first time she could see little but Ave's back. The second time, Ave having moved, she blinked at the broad hair-webbed chest of the sick man, noting a ragged looking scar running across his ribs which disappeared down his side and under his trousers.

She looked from Torville to Ave's tunic-covered back. Did

Ave have scars that looked like that? she wondered. Had he been wounded . . . badly wounded?

Ernie felt a strange sickness. Perhaps Ave had already suffered as Torville must have suffered when slashed that way. Perhaps he would again, would be wounded in some future battle, sick and with no one to care for him . . .

Slowly Ernie closed the door, leaned back against it. "No one to care for him . . ." she muttered. *Who had cared for him when he'd received the wound which left him with a limp? Who and when and where!*

She'd heard tales of the incredible misery of the field hospitals, the butchers who masqueraded as surgeons, or so the younger men said. More truly, too few doctors who did the best they could under impossible conditions, or so the older officers insisted when she'd questioned the younger officers' horror stories of reeking carnage harder to bear than battle in which the wounds were received . . .

Ave. Ave might find himself in the hands of those surgeons with their saws and knives. He might wake from that horror with one less leg or arm . . .

With no one to care for him . . .

Or he might never wake . . .

Ernie shut her eyes. Norry, according to Ave, had saved Jon's life. She'd found him, nursed him, cared enough to forget her own selfish fears and be there for him . . . *Where had Norry found that courage? How did one face the weaknesses inside one which told one to run and keep on running? Race against the fear of one's own pain and not worry about that of the man one ran from.* Again, Ernie saw, in her mind's eye, that long scar starting high across Torville's chest and crossing down . . .

Who had cared for *him* while he'd healed? she asked herself again. Who *did* care for the men and officers who fought and were wounded in battles? Then Ernie remembered Albert Bacon. The officers had their batmen. The common soldier? Perhaps they only had each other or the women who followed in the tail of any army . . .

Ernie shuddered, then drew herself together, hugging her arms close. Again she peeked into the kitchen. "Ernie?" asked her sister, hearing the door open. "Get blankets, please. And then, before you leave us again, check and see if that bark water is cooled."

Ernie left and promptly returned trailing blankets from both their beds. She gave them to the sister and turned to the table. "Not quite. I'll pour some into the honey jar, shall I?"

"A very good thought," said Ave. "Norry, where is Bacon?"

"I leant him to Lady Colonel Barton," said Norry and sighed.

"Which explains why you were alone when Torville came," said Ernie.

"I thought he'd finally given up," said Norry, with just a touch of impatience.

"His sort don't give up, although in this case I suspect he didn't exactly know what he was doing or, when he arrived tonight, why he'd come!" Ave turned to their patient who tossed and pushed at the blankets in which they'd rolled him. "Well, let's get a dose of that stuff down him while he's half-conscious and then I'll go get some men to carry him away."

"Where will you take him?" asked Ernie.

"Does it matter?"

"I just want to know that he's cared for," she said. Defensively, she went on. "I don't like him. I think him a fool and a blackguard. In fact, he's despicable. But he's still human and he must be cared for."

"There are physicians whose job it is. And they have orderlies to help them." Ave shrugged. "I'll also send a few messages. One to his batman who will know his history and can come and stay with him and one to his commanding officer with my suggestion . . ." Ave grinned. "I'll take a moment to tell you my notion. Such a good notion. I wonder why I didn't think of it long ago." His grin spread wider as he looked from one to the other. "Perhaps it will make you feel more the thing."

"Stop your teasing, Ave," scolded Norry who was attempting to get some of the bitter tasting medicine down Torville's throat. Far too much of it seemed to run out of the side of his mouth. She mopped up another spill. "Tell us or be still."

"It's quite simple, really," said Ave with what Ernie thought false modesty. "We'll give him the next dispatches to carry home to London—and include a message to someone there that they are to find excuses for keeping him around!"

"Keep him there until Jon returns," said Norry, modifying Ave's plan a trifle. She seemed unaware that Ave and Ernie shared a sudden sharp glance. She huffed, irritable, when more of another swallow ended up outside Torville than inside. "Graham," said Norry sharply. "Graham Torville, open your mouth. Now!"

The sick man's eyes fluttered. They opened. He stared at Norry.

"I have medicine for you and you are to take it. Now."

Obediently Torville opened his mouth. Norry somehow made him drink the whole glassful before she allowed him to fade back into unconsciousness. Ave lay the man back on the floor.

"I'll go now," he said. "You'll be all right?"

"Ave," said Norry, disgustedly, "you'd think I'd never dealt with illness or wounds or anything more taxing than my tambour frame and needle. Besides, in this condition he's no danger to anyone, so *go!* The sooner you come back with help, the sooner we'll be rid of him." Hands again on her hips, Norry stared down at her unwanted guest. "Usually he's just a great lummoxing fool, Ave, but, at the moment, he's just one more sick mortal in need of care."

"You shouldn't think of him as merely an awkward gawk. He's a dangerous man."

"Oh I know. He's bigger than I am. That makes him dangerous. Usually. But he is also a fool, a fumbling bumbling clown.

When in good health, that is. I cannot for the life of me see where he's gained his reputation as a rake. The only true rakes I've ever met were much more attractive, much more gentlemanly and *far* more interesting."

"Perhaps it is simply that you are shielded against his charm," suggested Ernie. "Your love for Jon, I mean . . ."

Ave turned a burning look her way. "Does that mean *you* can see his attraction?"

"No, but I've been angry with him for pestering my sister, so he never turned whatever charm he may possess my way, did he?" Ave blew a long breath out between pursed lips but Ernie didn't notice. She was looking curiously at Torville who had begun to sweat again. "You'd have to ask someone else why he's considered attractive. Good heavens, I've never seen a man sweat like that. Norry, should I find fresh rags and more water for rubbing him down?"

"You let Norry care for him!" ordered Ave. "I'll be back just as soon as I can," he added as he disappeared.

Half an hour later a surgeon and four of his men arrived. Norry explained what had been done for Torville—to which she received a grunt. Then Torville was wrapped in rough blankets and strapped onto a stretcher. They watched him carried away down one of the lanes.

"Well. Good. That," said Norry, with a certain obvious relief, "is finally *that.*"

"Do you mean Torville won't be back?" asked Ernie, turning back into the house.

"Exactly," said Ave. "As soon as he can travel, we'll have him off to London and, if nothing else can be arranged, a long leave of absence—although I don't really see a problem with my little plot. Actually his illness supports it." He grinned again. "We can quite legitimately claim he's in need of medical leave, can we not?"

"By nothing else, you don't mean a transfer to a unit based

in England, do you? Wouldn't that be a waste of a good officer?" asked Ernie.

Ave chuckled. "You mean because he's a come-on rather than a go-on? He's no bellamranger, Ernie. He'll be back. But, if I have my way, it won't be until we're ready to head into Spain again. Torville tends to get into mischief when he isn't actually worrying about his men during a campaign."

"Good riddance," said Norry.

"What's a bellamranger?" asked Ernie.

"Someone who malingers when he isn't really ill in order to stay away from the fighting," explained Ave.

"You've taught Ernie more cant than she should know," scolded Norry. "Enough now!" Then, to force the conversation into other channels, she asked, "How is the play coming along?"

"We may actually be ready to give it when the time comes!" said Ave.

"Assuming," added Ernie, mischievously, "the stage set is finished and we have costumes and . . ." She ducked Ave's playful backhand.

"It'll all get done." He frowned. "Ernie, Holles isn't still making a nuisance of himself, is he? I thought, at one point tonight, you kicked him!"

"You let me worry about Holles," she said and grinned.

He stared at her for a long moment. "You're up to something."

"Of course."

"And you're not going to tell me."

"I'm not such a fool."

"You fear I'll spoil sport?" he asked curiously.

Ernie was silent during a long moment's hesitation. "I don't know, do I? And I don't want this particular sport spoiled." The grin returned and she had difficulty repressing giggles. When she could she said, "I think what I have in mind may cure our amorous gentleman of trying anything similar in future, so you just leave me alone."

"That would be worth almost anything—so long as it isn't something which puts you into a difficult position . . . ?"

"I see no possibility of it disturbing me in any way," she said piously, but her eyes sparkled.

"Hmm."

"Let her be, Ave," said Norry. "Ernie's very good at fitting her revenges to the situation."

"Very well," he finally said. He eyed Ernie for another moment and then changed the subject. "We must make arrangements for going to the ball. It was why I returned with Ernie this evening—although I'm glad I did since you needed help, Norry." Before either woman could comment, he said, "I've arranged that you both stay with the Smiths. That was the easy part. But I'm going to be busy up to the last moment, I fear, so getting there may be something of a problem . . ."

"My plans are set," said Ernie. "I'll be riding over early so I'm very glad I may stay with Juana until time to dress. Brigade-major Osgood explained that a group will be going together that morning and I've agreed to go with them."

Now why, she wondered, did I make it seem as if I were going only as part of the group?

"I've been invited to ride with Lady Colonel Barton," said Norry quickly in an attempt to distract Ave from Ernie's surprise announcement. "It will take far longer, going by a route her coach can manage, but I've decided I will do it that way anyway."

After the Review at which Bertie and Maria were married Norry had finally decided she should no longer ride, that her pregnancy was too far advanced even for the ambling rides she'd allowed herself recently and that she must not take any chance of a mishap—so she'd made her arrangements with Bertha during one of their sewing days.

Ave looked from one to the other. "Is this your way of saying you don't need my escort?" A thundercloud formed, darkening in his features, his body not really moving but somehow changing—and suddenly Ernie realized that Ave Sommerton could be a dangerous enemy!

"We would both love to have you escort us to the ball," said Norry and slid in her next comment as smoothly as she could. "You and Osgood should coordinate times and so on, of course."

"Osgood." Ave dropped the name like a hot potato.

Norry and Ernie looked at one another. Norry made a shrugging movement indicating she'd done what she could and it was up to Ernie to explain the situation.

"Some time ago he asked to take me," said Ernie, trying to remember why, at the time, she'd thought it a good notion.

"I see." He stared at Ernie until she could stand it no longer and looked away.

"I doubt it," said Norry, drawing his attention.

For a long moment he transferred his glare to his oldest friend's wife. Steadily Norry stared right back. "Very well," he said as if responding to something she'd said. "But I don't like it."

Ernie didn't like it either, although she'd not have admitted it to anyone, and, least of all, to Ave. Not if he referred to her going with Osgood instead of himself, that is. Then, realizing the direction in which her thoughts were tending, she reminded herself that Ave was a soldier. She would not wed a soldier . . . would she?

A soldier who might be wounded and in need of her loving care?

Ave, with one more glowering look at Ernie, made abrupt adieux and left. Ernie, refusing to discuss the situation with her sister, turned on her heel and went to bed. She was angry with herself for another reason too: she still had not found an appropriate moment in which to ask Ave why he'd not come to stir the pudding! The longer she put it off the harder it would be to ask in a casual manner, too.

Life, she decided, was sometimes far too complicated for mere humans. It was really too bad one could not be *more*. But perfection was difficult and saints few and far between. Ernie, thinking about it, decided that she really wasn't certain she wished to be a saint—so, she finished the thought—I have to put up with doing things wrong from time to time, do I not?

But *had* she been wrong? *Could* she marry a soldier? And come to that, would she, now, ever be asked so that she might have the choice, or was Ave so angry with her he'd never again make those irritating predictions that one day she'd agree to wed him? And there was still that equally irritating point that he had *not* come to stir the pudding . . .

Complicated indeed, she thought and, yawning, she shifted to her other side and went to sleep.

The ballroom was a surprise. Ernie was rather shocked that they were expected to dance upon a beaten earth floor and doubted, ruefully, that the soles of her dancing shoes would last the night. Worse, part of the roof was missing. The hole was covered over by tenting material but it was a harsh reminder of the war which would be resumed in only a few short months.

But worst of all, there was a hole roughly in the middle of the floor. Could one dance under such conditions? Off to one side a couple of fiddles and a flute tuned up. At the end of the room a table was arranged with drinks—both alcoholic and not. Then, blushing furiously, a private dressed in his parade-best uniform, arrived to stand over the hole and keep people from stepping into it!

That, thought Ernie, would work so long as the ball didn't become a romp—which Norry had warned it might do later on and, she'd added, if it did so they were to leave immediately.

But even worse than holes in roofs and floors, there were *far* more men than women in the makeshift ballroom—even with the addition of some local women that Ernie suspected were no better than they should be and not suitable acquaintances for herself and Norry! But, because of the paucity of women, she feared she'd not be allowed to carry through with her resolve to dance with no one: having made a major error in agreeing to have Osgood for escort, Ernie had decided it would be best if she sprained her ankle so that she'd have an excuse for sitting out the rest of the evening.

That it would make Osgood angry was no problem if only such action would change Ave's tight-lipped stiff-backed overly-polite attitude. If only she'd no longer be in his black book which, for reasons she could not—or would not—admit, would be a very good thing. As things were, something made her feel small and helpless and unhappy.

Very unhappy.

She sighed. It wouldn't do. Under these conditions, her resolve that she not dance would be exceedingly selfish. Some of these men hadn't been back to England to their homes for a very long time. To remove even one woman from the too few decorating the side-lines, would be selfish indeed. Another solution to Ave's bad mood must be found . . .

"The waltz?" she said sharply, when Osgood took her card from her to sign for his two dances. "But no. I've told you I do not waltz."

"Then we shall sit it out," he said with the faintest of leers. "I will also have, of course, the supper dance." He scribbled his name twice and backed from the group already three deep around her. But before the first young man could open his mouth to ask her for a dance, a hand reached over her shoulder. It slipped the card from her fingers and, a moment or so later handed it back. She looked at it. Ave had signed for the dance—a waltz—after supper and, later, still another waltz . . .

Remembering Norry's admonishments that they would leave if things became overly wild, she wondered if she'd still be here for that last waltz.

Fifteen

The first few dances were enjoyable and Ernie's trepidations fled. To the devil, she decided, with Ave's sensitivities. She settled down to pleasing herself. She was having an excellent time when a young officer stopped before her and bowed.

"My dance, I believe," he said diffidently. "I'm Lieutenant Storrey," he added when she looked a question.

The music began but the young man didn't offer his arm as one expected. "Well, Lieutenant Storrey," suggested Ernie, "shall we dance?"

The lieutenant reddened, his tight collar seemed to pinch around his neck. "Er, well, you see . . ." His huge wide-opened eyes seemed to plead with her for understanding.

"You know," said Ernie kindly, guessing at his problem, "I've very nearly danced myself to a standstill. Do you think you might find me a glass of lemonade and we sit this one out? If you wouldn't mind . . . ?"

The young officer seemed to heave a great sigh of relief as he nodded and turned smartly toward the nearby table of refreshments. He returned almost immediately with her glass and looked around until he found another chair which he brought to set beside hers.

"I didn't want to admit it," he said softly, "but, you see, well, I'm not a very good dancer."

Ernie suspected it was worse than that and that he didn't dance at all but she refrained from twitting him, asking instead where he came from and about his family. It took her only a few moments to realize the boy—for he seemed no more to her—was desperately homesick. She sighed softly and asked another question—this time about his youngest sister, the one she'd guessed was his favorite among what seemed a huge number of siblings.

"She's such a bright little thing. I used to let her share my lessons, you know, and sometimes she'd have a better translation than mine and almost always her sums were more accurate. It was often embarrassing, but I'm very proud of her. In her letters she tells me she misses me and our lessons. You see," he confided, "my mother has made her cease attending with my brothers, saying she is much too old for such nonsense and must tend to her needle now and learn to be a good housewife—as if Mary were interested in such stuff!" He scowled. "It is really too bad, you know."

"I do know. Perhaps you might tell your sister to ask your mother if, assuming she does the work your mother sets her, she might join just one class with the tutor. A compromise, you see? Or," Ernie had another thought, "perhaps your mother fears your sister will develop a tendre for the tutor?"

Lieutenant Storrey gave her a startled look and then burst into laughter which Ernie thought good for him, since laughter seemed too far from his normal sober demeanor. "Oh, dear," he said. "Not *Mary*. Mary would stare to hear you suggest such a thing."

"But would your mother?" asked Ernie softly.

Again his expression approached that of a startled hare and again he chuckled. "You are correct, of course. Mother would only see that possibility. It wouldn't occur to her that Mary truly enjoys her studies."

"And perhaps it is also true that she disapproves those studies as being unladylike, perhaps fears your sister will become a blue-stocking?" prodded Ernie.

The lieutenant frowned. "I suppose she might. She herself does not even read novels which my other sisters enjoy. I'd not thought of that."

He cogitated for a long moment and Ernie allowed him his thoughts, looking to where Ave seemed to her to be enjoying, far more than was reasonable, a dance with a young lady visiting a married sister with the Smiths' regiment.

"I will do as you suggested," interrupted Lieutenant Storrey, "and I will remind my mother that Mary thinks the tutor a fat little snerp and beneath consideration and only barely adequate for teaching the boys what is necessary before they go to school. Perhaps she will forget her silly fears and allow Mary to have the one class."

"You might also tell her that all the best families have tutors for their daughters, or so a visitor with whom you discussed the situation told you. You might add that having only a governess is considered old fashioned."

"Is that true?" he asked, not certain if he should believe her.

"Well, in part." She smiled. "Not *all* the best families are doing it, but I know of two and I myself had a tutor for several years . . ."

The years before Bertie was sent off to school and his tutor, which she shared, dismissed . . . Ave was laughing now. *What had that young woman said to him? Would this dance never end?*

As conversation with Storrey continued, Ernie learned far more than she cared to know about the Storrey household. But the young man looked far more cheerful when her next partner approached, so she ceased to worry about him—although she continued to worry about Ave—as she and her new partner joined the Lancers. They danced with far more verve and enthusiasm than perhaps she should have allowed. She was fanning herself and wishing herself outside in the cool night air when Osgood came to claim his waltz and she realized the cool night air was the *last* place she could go—with *him,* at least.

"Thank goodness I will not be dancing this next one," said Ernie as she led the way to where Norry was seated. "Could you get me another glass of lemonade?" she asked when she noted Norry's frown. Osgood obediently went off for it which gave her the privacy to ask if her sister were feeling well. When Norry gave her a startled look at that suggestion, she asked, "What is it Norry?"

"It isn't that I feel ill, but I may decide to leave early even so. I've already talked to Bertha and she'll act your chaperon, so you needn't leave as well."

"You *aren't* feeling well," Ernie accused.

"Truly, I'm not ill. I just seem to be very tired and—Ernie, without Jon here to enjoy this with me, I don't really want to dance and it isn't fair," she said, echoing Ernie's earlier thoughts on the subject, "to sit out every dance when so many of the men have no partners. So I think I'll leave just before supper."

"You'll have Ave escort you?" asked Ernie, sharply, not liking the notion of her sister walking back to quarters alone.

"Yes. He'll see me to the Smiths' and be back before you go in for supper." Norry shook her head, smiling wryly. "Isn't it strange how such phrases remain even when they are inappropriate? In this case, you won't *go in* to supper—the supper will *come in* to you. They'll carry it in on boards—probably doors they've removed from somewhere—which will be laid across trestles to form buffet tables."

Just then a gray-haired woman bustled up in a flutter of hands and shawls. "You must d-d-do something, my dear Mrs. Lockwood," stuttered the woman, obviously laboring under strong emotion. "She has become quite w-w-wild. Very nearly hysterical," she added in a piercing whisper.

"Who?" asked Norry, rising to her feet and looking around— first toward where Juana Smith glowered at her husband who

flirted outrageously with a buxom woman. But Juana was neither wild nor hysterical. She was merely angry! "I don't see . . ."
began Norry.

"That Mrs. W-w-white. Quite, *quite* uncontrolled. D-d-do
come!"

"I don't know what I can do . . ."

"She a-a-admires you. She'll l-l-listen to you," Ernie heard
as the older woman led Norry away. "P-p-please hurry."

Ernie sighed. She'd hoped to have Norry for chaperon while
sitting out this waltz with Osgood. At least it was well started
before he managed to return with her drink.

"It has become far too warm in here," he said, standing before her. "Why do we not take this out into the entry where it
will very likely be cooler?" he asked.

"I have sat here quietly waiting for you and I'm no longer
too hot."

"I am."

"Then sit down and rest. You'll soon feel better. If you wish,
you may drink my lemonade," she added, a challenge in her
eyes.

A muscle jerked in his jaw. "I'd really like to speak with you
and who can speak in all this noise?"

"I have had no difficulty talking to my sister. Do sit down.
You look a perfect block looming over me that way."

Red tinged his cheeks, but he took Norry's vacated chair. "I
wish you would allow me a few moments in which to be private
with you," he said, leaning too near to speak crooningly into
her ear.

Backing off, she caught his eyes and held his gaze. "I am
not so foolish, sir."

The red spread to his neck and he could not look at her. "I
haven't a notion what you are thinking, but it's nothing of the
sort," he insisted. When she only continued to stare, he added,
"Truly!"

"Don't glower so. You make us conspicuous and I do not care for it."

Not that anyone was truly paying any attention to them, but the suggestion was enough to convince Osgood that if he could not lure Ernie away from everyone, it would be better to do as she asked. He handed her the glass and wiped all expression from his face although Ernie sensed he was not at all happy with her.

Ernie, having gotten her way, proceeded to make their conversation as light and stimulating as she could without once stepping over the line of what was pleasing—although it was something of a strain to do so when Ave seemed so well entertained by the local woman with whom he waltzed.

Osgood rose when her next partner arrived and grinned. "Forgive me?" he asked, all petulance gone.

"For trying your luck? So long as you didn't succeed I've nothing to forgive you *for,* have I?"

"I've enjoyed our talk," he admitted. "I look forward to having supper with you."

Ernie turned to her new partner and discovered it was Wellington himself bowing before her. "Sir!"

The field marshall chuckled. "I have startled you. No, do not rise. I will be quite honest and admit that I would prefer to sit with you for this dance and simply converse . . ."

Recovering her poise, Ernie nodded. Her conversation with the commander of the Peninsular armies ranged far and wide, was quick paced and exceedingly enjoyable. Twice she said something which roused the man's braying laughter and turned eyes their way. Both times Ave turned to stare as well—which didn't displease Ernie at all.

When the half hour ended, Wellington rose and lifted her hand for a quick kiss. He smiled knowingly, his pale-blue eyes twinkling. "I hope we'll meet again, my dear, but if we do not, have a good life in your new situation." He bowed again, winked, and disappeared into the crowd.

Ernie looked after him, startled. What could the man possibly have meant? There had been an undertone to his voice, a suggestive note—to say nothing of that wink—which led her to believe it was far more than the simple fact that she would soon be leaving Portugal with Norry and going home to their father where her life would return to one of daily routine—nothing new, either in situation or anything else. . . .

Ernie looked up, looked across the empty floor, and met Ave's gaze. He wore a questioning look and his eyes flicked toward where Wellington had joined several staff officers, turned back to meet hers. Ernie frowned, shook her head, her puzzlement complete. Ave seemed to think something might have passed between herself and his general—but what could it have been?

She recalled that she'd heard somewhere that Ave had recently spent a day at headquarters. Surely, she thought, he'd not have said anything to Wellington, of all people, about his intention to wed herself? Besides, if Wellington thought she might wed one of his officers, he would surely expect, in that case, to see her again. But if he did *not* have a wedding in mind, then why had he, now that she thought about it, come as near as made no difference to wishing her happy as he would if she were a bride-to-be?

Ernie had some difficulty pushing the conversation from her thoughts and found it necessary to put forth an effort to entertain her next partner. And then came the supper dance.

Her new chaperon swept up to her much like the proverbial ship-of-the-line in full sail. Ernie remembered watching those big ships in the convoy of which her transport had been a part when crossing to Portugal and had great difficulty in suppressing a giggle: whoever had first come up with that comparison had known ships that sailed with good following winds!

"Lady Colonel Barton," she murmured and, rising, offered the older woman her chair.

"You will dine with me and my husband, my dear."

"Brigade-major Osgood has the supper dance and I'm to dine with him," said Ernie, not quite knowing how to handle this man-o-war which had descended on her.

"He, too, then—and here he comes." The large buxom lady stared at the slim young officer until he blushed. "You will return Miss Matthewson to my side immediately after this dance has ended, Osgood."

"Yes sir," he said and the blush deepened. "I mean, yes, ma'am."

"Very well. Now enjoy yourselves. I'll be watching."

Ernie very nearly apologized for Lady Barton's presumption and might have except, just as she turned away toward the dance floor, she noted a distinct twinkle in the lady's eye and decided Lady Barton was not above twitting the young rake who was silently and very slightly pettishly going down the dance!

Inwardly Ernie shrugged. She wouldn't have allowed poor Osgood to sweep her off into a hidden corner or out a door so it really made no difference that the colonel's wife had sunk any plans Osgood had of that nature. But she did wish people would allow her to mind her own business and work out her own revenges.

Because, although he didn't know it, Osgood would not have tried such a thing more than once. In Ernie's coiffure was a long pin decorated with roses at both ends. It was a weapon she had learned to wear during her first season and it would have seen to Osgood's education as it had others with ill intent. A well placed pin, she'd discovered, could make a point far more firmly than mere words! In this particular case, since Osgood enjoyed going out with the hunt, it would have been twice as apt. He'd very likely not have felt like riding for some days. All of which assumed, of course, that he still had notions of attempting her seduction.

Ernie sighed. She almost wished she'd had the opportunity to use the pin! It was such a fitting lesson for a would-be rake who was hunting mad! She always preferred to fit her lessons to match the particular situation and this would be so particularly perfect!

It took most of the dance—given one had so little opportunity to talk when the figures were forming and moving apart and reforming—for Ernie to coax a smile from Osgood. When he chuckled, she felt relief. The notion of sitting down with a sulking man for the hour given over to supper was not high on Ernie's list of enjoyable social occasions!

Then Ave and Colonel Lord Barton came up to where Ernie and Lady Barton sat waiting for Osgood to return with Ernie's supper. The line was long and the two colonels must have been near the head of it before the dancing stopped because they had already brought a plate to Lady Barton and gone back for their own. They commandeered two more chairs and it was a lively group which Osgood found upon returning with Ernie's well chosen food. Then, reluctantly, he was forced to return to the line from which he glared, while waiting to get his own.

"That should put that fine gentleman in his place," said Lady Barton quietly when her husband and Ave were involved in a small argument.

"Who?"

"That Osgood. I have watched him again and again at these dances. He has succeeded far more often than one would think possible in luring some innocent miss away from the crowd." She looked thoughtful and then continued, "I don't think he goes much beyond kissing them, but, still . . . I am glad you have more sense, Miss Matthewson!"

"Very likely I've been on the town—as the saying is—longer than they. I've met far too many young men like Osgood. I think some men cannot resist chancing their luck and then others—well, I've decided, they feel they *must* do so or be considered failures—at least by themselves. I've never understood it."

"What can you never understand?" asked Ave abruptly, interrupting their conversation.

Ernie hadn't a notion what to say, but Lady Barton answered promptly. "The difference between strategy and tactics," she said.

Her ladyship's response made Ave's dark brows climb high up his forehead toward the thick gray hair which he'd combed into a Brutus. He turned his disbelieving gaze toward Ernie.

Ernestine couldn't help blushing. He and she had had a long debate only a few evenings earlier on just that subject and Ernie had shown no trouble distinguishing the two at all. She wondered if he'd reveal her unladylike knowledge—and then knew he would not. Not because he worried about twitting *her*, but because to do so would reveal that Lady Barton had lied and he was far too much the gentleman to embarrass the colonel's lady. She hoped he'd forget to raise the topic again later!

Osgood returned but was unable to discover another chair. He was forced to stand while he ate which is an awkward thing under any circumstances. Nor was he completely at ease with the two older men, his superior officers.

It had not been the best of evenings for Osgood and, now he'd had his two dances with Ernie and supper was nearly over, there would no more opportunity for him to improve it—especially since he guessed, and rightly, that Ave would be with them when he walked Ernie back to the Smiths' quarters at the end of the ball!

Then, as the supper ended and the small orchestra tuned up again, Osgood's cup of rue ran over. Ave, barely giving Ernie a chance to say that she *couldn't*, swept her into the waltz and she discovered she *could* after all. More, she discovered she enjoyed it—even when Ave pulled her a trifle closer than propriety decreed proper whenever he circled, which was often. Breathless, she stared up into his face and found he was looking at her with a gentle understanding look that made her knees go weak. If he'd not had his arm around her, if he'd not held her hand more than a little tightly, Ernie was quite certain she would have melted right down into the floor. How could she say no to a man who looked at her in just that way? Assuming, of course, that he ever asked her!

The last dance was also a waltz. This time Ernie looked forward to dancing with Ave, to the feel of his hand at her back, the feel of the other, a warm firm pressure around her hand, his thumb occasionally making a small movement against her palm. . . .

How, she wondered, could she be so conscious of that ridiculously small touch? It wasn't even as if his flesh touched hers since they both wore gloves! How could so little make her tremble and affect her breathing in such an odd fashion?

Again she looked up into Ave's face. This time she could not look away. How could eyes look hot? she wondered. How could they demand she draw near, that she raise her face to his, feel his lips taking, controlling hers . . . how above all could she know what he was thinking, wanting, wishing might be . . .

The dance ended and so did the fantasy of Ave's kiss—although his look had promised just that and, for the first time, Ernie felt a like desire, more, a need that this man keep the promise his gaze had silently made. Others had looked at her in a similar manner and she had felt either disgust or amusement or both. Now she wondered if any or all of those men had felt, inside, as she did at this moment when she blindly allowed Ave to lead her back to Lady Barton and . . .

Ernie blinked herself back to reality. Osgood was waiting, thin-lipped, to walk her home. He was, expectedly, unhappy when Ave joined them.

"I, too, am staying with the Smiths you know," said Ave, his voice just a touch too hearty. "In fact, Osgood, if you do not wish to go out of your way, there is no reason why I cannot accompany Ernie back to quarters."

"I am Miss Matthewson's escort and of course I'll see her home. You are undoubtedly tired, sir, I'm sure. Do not feel you must keep us company if you are in a hurry to reach your bed."

Ave threw back his head and laughed. He pulled Osgood a trifle farther away from where Lady Barton had cornered Ernie for some last words of advice and council. Ernie, half listening to her ladyship, wished she knew what Ave said to Osgood who first looked startled and then chagrined and finally wore a look of resignation.

Ernie gently but firmly brought her conversation to an end and joined the men. She looked from one to the other. Osgood offered an arm and, hesitantly, she took it. Ave offered his and even more hesitantly she took that. As they strolled down the village street toward the Smiths' lodging, Ave kept up a running monologue of light comments on the evening's entertainment.

When they reached it, Osgood said all the proper things and wished them good night before bowing over Ernie's hand. At the last possible moment and, with a quick defiant glance at Ave, he lifted her fingers to his mouth for an entirely improper kiss. Then he turned on his heel and stalked off.

"What was that all about?" asked Ernie, suspiciously.

"Does it matter? He's gone and I don't think he'll bother you again."

Was there just a touch of smugness in his tone? "In what way was he bothering me?"

"Was he not doing his possible to get you alone for a little love making?"

"And if he had that in mind, was it not *my* business?"

Ave was silent for a moment. "Was it? Entirely?" he asked quietly.

He gazed steadily down at her until she was forced to look

away. Ernie remembered that *look*. She recalled the way his thumb touching her gloved palm had sent sensations racing through her which she'd never felt before. For another moment she looked back, met his gaze. Without replying she turned on her heel and they entered to find Norry drinking a cup of coffee, her feet up, and staring into the fire.

All thought of Ave and her contradictory feelings disappeared as she hurried to kneel beside her scowling sister. "What is it Norry?"

"Why do some people make their lives so impossibly difficult?"

Ernie sat back on her heels. "Whom are you talking about?"

Norry sighed. "Mostly Mrs. White. She made a complete fool of herself tonight and the Rockinghams were required to leave early in order to take her home. It was most thoughtless of her and, worse, she was not at all repentant." Norry glanced toward a closed door and lowered her voice. "Also the Smiths. Poor Juana stormed in here a little while ago and I think is crying her eyes out, thanks to Harry's ridiculous and exceedingly public show of independence."

"What happened?" asked Ave. He too glanced toward the closed door. "With Mrs. White I mean?"

"You didn't see?"

"I expect my attention was elsewhere," he said with a dry look toward Ernie who ignored it.

Norry sighed. "She was flirting in quite the most ridiculous manner for such a recent widow. All the wildest rakes surrounded her. You might have assumed she'd never again in all her life see another man!"

"Do they not have assemblies in that place to which she's going?"

"I haven't the least notion but I should think so. Nor do I believe her father-in-law to be the sort to disapprove of such frivolities—from what I remember of his son, at least!"

Ave shook his head. "Sometimes the son will go as far as may be away from his parents' principles. Perhaps Mrs. White has reason to fear she goes to a completely sober household where she'll be expected to piously ply her needle, dress in widow's weeds forever, and join in family prayers six times a day."

"What do you think she was up to tonight?" asked Ernie.

"If what Ave thinks of her future is true, then I suspect she had hopes of finding herself another husband, one who would take care of her as White did," said Norry, exasperation clear in her tone.

"Impossible," said Ave. "Everyone who knew them pitied him far too much to put himself in White's place!"

"Ave, that wasn't kind."

"No, but the truth, nevertheless."

Norry took a last sip from her cup. "It is late. Mrs. White is a boring subject. We will go to bed. Come along Ernie."

"In a moment," said Ave, his hand grasping Ernie's when she would have docilely followed her sister.

"For *just* a moment, Ave," warned Norry, and shut the door to the small room she and Ernie shared.

As soon as the door shut behind Norry, Ave swung Ernie around. He didn't ask. He simply pulled her into his embrace, his hand tipping her chin, his mouth finding hers . . .

The kiss was everything she had been promised. She tingled from her toes encased in her worn-out dancing slippers right up to where her top-knot was falling loose, allowing long tresses to curl down her back. Idly, she reached for the rose-tipped decoration. Absently, she pulled it free. Languidly, she lay against him, feeling long hard thighs, a rather intrusive buckle and heavy brass buttons. Muscular arms encircled her, drawing her closer, more fully into the depths of his kiss. Ernie's arms tightened as well.

He moved, his hand making soft circles on her back, moving

slowly, insidiously, closer and closer to her side—until, with a muffled oath, he jerked away, setting her roughly onto her own feet. He clutched at his elbow, twisting it, looking at the back of his arm. Ernie, blinking rapidly, bemused, fell against the table which she clutched with one hand.

"Why did you do that?" he asked, obviously irritated.

"What? Kiss you?" She was totally bewildered. "Didn't you want me to? Wasn't I supposed to?"

"Don't pretend you don't know—you impossible minx!" He looked her up and down, noted the rose-covered pin and grabbed it away from her, studied it. "Good Lord, that's a lethal weapon!"

"It is? Oh. Oh, yes." Ernie looked from it to Ave, back at the pin. She felt heat rise up her neck. Another look at Ave's expression and her ears heated up as well. "Oh, dear, did it stick you?"

"Yes it did—as you very well know!"

Ernie reprehensibly giggled. "I didn't know." He obviously didn't believe her. "Ave, I *didn't*. Truly." She giggled again, putting her hand over her mouth when he scowled. "But . . . but it is funny. Laugh Ave! Please. I had it in my hair tonight for just such an occasion, you see! Ave? Can't you see how funny . . . ?"

After a moment his brows rose and he asked, "Osgood?"

"Of course. Or anyone else who might have gotten a little above himself and in need of reprimanding." She shrugged.

Ave was silent for a moment. "Me?"

Ernie stared for an even longer moment. "In this case," she said in a small voice, "perhaps the both of us? I'd better go in to Norry, or she'll come out demanding to know why I have not."

"I doubt very much she is wondering why not," said Ave. His voice exhibited the dry, slightly cynical tone she'd begun to hear in her head when she noted something she wanted to tell him, or saw something she wished to describe to him, or . . .

"Go to bed, my love," he said, reaching out to finger a long length of hair. "It's late and we must leave early."

Ernie, pulling the tress away from him, asked, "Where do you sleep?"

"I've a blanket and will roll up in it before the fireplace." He gestured toward where a small blaze gave the only light in the room. "Don't catch your lip between your teeth like that," he said and there was humor in his tone. "As absent-minded as you've become this evening you might forget and bite it. Ernie, you are not to worry," he added when she again cast a worried look toward the floor, "I've slept in far worse places in my time."

Ernie, realizing how true that must have been, nodded and quietly entered the small room. As silently as she could, she got herself ready for bed. Her sister had looked terribly tired when they'd come in and she hadn't even insisted Norry tell her if she were all right. Ernie sighed. This business of falling in love with an unsuitable party was a ridiculously self-absorbing business and altogether too time consuming. The sooner she and Norry left for England the better . . . or would it be?

Ernie remembered the tingles, the warmth, and the odd feeling in her bosom as if it were swelling and growing firmer and attempting all by itself to get closer to him. Were such feelings why some women married the obviously logically, wrong man? she asked herself. Did they become so desirous of feeling more and more of such sensations that they lost all pretense to owning good sense?

Surely one did not become a slave to one's senses? Surely one could put them aside and decide to wed on the basis of what was right and proper and the most sensible thing to do? Marrying Ave wasn't sensible at all. Marrying *any* officer would be stupid beyond permission.

So why did she have this vague and disturbing notion that she was weakening toward Ave, that her feelings had gone too far to be recalled and that she would, fighting and kicking all the way, eventually give into that part of her that wanted and needed to be with him?

Ernie lay as still as she could in the narrow bed so as not to disturb her sister—but it was a very long time before she could forget those odd and disturbing and much to be desired sensations Ave had roused with only a kiss.

Only a kiss? Had it truly only been a kiss? Ernie had a great deal of trouble believing it had not been far more—like the meeting and melding of souls, or perhaps the merging of mind and heart, or maybe . . .

Ernie caught herself up short, a new thought intruding. There was still the problem of why Ave hadn't come to stir the pudding.

Unfortunately, those odd sensations soon returned and Ernie finally drifted off to sleep still undecided as to exactly what had happened during that far too short eternity she'd been in Ave's arms.

Perhaps puddings weren't so very important after all?

Sixteen

Dressed in her fairy queen costume except for the filigree crown which she held in her hand, Ernie peered through a hole one of the actors had poked into a screen. The benches for the audience were filling up nicely.

A qualm hit her. She'd never played before so many people. At the house parties she'd attended, they'd usually put on a play twice—once for the servants and once for guests invited from the neighborhood. Never had there been more than thirty, thirty-five at most, but it looked as if there were already more than a hundred sitting out there gossiping and joking and generally anticipating a good time. Ernie swallowed. She was about to make a fool of herself. She was certain of it.

Then she felt a pinch through her gown and, without thinking kicked back. She missed and turned to find Holles leering at her. "You just wait!" Hands on hips, she glared at him.

"I can't wait," he said, dramatically, and reached for her.

Ernie slipped to one side and scowled. "I swear," she hissed, all too conscious of the growing audience, "you pull one silly trick once the play's begun and I'll show you tricks!"

"You better finish getting ready," he said pacifically, but his grin said he didn't believe her threats.

Muttering fiercely, she made her way to the back of the stage rounding the humped up area of pretend grass and flowers on which she was to recline as the play opened and went on out behind the screens painted to look like tree trunks with a few branches stuck with paper leaves scattered here and there to indicate a forest glade. Once behind the stage, she went into the room where the actors were to wait their cues and found Ave sorting out the props necessary for the first few scenes and, for one last time, warning worried actors to watch for his or her particular weakness.

"Ah, there you are," he said, sighting Ernie. "Aren't you ready yet? It is almost time."

"Almost time to make myself the biggest fool in Portugal. I can't do it, Ave."

"Stage fright?" His dark brows climbed toward his hair. "Nonsense. Not you. Ernie, some things are too serious for one to joke about them. You of all people should know that. Don't mention such a thing or I'll have a rebellion on my hands with every bit player here making himself ill!"

He looked at her sharply. Even under the stage make-up he could see she was a little pale and definitely a trifle wild-eyed. His teeth gritted together making a muscle jump in his jawline.

"Ernie, don't you *dare* let me down at this point," he ordered.

She took a deep breath. "Ave, I've never seen so many faces, all waiting and staring and ready to pounce on any error . . ."

"Ha! Don't be ridiculous. They may be staring and they are certainly waiting, but they are not about to pounce on errors. They get far too few entertainments to make them the least bit censorious. Besides, you'll do just fine. Now"—he reached for her crown and settled it firmly on her head—"you find a corner and read your first lines and before you know it, the play will be started and then, soon enough, all over."

Ernie didn't find a corner. Instead she went to the table which, with a borrowed mirror, was designated hers. Someone had put a rather rude screen across that corner to preserve the few women performers' modesty but no one else was there so Ernie had a bit of privacy, which she needed since the rest of the room was crowded.

Ernie peered around to make absolutely certain no one spied on her and then opened the box sitting on the table. She looked in and nodded. Everything she needed was there. Her first trick—assuming Holles didn't take to heart her warning to behave—involved sharp grit which she'd sprinkle into the boots he wore as Oberon. That man needed a lesson and Ernie planned to give it to him.

She wrote a note in block letters which read DON'T YOU DARE! and added a pin to it. She'd pin it to the back of her hillock and that would be her final warning. It should, if Holles had any sense at all, be enough. Next she put enough grit into her pocket to make the man very uncomfortable indeed—but only if he attempted to make *her* uncomfortable, of course.

Which he did. It seemed Holles could not overcome his belief that she was merely shy and unable to tell him how much she enjoyed his sly touches, soft pinches, the surreptitious grabs or his rubbing against her at all and any opportunity. And if she gave him none, he would invent one, a trick which upset everyone who had learned exactly where to stand and which way to turn at any given point in the play. All too often they discovered Holles was not where he was supposed to be.

When they came off-stage at the end of the first scene, Holles found himself facing an exceedingly angry Ave who, for the first time, revealed to the young officer, exactly what sort of temper he had. In fact, Ernie, who watched, was almost as surprised as Holles to discover the colonel had one, but, under the patience and control Ave normally presented to the world, there was quite definitely a temper.

Ernie listened with satisfaction. *Perhaps she should have let Ave handle Holles some time ago?* She put her hand in her pocket and fingered the grit, and grinned. She casually moved to where Holles's Oberon boots stood ready.

Ave, finishing his tongue-lashing, shoved Holles toward his

costume with only an instant to spare before the actor was due back on stage.

When Holles took his first step, he discovered exactly how Ernie intended fulfilling her threats to him. Painfully, he strode to his position center stage, wondering for the first time, if, maybe, Torville had been wrong about Ernie's feelings. No actor or actress who had any affection for another player would deliberately put grit into his boots!

Holles discovered it was necessary to concentrate completely to remember his lines and stage position while avoiding the possibility of the audience discovering anything was wrong. Because of that he behaved impeccably until he had a moment off stage and managed to empty his boots.

Ernie had actually enjoyed that scene. Without the necessity of maneuvering around Holles's irritating attentions, she remembered why she enjoyed participating in play-acting! Unfortunately, the scene was too short—at least from Ernie's point of view. And Holles, not admitting he had brought her revenge down on his head himself, was determined to get even, and was, if anything, more irritating than ever when he returned with grit-free boots.

When Ernie next had a moment off stage, she went back to her box. This time she chose a small bottle which she handed the props man with the information it was the wine for Oberon's glass which he would carry on during the next scene. He was supposed to wave the glass about and sip from it as he gave his speeches. Ernie suspected one sip would be enough—but what he would do, at the end just before exiting, when he was supposed to lift the glass and drain it—well, she'd wait and discover just how important acting was to poor old Holles. Would he or would he not? Ernie stifled a giggle as she took her place for the next scene.

Holles swaggered on in his role as Bottom, his ass's head firmly attached. In this scene, at least, he had no excuse whatsoever to come close to Titania for which Ernie was very glad. At the end, however, he invented one, following her from the stage with his ass's head resting on her shoulder and the rest of him far too close behind her for comfort. The qualms she'd begun to have about playing further tricks on him vanished.

Holles quickly prepared for his role as Oberon, grabbing the wine glass last thing before he returned, alone, to the stage. Ernie and Ave stood shoulder to shoulder watching from behind the scenes.

"What did you do to his wine?" asked Ave.

"What makes you think I've done anything at all?" she asked innocently.

"The props man didn't use the bottle *I* brought. It's standing there unopened. So, I ask again, what did you do to his wine?"

"It isn't."

"Isn't?"

"Wine, of course. It's vinegar."

"You didn't!"

At that exact instant Holles took a swig and discovered that for himself. He swung on his heel and, his back to the audience, made a awful face and stared unbelieving at his wine. The prompter hissed at him, fed him his line and, startled all over again, Holles swung back to face the lights. He stumbled half way through his soliloquy before he managed to pull himself together and back into the swing of things.

But, in the end, he proved himself a true actor. He changed the lines so that he could pour out the supposed wine in a libation to the gods of amour. It wasn't exactly William Shakespeare but it wasn't bad as such things go.

The look he gave Ernie as he exited, however, was one of undiluted disgust. "How dare you ruin my best scene that way?"

"How dare you behave as you've done when you've been told again and again to stop? Control yourself and you won't need to worry about another trick," she warned softly as he again changed the few bits which made him first Oberon and then Bottom. "Another amorous advance, however, and I'll retaliate. You'll never know when or how I'll strike, will you?"

For the next few scenes Holles kept a wary distance from her—but then he fell deeply back into the roles he played and once again he overstepped the bounds which Ernie had laid down for him.

This time, as Bottom, he actually laid his bare hand around her ankle up under her skirts as he lolled against her woodland mound far too near for her comfort. Casually rolling over, Ernie clipped him under the chin with her other heel and he let go.

But once again he was surprised and once again he forgot his lines. Ernie didn't try to cover for him, as she would have done for someone she liked. She merely stared off into the distance waiting for her cue—which he eventually heard from the hissing prompter and fed to her.

Ernie's revenge was going better than she'd hoped. Besides, playing her tricks meant she had no time for her own stage fright, something she realized and was grateful for the next time she exited and was face to face with an exceedingly green-in-the-face bit player!

She gave him an encouraging smile and continued to her box of tricks. The kick in the chin didn't really count, after all. What she wanted was something which would convince Holles he must permanently change his attitudes toward his leading ladies. Carefully she sorted through the two or three things which remained.

The long pin which she'd accidentally stuck into Ave's biceps must be saved for the last scene. She would show it to Holles before the scene began, of course, because she truly did not wish to do anything he could not, with effort, overcome and continue with his part. A pin pushed into one could not help but draw forth an involuntary response which would *not* be in character. If he knew the possibility, he could, if he would, avoid it.

Which left what? She picked up the pepper container which she had hesitated to add to her collection. Pepper would make him sneeze—which was again unavoidably out of character and not what she wanted. Besides, it might get loose in such a way the whole cast began sneezing! That would surely be disaster. Ernie grinned at the thought it might spread even further. What a sight if half the audience started sneezing as well! Which left only the honey.

What a mess it would make. Should she? she wondered. *Could* she? It would have to be done on stage and in view of the audience and she wasn't absolutely certain she could manage it without being seen . . . and if someone did see what she was up to? Did she care? Ernie thought about it and, rather ruefully, decided she didn't care a jot.

Whatever else resulted, Holles would never forget this production, she decided as she picked up the small jar of honey. Perhaps—although she thought it unlikely—it would make him more cautious in future about how he treated reluctant leading ladies. Ernie smugly hoped it would, but revenge alone was enough to keep her going.

The scene began with Bottom capering and showing off for Titania, the Queen of the Fairies. She lounged upon her little hillock and spoke her lines clearly as she awaited the moment when Holles would leave the stage and reappear as Oberon in complete kingly regalia—including sword and crown.

It was the sword she must get close to. Luckily it had a long handle and was carried in a baldric swung from one shoulder across to the other side. The handle would not be exactly easy to get near, but not impossible either. Not if she crowded in just a little bit closer than she had during practice. The only problem with that was that Holles might suspect her of being up to something . . . since it was not her habit to get near to him. She was much more likely to edge away! Well, either it would work or it would not. Soon she would know.

It worked. The scene arrived which Ave had written in which Oberon knighted Bottom (now without the ass's head and played by an extra) as an honorary fairy. Ernie, in her role of Titania, hovered in the background having a great deal of difficulty restraining a giggle. Then Holles grasped the doctored sword handle, froze, looked down at it and with a barely suppressed sigh went on with the scene.

As they all exited, preparing for the last scene in which Titania, having learned her lesson, promises Oberon that in future she'll be good, Holles licked some of the sweet from one finger and asked her, politely, if she had more trouble up her sleeve for him.

Ernie, who had stuck the long pin into her costume pulled it out. This time she looked him straight in the eye with no laughter in hers at all. "I have only one more trial for you, Lieutenant. If you step beyond the line so much as the width of a fingernail, I will use this on you without compunction. I will *not* be pawed or really kissed or anything else you have in mind for that reconciliation scene which took forever to get just right. Leave it exactly the way it is supposed to be and you are safe. One—just *one*—deviation will have you jumping all over the stage."

Holles compressed his lips. "You truly have no wish for my attentions, have you?"

"None whatsoever."

"I apologize. I still do not see *why* you feel that way, but I believe you do. You will have no need for that pin." He strode on into the dressing room.

"You've convinced him for now, but my guess is that he'll still misbehave with his next leading lady," said Ave softly from behind her.

"Unfortunately I agree. But, *if* she demurs, then *perhaps* he'll take her seriously?"

"One can hope." Ave's sober expression turned even more serious. "I wish to speak with you once the play is over, Ernie."

She stared up into his face, read his determination. Their eyes met, held, his gaze telling her things she didn't want to read but couldn't avoid. The time had come. He was warning her she'd have to make a decision. For a moment she thought of telling him she was too tired, of telling him that he would have to wait—but why should he? Why should she put either of them through more uncertainty when she'd already decided.

Hadn't she?

Ernie let her gaze fall to the pin she held in her hands. "Very well, Ave. You may walk Norry and myself home and we'll talk." She tucked the pin back into her sleeve and walked out onto the stage for the last scene.

Norry, yawning, left them in the kitchen which was still warm from the partially banked fire. Ernie busied herself building it up, adding kindling and then wood as Maria had taught her. She set the tripod over the heat and set the kettle on to boil. Finally she had no more excuses. She rose and turned to face Ave.

Ave had seated himself at the table. He gestured to a stool across from him and Ernie took it. At least, she thought—and wondered why she felt the teeniest little bit of chagrin—he was not going to cheat by taking her into his arms and using what he could so easily make her feel to his advantage.

"I love you," he said softly.

"I . . . love you, too, but it makes no difference." Or does it? she wondered.

"It makes all the difference in the world." A muscle clenched in his jaw, relaxed. "You would cheat us, Ernie, of something very special, something far too few find in this world."

"Cheat us?" He was accusing her of cheating just when she had absolved him of doing so? Blast the man! Then, thinking, she shook her head. "The cheat is your profession, Ave. You would have to, again and again, chance that something being taken from me alone. Only I would be left to suffer for our love."

Chance death, she thought, yes, but also chance being gravely wounded . . . "It is too one-sided, too unfair . . . it is the women who suffer . . ." she insisted.

But wounded, who would care for him? Would he be looked after properly? Could she bear to be elsewhere and not know for weeks and weeks after a battle whether he lived or died . . . ?

"Life is not fair, my dear," he said, interrupting her rampaging thoughts. "Where did you ever get the notion it was?"

"You would wish such uncertainty to be my part in life?"

A muscle clenched in Ave's jaw. He could, he thought, so simply cut short this argument by telling her she need not concern herself. Why did he not do so? Why must he be so stubborn . . . ?

When he didn't respond immediately, she dropped her gaze, looked at her clenched hands lying on the table. "Ave, something rather ridiculous has been bothering me very much." She looked up, met his questioning gaze. "Why did you not tell us you were not coming to stir the pudding? I told you it was ridiculous," she finished in a rush when his eyes widened and she saw a growing astonishment. She looked away. A moment's silence ensued which drew her eyes back to his.

"But I did," he finally responded. "I gave a note to—"

The astonishment changed to anger and the string of swear words issuing heatedly from his mouth had Ernie burning red in no time at all.

"Ave!"

He glanced at her, shut his mouth. After a moment he shook his head. "Of all the stupid things. I don't know if I'm swearing at myself for being so idiotic as to give that note to Holles to deliver or if I'm swearing at him for disobeying what was, after all, a direct order!"

"You're saying you wrote . . . ?"

"Of course. I've not forgotten all the niceties I was taught as a youth! It would have been exceedingly impolite to have gone off that way without excusing myself from a promise to you." Something between outrage and chagrin tinted his expression. "If you had any idea at all of how *much* I wanted to be here!" He reached across the table for her hands and his expression softened. "Ernie, love, I had an order from Wellington himself that I was to waste no time appearing for an important conference. When he and I were finished, I spent hours and hours with several other officers planning the logistics for the implementation of the orders he'd given me." His warm clasp tightened slightly around her hand.

"I see. That at least explains *that.*" Carefully she freed her hands and again clasped them before her. "But it is another point of suffering for any woman stupid enough to follow the drum, is it not? She'd never know from moment to moment when some stupid order would take her husband away—very likely with no knowledge of where he'd gone or for how long he'd be away."

"Yes, that is possible."

She blinked that he'd not tried to tease her out of her complaint or give her facile promises that he guaranteed word would be brought to her by someone. She drew in a deep breath. "You are asking that I wait as Norry waits for a return that will not happen?"

A wry smile flickered across his face, disappeared. He sighed. "You forget that Jon will come—according to your sister." The smile was sad when it reappeared. "I talked to Norry while we waited for you after the play? She says some may consider it a Christmas miracle, but she knows it is merely that he has finally been allowed to come home to her. Jon will, she says, arrive in time for dinner day after tomorrow!"

It was Ernie's turn to reach for his hands. "Ave, you will not desert me when she must finally accept he's not coming? I . . . we . . . we'll both need you then, I think."

"Whatever comes of *us,* my love, I have promised to help you with Norry and I will. She is my friend, too, you know."

"She *is* my friend, is she not? As well as my sister? Sometimes I forget that."

"Hmm. But speaking of Norry and her problems settles nothing between us, does it?"

"I'm so torn, Ave. I fear to leave you for fear you'll need me. I mean, if you are wounded again, I should be here to nurse you."

"I have other needs which only you can . . . heal." He grinned when she went crimson and jerked her hands from his. "I should not tease you so, but it is a part of marriage, the loving. You must *not* leave it out of your very logical calculations when deciding what we'll do."

"I . . . decide . . ."

"I," he interrupted, "have decided what I want. You know what that is, Ernie. I want to marry you. Now it is your turn, my dear. *You* will make *your* decision and that will be for both of us, will it not, my love?"

Ernie felt a tremor in her hands and clasped them tightly to hide it. Forcing herself, she once again met his steady gaze. "I do love you. I cannot pretend any longer that it is merely an affection or an infatuation." She made the admission in a whisper.

He held her gaze steadily. "And, if you go home to your father, will you forget me easily?"

"Ave! No! I may never forget you . . ."

"Ah." A certain amount of speculation colored his expression. "You mean you'll suffer if you leave me and go home?"

"Suffer." The word registered. "If I go home I suffer . . ." Again she looked up and this time noted the faintest gleam of amusement in his eyes. "Avenel Sommerton, that was unfair!"

He chuckled and chuckled again when he realized his laughter angered her. "But only the truth, was it not?"

"Yes, damn you." Ernie glowered, her lips tightly compressed, unable to say, quite, just why she felt the anger!

"So," he continued, his tone suggestive, "if you go home your suffering begins immediately. If you stay, your suffering may begin during any battle I have to fight. On the other hand, I've fought a lot of battles and have taken very good care of my skin. I will continue to do so—especially since I'll have new reason for such care! Do you think I *want* to die, Ernie, my love?"

"No. Of course not." Her lips compressed and she scowled. "You say that I either suffer for certain or I suffer in anticipation. It doesn't seem to me to be a very good choice, Ave."

"No, but there are compensations if you choose the latter," he said softly, insinuatingly, and again chuckled softly at Ernie's reddening skin. "Yes, I referred, again, to our marriage bed, but, think, my dear, there is so much else as well. We'll have the companionship and friendship and togetherness which is so important to a loving relationship. We'll share our burdens and enjoy our victories—whether they are in battle or in our daily life. We will be *together,* Ernie."

Ernie weighed her fear against her love and finally realized she had no choice at all. She sighed and raised her eyes to his. He must have read there what he wanted to know because, even before she could speak, he had risen, pulled her up and around the end of the table and into his arms. He held her tightly, his hand pressing her head into his shoulder.

"Ernie," he mumbled into her hair. "Ernie, Ernie, my very best friend, my help-meet, my love, my lover . . ."

Finally, he tipped her face up to his and kissed her.

The kiss went on and on and, although it started from the welling up of love and caring, it moved very quickly into the realms of passion. Ernie, her emotions roiling and boiling and filling her with such pressure as she'd never known, tried very hard to become part of Ave, pressing closer, rolling back and forth against him, trying to feel him with all of her . . . and coming very near to blacking out from it all—and then did just that as the conflict between what she wanted to do and what she should do fought to a stand-still within her.

"Ernie? Ernie . . . !"

Ave held her limp form, returning quickly from the very far-ther-most borders which, once passed, one may not cross again until passion is satisfied. Carefully, Ave seated himself and ten-derly he cradled his love until her eyelids fluttered and she stared disbelievingly up at him. His expression revealed more than a touch of concern.

"Love?" he asked. "Are you all right?"

"I don't know, do I?" she asked after a moment's thought. Then, after another thought, she raised startled eyes to his. "What happened? What have we done?"

He smiled. "Not that. Not that we didn't both wish to do so. I think it was your conscience telling you that you must not and fighting with your emotions which told you you *must* which made you swoon for a moment."

"I guess you were right, were you not?"

"I was?" he asked cautiously. "About what in particular?"

"There will be compensations!" Something very nearly an old Ernie-grin crossed her face as she struggled to sit up. "You'd better go, Ave."

He tucked her back into his arm, held her close, his chin nuzzling her hair. "I don't want to."

"No, I don't suppose you do. If I were another sort, I suppose I could ask you to stay . . . but I won't."

He sighed. "No. And if you were the sort who would, then I very likely wouldn't love you as I do, would I?"

"Very likely that's the case."

"Are you resigned to marrying a soldier, love?" he asked.

"I've come to the conclusion I've no choice. I don't know how you did it, Ave, but you managed to get around or over or under every defense I raised against falling in love with you. I swore I would not fall in love with you. I swore I would not marry a soldier, too, did I not?" She tipped her head. "Maybe I'd better give up swearing?"

"Not until you've made one last oath, my dear one. I'll have our vows said before the altar before you give up swearing!"

"Ah. Well. Once more then."

Ave kissed her again. Again it began as the tenderest of loving kisses—and again it changed, took on warmth and blossomed, turning into something of an entirely different nature. This time it was Ave who stopped their passion but again not by conscious choice. He slipped off the stool and they landed, with a thump on the floor!

Ave, still holding her, blinked in shock. Ernie, roused to something approaching sanity, noticed the look and laughed. For a moment Ave couldn't see the humor or understand why she laughed. Then he too chuckled, shaking his head ruefully.

"You'd better go, Ave."

"Yes. I really must go."

He set her off his lap and stood up, holding down his hand to help her to her feet. They moved into the front room and he was about to go when he turned to her, taking her hands.

"Ernie, you do believe I love you? You believe that whatever happens in the future, I have, tonight, done—and said—nothing I haven't believed deeply?"

"I believe you."

He sighed. "Yes. And I believe as I have for a long time now, that you love me. I just hope, my love, that you love me enough."

And with those ominous sounding words, he went, closing the door softly behind him.

Seventeen

Christmas Eve was the coldest night yet, but there was no wind and the huge bowl of sky overhead was so clear Ernie couldn't believe the star-studded sky was real. She'd never seen so many stars. Nor had they ever seemed so close, some hanging so near she felt she could reach up and pick them as Bertie had oranges from a tree her first day in Portugal.

"It's glorious," she whispered to Norry who stood beside her wrapped in the fur-lined cloak Ernie had given her. "It is so incredibly beautiful."

"It always is," whispered Norry in turn. "I like to think the night sky over Bethlehem looked like this when the angelic hosts came down to the shepherds."

"A night so full of love one can almost feel it."

"Hmm."

"Norry . . . ," said Ernie urgently, after a moment's silence.

"You want me to promise to come home with you," said her sister.

"Yes." When Norry didn't reply, Ernie insisted, "You must. You cannot stay here forever. You say that Jon will come home. Today you said he'd come tomorrow—and tonight I'll admit I can almost believe in that miracle—but, Norry, what if he doesn't . . . ?"

"If Jon does not come home by the new year we'll pack and go home," she answered softly, her arm going around Ernie.

Norry pulled her younger sister close, wrapping Ernie into the fur and warming her.

Ernie was again silent for a long moment. "You know something, do you not?"

"Yes. I *know*," said Norry softly. "Don't worry about it, my dear. Think about Christmas instead. See? There's the Reverend Stark. The service is about to begin."

Ernie struggled with her need to argue, let herself lose. "He's very young," she said.

"But very right for an army of young men. Shhhh."

The service began with the reading of the beautiful words from St. Luke, Chapter two, verses one through twenty. A strong but husky baritone rang over the hillside and Ernie wasn't at all surprised to discover it was Ave, Colonel Sommerton's voice. The reading was followed by the Christmas hymn, Oh Little Town of Bethlehem.

And so it went. Simple well-known hymns even the least religious could sing from the heart. A brief sermon about God's wonderful gift to man. Short deeply meaningful prayers asking that peace be allowed to return to earth and to mankind and to these soldiers in particular who were so far from home and family.

The service was breathtakingly simple and simply breathtaking. Ernie felt tears in her eyes and hoped they wouldn't affect her voice when she sang.

Candles had been passed out as people arrived. Toward the end the young clergyman asked that they be lit. A scramble ensued while, here and there, men crouched down and took out flint and tinder. Soon a few carefully shielded candles glowed. Each lit candle lit another nearby, the points of light spread and spread until the hillside glowed softly.

When everyone was quiet again, the minister suggested that each person say his own personal Christmas prayer, silently, and then, after the final prayer, everyone could return to his bivouac, singing carols. Reverend Stark suggested several more old favorites which they might begin with while everyone walked back together.

"Norry," said Ernie some minutes later as they began the short trek home, "I'll never forget this night."

"Nor I. I'm so happy to have shared it with you. If only . . ."

"Don't say it, Norry. Either you believe he'll come home—or you don't. In either case, although I'll admit I didn't get to know him well, I don't think the Jon I remember would wish you to allow anything to take from you the least bit of wonder, the awe and love we've felt here tonight."

"You are perfectly correct, Ernie. He would not." Norry raised her head and her clear soprano joined with the chorus of male voices singing *Good King Wenceslas*.

They reached the edge of town and then the cottage. A number of voices wished them a happy Christmas and a joyous New Year and they replied in kind but closed the door quickly against the sharp cold. Norry headed straight for the kitchen where Albert had left fresh water and a fire, banked and waiting. She set about making them a final pot of tea. Ernie found cups and saucers and was setting them on the kitchen table when a chorus of voices coming from the square beyond their balcony made her turn to stare at Norry.

"Carollers? At this time of night?!"

"I don't think they'll stay long." Norry went to the shelf where she'd put the balance of the bottle of brandy they had used for Christmas cooking. She checked it and shook her head, heaving a sigh. "Not enough, I fear. I should have thought of this possibility."

She picked up one of the bottles of wine she'd purchased for Christmas dinner and a glass and headed for the door, pausing to slip on the fur-lined and hooded cloak. She smiled at her sister. "I'm going to love this, Ernie," she said and touched the soft wool of the outer layer. "Thank you more than I can say."

Again she headed for the door and stepped out. The singing

came to an end and, with a toast, laughter and many good wishes, the men soon drifted away.

All but one of them, that is. Ave entered the house behind Norry, the accouterments of his dress uniform jingling and clinking. He looked across the cold parlor at Ernie. "I'd like to talk to your sister, Norry." That muscle moved in his jaw. "Alone," he added.

Norry hesitated, looked at Ave for a long moment and shrugged. "Well, now that you're engaged, I see no difficulty with that."

Ernie saw the muscle in his jaw tighten still again and wondered what was coming. She accepted the cloak Norry handed her before her sister returned to the much warmer kitchen. Swinging the garment around her, she went to the table, sat down. "What is it, Ave?"

"I have done a terrible thing, love."

"Have you?"

He sighed, paced the small room once and then came to sit across from her. Reaching for her hands, he held them against the scarred wood, lifted them, played with her fingers, held them together and laid them back down.

"I didn't think this would be so difficult," he said and sighed again. And again.

Ernie waited with growing anxiety, allowing Ave to play with her hands as he struggled for words.

"Perhaps," he said, disgusted, "I should just forget the whole thing and stay in the army where I belong."

Ernie's hands stilled beneath his. "Ave, I think you'd better just say it and be done with it. Why would you *not* stay here?"

He raised his eyes, caught hers and held her gaze with his. "Do you remember I said I hoped you loved me enough? I meant enough to forgive me. I've told you about my father, Ernie. I've had word he died."

About to ask sharply what she had to forgive, his words concerning his father shocked her into forgetting. "I'm so sorry, Ave." Her hands turned, tightened around his.

"You needn't be. We were never close. I regret that I cannot grieve for him—that we didn't have the sort of relationship we should have had as father and son . . ." Ernie, remembering all Norry had told her, tightened her hands around his again. He drew in a deep breath and continued, holding her fingers tightly. "But what it means, Ernie, is that things are different than you've believed. I cannot stay here. With the army, I mean."

She nodded, pulling free and clutching the cloak more tightly around her shoulders. "What you wish to say, then, is that you must take leave—perhaps a long leave—go back and straighten out the mess he'll have left."

"That's not quite it." Ave pursed his lips and whooshed out a breath. "I've a confession, love. And if you can't forgive me, I suppose I'll survive, but I don't quite know how."

"Ave, you frighten me," she said, her heart pounding, "Please, don't keep me in suspense."

He bit his lips, looked over her shoulder, then back. "I was selfish. I wanted so much for you to agree to marry *me*. Marry the man I am and expected always to be . . ."

"Ave-the-soldier. I know." She nodded, although still without understanding. "And I have done so, have I not?"

"Yes. Reluctantly. And only after a great deal of argument." He grinned briefly, remembering her struggle and sobered again. "Ernie, I know it wasn't an easy decision for you. I know you are still full of fears . . ."

"Terrors," she interrupted.

"All right, terrors, if you will." He again reached for and clutched her hands tightly. "I knew how you felt and I've let it happen when it wasn't necessary. Don't hate me."

"Ave," she said, pulling away for the second time—but this time because she needed the physical space between them which would make it possible for her to think clearly, "I begin to think you are a go-on and not a come-on after all and in that case I needn't be so fearful when you go into battle! Do get on with saying what you wish to say!"

He leaned back. "Right now I face the fiercest battle of my life and, yes, I'm suffering mulligrubs and am thinking of turning bellamranger. Ernie," he finished in a rush, "I've known practically since you arrived that I must resign my commission and go home, but I didn't tell you—or anyone else, for that matter."

"What you"—she frowned trying to remember—"or *somebody* told me was that there would be nothing for you to go home *to*."

He nodded. "So I've always believed."

"So how is it different now?"

He grimaced. "It never once occurred to me that my father would be at high tide when he stuck his spoon in the wall."

Ernie frowned again, trying to absorb the meaning behind the words he spoke. "He died wealthy?"

Again Ave pursed his lips. "Ernie, if only I could say he'd left me a wealthy man, then I'd not feel like such an idiot for doing what I've done to you. He didn't. On the other hand, he'd won enough there is hope I can save much of the estate, maybe most of it. But it won't be easy."

Ernie frowned. "I was told everything is heavily mortgaged, was I not?"

"It is. Was . . . well, I've had some of the mortgages paid off entirely and some paid down and have left myself barely enough I may make a beginning on all that must be done. Ernie," he said intensely, leaning forward to put his elbows on the table, steepling his fingers. "I doubt there is a house on any of the three estates with a whole roof. I don't think anything has been replaced or repaired since my father became earl. I pray I'll live long enough to pass on to my son a well-run and profitable estate."

This time Ernie reached for and caught one of his hands, her emotions caught by the depth of determination, of hope, of fear which he was feeling.

"In short, my love," he said, tightening his grip on her fingers, "I'm offering for you all over again and this time I swear I'm offering a harder life than that you'd have had with the army!"

"Offering all over again . . . ?"

Ave ran fingers through his gray hair, ruffling it in the way Ernie liked. "Love," he explained, "if I am at all honorable, if I am to live with myself, I have to release you from your promise to wed me and then ask you *again* if you will have me now you know the truth . . ."

Ernie stared at him. "Release me . . ." she said faintly.

"I need you, love. Going home to run an estate I never believed would be mine, I need you more than if I were to continue as an officer in the King's Army. Ernie, I *know* how to be an officer," he said, that intensity returning to his voice. "My love, I haven't a notion how to be an earl! I don't know what must be done to retrieve the estates from ruin. I don't know *how* to begin or *where* to start or, for that matter, whether it is even possible." The grimace touched his features again. "What I may do is go home, take one look, turn yellow belly, and run away to the Army all over again . . ."

"Live with yourself . . ." Ernie stared at him her mind in turmoil. "Ave, I don't understand. Did you say you've known this—that you'd have to return to England—for weeks now and you didn't tell me?"

Ave stared at her, let his eyes drop to his hands. "Perhaps I was a fool, Ernie, but I had to do it this way for my peace of mind. You were so insistent you'd not marry a soldier, but that is what I am, what I've always been and what I expected I'd always be. I still can't believe I'll not live my life as one. Don't you see, Ernie? I had to convince you to marry the man I am. I *had* to."

"I don't see that at all. If you loved me, why would you wish to put me through the pain and conflict I've suffered? If you truly loved me, why should you not have told me the truth immediately?" Deeply chilled by more than the cold of the room, she again freed herself and pulled the warming cape more tightly around herself although it couldn't reach in to where she was chilled.

"I love you, Ernie. I love you as I never expected to love any woman. Can't you see that it is *because* of that that it was important to me that you agree to marry *me?* Me the soldier. Not some title, not the earl whom you would expect to take you home to an easy life. Not when I *know* that won't be possible?"

"Ave, haven't you understood that it is not the *way* of life which has bothered me? Do you truly think I would balk at living as Norry has described her life? It was not *that* which frightened me, but the thought of losing the man I love in battle. Surely you can understand that."

"You could just as easily lose me when crossing a busy street"—his chin jutted in that stubborn way it had—"as my father died, by simply walking out in front of a half-trained horse and making it shy. That's all it takes, Ernie."

She shook her head. "Perhaps soldiers must forget about death, must never think of it as something real and possible. Perhaps that is why you refuse to admit that death is far closer to you here in Iberia than it would be at home . . ."

He drew in a deep breath. "Are you avoiding making a decision, Ernie?" She didn't respond and he added, "Have you forgotten I've once again asked you to wed me?"

"Have you?" She eyed him, dropped her gaze to the table and then looked back to the worried face across the table from her. *Worried. Well, he deserved to be worried!* Ernie's lower lip pushed out in a gentle pout. She tipped her head. "Yes, I believe you did ask. And with no more flowery speeches or romantic promises than the first time." She crossed her arms and turned sideways in her chair. "You don't learn very quickly, do you Ave?"

Ave, for the first time, felt there might be hope. Quickly he rose to his feet, circled the table and pulled her up into his arms. He kissed her, then pressed her head into his shoulder.

"Flowery speeches aren't my strong point, Ernie. I don't know how to make them—even when I feel my love for you so deeply it has become the major part of my whole being. It would nearly kill me to tear it from me now, I think."

He tipped her face up. "No pretty speeches, love. And no promises—except that I'll always love you. Only you. *Love* I can give you, but will I ever be able to give you the life you deserve? Will I ever be in funds so that I may dress you as you should be dressed? So that I can give you a season each spring in London where you would shine in society and become a hostess envied by all? Give you enough servants, and well furnished homes, settings in which you would be the jewel that made everything perfect? Ernie, I can give you neither pretty speeches nor fancy promises. All I can tell you is that I love you and need you."

Ernie pushed back into his loosened embrace. Her eyes shone. "I was wrong. You learn very quickly indeed."

"Will you marry me? Even if I don't know how to court you properly?"

"Yes . . ."

"You will . . . ? *You will,"* he repeated firmly while looking into her glowing eyes. He kissed her deeply, then hugged her.

"Not that it matters," she teased. "but now that I'll not be Lady Colonel Sommerton, just whom have I agreed to marry?"

"You will be Lady Mowtrey, my dear, for what it's worth." He frowned. "You have understood that life will not be easy? That it will take years to return the land to what it should be, to repair and modernize and that every pence which is earned must be poured back into repairing roofs and . . . and draining fens and . . . and I haven't a notion what is needed."

"Where is this estate, Lord Mowtrey?"

He frowned. "Don't call me that."

Ernie smiled, leaning back into his hard embrace. "You'd better get used to it, my dear. Once in England, it is all you'll hear from both friends and strangers. Now, tell me, where?"

"There are three estates, but only Sommerton Hall is truly important to me. It is no more than fifteen miles from Chatsworth of which you'll have heard, and which"—again that jaw jutted and a faint frown marred his brow—"I believe, was the ruin of my father who wished to live in that style when he'd nowhere near the resources needed to do so."

"Hmm."

"You've a thought?"

"My father corresponds with a man in that region," she said slowly, "who turned around his estate by building a canal."

Ave looked astounded. "A canal?"

"You know," she teased. "One of those things through which water flows?"

"Of course I know what a canal is! But . . . a canal?"

"It is only something to think about. They can be quite profitable if your land lies in just the proper area," she said and added, "which yours may *not,* of course."

"A *canal?"*

"Don't worry about it," she soothed. "We'll come about one way or another. My dowry will help make a beginning."

"Dowry? *Dowry.* Ernie, I'd not even thought about that possibility." He frowned, worried. "Is it very large? Will I be accused of being a fortune hunter?"

She chuckled. "It is considered reasonably adequate but not so large you need fear that particular odium. In fact," she said as she attempted to disentangle herself from his arms, "perhaps you should *not* marry me, but *should* look about you for an immense dowry . . ."

He cut off her words with another kiss, stilling her struggles. When she settled, he said, "I will marry you or no one. Never suggest such a thing ever again." He loosened his embrace and leaned until his forehead rested on hers. "I'd better go or I'll be kissing you still at sunrise."

"Yes, you'd better go," she agreed, but reluctantly. She brightened. "But maybe we should first tell Norry we've become re-engaged and send her to bed?" It would be a few more minutes with him—but then Ernie yawned and, embarrassed, looked at Ave only to discover he too was suffering from a jaw-cracking, gaping, yawn. "We have a big day tomorrow and it is already long after midnight."

"I'll leave. It isn't as if Norry need know I had to ask you all over again. Good night my dearest love." He'd not let her out of his embrace so it was simple enough to raise her head with a thumb under her chin, to lower his mouth to hers . . . to become far more involved than he should have done.

A throat clearing itself loudly and a tapping foot broke into their bemusement. "I think I should perhaps have come out earlier," scolded Norry, "but I heard you talking so seriously I didn't feel I should intrude." Norry glared from one to the other. "It is only that I know you could not have been talking and also behaving the rake as you just were that I do not become very angry with you, Ave."

"Wish me happy, Norry," he said with a grin, not the least bit discomposed by her scolding. Dropping another kiss on Ernie's nose and, still grinning, he left them. Then he reopened the door before Norry could bar it and said, "I almost forgot. I've six bottles of an excellent wine and two of *fino,* which I'll bring to dinner tomorrow. Good night again."

"What did he mean, I was to wish him happy?" Norry turned

to lean against the door. "I already wished him happy. Did I not?"

Ernie grinned. "The silly man. He released me from our original engagement which he'd inveigled me into under false premises. Then, after long explanations about his current situation, dire warnings about how hard life will be—and promises to love only me—he asked me all over again."

"Current situation?"

"Congratulate me, Norry," said Ernie dryly. "It appears I'm to be Lady Mowtrey, lady to the impoverished Lord Mowtrey, who has hopes, after all, of retrieving his estates. He's decided he must resign his commission and return home."

"I'd looked forward to having you here, but that means"— Norry's eyes widened—"Ernie, the two of you will be going back to England."

"Yes. It will be necessary to look into the situation very carefully. Apparently his father ran everything into the ground. From what Ave said, I think he believes we may have to sell at least one of his two minor estates in order to save the rest, particularly the family seat for which he seems to have an affection."

"It's a ruin—or so Jon told me."

"Ave said he didn't think there was a roof anywhere which did not leak. I thought he meant the tenants' houses, but you're suggesting that includes his home as well, are you not?"

"*Especially* his home. Ave's father hated it and wouldn't spend a groat on it." Norry yawned. "I'm to bed. Tomorrow will be a very special day."

Ernie suddenly remembered her sister's belief Jon would return on the morrow. "Norry . . . !"

Her sister turned, grinned, backed toward her door. "Remember, Ernie," she coaxed. "Miracles happen. Especially at Christmas."

Ernie looked around the living area which they'd decorated the previous afternoon. It looked festive with greenery tacked up and bright red ribbons tied in bows. Best of all it *smelled* like Christmas, something Ernie had feared would not be the case, but Bertie had found the proper sorts of evergreens and all was well in that respect.

If only Norry did not believe so thoroughly that Jon would return in time for Christmas dinner! Her disappointment when he did not come would very likely be more than anyone could bear to see . . .

Perhaps more than Norry could bear?

Ernie shook her head and took herself to her narrow cot. As she lay snug under heavy covers she forced her mind from Norry to Ave. She wondered how soon she would be sharing a bigger bed with him and wished it would be very soon—knew it had *better* be soon! Tonight his kisses and his touch had very nearly led them to forget propriety, to forget everything. It was, Ernie, supposed, just as well Norry had come in to stop them, but oh, how she wished . . .

Dreaming about what she wished, Ernie fell asleep.

"What time," asked Ernie, as she peeled what seemed a mountain of vegetables, "will our guests begin to arrive?"

"Not until nearly three." Norry's hands were busy wielding the pole churning precious cream from which she was making fresh butter. "Will you turn the ham and baste the goose, please? I don't dare stop this just now."

Ernie did so, and went back to her vegetables. "Did Maria say she'd be bringing her Spanish stew?"

"Yes. Everyone will bring something. It will likely be an odd assortment before we're finished, but it will all be delicious and no one will care if it is not at all traditional."

"Does everyone know about the pudding?" Ernie grinned. *"That* will be tradition! It's hardly Christmas without a proper pudding."

Later Norry came out of her room wearing a dress Ernie had

never seen. It was a traditional Spanish design with full tiered skirts and a snug waist—which didn't quite close, but the long fringed shawl hid that fact unless one looked for the gaping seam where laces crossed and recrossed, revealing Norry's shift beneath. The dress looked a trifle odd to Ernie who had become used to the higher waists and slimmer skirts which were all the mode in England.

"You look beautiful," she told her sister—although it took her a moment to decide that that was so.

"Thank you." She turned, spreading her skirts. "Jon bought this for me before we left Madrid for Burgos." Her eyes sparkled with the memory. "We had such a lovely time in Madrid. You wouldn't believe how generous the Madrilenos were."

"I've heard they weren't so happy when the British were forced to leave Madrid," responded Ernie.

"No. But what else could Wellington have done? It was a Spanish general's disinclination to follow orders which led to disaster after all. We had to retreat."

"Wellington, it is said at home, is very good at retreat," said Ernie, only half teasing.

Norry's lips pressed together into a firm disapproving line. "Those fools are not here to see how it is. Wellington has been out numbered in every battle. He has had to choose his ground carefully. They don't *know* the problems he's faced."

"Then that will be something else Ave must do."

Norry blinked. "I thought you were going to England. What can he do there about Wellington's problems?"

"Once we're in England Ave must take his seat in the Lords and tell them how things are," explained Ernie and shrugged, as if it should be obvious. She sighed. "It is too bad Parliament convenes in the spring just when one is most needed on at home in the country. We'll not really be ready to go to London but he'll have to do so so he can convince people that Wellington needs support, not criticism."

It was Norry's turn to shrug. "Perhaps it will not be necessary. With any luck at all, his lordship may not need help. I've a presentment this year will see the end of the war and Napoleon's defeat."

"So we shall hope." Ernie looked around. "Have we enough candles do you think?"

"I think you bought up far too many when you went to the sutler's market in Frienada the other day. Poor Albert had an awful time getting them home, I was told."

"He certainly complained about the weight. Wax is heavy, of course, but for Christmas we needed proper candles. Can you think of how awful to have so many guests when the smell of tallow candles permeates the room? We'd not be able to breathe, I think." She looked with satisfaction at the dozen simple candle sconces she'd had Albert put up on the walls around the room. There would, for once, be light!

"You should not have spent so much on something so frivolous," scolded Norry. "It was a waste."

"Very likely, but we'll leave soon, and Father was generous."

"Ernie . . ."

"Shh. I'm sorry I said anything."

Norry sighed. "It is just that you refuse to believe me. Jon will be home today."

"And if he is not?"

"Then he'll arrive before the new year . . . but he'll be here." Norry looked at the place setting she'd put out for Jon. Stars lit her eyes again and she smiled. "Oh, Ernie, I can barely wait. It has been so long and I've so much to tell him."

If only that miracle would happen, thought Ernie, fearing the disappointment her sister faced. "I'm sure you do," was all she said, turning away and going to the kitchen to turn the ham again and again baste the browning goose. She felt a trifle embarrassed about the ham. The Portuguese did a very nice ham, although quite different from the English in flavor and texture—

so at least this one would be another touch from home which, she thought, would be appreciated.

Nearly a dozen friends would crowd around the makeshift table with its mismatched settings and oddments of glassware, borrowed from wherever they could find it. Only one set of glasses matched. Ernie had made another purchase in the bigger market, a set of gorgeous red goblets with clear but twisted stems which had traveled all the way from the glass blowing center in Venice. She meant to give them to Ave for Christmas—but not until after they had been used for toasts at the end of Christmas dinner!

A knock brought her back into the living room to welcome Bertie and Maria. The Spanish girl's father followed, handing Norry a bouquet of flowers which could only have come from the low lands near the coast. Nobody asked how he had achieved that small miracle but Ernie guessed he'd dispatched one of the men she had seen the day the Spaniard accosted Ave and herself. The flowers were gorgeous.

Norry found a vase and put the flowers on the trestle table which would hold the viands. After being served their first course, people would get themselves seconds. Maria disappeared into the kitchen with a far larger panella than Ernie had yet seen which she set near the fire. Ernie sniffed the wonderful aroma of her rabbit stew which was always so good—and which Norry said was a favorite with Jon.

Ernie wished she had not thought of Jon. She didn't manage to put him from her mind until Ave arrived, kissing her on the forehead and handing her a small package.

"It isn't much," he said, a spot of embarrassment coloring each cheek. "When we return home—assuming my father respected the entail and didn't sell it—I'll give you the traditional bridal ring which is saved for each heir's bride." He waited while Ernie opened the small packet, relaxed at her pleased gasp of surprise.

"But this is lovely, Ave. How could you have found such a thing in a village the size of this one?"

"I didn't find it here. I had it sent up from Lisbon. You do like it?" he asked, needing reassurance.

Ernie held up her hand. A rectangular ruby the size of a small beetle had, on each side, small round emeralds which were set off by a curve of even smaller diamonds. The jewels flashed in the candlelight. "It is very different from anything I've ever seen and I like it very much. It will become a new family treasure, Ave."

Norry looked at it and nodded approvingly, but she had no time for comments. Their next guests arrived, a couple Ernie had not met because they came from another regiment. Then still others arrived and soon the small room was full to bursting, the noise level rising higher and higher, a joyful sound of friendship and of the season.

Norry calmly refilled glasses as they were emptied but, occasionally, Ernie saw her glance with a small frown toward the door. She sighed. What would Norry do when she had to admit that Jon was not coming? Ernie wondered. How would she react? Would there be tears or hysterics? Would she collapse? If only one could save her from such terrible disappointment. If only one could make the miracle happen which would bring a living man home to her . . .

Ernie looked around, found Ave in a small circle of strangers and went to his side, slipping her hand into his arm. He glanced down at her, his eyes asking a question. She shook her head slightly and looked pointedly toward a woman she didn't know. Ave introduced Ernie as his betrothed and soon the whole room was bubbling with congratulations and best wishes. He looked at her ruefully.

"Beast," she said softly. "I'd a plan that you'd announce our engagement toward the end of the meal. I bought a lovely set of glasses which would go with your special *fino* for proper toasts!"

"We can still do it properly when the time comes," he soothed and turned to introduce her to yet another officer, a major.

The major announced Ave was a lucky dog and didn't deserve such a jewel of a woman and it was too bad of him to have hidden her away before she'd had an opportunity to meet a real man. Himself, of course . . . the bantering went on for some time, embarrassing Ernie somewhat.

Finally Norry calmly organized people, urging them to seat themselves at the long board made by putting several borrowed tables end to end. Then she and Ernie and Maria brought in the food and set it upon the buffet around Maria's father's lovely flowers. Once everything was in place, Norry urged Maria and Ernie to their places.

When they were seated, Norry called for attention and waited for the buzz of conversation to taper off. She folded her hands, bowed her head and everyone quieted. She said a simple, but moving grace, asking the Lord's blessing on each of them in the coming year.

She finished and, with one more worried look toward the door, her belief Jon would arrive in time for dinner obviously wavering, she moved to pick up the huge bowl of soup which one of the women guests had brought.

Suddenly a knock sounded at the door. Immediately Norry set the bowl down and rushed to throw it open. Before anyone knew what was happening she was in the arms of the tall ragged looking heavily bearded gentleman standing there.

"Jon my dear," she said after a long moment, stepping back to look up at him. "I'd begun to believe you'd not, after all, make it home today. Come in, come in, beloved." She turned, her face glowing. "Everyone? Here's my Jon! He's a little late and you'll have to wait a moment or two longer before we eat." Still clutching Jon's arm, she turned back to him. "Jon, I was certain you'll wish a few minutes to freshen up and I've put hot water in our room. Come along, my dearest. I've laid out fresh things for you," she said, pulling the tired-looking officer into her bedroom and closing the door.

The people seated at the table threw stunned glances at each other. Ernie, the most stunned of all, simply sat there blinking.

Ave touched her hand. "Love?"

"She said he'd come. She insisted he'd be here."

"Yes. I know."

Ernie turned to stare at him, her eyes painfully wide open. "Did *you* believe her when I did not?"

"No, of course I didn't believe her."

"But here. It's a miracle," said Ernie into the silence around her.

Everyone raised their glasses simultaneously. "To the miracle of my oldest friend's return," said Ave softly. Everyone drank.

From the room behind them which had been surprisingly quiet—or perhaps not so surprisingly quiet?—Norry's voice was finally heard.

"Oh, my love," she said softly, "I'm so happy you're home. It's been so hard waiting for you . . . and I've a surprise for you, my darling. It has been so hard not to tell others of my joy, but I wanted you to be the first to know. We're going to have a baby, Jon."

Once again there was silence from behind the closed door. And once again glasses were raised. This time the toast was silent, but everyone knew it was to new life—both to Jon, a man who had come back to them when they'd believed him dead and to Jon's child.

Tears shone unashamedly in eyes all around the table. They ran silently down Ave's cheeks, his wide grin telling one and all they were happy tears.

They filled Ernie's eyes, making them shiny in the candle-light. She was full clear up to her tight throat with happiness for her sister whom she'd been certain would finally have to accept her grief—only to discover Norry really had known all along that Jon was alive.

Another sort of miracle, that? Norry's ability to *know?* Or perhaps that was a talent which was a blessing only when it brought good news, as it had when it told Norry that Jon would return today.

The silence was broken by Maria's father. "But that is the English officer I have seen with my brigands—the one they have tried to hide from me—the one I'd thought to help once Christmas was over and I had time to think of ways to organize his escape!" There was a rash of comment and question from around the table.

Ave rose to his feet, quieting one and all. A dry note coloring his voice, he said, "I suspect Jon and Norry may be awhile." He looked around, a grin widening as others had the same thought. "Perhaps we might be more comfortable conversing until they are ready to join us?"

Maria and Ernie put the food which needed heating back near the fire in the kitchen and Maria returned to the front room but Ernie did not.

Ave opened the kitchen door and looked in. "Ernie?" he called. When he saw her, her shoulders drooping, standing near the window, he came on in and went to her side.

"I didn't believe her," said Ernie, turning her head into his shoulder. "It hurt her that I didn't believe."

"But aren't we all a little slow to believe in miracles?" he asked softly, holding her close.

"She is my sister. I should have believed."

"I did not and Jon is my closest friend. If we must chastise ourselves, than I am worse than you, Ernie. Unlike you, I've seen that special thread which ties them together at a level so deep mere mortals cannot understand it. Remember, I was there when she once went to his side through the chaos of a battlefield in order to save his life. I knew and accepted that she knew he'd

been wounded again at that last battle—but, when she said he'd recovered I did not believe her. Why did I not?"

After a long moment in which they merely held each other, Ernie offered, "It is not easy to accept that miracles still happen, but it has been a season of miracles, has it not?"

"More than that Jon has come back to us?"

Ernie turned in his arms and they closed more tightly around her. "Yes. It is also a miracle that I accepted I cannot live without you whatever sort of life it is you must lead." She looked up, a worried expression in her eyes. "I am a very stubborn woman, Ave. I do not often change my mind once I've made it up."

"So unlike other women, then?" When she didn't do more than nod, still serious, he added, "You mean it is a miracle that you agreed to marry me at all."

"Yes."

"That is two miracles. Are there more?"

"I think so. Isn't one that Maria's father came to her just when she needed him?"

"Yes, perhaps that *could* be considered a miracle. I hadn't thought of it that way—judging it merely one of those odd co-incidences that seem too pat to be believed! But isn't that part of the essence of a miracle?"

"I think so. Then, the fact Lieutenant Torville came down with The Fever just when Norry thought she might no longer be able to save herself from his importunities, when he was about to take extreme measures to have his own way, I think that a miracle."

Ave chuckled. "You are saying that a *fever* is a miracle?"

Her chin could look as stubborn as Ave's on occasion and this was such a time. "In this case, yes."

"All right, then. That is four. Are there more?"

"Hmm. That we ever met, perhaps?"

"No," he said in a very decided tone.

"No?" she asked, tracing a line along his jaw.

"No," he repeated and added, "because I'm certain that if we'd not met *now* we'd have met somehow, sometime, somewhere. That was not a miracle." He smiled down at her. "We were destined to meet and we did."

"No miracle."

"Not that."

He kissed her. Somehow the kiss grew and changed and deepened. Finally, behind them, a throat was cleared. A foot tapped against the tile floor. Ernie and Ave looked at each other. Bemused, they turned their heads until they faced Norry.

"You want something, Norry?" asked Ernie.

"We all want something," said Norry, unable to maintain her disapproving stance. Laughing as she used to laugh, and for the first time since Ernie had come to Portugal, she added, mischievously, "We want our *dinner*—if you do not think that's asking too much?"

"Another miracle," said Ave, softly.

"Another one?" asked Ernie. "You mean that Norry can laugh again?"

"That, too, perhaps. But what *I* had in mind is that, despite the delay, not a single thing appears to have been over-cooked or dried out or otherwise ruined!"

He pointed to where the food, set near the fire, awaited their attention.

"Now *that* is truly a miracle worthy of a tale to tell our grandchildren. Is it not?" he asked, looking around.

Dear Reader,

My husband suggested we visit Portugal while I worked on this book—for which notion, bless him! The landscape is very different from what I'd imagined. I've tried to give a flavor of how it was when Wellington went into winter headquarters in Frienada: A plaque is fixed to the side of the building in which he lived during the winter of 1813–1814. It was a wonderful week.

My next book, *A Lady's Deception,* coming in June 1995, concerns one of those grief-stricken women Ernie fears to be: Tacye Alington's twin brother died at the battle of San Marcial. Not only must Tacye deal with normal grief, but also the extra grief specific to some twins who feel they've lost half themselves. Since she's always believed no man could mean so much to her as her twin, our heroine isn't interested in a husband for herself, but her younger and much lovelier sister, Damaris, must have a season, even if only in Bath.

Damaris must also be seen to be protected and our heroine, who has all her life dressed in men's clothing when possible, decides to escort the younger girl in male disguise. The girls' blind chaperon, Aunt Fanny, goes also. There are enough heroes to go around, a ghost-fearing ex-officer—who, when he sees Tacye thinks it her brother come back to haunt him—and several villains. In the end, each finds his particular reward or comeuppance.

I hope you enjoyed *A Christmas Treasure* and that you'll find my new book equally amusing. I'd enjoy hearing your views and will respond when you write if you include a self-addressed, stamped, envelope.

Jeanne Savery
P.O. Box 1771
Rochester, MI 48308